# A Shroud of Leaves

## REBECCA Alexander

**TITAN** BOOKS

A Shroud of Leaves
Print edition ISBN: 9781785656248
E-book edition ISBN: 9781785656255

Published by Titan Books
A division of Titan Publishing Group Ltd
144 Southwark Street, London SE1 0UP

First edition: July 2019
1 2 3 4 5 6 7 8 9 10

A CIP catalogue record for this title is available from the British Library.

Printed and bound in the United States.

**TITAN**BOOKS.COM

# Praise for *A Baby's Bones*

"An intricately plotted mystery…bittersweet and haunting." LIBRARY JOURNAL

"Steeped in dark drama and rich historical detail."
M.L. RIO

"An engrossing read that perfectly blends the historical and contemporary for a brilliant story."
THE CRIME REVIEW

"Enthralling and immensely satisfying."
KAREN MAITLAND

"One of my favourite reads of the year."
CRIMINAL ELEMENT

"A compelling read." MAUREEN JENNINGS

"Gripping, atmospheric and emotionally satisfying."
RUTH DOWNIE

Also available from Rebecca Alexander and Titan Books

*A Baby's Bones*

*For*
LILY ALISON BAVE
*who made me a grandmother.*

# 1

The victim had been buried in a carved hollow in the grass and shrouded in fallen leaves. Dr Sage Westfield accidentally brushed one slate-blue hand, which the pathologist had uncovered. Even through gloves, she could feel the cold, waxy flesh, unlike anything she had experienced before at an excavation.

'Sorry,' she breathed, as much to the corpse as the pathologist.

Dr Megan Levy grimaced back. She was a sandy-haired woman who looked like she was in her forties. 'I'm guessing this is your first burial scene?'

'The first one less than a hundred years old, yes. I've done a lot of classes and observed a couple of recent post-mortems, but I wasn't expecting to be called to a recent murder.' The grave reminded Sage of an Egyptian sarcophagus, rounded at the head end and tapered to the feet. The forensic suit rustled when she moved; she was wearing a hood and overshoes as well. The investigation team looked like ghosts drifting in the late afternoon gloom; pools of artificial light from lamps sharpened the silhouettes of the people huddled around the grave.

She checked her field bag again. Camera, extra batteries, notebook, tablet, phone, charger for the car. Evidence bags in different sizes, trowels, labels, marker pens, brushes, hand lenses. Most of her classes were about the law and rules of handling and preserving evidence; she didn't feel at all prepared for an actual burial that wasn't hundreds or even thousands of years old. It was all about local, recent stratigraphy of soil layers; how someone had dug the grave and covered it up. Her supervisor, Trent, was probably just there so the police could prove they had covered all the bases. She glanced up to see an older man, stocky, staring back at her. He gestured with a curled finger and she stood up.

'Dr Westfield?' She nodded. 'The archaeologist from the island, I presume. Where's Trent?'

'I'm one of his students. Well, I've known him for more than a decade – we trained together.'

He looked over his shoulder. 'Stay out of the woods!' he barked at someone working beyond the scrubby lawn, towards the trees that encroached on the space in front of the house. 'And lay some more forensic pads.' He turned back to Sage. 'I need the real thing, not a student. I want to know how that grave was dug, what it means.'

Sage swallowed the first three things she wanted to say. 'I phrased that badly. I am a fully qualified, experienced scientist. Until last year I was the county archaeologist for the Isle of Wight, and I lecture at the university with Trent. I'm completing additional training in forensic techniques.'

He stared at her a bit longer, until she felt uncomfortable. 'I'm the SIO, DCI Lenham.'

SIO, DCI. Senior Investigating Officer, Detective Chief Inspector Lenham.

She looked him in the eye. 'Trent is supervising me. He's working on the road verge; he's found some anomalous tyre impressions.' All around was the New Forest, a national park on the south coast just a few miles from Sage's home on the Isle of Wight. The property was a large one, an imposing Victorian house in a garden with woodland all around. Originally, the rank grass would have been part of about an acre of lawn, possibly surrounded with flower beds. Now straggly shrubs were intertwined with brambles and spindly trees.

'OK, then. Yesterday we had a missing girl and at fifteen years old, the most likely scenario was that she had run away.' He turned to look at the house. 'Now we have a body, found by a local woman walking her dog. Megan, let me know as soon as you find something. First impressions, anything. Trent thinks there might be footprints into the trees; I'm keeping everyone else out.'

Sage knelt down on the plastic sheet beside the grave, avoiding Dr Levy. 'Charming,' she muttered to the pathologist. 'What do you need me to do first?'

'Don't mind Graham. He's a good man, really experienced, just a bit impatient. This might be quite an easy investigation. They'll interview the owner of the garden first – he's top of their list as a suspect, then family and friends. That normally identifies the main suspects. What I need you to do is catalogue all the materials covering the body, systematically, so the prosecutors can build the case.'

Sage sat back on her heels. The corpse was covered in thousands of leaves, mainly, it seemed, holly and ivy, which looked deliberately placed. 'We can't number each one.'

Megan raised a sandy eyebrow. 'We sometimes have to, but honestly, I think some are falling apart and there are too many. No, you photograph stacks in situ, lift, bag and catalogue. The person who buried her had to do that; they couldn't have carried the whole lot. That way if we find anything anomalous we can say where it was in relation to the remains.' She smiled at Sage, the white light gleaming on a crooked tooth. 'We'll chill the leaves down to preserve evidence. Then you and the forensic team can examine them in the lab for fibres, fluids, even fingerprints if the glossier leaves will hold one.'

Sage took out her camera, checked the battery and focused on the leaves at the head end of the grave. 'OK.'

After a few flashes and some more taken under the light from the lamps, she was able to lift a small stack of wet leaves, pressed together and smelling musty. She wrote the picture numbers and location on the bag as she'd been taught. She stood up to take a larger picture of the whole site and added a grid to the image.

Megan asked to see. 'Nice idea. We use laser scans but they are always moving. I have to make measurements on the ground. Send me a copy and I'll use the same grid for my observations too.'

Sage started snapping a handful of leaves near the body, the flash picking up the first threads of blonde hair underneath.

Megan was crawling over the plastic sheeting on the other side, peering at the exposed hand. There was glittery nail varnish, a little flaky and growing out, and three parallel scratches. 'I think we can say it's probably a female from the small hands and the polish,' the pathologist said. 'We can't be certain yet, but Lenham suspects this is River Sloane, the missing teenager from Southampton. I wonder how she ended up here, in the forest.'

Sage swallowed and looked away. The fingers were swollen; they didn't look real. Her experience as a county archaeologist was mostly about bones and artefacts. This was too real, someone that she could have seen on the street a few days ago had actually died. 'What happens when I've got all the leaves off the top?'

'We'll remove the body, then you and Trent will start working on the grave cut itself.'

Sage looked around. 'It's not obvious where they put the spoil. There should be some pieces of hacked-off turf somewhere around. It's very neat, deliberate.'

'We'll have to identify anything they moved,' Megan said. 'Log all your observations as you go. I use a voice recorder but your phone will do. Send in the file along with your finished notes. We want everything.'

The remains had been nested in a blanket of leaves, laid in a cut roughly the shape of the body. It widened at shoulders and hips. Sage lifted a few more leaves, revealing the purpled chin, and tried to avoid touching it. The colour made the areas of exposed skin look stretched by gases building up, and Sage knew that the faint smell heralded a cascade of decomposition processes. She glanced at the face revealed as she lifted the next batch: definitely female, young, the milky eyes staring up at the sky, beginning to bulge. Textbooks and research on forensic archaeology hadn't prepared Sage for the sadness, the horror of it. Even mortuary visits had been distant, factual. This was intense. She bagged more leaves, trying not to touch the body, and wrote on the label.

Megan leaned forward to zoom in on something. She sat back and breathed out, making her mask billow. 'OK, Sage. What can you tell me from our initial survey?'

'She's covered with leaves. I suppose that's odd, not to

cover her with the soil they dug out.'

'Which means?'

Sage thought. 'I'm not sure – maybe they wanted her to be found quickly?'

'Maybe. With all this work they could have buried her deeper in the same amount of time. And something else.' She eased a few large leaves off the neck. 'Look at these leaves. They weren't shovelled on, they were placed very carefully.'

'Overlapping, almost tenderly?' said Sage.

'That's possible,' Megan said. 'Although in some murders it would mean the killer wanted to revisit the body. The "ick" range of tenderness. We worry more about a sexual motive if the body is undressed.'

Sage looked around the slight mound of leaves. 'Oh.' She lifted more piles of leaves, took photographs, bagged them and recorded their location. Slowly, the body emerged, naked so far. On the right side of the face were dark smudges. The regular pattern caught Sage's eye and she leaned in. 'What is that?' Trying not to touch the skin, she pointed at a few dark spots in a line. 'Bruising?'

'You've got a good eye,' Megan said, snapping a few close-ups. 'I don't know what caused it. It could be something she was hit with, or fell onto. It's diffuse and looks ante-mortem. Sometimes marks on the skin develop further in the morgue. I'll look into it at the post-mortem examination and we'll swab it for trace.' She smiled up at Sage. 'Well done.'

Sage bagged another stack of leaves and sat back to write up the label. The grave was beyond the house, away from the road. Sage could see a glazed door in the outbuilding that might have looked over the garden originally, but several of the panes were missing and filled in with cardboard. The looming house had a dozen windows along the front, the painted sashes were peeling and there was cracked glass on the top floor. Someone had carried the body past the front door with its stone steps, past the dark frontage and the outbuilding, and buried it without being seen.

As Megan adjusted the light Sage could see purplish-red stippling on the opposite side from the bruising. Sage understood the post-death processes from recent reading but the reality was making her shiver inside. For a moment, she remembered finding her dead student the year before and her heart pounded in her ears. The pathologist flexed the girl's fingers, moved her jaw. 'Rigor mortis isn't completely gone. In these temperatures, I wouldn't expect to see that before thirty-six to forty-eight hours, but with a wide margin of error. Her temperature is less than six degrees, a little warmer than ambient because soil retains heat. Can you see the post-mortem staining there?'

'Livor mortis.' Sage had to swallow hard again as she caught another whiff of something from the body. Maybe it was just the mouldering leaves. The girl looked as if she was emerging from the forest floor like some sort of tree spirit. 'Hypostasis,' she managed, looking down at the plastic sheeting, trying to get her emotions back under control. 'Where the blood has pooled and stained the skin.'

'Exactly. Here it's on the left side of her face.' The pathologist gently lifted a few more layers of covering and shone her torch underneath.

'She does appear to be naked,' Sage said, concentrating on keeping her voice steady as she lifted another pile of leaves. 'Does that mean a sexual motive?'

'Possibly but it might also be a forensic countermeasure. Even criminals know about transferred trace evidence and DNA now. Look here, on the left side of the torso. Why is there no post-mortem staining on her shoulder?'

'Pressure stopped the blood concentrating there,' Sage said through rising panic from flashbacks of a face in the black water of a well. 'Maybe she was lying on a hard surface on her side? The blood would have collected in the lowest tissues, except where the blood vessels were compressed.' She counted the flashbacks away.

'Deep breaths,' Megan said, staring so intently at the body that for a moment Sage thought she was talking to the dead girl. 'Deep breaths will help you avoid the dizziness. We tend to hold our breath because of the smell and dizziness can make the nausea worse.' She glanced up. 'Pathologist's trick. You were looking a bit blue.'

Sage took a few breaths, closed her eyes and accepted the definite sweet-vile hint in the air. It smelled like rotten meat somehow sprinkled with cheap perfume. 'It's just cadaverine and putrescine,' she murmured, half to herself. 'Just chemicals, normal breakdown.'

Megan half laughed. 'Honestly, this is nothing. Try and focus on the smaller tasks and the bigger picture fades.'

The details burned into Sage's brain, like the plastic bags Megan was taping onto the hands, like the insect scurrying along the girl's lips to hide away in her mouth. Sage swallowed and looked up. She saw Trent, her supervisor, approaching.

'So, what do we do after we have collected all the leaves?' she asked him as he knelt beside her on the plastic sheet.

'Well, as you know, our job is to tell people what we need them to leave as part of the primary forensic survey. The initial briefing divides the evidence into what each specialism will concentrate on.'

Sage thought back to her classes. 'So, the pathologist gets the body, obviously, and records the position and relationship to the grave site. Forensics will look for any transfer, footprints, fibres and fingerprints. We do the grave and surrounding areas.'

'The layers of covering materials like the leaves need to be documented and preserved,' he said, nodding. 'You've made a good start. We'll make a site plan of the scene and advise what samples need to be taken. Someone dug the hole; we need to be able to say how and what with. What they covered her with will say something about what they were thinking. Archaeology will tell the investigation what was there. The police and other investigators will read that evidence, suggest why it was done. Sometimes we use a forensic anthropologist too.'

'OK.' Sage struggled with the taste of bile in her throat. 'Sorry. The smell is getting to me a bit; I'm used to historical sites where we only date to a century or so. Do you have an anthropologist involved?'

Trent half smiled in sympathy. 'No, so we're doing both jobs here.' He lowered his voice. 'If you feel sick, there's a bucket in the car. If you can't make it, throw up in an evidence bag. We can't contaminate the scene.' He bagged a few more leaves. 'I still feel rough, occasionally. Kids are harder. We probably won't need an anthropologist, there's a lot of crossover between us and them. We do know about burial rituals, so we can look for evidence of religious or cultural traditions as well.'

'OK.' Sage swallowed, hard. 'I'm OK.' She looked across the mound of leaves and twigs. 'There's evidence of some digging in the surface area around the site. We should photograph that. And take samples, in case they covered her up with soil from somewhere else. I can't see any trees that these leaves might have come from.'

The pathologist took a few more pictures, the flash whitening the skin.

The sound of a keening, animal cry reached Sage. She jumped and looked around. 'What's that?' The garden was waist high with bracken and brambles in places. The sky was darkening, the clouds gathering a purple tinge as the March daylight faded. Technicians were pulling the tent over the grave, putting more lights in place.

Sage stood awkwardly, making sure her booties didn't touch the grave edge, and followed Trent away from the burial. A few gulps of air got her nausea under control. The wailing had turned to wrenching sobs, coming from a huddle of people beyond police tape that was keeping press and locals at bay. A woman was supported by a bearded older man, a teenage girl beside them. The girl turned her head to stare at Sage, her expression blank. The woman screamed again, then subsided into hoarse sobs. The man was crying, the lights catching the tears on his face.

'Family,' said Trent, his lips tight. 'This is the hard bit.' He snapped a few pictures of the grass around him.

'How did they even know? I mean it might not be their daughter.'

'The radio and TV reported that a body had been found and a road sealed off three hours ago. The family recorded an appeal with the press last night.' Trent frowned. 'The psychologists will be looking at that, frame by frame.'

'I suppose they have to assume the family knows something.'

Trent grimaced. 'Do you know what percentage of child murders are done by parents? We have to be careful not to give away anything we find out. Everyone's a suspect at this point. Obviously, the owner of the house. Also, teachers, friends, neighbours – but mostly parents or their partners. You better get back before the press get a picture.' He moved away, taking more pictures of the crime scene as he went.

A scuffle behind her made Sage look towards the house. Two police officers were wrestling a tall, heavy-set man from the front door to the road. He fought them, falling onto his knees until they almost carried him along, sweating and struggling. DCI Lenham helped drag him towards the police vehicles.

'Mr Chorleigh, this isn't helping. Let us get your statement, then you can come home,' Lenham said as the big man shook him off.

A small dog barked around them until one officer nudged it hard with his foot and it yelped.

'The little bugger bit me,' he said, and Chorleigh swore and fought the officers until they snapped handcuffs on his wrists.

Sage moved forward and crouched down and called to the dog. 'Here, puppy. Over here, there's a good boy.' It froze, watching her, then trotted over. She caught it by its collar. 'Who deals with the dog?' she asked, but Lenham was pulling the man to his feet.

'RSPCA or kennels,' he said, out of breath. 'If we can't find a relative or neighbour.'

'I haven't done anything wrong!' the man howled, fighting them. 'And it's not his fault.' He was dressed in several layers of old jumpers with a shabby coat over the top. It was hard to guess his age; he looked old and ill but could have been as young as mid-forties.

A young policewoman held out a tattered lead and Sage clipped it on. There was something about the man's fear for his dog that touched her. 'I'll make sure he's looked after. Is it a he?' It was difficult to tell under matted hair.

Watching her, Chorleigh seemed to calm down a little. 'Hamish. He's only two, he's a bit boisterous. He's allergic to fish.'

'I'll tell them.' The man passed quite close to Sage as he was hauled to the police vehicles. In the distance someone shrieked, a man bellowed – perhaps they had caught sight of the suspect. Sage picked the dog up. It was a white terrier, with long greasy fur. It strained to reach its owner, to lick his face. 'He'll be fine.'

'I didn't do anything,' he started to say as he was dragged into the van. 'I haven't hurt anyone.'

'You said that last time,' Lenham muttered under his breath. He lifted his hand to touch the dog, then pulled it away. 'He's filthy. You'll need a clean suit.'

Sage had a good look at the front paws of the animal. 'You'd think he would have dug around the body. As – you know, it started to smell. They have a great nose for decomposition.'

'Good point.' Lenham waved to one of his colleagues. 'Get the dog taken over to the station and examined in case he touched the body.' He turned back to Sage. 'How's the retrieval coming on?'

'Trent is just taking a few more location shots while we work on the grave itself. Megan says she'll take the body to the mortuary in the morning at the earliest; we'll be working late. There's a lot to document.' She hesitated. 'What did you mean by "last time"?'

'Teenager went missing in 1992, right here. Alistair Chorleigh was the last person to see her. She was never found.' His voice was clipped. 'We need that body if we're going to solve this murder. You'd better get on with it, then.'

Sage walked back to the tent, changed her forensic suit for a clean one, and knelt by the corpse again. She reached for a few more leaves at the side of the body and brushed the girl's hip. The distant sobbing of the woman at the gate was chilling, and the flickering lights brought movement to the gleaming eyes of the dead girl.

# 2

'I first heard of Chorleigh House and its ancient burial mounds from my friend, P. Chorleigh, Balliol. I intend to help him excavate the barrows with as little disruption as possible, using my training in archaeology. We hope to add to the sketchy knowledge of earthworks within the Royal Forest.'

Journal of Edwin Masters, Saturday 22nd June 1913

The invitation to excavate an ancient barrow had come at the right time, at least for me. My mother, laid low by a fever, was being nursed by her sister. There was no room for me in our rooms. Instead, I would have been forced to stay in my study in Oxford, and survive on what little work there was clerking for a firm of solicitors. Instead, I was greeted by Peter Chorleigh's excited note, dashed off with a rough sketch of what he believed to be Bronze Age earthworks. They were in the grounds of his family home in Hampshire, but he had never thought of them as so old or interesting before. I didn't hesitate, but wrote a letter to my mother and bought a railway ticket to Southampton. I changed there for the halt at Holmsley in the New Forest.

My first view of Chorleigh House was when the driver dropped me off in his horse and trap. It had been a long rattle over forest roads to the house, the drive arching in through a double gate with massive gateposts. The house sat side-on to the road beside a huge striped lawn and shrub beds already covered with roses in bud. The property itself was built of grey stone, the front door under a portico at the top of three shallow steps. Pairs of windows looked out over the garden, and I could see a couple ran through the house to give a view of treetops and sky beyond. A grass tennis court appeared to run along the furthest side of the house beyond an outbuilding or two.

'Here's Chorleigh,' the driver told me, pulling his horse up on the wide circle of gravel in front of the house. 'That'll be three shillings.'

I gave him four; I had enjoyed the drive through the forest from Holmsley Station.

'I suppose you must get a bit of work from the Chorleighs?' I said, dragging my leather bag off the back.

'Not much,' he answered, somewhat curtly. 'They got motors. Bloody things, shouldn't be allowed in the forest, that's what I say. They scare the horses. Two ponies had to be shot last month after they were run down.'

'I'm sorry to hear that.' I lifted my satchel off and stood back. 'Thank you, anyway. I plan to stay a month, but perhaps I shall see you when I leave.'

'You can get me through the station, they've got a telephone there.' He snapped out a number and started to turn his horse towards the road. Then he stopped, and curiously, looked back. 'If you need me in a hurry, my niece, Tilly, she'll always get a message to me. She works in the kitchen here. Mr Chorleigh, he's a hard man. He's got a bit of a temper.'

'I'm sure everything will be fine, but thank you.' I was baffled by the offer, but thanked him anyway. Then Peter appeared in the open doorway at the front of the house and yelled, 'Edwin!' and I was swept off my feet in a bear hug.

Peter is a year younger than me as I started my degree late, and we didn't seem to have much in common. But in the last years, as we studied our degrees and shared a college, we became close. 'Comrades under fire,' Peter called it, as we shivered under the scathing criticism of one of our teachers, the great Sir Charles Latterby. Now our essays are marked, our final examinations are over and we are to spend the summer putting our knowledge to the test before I must return to my mother's house and find suitable employment.

He led me through a large door into a spacious hallway, with two staircases curving up to a half-landing above.

'Peter!' a voice exclaimed, and I turned to see a young

woman who resembled him so much I knew she must be his sister.

'Oh, Molly, there you are!' He hugged her briefly, and for a moment their faces were close together. She looked like a delicate, feminine version of him, and he caught her arm to draw her towards me. 'This is Edwin, my closest friend from Oxford.'

Molly held out her hand; I noticed it had smears of paint or ink on it. She almost withdrew it, but I clasped it anyway. She blushed. 'I'm sorry,' she murmured. I could see an older man behind her, as dark as his children were fair and even taller than Peter.

'My father, Mr James Chorleigh,' Peter said, stooping to pat the two dogs that curved around his feet. 'Edwin Masters, Father.'

I shook Mr Chorleigh's hand.

'You're welcome,' he said. 'Peter, get your friend settled in, then go and see your mother.' He turned to me, 'I know you won't mind my wife not greeting you. She has been unwell.' I knew she had been ill; a nervous collapse, Peter had said. The youngest child of the family had died from diphtheria the year before, a terrible time for them all, and Mrs Chorleigh had taken to her bed. 'We are looking forward to your historical discoveries in the grounds. But I don't want my wife disturbed.'

'Of course, sir,' I said. 'And we won't spoil your grounds too much.'

He nodded to me and turned away. Peter hefted my leather bag.

'Come up, Ed, I'll show you your room.'

'Then come down for tea,' Molly said, blushing again.

As we walked up to the landing, I could see it was beautifully lit from above by a domed lantern in the ceiling. It shone on the polished parquet flooring below. 'This is lovely,' I managed to say before he caught my arm and dragged me towards one wing.

'Nice enough. My grandfather put in the wooden flooring downstairs; it's better with the dogs than carpets everywhere.' He dragged my case into one of the bedrooms. 'I've put you in here, next to me. My mother is on the other side of the house; she likes the quiet. Now, wash up and come down for some tea,' he said, putting the bag on the bed. 'There's the bathroom across the hall, there's a towel somewhere – ah, here. I'll go and see Mother.' He grimaced. 'Poor Molls, she's become Mother's companion. She doesn't get out much since Claire died.'

'That can't be easy, at her age.'

He leaned against the doorjamb. 'That's why you're here. You will liven us all up with your discoveries and scholarship.'

I almost laughed at that. 'Me, old sobersides, to liven anyone up?'

'Well, you'll liven me up anyway.' He grasped my arm briefly. 'I've missed you, Ed.'

# 3

*Tuesday 19th March, this year*

It had been a long evening's work uncovering the body and Sage didn't get back to her mother's house in Winchester until past midnight. She half registered that Nick was asleep in the spare bed and Max, her eleven-month-old son, startled in his cot when she walked in.

It was a pleasure to lift him, feel him snuggle into her. It didn't seem possible that River Sloane had ever been alive like this, but the idea made tears gather in the corners of her eyes. Max laid his head against her shoulder and subsided back into sleep. He smelled of shampoo and clean pyjamas and baby and if Nick hadn't been taking up half the bed, she probably would have snuck Max in with her. She nestled him back between his soft toys and covered him with a blanket. He turned his head and whimpered and she stroked his back.

'How did it go?' Nick's whisper just reached her, but

she waited until the baby was completely asleep before she answered.

'OK. It was all right,' she murmured back, sliding out of her clothes. She ached from kneeling over the grave for so long. 'Sad.' She couldn't face looking in her bag for more clothes so decided to sleep in her T-shirt. When she slid under the duvet Nick reached for her and curved his body against her back. He was warm; she realised how cold she'd got. 'Go back to sleep. Love you.'

He buried his face in her hair and kissed her neck. 'Mm. You too.'

Sage woke with a start; she must have crashed straight into sleep, and it took a few moments to work out where she was. Mum's house, the body in the woods, Maxie, Nick. She checked her phone: barely six-thirty, it was still gloomy outside. A tangled memory of running, a body in a well and the girl in the leaves haunted her.

The bed next to her was empty, as was the cot. Nick must have taken the baby downstairs with him. Sage could shower and dress in peace. She could just hear the odd burst of conversation from downstairs, laughter, as she got ready for work. Mum loved Max and he adored her. His giggle met Sage as she walked towards the kitchen at the back of the old terraced house.

Nick appeared in the doorway with a spoon, holding the

baby. 'Put Maxie in his high chair, will you? And taste this.'

She smiled at Max and tasted the porridge. 'That's delicious. Hi, baby boy. Do you want some maple syrup like Mummy?'

Max lifted his arms towards her. It was still a wonder to be able to hold him, feel his weight against her. He was just starting to wobble across the room on his feet, which to Sage was a small miracle every day.

'He eats it as it comes, like me,' Nick scoffed. 'It's just you that needs to drown it in sugar.'

Max waved and burbled something to her. She pulled the high chair out from the wall beside the table. 'Really, Maxie, are you hungry? Sit in your chair and Nick will get you something to eat. Where's *Sheshe?*'

'Just putting the bin out.' Nick carried bowls over. He put some toast soldiers on the tray for Max to pick up and drop and throw about, and handed Sage a baby spoon. 'It's your turn to get covered. I was still getting porridge out of my hair at lunchtime yesterday.'

Sage's mother, Yana, walked in and opened her arms for a hug with her daughter. 'You're OK?' she asked after a moment, pushing Sage back to study her face. 'Saw the case on the news. Terrible.' It always amazed Sage that Yana had never lost her Kazakh accent, despite living in the UK for nearly forty years.

'Very sad,' Sage said, looking at them. Her favourite people, all together. 'How's Maxie been?'

'No trouble, never.' Her mother beamed. 'Nick and me, we took him to park.'

'When do you have to go back to the crime scene?' Nick mumbled through a spoonful of porridge.

'I need to be there early. Maxie?' The baby opened his mouth like a bird and took the porridge off the spoon. He slapped the toast on the tray, some of the bits flying across the table.

Sage's phone pinged and she reached for it. Trent. *Check the 24-hour news.*

'Sorry, *Sheshe.*' She switched the small TV on over Yana's protests. 'It's just work.'

She could hear Nick talking to Max. A couple were on a long table flanked by police. Both looked exhausted, red-eyed with fear, especially the father. A voiceover was dispassionate. 'On Sunday 17th March, Owen and Jenna Sloane appealed for the safe return of their daughter, River, who went missing on Saturday afternoon after 12.30.'

'If anyone knows anything, please let the police know,' the woman said. 'We're just so worried. She didn't even tell us where she was going.' Her face was creased with anxiety, fear, threaded with hope. The father buried his head in his hands and was comforted by his wife. A group portrait flashed up, of the smiling parents, River, another young girl she recognised from outside the garden at Chorleigh House, and a small boy. It took Sage a moment to equate the family portrait with the still, grey body in the leaves. Sage couldn't imagine how the family were feeling. It must have been terrifying being caught up in a room full of journalists and police; the cameras showed the mother collapsing in tears. The banner scrolling across the bottom of the screen caught Sage's eye. 'Body found in New Forest…' The shot cut away from the appeal to the distant five-bar gate of Chorleigh House. 'Police are unable to confirm the body found at an address in the New Forest…' She switched the TV off.

'That's awful. I can't imagine how the parents are coping,' Nick said. 'How long will you need to be at the site?' Nick shook his head at Max, who was cramming his fingers into his mouth after the porridge. 'You're going to need a bath, little man.'

Sage gulped a mouthful of tea. 'They were there yesterday, crying behind the police barrier. I don't know how long it will go on for. We hadn't even finished uncovering…' She looked at Max. 'Retrieving the victim. Then we have a lot of lab stuff to do.'

'You do remember I'm going away too?'

'Of course, that's why I asked Mum to babysit Max.' Which was all true, it's just that where he was going and the reason had slipped her mind. 'Conference, right?'

He looked back at her, his face grave. 'No, not a conference. I'm going to see a team ministry. It's a particularly successful model for other deprived rural areas. I want to see how it works. For the future, if I go for another job.'

Sage filled a spoon for the baby and retrieved bits of chewed toast from the floor. Five-second rule, she decided, and put a couple of the least fluffy ones back on his tray. 'Porridge, Maxie.' The baby was adorable; Sage's whole body seemed to relax when he looked at her. 'We're OK living where we are at the moment; we can manage a bit longer. You're happy at Banstock and I'm finishing my training. Maybe we should move a few things around to make the flat more comfortable. Let me get back to work properly, get the job situation sorted out.'

Yana exchanged looks with Sage and walked out into the hall. Oh. It's going to be one of those talks. Sage took a gulp of tea to fortify herself.

'Spending two nights a week in a one-bedroom flat?' Nick said. 'Making love on a sofa bed because the baby shares the only bedroom? You visiting the vicarage a few times a month?'

It had all been said before. Sage leaned forward. 'I love you, you love me. That's all we have room for at the moment. It's Max's home and I have a mortgage. I can't afford to buy anything bigger and you earn peanuts as a vicar. I still have to find a new career I can fit around a baby. Hopefully, forensic archaeology will work for me and I can look for a permanent job on the mainland. Then we can move in together.'

'How about Maxie, Sage?' He sat next to her, looking down at the baby. 'He's nearly eleven months old. How does he know who I am if I only visit?'

'He doesn't need to see you every day to love you—'

Nick looked down, his face sad. 'I want to see you every day. And I want to be Max's dad. I miss you both in the week.'

'I miss you too—' Her mobile phone rang. 'I'm sorry, I need to get this, it's Trent.'

'Sage?' The signal wasn't good. 'I need to do the survey at Chorleigh House before the dew goes. Will you be there?'

'On my way, should be half an hour.'

Nick silently handed her the phone charger and her work lanyard. She wolfed down the last of her porridge. It had gone cold.

He put his hand on her shoulder. 'I'm still not sure that working on a murder won't bring back stuff from last year. Flashbacks.'

Just the word felt like a cup of cold water down her spine. 'I know,' she said, stalled. 'I've been studying forensics to get it out of my system. I think this will help, I really do. It's sad but it's someone else's child, you know?'

He reached his arms around her, holding her until she curved into him and hugged him back. 'I remember how you were when you found the body in the well last year. It's bound to remind you.'

She smiled at him, having to tilt her chin up as he was a little taller. 'It might be a good thing. Then I'll have something to tell that counsellor you're always telling me to see.' He smelled like the sea, fresh scents coming off his clean jumper. 'I'll be careful, and I'll tell you all about it.'

He kissed her. 'I love you, Sage.' He let go slowly, leaving her a bit puzzled.

'I love you too. Are you OK?'

'Just not looking forward to the long drive. I'll be in Cambridge tonight seeing my parents, then I'll do the rest tomorrow.'

She couldn't even remember where he was driving to, and didn't want him to think she didn't care. God, I've become so selfish. 'Well, I hope you have a great time. I better go, I don't want to be late.' She kissed Max on the top of his head, the only part of him that didn't look sticky. 'Love you, Maxie Bean. Be good for Nana.'

The New Forest looked lovely in the early morning light. Leaves were just starting to unfurl from some of the saplings at the edge of the road, and there were catkins everywhere. Sage could feel the tension building as she turned towards Fairfield then into the lane where Chorleigh House was set in the forest. A dozen cars were pulled up on the grass verges along the road and a line of police tape held back people with cameras, some even snapping a few pictures of her as she was waved through and pulled into the drive.

The property had a paling fence held together with wire and a wide drive with two brick gateposts, both in poor repair. The five-bar gate was pulled partly across, narrowing the gap onto a large expanse of gravel. The area was full of weeds and brambles encroaching from the edges. To the left was a raised bed built of the same stone as the house, rampant with the frost-blackened skeletons of bracken. On the right the house was grey, the windows dark.

As she walked in the low light she realised how fresh the air was, the breeze cold on her neck. A tall, thin man was pacing across the drive, counting each step aloud. 'Trent!'

He grinned at her through a dark beard. 'There you are. How did the grave site work go?'

'It's still going on. We got most of the leaves last night and they are hoping to retrieve the body this morning. What are you doing – have you started the survey?'

'No, I'm getting ready to attempt an aerial assessment before the frost melts and the dew dries. They are highlighting the footprints into the woods.' He squinted up through his glasses. 'The sun's starting to come over the hill, these shadows won't last much longer.'

'Drones. We didn't use them in my training,' Sage said as they moved onto the grass. She looked along Trent's arm, pointing into the woodland. A number of footprint trails converged on the area of the body, clearly visible in the frost. There was a flattened path leading between the bare trees.

'There are about thirty-eight acres of woodland associated with the property,' he said, pulling a map out of his backpack. He shook it open and folded it so she could see the area better. 'All of this belongs to Chorleigh House.'

His finger circled the irregular shape, then pointed at two star shapes. 'These are the historical barrows, probably Bronze Age. They were excavated a hundred years ago. I've been trying to get to see them.'

'Wow. How much is left?'

Trent grinned at her. 'Quite a lot. Back in the early nineteen hundreds an archaeology student dug up a burial in the complete earthwork. They "restored" the mound afterwards, which probably means they just chucked the soil back.'

Sage looked back at him. 'I'm guessing this was not a permitted excavation?'

'No, but they hadn't even identified it as a scheduled monument at that time. But there's a real legend around the barrows.' He looked up at the house, which looked like it was leaning over the garden. 'The archaeologist in charge of the dig vanished. The locals call the place haunted; they claim he disturbed an ancient curse.'

She shrugged. 'I don't believe in curses, ancient or otherwise. The earthworks look like they are right on the boundary of the adjoining farmland. There could be banks and ditches associated with the barrows. I wonder how much has been ploughed away. Do we know if they found anything on the original dig?'

'That's the strange thing,' Trent answered. 'I haven't found many records yet. And the family was cursed in a way. Alistair Chorleigh's having a tough time of it; he's been interviewed all night but they have to release him later or apply for an extension. They just don't have enough evidence yet, which is where we come in.' He looked up. 'Do you see where the leaves came from?'

She turned around, looking for evergreen trees that weren't just covered in ivy. 'None nearby but it's dark in the woodland. There's been a lot of foot traffic in and out along that path. Oh, DCI Lenham.'

Lenham stepped onto the pad behind her. 'Good morning. The old lady who found the body said she only went as far as the grave to get her dog.'

Sage looked back across the long grass and bracken. 'Did her dog touch the body? There are scratches on one of the hands.'

'Yes, the owner said it ran off and wouldn't come back.' Lenham shivered, shrugged his coat around his ears. 'She didn't like to trespass because Chorleigh has got a bit of a nasty reputation locally. When she couldn't get it to come back to the road, she had to go in to get it. The animal had taken the leaves off part of the girl's hand.'

Sage surveyed the woodland. It was dense and didn't look well managed. Brambles had filled in most of the undergrowth and she could see rabbit and deer droppings on the slight path. There were definitely discrete areas of flattening in the shimmering white over the grass.

'Are those the footprints you saw last night?' she asked.

'Yes.' Trent pointed up to the sky. 'I'll get the drone up

and we'll get some footage. Can Megan spare you for half an hour?'

Sage looked around the garden. 'I'm sure she can, I came early just to help you.' Apart from islands of overgrown shrubs in the bracken and grass, there was little evidence it had been cultivated recently. The trees gathered into a wall of shadows. 'I can see how a view from above will show features you can't see from the ground.'

Trent grinned at her. 'The police love our aerial shots. I want to get some before they start exploring the grounds.' He turned to DCI Lenham. 'If you could get your officers to stand back, I can get the drone up.'

'No problem.' Lenham hunched his shoulders up. 'This place gives me the creeps.' He walked towards the front of the house, waving at three officers who followed him.

The long grass and bracken were covered with a shimmering lace of spiders' webs hung with droplets as the frost melted. A few lime-green buds were just unfolding. Sage could see some areas were flattened in ovals in a staggered line of prints, still visible in the light frost. Trent started to set the drone up in the centre of the lawn.

He waved at Sage. 'Stand well back. I'm taking off.'

The drone whined and started hovering over the grass where he had placed it. The grave site itself was still covered with the forensic tent. As the machine rose Trent showed her the white tent in the green of the grounds on his tablet. 'Look.'

Greener areas had less frost, and as the image sharpened Sage could see footprints criss-crossing the shaded grass into gaps between the trees. They were roughly oval and the flattened grass distorted the shape.

Sage pointed at the screen. 'How do we know they aren't animal prints?'

Trent brought the drone down until it hovered a few metres over the edge of the woodland. He zoomed in on one of the marks. 'There are heel and toe impressions on a few of them. Not to mention there's just one pair of prints, no back feet. Although you're right, that doesn't always mean a biped; deer often walk in their own prints. They are fuzzy – they've been here at least eighteen hours and possibly from the night before, they are just rough shapes. Quite a long stride. Hopefully the ground will give us a better impression if we can find a muddy patch and we might find a trace.'

Sage bounced on her heels, rubbed her hands down her arms to warm herself up. 'Maybe they went into the wood to gather the leaves?'

'It's possible.' Trent manoeuvred the drone so it swooped over the ground towards the drive. 'My guess is they drove here, parked maybe on the drive or the verge along the road. The gravel wouldn't leave the same prints as flattened grass and the gate's always open but it would make a lot of noise.'

'They then carried the body across the garden? Anyone

driving past could have seen them. And what about the homeowner?'

'I suspect it was dark, in the middle of the night, and a quiet road because that's how most people dispose of victims. And the homeowner is a suspect himself. But look what I found yesterday.'

The drone swerved along the drive over the road, absent of cars as it was still closed off, the press kept behind police tape. It slid east along the grass verge, then turned back and covered the area to the west. There were multiple tyre lines diagonal to the grass verges but only one parallel to the road. They showed patches of white, like paint.

Trent pointed it out. 'The police made a cast of these tracks. We'll check to make sure these aren't from the press or the dog walker, but I think the perp could have parked outside, carried her in. She didn't look heavy.'

'Chorleigh wouldn't have needed to park on the verge. He could have pulled onto the drive.'

'Yes, and anyone could have driven onto the grass since we last had heavy rain. Walkers, or someone who stopped to look at a map or got a puncture. But they look fresh.' He swung the drone around again, letting it alight gently on the lawn. 'You don't fancy Chorleigh for it, then?'

'I don't know. It seems stupid, to bury the body in your own garden and just a foot deep.'

'Stupid, yes. Unlikely – I don't know. Murderers are stupid, in my experience. He might not have been thinking straight, he's a drunk. Who knows what he was thinking? The leaves could have been laid on with remorse.'

Sage looked back at the white tent. 'She was found by a dog walker, you said. Why not by Chorleigh's own dog? Surely he would have smelled a stranger, let alone a body.'

'According to Lenham, Chorleigh says he doesn't let his dog off the lead at night because the gate is always open, apparently it's stuck. The walker couldn't get her collie to come back so she came in to get it. When she saw what her dog had uncovered she panicked, flagged down an elderly motorist. She was in such distress he called an ambulance and the police, in case her story was true.'

'It's a good job the dog didn't disturb the burial too much.'

Trent raised the drone high above the trees to get a wider view. 'We see animal damage a lot. Foxes and badgers can disarticulate a body quite fast in the summer.'

She felt queasy again. 'Enough information. Do we know when they can remove the body?'

'It won't be long. Forensics want another look at the grave in daylight before we start excavating the cut itself, the digging.'

'Do we need to be involved in that?' Two more people were walking down the drive, dressed in forensic suits. She looked back at the dark windows of the house.

'They look at it primarily as a source of trace evidence, so no, they won't want us. They'll look for clothing fibres, as she was undressed, and anything the murderer might have dropped. We'll look at the wider scene, how the hole was dug, where the spoil was dropped, how the hole was filled in.'

'In this case, where did they get the leaves from?' Sage said. 'I don't see many evergreens.'

He looked around. 'Not from this area, anyway. We'll search the whole grounds. We will also look into whether they left any more footmarks or evidence, and do the wider survey to create an accurate site plan.' The drone's engine, hovering overhead, hummed like a large bee. The machine lifted high above the trees, and Trent flew it a few hundred yards south of the drive. He held the tablet out to Sage. 'Watch this.'

The trees looked odd from above, the branches reaching for the drone. It disturbed a blackbird which took off with angry screeching. A jay flew under the camera in a flap of black, white and peach feathers, a flash of blue. She watched as the drone slowly moved along the boundary of the woodland and the field beyond. 'Are those – the barrows?' There were two raised areas, one classically a round-ended, elongated rectangle, and the other about half the size with an oval end. The smaller one had a few small shrubs leaning from one end and a large flat area on the surface.

'Yes,' Trent said. 'The site's called Hound Butt on Victorian surveys. It was pretty well vandalised in the early nineteen hundreds, by modern standards anyway.'

'Vandalised? Do you mean when the archaeologist who went missing dug it up?' Sage followed the view as the drone swooped over the intact one.

'The family who owned the land excavated it with a few volunteers, that archaeologist and an Oxford history professor. They made a bit of a mess of it.' He swung the drone around to the east of the long barrow. 'There's what looks like the second one. Or what's left of it, it looks like it's been hacked in half. You can see the internal architecture.'

The eastern end of the feature was a stone wall of two parallel slabs, green with algae and moss. A narrow stream dribbled around the bottom of the cut edge into a brown patch of what looked like mud, which trickled under the wire fence and into a ditch. The other side was a gentle slope running almost to the edge of the other feature, dotted with scrubby gorse and bracken.

'Yes,' she said, unable to make out the details. 'There's no idea of height from above. Can we go and see them?'

'We must stay strictly within the warrant but yes, we should be able to get to it. There are a number of possible places where there could be evidence. We can also do this.'

He brought the drone down through a space in the canopy over the smaller feature and Sage leaned in to see the screen as it hovered a couple of metres off the top. 'The barrows look barely fifteen, twenty metres apart,' she said. 'They could have been part of the same feature originally.'

'Scale is misleading with this thing.' The stones that

covered the top were thick with mounds of velvety moss. 'We need to look on the ground, I don't want to risk my drone on these trees.'

She watched as he flew it back up. 'That's amazing detail on the footage. Do you know anything more about the dig?'

'There were a few mentions in the local paper, a local investigation into the man that went missing, that's all.' He landed the machine on the lawn before he looked at her. 'It started OK. They dug it over the summer of 1913, uncovered a few finds – bones, bronze wire, that sort of thing. Then the family lost interest in the excavation and threw the spoil back over the burial chamber.'

'I'd love to find out more,' Sage said. 'Are there any recorded remains, bones in the local museum maybe?'

'I don't know. But the whole family was cursed, according to the legend. It's local history, you can look it up online.' He started the drone again, and it lifted to about three metres off the ground. Sage fell into step with him as he followed the machine. He halted at the edge of the woodland, and positioned the drone over the narrow path. 'I've been trying to get permission to see the barrows since they showed up on a LiDAR scan of the area. Look, more footprints, back and forward along that rabbit path.'

Sage peered at the screen and pointed at a dark square. 'What's that rectilinear feature?' The shadow on the screen was almost covered with evergreen foliage, perhaps the same as the leaves from the burial. 'We need to have a look at it.'

'It could be a large shed or workshop,' he said. 'Maybe a garage or stable, left to rot. I'm no gardener but it doesn't look like anything's been done to the grounds for twenty, thirty years.'

'It's covered with branches.' When Trent brought the drone down she could see the dark leaves. 'That could be the source of the holly over the body.' She turned to see DCI Lenham standing by the forensic tent making notes, and waved him over. 'DCI Lenham! We've found a possible source for the foliage.'

Lenham took the screen from Trent. He was tall and heavy-set, his hair more white than grey at the sides. He glanced at her sideways, catching her staring, and frowned. 'What is it?'

Sage pointed to the shape in the trees. 'There's some sort of building, in the trees a few hundred metres from the boundary. It seems covered in the type of plants that were used to conceal the body – ivy and holly.'

'OK. We'll have a look at it.' He pointed at the screen as Trent brought the drone over the site. 'What am I looking at? That looks grave-shaped.' He studied the image of the barrows.

'It's too big to be a burial – there's no scale on this thing,' she explained. 'Trent was telling me it's an ancient earthwork; it was picked up on LiDAR and it's on the maps.'

Lenham looked from Trent to Sage. 'LiDAR?'

Sage answered, as Trent navigated the drone over the

building again. 'LiDAR is a laser scanning technique. It's been used to survey the New Forest looking for features that might otherwise not show up on aerial photographs.'

'Can it show anything unusual?'

'It can read the landscape under the vegetation and see even tiny features or fairly flat ones that don't show up on satellite images.'

Lenham looked interested. 'It would be worth looking at those scans to see if there's any sign of a burial from the nineties. We never got to really search the grounds thoroughly when the teenager Lara Black went missing.'

*Permission to look at the barrows.* Sage was excited but tried to keep it out of her voice. 'We could follow up with a closer look on the ground.'

Trent brought the drone back, allowing it to land gently by its case. 'You can see there are recent footfalls leading in and out of the trees. We need to follow up the prints you can see in the dew and we'll create a plan of the whole site.'

Lenham looked around at his officers. 'Just be finished before this afternoon, because my officers will need to do their own ground search and survey. Your drone footage will be useful, though. Mapping's always difficult with so much undergrowth. We're making a list of possible suspects at the moment.'

Sage looked at him. 'Are there many? I mean, how many people might want to hurt a fifteen-year-old girl, unless it's a predator.'

'You'd be surprised how many motives there can be. She lived with her mother and stepfather, a stepsister and half-brother, so there's lots of family dynamics to explore. Her own dad isn't around much. She had friends, an older boyfriend, and was into animal rights campaigning.' He managed a humourless smile. 'That could have created tensions for the parents. She and her stepsister don't seem close, either.'

'How old is the boyfriend?' Sage said.

'Good question,' Lenham answered. 'I'm not sure I'd like my fifteen-year-old dating a nineteen-year-old lad.'

Trent interrupted. 'How far can we extend our search of the estate?'

'We have a warrant that covers the house, car and all the grounds.' Lenham looked back at the screen. 'Where do you want to start?'

Trent pulled up an image. 'There's the building through the trees that might be useful. There could be a solid floor inside, maybe a stable yard outside. I can't see anything from above except these footprints…' He explained the images to Lenham. 'But first, we need to catalogue the information from the grave itself. I'll get Sage to concentrate on that.' Trent waved her towards the forensic tent. 'Sorry. Back to your mouldy leaves.'

# 4

'Lastly, from its very nature, the New Forest is ever beautiful, at every season of the year, even in the depths of winter. The colouring of summer is not more rich. Then the great masses of holly glisten with its brightest green; the purple light hangs around the bare oaks; and the yews stand out in their shrouds of black.'

*The New Forest: its History and its Scenery*, John R.Wise (1885)
Copied by hand in a book of field notes, Edwin Masters, 22nd June 1913

Dinner was a sombre affair. Mr Chorleigh barely acknowledged my presence after a scathing stare at my lack of proper formal attire, and didn't encourage much conversation while the food was served. I had time to observe Peter and his sister communicating by the odd word and a few smiles.

Molly is pretty, slight, and looks younger than her
seventeen years. Last summer Peter came to stay with me and
my mother in our rooms in Colchester, while his sister Claire
was ill and infectious. He stayed a month, until the poor girl
died, and the time together strengthened our friendship. We
talked late into each night about his dreams and his fears for
his family. I missed him when he left for the funeral. Through
him, I felt I already knew his sensitive, grief-stricken mother
and his bookish younger sister. He didn't speak with as much
affection about his father, but he had a great deal of respect.

After dinner, Peter and Molly took me out to see the
grounds. The family have about forty acres of forest, and
it seems pleasant and open to me. The back of the house
looks over a handsome paved area covered in Grecian-style
statues, scantily dressed nymphs and a rather fat Pan. The
whole terrace has a view down a gradual incline, lightly
forested, to the river. The house has a grand reception room
with three sets of French doors, which Molly told me can
hold forty couples dancing or even more. They prefer to sit
in the south drawing room, which also has river views and
catches the last of the evening sun. The weather had been
sunny, and was becoming sultry.

'The sea is just a short trip in the motor,' Peter told me,
pointing at a garage that we passed between the house and
the tennis court. 'And we swim in the river sometimes; it's
tidal. There's a beach and a boathouse through the trees.
We drive out to Lymington if we want to sail. Father has

a three-year-old Starling motor, and there's a wagonette brake we use for hunting and shooting parties.'

It was a reminder that Peter's upbringing was very different from my own. Some diffidence must have shown on my face, because Peter nudged me with his elbow. 'Cheer up, Ed. If anyone acts snobby you can trot out your great-uncle, the general.'

I smiled, but hardly thought the relative I had met once when I was a child was equal to all this splendour. 'It is rather different.'

'I've stayed with your mother, and she couldn't have been kinder. It's no different here, we just have a bigger place. Anyway, don't be a chump, let's go and look at the barrows.'

I followed him and Molly out to the grass tennis court and along a well-kept path mowed through the trees. We walked down to the gardeners' shed. Beyond it the path narrowed to a track. We wove through trees and bushes, past a huge stack of felled logs, and the sounds of birds became louder.

Molly turned and put her finger to her lips. 'If we're very quiet, we might see them…'

She tiptoed down the path with Peter and stopped when he raised a hand. I crept up to them and saw a magnificent sight: fallow deer, five of them, standing on a hillock. They lifted their heads and froze for a moment. I held my breath. Then the nearest one sniffed at the air and our human scent must have frightened them, for they were off, bounding into the trees and away from us.

'They're often here, but not normally so early,' Peter said, walking out onto the foot of the slope. 'It's because Molls and I have been away. They don't get disturbed much. This is the barrow.'

As I ducked under the foliage, I came into the clearing and the full scale of the mound was revealed. It was some eighty or a hundred feet long, and twenty feet across at its widest and covered with grass. It was about five or six feet high.

'Isn't it magnificent?' Molly shaded her eyes against the late sun. 'And there's the second one.'

I hadn't noticed the second barrow because it was at a slight angle and half obscured by small trees. The slope rose up, more steeply, and was covered with brambles and gorse. It seemed to end abruptly; Peter had warned me it had been chopped about badly. He led the way, squeezing past stinging nettles and bracken along the side.

The second barrow *had* been cut in half. The whole of one end had gone, exposing two stone slabs that had once formed some sort of chamber within, like double doors. The barrow was a little taller than the other one, and narrower, like a wedge of cake covered in grass. Below, the ground gave way to dried mud. It looked as if there was some sort of pond here in wet weather.

Standing on the rutted ground, I could just reach the top of the slabs, where I could feel an open space like a letterbox but wider. 'It's been cut about as if it was another barrow. Was it ever excavated?'

Peter shook his head, walking carefully over the edges of the dried mud. 'It's been like this since the farm owned it, and they say it went back to the Middle Ages at least.' He rested his hands on the two upright slabs that formed a barrier, holding back the inside of the barrow. 'I always imagined this was a portal to a great treasure chamber within. I thought one day I would find a way to open it.'

'Is it hollow?'

Peter pointed at the top of the stones, obscured by hanging ivy and plants. 'There's a huge flat rock roof on top, under the grass. That slot goes right under the top stones. When I was a child my father forbade me climbing up inside in case I got stuck. It does echo so maybe there's a deeper cavity in the middle.'

'Perhaps we should investigate this one instead,' I said, suddenly anxious not to damage the intact earthwork.

'My father's expecting a gold hoard, at the very least,' Peter said. 'If there was any treasure in this one, someone has already had it.'

I looked back at the serene burial mound behind us. 'It sounds silly, but it makes me a little uneasy to disturb whatever's buried there.'

'Exactly!' said Molly. 'Don't disturb the curse of Hound Barrow.'

'Hound Butt,' corrected Peter. 'And there is no suggestion of a curse.'

# 5

While Trent packed the drone away and downloaded the data for analysis, Sage went back to help collect evidence from the grave site. She found Megan outside the tent, holding out a forensic suit pack.

'We're finally ready to take the body to the mortuary,' she said. 'It was more complicated than we thought with all the leaves, and the press have been questioning how long we're taking to move her. They want a definite confirmation that it is River, which Lenham will give at a press conference once all the relatives have been told.' She brushed her hood back with a gloved hand. 'I've been here since five and I didn't get to bed until one last night.'

Sage noticed the dark rings under the pathologist's eyes. 'You must be shattered. Trent sent me to help. What can I do?' She followed Megan into the tent. At least the body was now covered with a plastic sheet. Sage lifted up one of the last piles of leaves from above the girl's head. They were moulded together into a stack by moisture, white threads of mould running through them. 'These were piled up somewhere for at least a few weeks.'

Megan stood back, rubbed the base of her spine. 'We need to find where they got them. It's unlikely they brought a car full of leaves with them, but you never know.' She smiled as DCI Lenham pulled back the tent flap and slid just inside.

He leaned towards the grave. 'Before I talk to the press, is there any doubt that this is River Sloane? DNA will confirm it, of course.'

Megan reached forward and drew back the sheet carefully. 'What do you think, Sage? Is there anything which would contradict that conclusion? It helps if we all use the same basic procedures.' The pathologist stared at her, and Sage felt like she was twelve years old in a French verbs test.

The body looked so pathetic in its grave cut, the soil appearing almost black. 'Well, it's a female, obviously, and the length and colour of hair and make-up residue seem to match the photos I saw on the news. She could be as young as twelve, or as old as twenty – post-mortem changes to the face make it hard to tell with the swelling. She had shoulder-length blonde hair, bleached a few weeks ago; her roots are dark blonde, mousy.' Sage had a flashback to seeing Steph's face, floating in a haze of pale hair from the year before. She blinked the memory away. 'She has two piercings in the right ear, three in the left, all in the lobe. Her eyes are… um, I'm not sure.'

The pathologist lifted one of the eyelids with a probe. They had a pearly sheen. 'Blue, I'd say. Maybe green. We'll be able to be more definitive at autopsy.'

DCI Lenham consulted the note he was holding. 'Height?'

When Sage couldn't answer because she didn't have a measuring tape to hand, the pathologist answered for her. 'Four-ten to five-one, maybe. Short, slight, as you can see. It's almost certainly River Sloane, although the swelling of the face and extensive bruising makes a visual ID tricky. Fingerprints match exemplars in her bedroom and DNA will be later.'

Lenham stared down at the girl. 'Poor kid. Was there something you wanted to show me?'

'Here's a bruise, triangular, left temple. What do you make of it?'

He peered at it. 'I don't want to pre-empt the post-mortem. But I've seen those kind of bruises before.'

Sage collected another handful of sharp holly leaves and put them in a large evidence bag. 'Oh?'

Megan started bagging leaves from above the head. 'Blunt instrument with a wedge-shaped profile? We see them occasionally; they are sometimes the cause of accidental deaths.' She swung an imaginary golf club. 'Golf balls can kill, too, although I've never seen a case.'

Lenham was about to leave when he turned back. 'Dr Westfield, do you know Felix Guichard?'

'I do, he's an anthropologist I've worked with before. Why?'

'He's coming down to see me. When I mentioned your name, he said you were a meticulous investigator. That's the word he used, meticulous.' Lenham's voice was gruff and he turned away.

'Why is he coming?' Sage couldn't see a connection with Felix.

Lenham stopped but didn't look around. 'Old case,' was all he said as he walked away.

Sage checked the location code before she wrote up the last bag of leaves from the body. 'Do you know what that's about?'

'It's the missing girl, Lara Black,' Megan said. 'She disappeared from the bus shelter right opposite the house, twenty-odd years ago. If you can clear that edge we can lift the body out, get her to the morgue. Then you can collect the rest of the leaves.'

'OK,' Sage said. 'Underneath, there's a border of the turf that we were looking for yesterday, it's been rolled up tightly around the edge. I'm conserving that, too. Have you ever seen that before?'

'There's a lot about this burial that's new to me,' Megan said. 'It's more like a display case for her. Strange.' Megan turned to Sage. 'What made you think about forensic archaeology?'

'When I came back from maternity leave I realised I didn't want to be the county archaeologist any more. I had a lot of time to think about how I would fit in childcare so I did a couple of post-graduate modules while I was teaching at the university. I thought I could take a few cases here and there, fit it all in around the baby.'

Megan smiled. 'That's why I went into forensic pathology, to spend time with my children. In practice I get called out at all hours and hardly see my kids.'

Sage winced. 'Hopefully this will give me lots to write about for the dissertation. If I can find enough time to work at the laptop.'

'Does your partner help with childcare?'

Sage managed a small smile. 'He does, but Nick works very long hours. He's a vicar – we don't live together.' It felt awkward, chatting about Nick. 'After what happened on the island last year I wondered if forensics might suit me.' She could feel her heart thumping, her palms sweating at the memory.

'A crime on the Isle of Wight?' Megan said, half smiling. 'You never expect it, do you?'

'I was looking into a murder, but a very old one. Fifteen-eighties,' Sage added, watching a frown wrinkle Megan's forehead.

'And that's when you were attacked? Trent said something.'

Her words sent a shiver down Sage's back. She nodded, and tried to keep her voice neutral. 'Yes.'

'I would have thought that might have put you off forensics.'

Sage half smiled at the thought that *this* case might. She looked away from the shrouded body. 'Maybe it should have. I'm hoping it helps me work through it.'

A young police officer poked his head around the tent flap. 'Dr Westfield? I was wondering if you could have a look at something out here.'

Megan waved at her. 'Go with PC Stewart. We're ready to move the body, anyway.'

It was a relief to stand up in the open air. 'What can I help you with?'

'It's over here.' He glanced curiously as she sighed with relief. 'I suppose you've seen dozens of bodies.'

'Not really.' Sage followed him along the front of the house. 'I mean, I've excavated a lot of burials, but they were usually hundreds of years old.'

'I thought you were with pathology?'

'Forensic archaeology. I'm thinking of specialising in crime investigation.'

The officer smiled at her. 'I would have thought proper archaeology would be fascinating. *Time Team* and all that.'

She smiled but shook her head. 'It doesn't fit in very well with a baby. Forensic archaeology is mostly lab work, in office hours.'

'Except for the evidence retrieval.'

'In my old job I had to do planning permission for extensions, roadworks, that sort of thing. A lot of site visits.

This will be a couple of days in the field and six weeks writing up reports. I might even do some of it at home.'

Stewart crouched down next to something in the rough grass. 'I saw this on the way over. What do you think it is?'

Sage leaned down to look. It was a block of stone half buried at the edge of a moss-covered path, draped with the long stems of a neglected rose bush.

'I don't know. Some sort of marker, a pet grave maybe.' She reached in her pocket for a trowel. 'Hang on – ouch.' The thorns latched into the skin on the back of her thumb, and she had to retreat gently to stop it cutting further. With more care, she scraped away at the moss and grass growing halfway up the stone. 'In Memoriam…' She squinted in the shadow until the officer handed her a torch. She knelt beside it, scrabbling along the base of the marker. It had sagged into the soil around it. 'It's angled down, I don't know if there's any more.' She scratched around the base. The young officer bounced to his feet as if coming to attention and Sage looked up to see Lenham.

DCI Lenham nodded to the officer. 'Stewart. We're ready to search the house,' he said. He looked at Sage. 'What have you got?'

'A memorial stone, I think. It's old, more than fifty years, I would guess. It has sunk into the grass.'

He crouched down to look. 'It's too old for our investigations. Leave it.'

'What about this old case Felix was involved in?' Sage

said, scratching at the edge under the soil level.

'I said, leave it. You said it was old.' He walked away, leaving Sage to stare up at Stewart.

He shrugged. 'We ought to focus on this girl,' he said. 'That's what we're here for. There's coffee in the van.'

'Great,' she said. Sage got to her feet and followed him to a police vehicle with the back doors open. Trent was already there, bundled into a ski jacket and warming his hands on a paper cup.

The pathologist joined them to shelter from the wind. The traffic had been stopped down the country road with crime-scene tape, and Sage could hear questions shouted out from the press beyond the barrier.

Sage wrapped her fingers around the hot paper cup. 'So, at least we're certain who she is.'

'River Sloane, aged fifteen and a half.' Trent stirred sugar into his coffee. 'She's been missing since Saturday afternoon, her mother called it in about half-two.'

'The actual time of death is very provisional but I think it's late Saturday evening,' Megan said. 'We'll get her back to the mortuary and have a closer look to establish it. Scenes of crime are doing a fingertip search of the grounds to go with your drone footage.'

Trent sipped his coffee. 'We don't want to get in the way of the SOCOs. We should have a complete site map by this evening. I'm going to get a look at the barrows when I get a chance, too.'

Sage smiled. 'Let me know what you find.' She turned to Megan. 'An archaeologist's dream find: Bronze Age barrows that haven't been properly surveyed before, on private land.'

Megan nodded. 'Meanwhile, we'll be collecting evidence. Hopefully the meteorological information will be ready for me when we get back. We need to know temperature, rainfall, that sort of thing.'

DCI Lenham appeared, poured himself a cup of coffee from the large urn. 'I have to get back to the interviews, but I came to look around the house first.'

Trent looked at him and raised an eyebrow. 'For anything particular?'

'Spade, wheelbarrow, anything used to dig the grave. Her clothes and other belongings would be crucial, obviously. But Chorleigh basically camps in the kitchen; the rest of the house is filled with rubbish. I don't know what we're supposed to find, especially as we're also looking for evidence of the disappearance in 1992 as well.' He shrugged his shoulders. 'The family contacted Guichard – we used him on the original case. He's an anthropologist, studies human weirdness. They knew he'd been looking into the animal attacks.'

Sage stared at him, trying to read his tense face. 'What was Felix's involvement?'

'He was consulted by my senior officer to look into some stabbings of ponies and cattle across the forest. He got called back when Lara disappeared because he'd said the animal attacks could escalate to humans. The investigation was redirected back to Alistair Chorleigh.'

'But you don't know for sure that she died.'

'Exactly,' Lenham said, and drained his cup. 'It wasn't a murder investigation but we did have enough to question Chorleigh. If his father hadn't employed the best lawyers he would probably have been charged with lying repeatedly to the police. He came up with several stories, none of which made sense and all of which declared him innocent, even though we didn't have a crime. He'd just come out of hospital after a head injury at the time we spoke to him; he was confused and we couldn't hold him. We also couldn't get a warrant fast enough to search the grounds properly. He could have moved her anywhere, even if she was killed here. It's a huge forest and it was still a missing person investigation.'

'But not like this case,' Sage reminded him. 'This is different. River's not missing and she's definitely dead. Why half bury River in Chorleigh's garden?'

He grimaced at her. 'If I wanted to deflect attention from my involvement in a murder, I'd stick it in Alistair Chorleigh's garden too.'


Sage grabbed a handful of evidence bags and headed back to the grave site. Trent was her supervisor, he could be exploring the barrows, but she had to concentrate on the murder investigation. She knelt on the plastic beside the grave site. The body was gone but the depression it had been laid in was a mirror for its shape with a raised border around. The killer – no, not necessarily the killer – the person who concealed the body, she reminded herself, had carefully dug the shape of the girl's shoulders and hips into the ground. Scraped was actually more accurate – the hole was barely deep enough to hide her. Thirty-seven centimetres at its deepest, she noted, measuring and marking on the diagram. The turf around the edge created a border a few centimetres higher. The scanning equipment would come back with more accurate measurements. The compacted soil held the impression of the tool used to cut into it. A curved blade, blunt, some fourteen centimetres in length. *Garden trowel?* She took more pictures with a scale marker.

Megan had left the outside layers of debris on a tarpaulin for Sage to record. She lifted another stack of leaves from adjacent to the grave, as compacted as a deck of cards. The ones on the bottom were more degraded than those on the top, suggesting the leaf drifts had been undisturbed as they slowly rotted away under the trees. She consulted an online identification guide to classify them. The decayed skeletons of birch, curling beech in good condition, field maple and hazel, and many blackened holly leaves. There was also crisp ivy, some oak, and a few gnawed acorns still in their cups. It should be easy enough to find where he took the leaves from.

Sage started clearing the loose debris from the bottom of the grave, centimetre by centimetre, recording as she went down to compacted soil. She was surprised to find a piece of bone under the hip area, especially as it was dark brown and looked ancient. More brushing revealed gravel, several tiny fragments of bone and a tooth that looked like it belonged to a dog or fox. The grave itself was dug into long-established grass, she decided; the layers hadn't been disturbed for decades. But there weren't any tree or shrub roots. Turf developed its own profile, and this looked like park. She looked out of the doorway of the tent. There was about an acre of grass in what had been a lawn in front of the house, with the remains of borders. This secondary area at the side wouldn't even be visible from the front of the house, and the path around it into the trees looked well established.

She started finding more pebble-sized pieces of something – pottery. They almost looked like clay that had been shaped by ploughing and harrowing on the surface of a field, but they were smoother. She held one up to the light, rubbed off the earth with her thumb. They looked old, like Bronze Age pottery. One piece was unusual with a twin inscribed line on the outside. They were worn smooth in places, by the action of a mower perhaps.

She was so involved in collecting more fragments that she didn't notice PC Stewart enter the tent. 'We found something,' he said. 'DCI Lenham told me to show you.'

She looked up with a start; he was holding something flat against his body, like a small picture.

She hesitated before answering. 'I've found something too. Some old bone fragments, maybe animal, and there's pottery here, probably from the Bronze Age. Trent showed me the barrows in the woodland, which were excavated a hundred years ago. The pottery and bone might come from there.'

'Is that where Trent's gone? He seemed pretty excited.'

She showed him the tiny piece of pot she was holding. 'This looks very old to me. There are quite a few bits of it with a few fragments of bone. I can't tell if they're animal or human.'

Stewart peered at it. 'OK. How does that relate to the murder?'

She wrapped the piece carefully in a square of bubble wrap and tucked it into the box. 'I don't think it does. It just means he – or she – didn't dig very deep. They only took the top layer off, the turf and a bit of soil. They laid it around the edge to frame her. Then they covered her with a thick layer of leaves. It seems very ritualised and deliberate. I'm just a bit puzzled about this ground. It looks like lawn in section but it's stuck on the side of the house.'

He held the picture out for her to take. 'I found this on the wall inside the house. It shows the grounds with the side of the building behind.'

She looked closely at the old photograph, lining up the

outhouse, the corner of the big house. 'This bit used to be a tennis court?' That made sense: the incessant rolling and mowing would have compacted it and smoothed off any loose clay or bone.

PC Stewart took it back. 'There are several old photographs of the gardens from the beginning of the twentieth century. This bit was a grass court.'

'This soil is typical lawn, not vegetable patch or shrubbery, or flower border. It hasn't been dug over recently but the grass is preserved even though it's been neglected for a long time.'

He crouched down to look at the edge of the grave. 'None of this makes much sense. If someone killed her because they like to hurt young girls, I would have thought she would vanish altogether or be laid out, displayed to taunt the police.'

'Have you been involved with many murders?'

He shook his head. 'I've studied some, obviously. We're trained to look for anything that's unusual.'

'And this?'

'They say deliberate burials like this one suggest remorse, a personal relationship with the victim. DCI Lenham would love to prove this was Chorleigh. It would be neat, simple, especially as they never found the other girl, Lara.'

Sage sat back and rolled her shoulders to ease the stiffness. 'Was that his case too?'

'Years ago, when he was my age. If we could find Lara

Black we could build a profile of a man who likes to attack young girls. Maybe he did kill her, sobered up, put her in the ground without really thinking about the consequences. His alcohol level was eye-wateringly high when we breathalysed him; they had to wait until he sobered up to talk to him.' Stewart sighed. 'Do you know if there's any evidence of sexual assault?'

She shook her head. 'None so far but we're waiting for the post-mortem results.'

He nodded. 'At the briefing DCI Lenham said Lara Black disappeared right here on September ninth, 1992, after she was seen talking to Alistair Chorleigh at the bus stop along the road. Lenham concluded she just ran off with someone. She was estranged from her parents, into all sorts of illegal stuff, as well as animal rights like River. Both girls had a connection to Chorleigh House, which would be a bit of a coincidence.'

Sage stood, eased her back. 'There's another coincidence.'

'Oh?'

'The archaeologist who dug up the barrows went missing here, too.'

That caught his attention. 'When was this?'

'That's the odd thing,' said Sage. 'More than a hundred years ago.'

Stewart relaxed. 'I think we can assume we don't have to solve that disappearance.'

Sage knelt back down to carry on scraping. 'Well, I

think it's strange that two people disappeared on the same land. Felix Guichard was consulted back in 1992. Do you know what he said about Lara Black at the time?'

'It came up at the first briefing. I don't think the DCI liked him very much,' he said. 'He was interviewing some of the animal rights nuts, people protesting outside fur farms, animal testing labs, that sort of thing. People who were hassling us to solve the animal abuse case, anti-hunt campaigners, pagan groups, travellers living rough in the forest. I wasn't even born then.' He smiled at her. 'Guichard believed Lara was still here, buried somewhere. He thought there was some connection between the abused animals and the girl. His report didn't do DCI Lenham's career any good, by the sound of it.'

Sage brushed loose soil away from a tree root. 'Who else did they talk to back then?'

'Parents, siblings, friends, teachers, boyfriends, neighbours, just like River's inquiry. I think they're considering reopening the Lara Black case. Maybe if we give it some publicity she'll come forward – if she's still alive.'

# 6

'Sepulchral tumuli are not uncommon but as the usual
form of earthwork in Hampshire is round, the Hound
Butt mounds are different. One is intact and therefore
most worthy of study.'

Journal of Edwin Masters, 24th June 1913

I finished inking up my pencil sketches of the complete
barrow this evening. It is unusual in shape, being
somewhere between oval and rectangular, but the edges
may have been ploughed away over the centuries. I sketched
a plan to measurements with Peter's help, although he was
more interested in showing me where he and Molly used
to slide down the sloping side on an old carpet. He is a dear
friend, he makes me feel welcome. I like Molly too, she is
very like him and kind to me.

Peter's father was good enough to give us a number of pieces of pottery the gardeners have dug up in the flower beds. They look ancient to me, although smoothed over years in the elements. I have asked Professor Conway to take a look at them; he has always said I may send him finds, although I have previously been reluctant to disturb him. Mr Chorleigh also had a small Roman coin, picked up along the river foreshore, although I am unsure as to its date. There appears to be an emperor inscribed upon it. It's such a shame they all look so similar.

Peter is much liked in the village, and it is easy to see he has the same affection for everyone. His family have hopes that he will marry a local girl – the daughter of a retired admiral with his own marine engineering company – but he tells me that they were raised as brother and sister. Her name is Beatrice Marchmont, and they call her Trixie. They have been unofficially engaged these last four years but Peter speaks of her as an old friend.

We have laid out strings in a lattice pattern, ready to dig the barrow. Beside it is the ruined earthwork, watching over us. We used the slope to put a little shade up, where we can leave a basket of provisions and our bags of tools while we explore the complete mound. Molly has started drawing from the stony summit, as it is the highest point nearby. There appears to be animal workings on the field side; perhaps it was undermined generations ago by rabbits or badgers and collapsed, or the earth was washed away. There is certainly evidence of water carving out the facing stones and running into the boggy ground beyond. Water has created a channel under the fence into the field ditch, fully two yards across. Peter tells me the water table is high here; he has seen the mud flooded a foot deep before it flows into the field. I wondered if there might be finds in the soft soil, but he is eager to mark up the main barrow to establish the best place to dig our trench.

Peter has taken some photographs and we are waiting for them to be developed and printed by the chemist in Lyndhurst. He got a few snaps of Molly and me, for posterity. It helped him use up the roll, as he thinks there might be a picture of his younger sister Claire in the camera too. I hope so – it would be a nice memento for Mrs Chorleigh, as I believe Claire was not photographed in the last year of her life. Peter has said nothing to his mother in case she is disappointed. I have only caught glimpses of Mrs Chorleigh, sat on a sofa in the library with a book she never seems to read. Molly says she would like to meet me when she feels stronger, but she sounds doubtful. Poor lady, she apparently suffered a complete collapse after her daughter died, and Peter says she has never been strong. Mr Chorleigh hardly looks at me either, and rarely speaks directly to me. I think he has little patience with Peter's interest in history.

* * *

Letter to Professor Robert Conway, 22nd June 1913,
Balliol College, Oxford

Dear Professor,

I would be most obliged if you could give me your
opinion on the pottery fragments enclosed. They belong
to one of my friends, P. Chorleigh (Balliol, History), who
lives in Fairfield in the New Forest. I believe they may
be early, and the site includes an undisturbed barrow
from, if I am not mistaken, the Bronze Age. The pottery
looked, to my inexperienced eye, to be crudely made
and unevenly fired. There is a single finger impression,
as you will observe, which I took to be decoration.
There is another mound, perhaps of ancient provenance,
beside the barrow. It is unusual, being comprised of two
upright hewn slabs, parallel, each perhaps of thirty-
eight or nine inches average width, with a massive
stone perched on top, leaving a gap like a letterbox (see
my sketch, apologies for its crudeness). Water can be
seen dribbling down the gap between the middle of the
uprights and I wondered if this natural spring may have
excavated the earthwork over the millennia, leaving
just the internal architecture remaining. I also enclose
a coin, Romano-British I believe, which is much worn
but may be of interest. I should value your opinion.

Yours sincerely,
*E. Masters*

# 7

By the afternoon, Sage had bagged up and logged the remaining leaves with the help of one of the forensic technicians. DCI Lenham had reported back that his superiors had officially ordered him to reinvestigate Lara Black's disappearance alongside the death of River Sloane. They weren't officially assuming a link between the two cases but the coincidence of the location and Alistair Chorleigh's presence couldn't be ignored. The press had also made the connection between two young women, both blonde and of a similar age and build, who disappeared or died at Chorleigh House. When Sage watched the news on PC Stewart's tablet, DCI Lenham confirmed River's identity but wouldn't be drawn on whether the cases were linked.

'Well, he won't, will he?' said Stewart. 'He spent so much time saying she was just a runaway.' The police appealed for anyone who had seen a car in the area between midnight and six a.m. to come forward, and Lenham asked if Lara could contact them, in confidence. Sage decided to head towards the barrows to look for Trent.

She found him on top of the complete earthwork, Hound Butt. It was covered in shorter grass than the surrounding scrub. The middle was lower, as if an internal structure had collapsed.

'This is amazing,' he said, as she joined him. 'It looks like someone dug the whole thing out but they didn't put it all back.'

'Maybe there was a cavity inside that they filled in?' she suggested.

Trent brushed the grass aside from the edge of a stone. 'Maybe. You found some pottery from the grave? Perhaps it came from here.'

She shook her head. 'Not recently – I think it went in when they built the tennis court. It's not Victorian, it's less refined clay. There were fragments of old bone under the grass, too, which could be animal. Perhaps there was a settlement in this area.' She looked towards the other earthwork. It was taller, the slope steeper, the cut edge abruptly lined with stone. The whole thing was dense with bushes and brambles; it would be difficult to get up there. 'Should I concentrate on the leaves?'

'They will go into refrigeration when we take them to the lab, they can wait. I don't know how long we have to search the grounds and Lenham wants us to rule out a burial in 1992.'

'The building in the woods?'

'I think it's too far back from the road to be a garage; it looks like a stable or workshop. It might have a concrete floor which would be of interest if it went down around 1992 – maybe Lara Black is buried underneath it. We have ground-penetrating radar equipment back at the office. We could have a look underneath with GPR and a metal detector tomorrow. It's taped off; the police are advising the building looks dangerously unstable. Unstable stable – funny, huh?'

'Hilarious. So, what do I do while we wait?'

'We have to check with the pathologist so she can ask any relevant questions. It's a good learning experience for you, too.'

'Do you normally go? To talk to the pathologist, I mean.'

He shook his head. 'Not always, not unless the remains are scattered or skeletonised. But this case is very unusual, the grave cut and fill is puzzling us. Why bury someone if you want them to be found?' He managed a wry smile. 'They never ask much, they just like to make sure an archaeologist is consulted. The defence teams check that all the experts have been questioned.' He scrambled down the end of the slope and halfway up the next one, crushing gorse and brambles underfoot.

She climbed down and walked around to look up at

him. The barrow terminated at a stone wall set upright in the soil, covered with mosses and lichens. At the base was the remains of a puddle, almost a pond, sticky with mud. 'We could probably get a good look inside the barrow from here if we had a ladder. What can you see from up there?'

He shaded his eyes with one hand as he looked back into the woodland. 'A lot of trees, some evergreen. I can just see the top of the wooden building to the east – there's a clear space covered in leaves at this end. I suppose it could be the roof we saw from the drone.' He kicked a bramble aside. 'These thorns are nasty. I don't suppose the owner would let us clear the scrub to have a proper look at the barrows?'

'I doubt if he'll be co-operative seeing as he was dragged off by the police and interrogated all night. Can we do it anyway?'

Trent struggled forward, crushing a couple of ferns until he found a clear spot on the edge of the stone wall. 'Possibly. There's some sort of slab underfoot.' He leaned over to look at the slot at the top. 'I could get a look in there, I think. Maybe I can argue we need to explore all of it to look for Lara Black. You get off to the mortuary, I'll head back to the grave.'

Sage took a deep breath. 'What should I watch out for at the mortuary?'

He looked down at her. 'Check that the pathologist doesn't have any questions for us. Mention everything we found, the leaves, the old pottery and bone, anything that gives context. We could be asked to comment in court about anything we've seen.' He grinned. 'Don't look so worried. We're hardly ever called to be witnesses. We're just covering the police's arses, establishing the provenance of everything the prosecution might use as evidence.'

'Oh.' She looked at where he was balanced on the top of the slabs of stone. 'If that's been excavated out it could be unsupported. So – speaking as an archaeologist, now – you need to come down and do your investigation on terra firma.'

He smiled at her. 'Coming, Mum.' He walked down the slope, jumped the last couple of feet and landed in the soil and leaf mould with a squelching sound.

Sage stepped back, feeling the earth pull at the soles of her boots. 'It's wet, isn't it?'

'It's a bit boggy this side. There's a stream coming out between the slabs. It looks like some sort of spring; maybe it's built around a natural water feature.' Trent led the way around the side. Water seeped down an algae-covered mossy edge between the slabs.

Her interest was caught. 'It could be some sort of cistern, or a well head. Which would be very unusual, especially if it's Bronze Age. Or it could just be the remains of an excavated barrow.'

'I don't think so. It's on a slightly different alignment from the big one. I'll be back in the tent in a minute.'

Sage glanced up at the clouds overhead. 'How long will

they leave it up?' Rain had periodically spattered the tent all morning in spite of intermittent sunshine.

'A few days. We may see different layers as it dries out and it stops the press taking their pictures before we fill it back in.' Trent picked up his rucksack. 'I'll carry on with the site survey. You can go home from the mortuary if you like, we'll be losing the light by the time you finish.'

Sage and Trent packed the boxes of evidence bags into her car. She was a little nervous about seeing the body again, but she was curious about what happened. Perhaps Megan was going to find the reason for the murder.

Trent wedged in the last box of bagged samples and she shut the boot of her car.

'I'll let you know when I'm finished,' Sage said.

'Great. I'm going to look for any evidence left by the person who made those footprints leading to and from the grave.'

She took a deep breath, pulled her shoulders back. 'OK. Have you found a good print yet?'

'A couple of bits of textured trainer. The size is about a ten. The ground's not wet enough to get all the edges but we've preserved what we can. The mortuary is at the back of the hospital; there's dedicated parking. Just leave your badge in the window so you don't get wheel-clamped. Oh, and your friend is there. That anthropologist guy Lenham was talking about.'

'Felix? He got here fast.' The thought lightened her nerves immediately.

'I think Lara Black's family called him in when they heard about River.' Trent smiled, but he didn't look amused. 'Don't worry about the mortuary. Tell yourself it's just a body, another specimen.'

'I'll get used to it, will I?' she said wryly.

His smile was twisted. 'No, not really. Which is why I'm making you go.'


It took Sage most of an hour to drive to the hospital and park, and the light was fading. The mortuary was rather as she had expected: lots of gleaming stainless steel. She was directed to a conference room. A tall man with longish hair was leaning over a table. He was staring at a spread of A4 printed sheets of the grave site.

'Felix!' It was lovely to see him. He swept her into a hug.

'Sage. It's great to see you, even if it is under these rather horrible circumstances.' He let go, and stared down at her with his intense green eyes. 'How are Nick and the baby?'

She hesitated before she answered. 'Nick's fine. Max is nearly one, he's great. We're both staying with my mother in Winchester this week. How have you been?'

Felix lifted an eyebrow but didn't say anything. 'I'm OK.'

'You got here quick.'

He glanced up. 'I was already here. Lara Black's family called me.'

'DCI Lenham said you were involved in the original investigation.'

He nodded. 'Many years ago. There are some similarities with the present murder.'

'Like?' Sage turned one of the pictures around. 'They never found a grave.'

'River was almost sixteen,' he said, 'Lara was only a few months older. They looked alike: fair-haired, short, slight. They were both last seen in the area of Chorleigh House. Alistair Chorleigh was seen talking to Lara at the bus stop, then River was buried in his garden. They even shared some interest in animal rights.'

'I thought there were some unlikely coincidences.'

'I've never felt justice was served for Lara. We never heard from her again, which is unusual in such a young girl. Most runaways turn up somewhere, either paying taxes or getting benefits. Her family have never given up trying to find out – we've kept in contact.'

'Heartbreaking for them.'

'Yes. I became involved back then as I was already here, looking into a series of attacks on animals. They looked ritualistic and I had some experience of investigating sacrifices in my studies.' He shuffled the papers into a neat pile. 'We thought it was possible that someone, probably male, could have escalated from cattle and ponies to a human victim. I predicted that might happen in my report. The attacks were frenzied, need-driven, compulsive. I didn't think the attacker would just stop.'

Sage looked up at Felix. 'When did the animal attacks end?'

'They stopped right after Lara disappeared, which suggested the abuser could have moved to a human victim. I think we owe it to the victim and her family to find her body, if possible.'

'It must have been hard for Lara's parents.'

'It got worse. The press went to town on Lara's family and friends, but no one stood out in the investigation. She was interested in environmental activism and ecology, and she was wild camping on land owned by a local witchcraft group, all of which made headlines. She protested road-building at Twyford Down and was arrested several times. She made a claim of assault against two security officers there, and was arrested trying to lead a spellcasting against the construction company.' He sat down. 'We don't even know whether Lara is dead. But twenty-seven years later we have to assume she is, which brings us back to the last person seen talking to her – Alistair Chorleigh.'

Sage sat opposite him. 'But to completely disappear at that age – there must have been a presumption of death at the time.'

He nodded. 'The fact that she left her bag at the bus stop was highly suspicious, I felt. The police argued she could have got into a car, been abducted or run away with a friend. She left her bus pass, bank card, cash, make-up, purse. ' He shrugged. 'They also found her camera case a mile away, through the forest, nowhere near the road. If she went that way, why didn't she take her other things?'

Sage stood back from the pages of images, looking for something that would make sense. 'Police. You mean DCI Lenham.'

'Detective Sergeant Lenham at the time. He didn't like me much.'

'I'm not sure he likes you now,' she said, remembering his expression when he spoke about Felix.

He smiled down at her. She liked the way the skin around his green eyes crinkled, as though he smiled a lot. She noticed more grey in his hair than there had been last year, when he came between her and a mentally ill man, when he administered first aid to Nick and saved his life.

'The thing is,' he said, 'there was once a famous coven of witches in the New Forest. Lara was connected to some well-known people.'

'OK.' Sage couldn't help the scepticism reaching her voice.

He smiled again but carried on. 'There are still groups who are descended from the coven. It's a nature cult but several members are still politically involved in environmental issues. They have already contacted the police offering to help because they heard a dead girl had been found and thought of Lara. Here's another similarity for you – River was a supporter of several organisations that campaign against animal testing on social media.'

'How do you know that?'

'I live with a teenager who is a computing wizard.'

Sage laughed, a little nervously. 'And how did the police respond to the offer of help from a coven of witches?'

'Needless to say, they weren't interested in talking to a group of New Age pagan hippies and weirdos – their words, not mine – no matter how established their group is.' He tidied up the papers and put them back in a folder. 'But if the coven knew Lara, the police need someone to interview them about River. They don't expect the coven will be able to add anything to the inquiry, so they're sending me to do it. Do you want to come?'

'I would, but I have to talk to the pathologist first.'

Her face must have given away her concern as he said, 'Shall I come in with you?'

'Does that make me pathetic?'

He gave a little cough of laughter. 'No one finds it easy, I promise you. Even the pathologists don't like working with kids. I ought to have a look at the body anyway; there appears to be some ritual associated with the burial. I've been asked to look for ceremonial or psychological features they can search the databases for. The interviews can wait until tomorrow.'

Sage pushed the door open a few inches. 'I'm just worried I'll throw up or faint,' she said quietly.

'Maybe you will. But you won't die.'

She frowned at him. 'Not helpful.'

'I mean it. A child is dead, and others may follow. Whatever answers you can give the pathologist will add to the evidence suggesting who did this. Even if it's uncomfortable for us, we might be able to give another perspective, ask the right question.'

'It must be really annoying for your friends. Always being right.'

He laughed. 'I live with a teenager. I'm never right.'

Any humour faded as she stepped into the inner room. The naked girl had been laid out on a metal table and Megan was photographing her, snapping shots from her feet up. It seemed wrong, voyeuristic, even. An older man made notes.

'Ah. Afternoon, Sage.'

'Hi, Megan. I'm guessing you've met Professor Guichard?'

'We passed in the corridor.'

Felix stepped forward. 'Felix, social anthropology.'

'Your reputation precedes you, Felix. I'm Megan and this is my colleague, Warren. I don't need you two for the internal post-mortem but I have a few questions about the burial.' She smiled as Sage exhaled with a grateful whoosh.

Sage could see purple and red marks on the slight body. The girl looked like she'd been beaten from head to toe. They didn't all look post-mortem as she'd thought at first, but she waited for Megan to confirm it. 'What can I do?'

'Don't worry,' Megan said, scribbling a few notes.

'Your presence is mostly for the prosecution in case they get questioned by the defence about why the scene wasn't examined fully by an archaeologist. We only call a forensic archaeologist in about ten, twenty per cent of cases.'

'Why did you call on us for this one – because of the unusual burial?' Sage looked away from the swollen face.

'Yes, the grave site was so atypical I thought we should have an expert on excavation and burial behaviour,' Megan said. 'I don't think we'll need an anthropologist, but if you see anything, speak up.' Felix nodded and she continued. 'I'll tell you what I see and if I have any inconsistencies, I might ask for your observations, Sage. The whole lot is recorded for the court. From now, then.' She nodded to Warren, who pressed a button on the overhead recorder. 'Present, Dr Megan Levy, pathologist. With Dr Sage Westfield, forensic archaeology, and Professor Felix Guichard, social anthropology. Also Warren Tindall, assistant pathologist.'

She pointed to the girl's neck and Warren took a photograph, the flash bouncing off the white walls and stainless-steel table. 'The body is of a well-nourished female whose appearance is consistent with an age of fifteen years and nine months, her formal identification as River Sloane was confirmed by fingerprint comparison, pending DNA. The body was discovered by a dog in the garden of—Sage?'

'Chorleigh House, Fairfield Road.'

'—Chorleigh House, Fairfield Road. She was buried in a shallow excavation of dark-coloured loam and established turf, then covered with leaves.'

When Sage opened her mouth to speak, Megan held her hand up and carried on.

'When I initially saw the body in situ it was loosely covered with rotted leaves and part of the face and right hand had been partially exposed by the actions of a dog and its owner. It wasn't obvious where the top covering was from. Dr Westfield?'

'I – I mean, my colleague Dr Trent Reynolds and I looked at aerial photographs of the grounds and noticed footprints going to the back of the property. There's some sort of structure there covered with evergreens. We will be examining the area for holly trees and other leaves.'

'Did you recover all the covering materials?' Megan asked.

Warren took more photographs as Megan pointed to a scrape on the skin.

'We did retrieve all the leaves,' Sage said. 'They were laid in layers, not thrown onto the body. Most of them were from the top of a pile, taken in handfuls.'

The pathologist leaned towards the girl's face to get a closer look, and Sage took in how young River looked. 'These areas of bruising on the right side of the face, they look regular, like a pattern, as Dr Westfield pointed out in the field. Possibly a shoe print from a kick, but it looks curved. They are diffused, they happened some hours before death. We'll keep an eye on them, bruising can develop over time. The staining on the left side is post-mortem. Photograph here, please.'

Sage recognised the patchy red staining, the pooling of blood across her torso, except for a vivid white patch across her ribs and on one shoulder.

'She was laid on her side.'

'As Dr Westfield suggests, livor mortis appears to indicate that she was initially left on her side after death, her body laid over her left arm.'

Sage watched as Warren snapped a dozen more shots of the body.

The pathologist picked up forceps and probed the girl's nose. Sage looked away and Megan continued to dictate. 'This would suggest that she had been laid on a hard surface. There is evidence of fly eggs in her nostrils and the external corner of her right eye, indicating there were insects in the vicinity. Shall we have a look at the back?' She gestured to her colleague.

As Warren and Megan rolled the body onto its side, it made a soft squelching noise and Sage's nausea was back. The faint smell in the room increased considerably, even driving Felix back a step. Warren picked up the camera and took more pictures.

'She was likely naked or partially undressed when she was left after death,' Megan continued. 'Flies can detect the beginnings of decomposition within hours. There are fly eggs back here, too.'

Sage stared at the girl's thin back. 'Are they – bruises too?'

'As Dr Westfield observes, there are bruises on the skin of the torso that suggest repeated impacts. The patterns may relate to the soles of boots or shoes; the bruises are diffused but there is a pattern of ridges with high points.' She turned to Warren. 'Different light sources might reveal more details of the footwear. I'd like the skin swabbed as well, it might tell us where they have been.' She turned back to the recorder. 'This suggests the deceased survived the fatal injury for some time, evidenced by the developed bruising and swelling. This, with rigor mortis and temperature evidence, suggests time of death between eight p.m. Saturday evening and two a.m. Sunday morning. The time of injury could be any time from when she was last seen at home.' Megan helped Warren lay the girl down gently onto her back. 'Thank you.' Megan nodded to Warren who turned the recording machine off.

Sage leaned forward to look at the pattern on River's cheekbone. 'Can you estimate the size of shoe, if it's a shoe print?'

'The texture only shows up where there's an underlying bone, but I'd guess small. But I can't be sure, the bruises are diffused because she lived for some time after injury. We haven't ruled out more than one attacker at this point. She was found buried in a shallow depression. How deep?'

Sage consulted her notes. 'The grave was between twenty-eight and thirty-seven centimetres deep. The leaves were mounded over the top, up to thirty centimetres deep in places. It's in our report.'

'What can you tell me about the shape of the excavation?'

Sage swallowed back down the coffee she'd had outside Chorleigh House; she hadn't wanted lunch and now she felt sick. 'It had been carefully cut out in the shape of the body using some sort of sharp, curved edge to slice through the turf, which was then laid around the shape of the body forming a ridge. The loose soil was also piled around her.' She paused, took a breath. 'River. The body.'

'Take your time.' Megan smiled at her, a wry half-smile.

'Underneath the grass roots we found a compacted layer of subsoil; it must have been much harder to dig. I also found some small pottery fragments that look prehistoric. The grave was cut into an area that was once a tennis court – the police showed me photographs from the house. What I mean is,' Sage went on, 'there must have been many better places to bury her than right by the house. Deep in the woods where no one would have found her, or maybe on the common land somewhere.'

'I hear you. But we can't predict what people will do under the stress of dealing with a body.' Megan scribbled something on her notes. 'Right to roam in the forest means dogs have access to most of the land around, I think she would have been more easily found than on a private estate. But I agree, why in the open, right by the house? I don't think we can rule out that this was an attempt to incriminate the homeowner.'

'Do you know how she died?'

'We can't confirm cause of death until the post-mortem is complete. But the swelling on her face and the back of her head suggests head injury, and X-rays revealed a depressed skull fracture. A severe beating, perhaps, and the bruises do look like boot marks on her face. I may take a section for microscopal examination to distinguish between lividity and injury. It also appears that she might have lived some hours on a very cold night, so we have to rule out death from hypothermia. We'll check for sexual trauma and activity, too, although there's nothing obvious yet. You don't want to be here for that.'

'No. No, I don't.' Sage took a deeper breath.

'The toilets are on the other side of the corridor,' Megan said, in a matter-of-fact way. Sage only just made it.

# 8

'If we take the Fairfield–Lyndhurst road to Blazeden Farm we find a lightly wooded site with two small earthworks visible from the meadow. The stream beyond is clearly marked and follows the line of the ancient ditch.'

*Field Archaeology of Wessex*, J. L. Foreman (1908)
Copied into excavation notes, Edwin Masters, 25th June 1913

We marked out the trench we intended to excavate, hoping to find remains above the forest floor level that may have preserved them from being saturated by acidic groundwater.

Taking the turf off was an arduous task. The head gardener, after much fussing, helped us to lay the turf upside down and water it well, leaving it in the shade of the trees. We were to replace it as soon as possible. With the gardener and his men's help we got it all done by midday. Almost immediately, Peter found a flint arrowhead.

'Look, Ed!' he shouted, running and sliding down the hard-packed soil, with the little gem in his hand. It was so sharp it slightly cut him when he landed, as we all (Molly was helping too) bent over it.

Molly took it from him with exaggerated care. 'Does that mean the mounds are even older than we thought?' she asked.

'Not necessarily,' I assured her. 'Stone was probably in use for many generations after metalwork was introduced. And perhaps this area had been settled for hundreds of years before the barrows were built. It might just have been in the soil when they built the barrow.'

'There's a huge prehistoric hand axe in the museum in Christchurch,' Peter said, pushing his hair out of his eyes. 'I remember seeing it when I was a boy. There were definitely ancient settlements here.'

'Can I try with a trowel?' Molly asked me, smiling from under a rather fetching hat. I went to my kit for a smaller trowel.

'This is for fine work,' I said, showing her. 'You can scrape away harder than you think, just stop if there's any kind of change in colour or texture. You sort of feel your way layer by layer. And don't be surprised if you find quite modern things. People often lose even valuable things out of their pockets, or drop the odd item and it gets pressed into wet soil. Some gardens have whole rubbish dumps in them, hundreds of years old.'

She started scraping, and I went back to the area I was working. Peter began digging, carrying away more of the spoil to put through a garden sieve. After a few minutes he brought something over. 'Is this Bronze Age? It looks jolly early…'

It was a piece of pottery, a little smoothed by the passage of time, or ploughing. It had a curve on it, and just the suggestion of the rim of a pot.

'Let me see,' Molly interrupted, and I dropped it into her fingers.

'I think Peter has found a proper piece of Bronze Age pottery,' I said, prodding it to lie face upwards. 'And it has decoration. Wait a minute.' I ran over to the basket and pulled out half a bottle of warmish water. I poured a little into my cupped palm and rubbed the surface with my thumb. The dark grey gave way to a distinct blackish line, just across the corner, and the hint of a second line above it.

She looked up. 'Look what Peter found!' Her father was standing beyond our spoil heap.

'Some very grubby youngsters,' he said, but it seemed he was in better humour today. Molly took the potsherd over to show him.

'This is very useful dating evidence,' I explained. 'This was possibly made in the Bronze Age, although it could be earlier. This area was probably also inhabited by Stone Age people, what we call Neolithic. Peter found an arrowhead.'

'Have you found anything of worth?' Mr Chorleigh bent to look at it. 'You know they found a golden torc in the river not a mile from here.'

I nodded. 'That was a Celtic artefact, sir. These remains are from an earlier age.'

He turned away, having already lost interest. I have noticed that rich people are the most interested in the monetary worth of things. We were uncovering the history of perhaps four or five thousand years ago. Peter and I knew the importance of the information we were gathering.

Molly turned around and lifted her sketchbook off the ground. 'I drew this before you started digging again. Is this correct?'

Molly's drawing was wonderful, showing the mound as it had been revealed by the removal of the turf, layers of different colour just suggested by shading in places. Somehow she had managed to draw the site as if Peter had not been there. On the facing page of her notebook I saw a quick sketch of her brother, laughing up at her, holding his trowel out as if to ward her off.

'That is an excellent picture of the barrow,' I told her, being rewarded by a wide smile, so like Peter's. 'I like this one, too.' I pushed my knuckle towards the sketch so I wouldn't smear it. 'I should like to have that.'

'Of course,' she said, scrambling back up the bank.

Mr Chorleigh walked away, swishing his stick through

the long grass. I felt lighter once he had gone; I found him oppressive.

'Gosh, it's thirsty work, isn't it?' Peter said, wiping his forehead on his arm.

My throat was dry; the sun had lit up the spot we were digging. I fumbled in my bag. 'I have barley sugars if that will help.'

'A drink would be better,' Peter said, blowing the fringe out of his eyes. It was oppressively hot by now, the buzzing of flies and bees humming from the long pasture beyond. 'I think Cook put a few bottles of her lemonade in the basket with the sandwiches.'

She had; they were lukewarm and starting to fizz but their corks were still in. I sat on the grassy edge of the dig, drinking deep from one of them. Peter put a hand out to help Molly sit beside us, and she accepted a fresh bottle. She stretched the umbrella over my head, too, and it was a relief for my eyes. She handed me a sandwich wrapped in paper.

'Perhaps we should get out of the sun until later,' she suggested. 'I'm already a bit pink in places and Peter's getting burned.'

'Unlike Edwin, who just goes as dark as an Arab,' Peter said, before downing his lemonade. The brew was sharp and refreshing. 'We could put up the awning, like we do for swimming parties.'

Molly answered him. 'I think people are using it this afternoon, by the river, at high tide. We could go for a swim, and come back when the sun goes down a little.'

That's Molly, filled with common sense and four years our junior. I'm sure I would have stayed all day until struck down with heatstroke. So we finished our lunch, covered up the remains from the prying eyes of the staff and the Chorleighs' young friends, and decamped to the river to join the swimming party. Trixie was already at the house, cool in some chiffony dress, putting her hand in Peter's and allowing him to hand her up the steps of the shooting brake to drive to the river. She was like a gilded statue, her skin and hair pale gold, her attitude as if a breeze would have blown her away. She leaned on him and whispered in his ear. She made him place the awning, an old sail, between two trees then patted the deckchair beside her.

He grinned then at me, turning to her. 'It's scorching, Trixie, I'm as hot as a racehorse. I'm going for a swim. Come on, Ed, let's cool down.'

I threw off my shirt to jump into the water with him and Molly. We gambolled in the shallows, then the Chorleighs set out for a serious swim, and I returned to the chairs and a towel.

'I'm glad to know one of Peter's university friends,' Trixie said. I was surprised because apart from a 'how-de-do' she had never spoken to me before. 'His last summer as a boy, a dear boy, of course. But now he needs to think about his future. Did you know he's been offered a position in my father's firm?'

'I – I didn't. I thought he might do a master's degree.'

She waved a fan in front of her face. 'I think we have both waited long enough to be married. We've been engaged four years, you know.'

I did know Peter didn't consider it a proper engagement at all. 'I worshipped at her feet, we all did,' he once told me. 'She's a goddess, too good for me. She'll probably marry a viscount.'

I looked across the river, seeing the sleek heads of Peter and Molly, diving and breaching like seals. He waved at the shore and I waved back.

'Molly is a dear girl, don't you think?' The goddess was talking at me with her eyes shut. 'She's a bit young, of course, but such a loyal, sweet thing. She'll miss Peter once we're in London. Unless she has her own friends, of course.'

'I believe Molly means to study at university,' I answered, a little more curtly than I had intended.

'Indeed? I had thought her too pretty to go to university.' The conversation appeared closed as she turned away and addressed a languid remark to one of the other fellows in the party, one of the Chorleighs' neighbours.

I felt, as I always did, out of place without Peter there. Life in a country vicarage had not prepared me for the social life of the wealthy middle classes.

# 9

After a disturbed night Sage woke up gasping, then the image of the knife buried in Nick's chest faded back into the nightmare. She shook the dream off, got ready for work and picked up the ground-penetrating radar equipment from Trent's office. She headed back into the New Forest. Trent had left a message. 'I have an odd case, what looks like a sleeping bag with human remains buried in a back garden. It's probably just an illegal burial to save the funeral and keep claiming the pension; I had one of those when I was training. Ask DCI Lenham if you can do anything, but hold off with the ground-penetrating radar, I want to be in on that. See you soon.'

But DCI Lenham didn't have anything for her to do. 'SOCOs are sweeping for trace evidence around the grave site and along the path to the shed, so we have to stay clear. I have several interviews today anyway.'

'Should I start on the leaves?' she asked.

'Actually, forensics still need the lab so they will have to wait as well. Your friend is here, though,' he said. 'The professor. He asked if you could go with him. He's going to interview those weirdos in Chilhaven, Lara Black's friends.'

'Oh?' Sage looked over the overgrown grass to where Felix was examining the marker stone on the ground in front of the house. 'Don't the police want to talk to them?' Though she knew full well from Felix that they didn't.

Lenham shook his head. 'Guichard was originally consulted in 1991 to investigate animal mutilations because they looked ritualistic. We had everyone on that – psychologists, police, the bloody RSPCA. He gave us some ideas but eventually it just stopped happening. The Wildwood people wouldn't talk to us so we sent Guichard.'

'You never solved the animal mutilations?' said Sage.

'No, but we spent a lot of money looking in some very odd places. Like the Wildwood Coven and a couple of random satanists who turned out to belong to a metal band. Guichard sent us on a wild goose chase – he was convinced the attacks would progress to humans one day.'

Sage turned back to Lenham. 'Did they?'

'No. Unless Lara Black's disappearance was related, which is unlikely. We don't even have evidence she's dead.' He was snappy. 'And the press wrote about Hampshire Police calling in psychics and reading tarot cards. Which didn't do my career any good at the time.'

Sage turned to leave but remembered something. 'I promised Mr Chorleigh I would make sure his dog was OK.'

'He's fine. We took swabs from his claws but didn't find anything obvious from the body, and we don't think he scratched River. I passed on the message he was allergic to fish, before you ask. After the kennel removed about a pound of fleas.' As Lenham looked away, Sage thought of something else.

'The animal attacks ended after Lara went missing.'

He stopped, looked back over his shoulder, frowning. 'Yes, Guichard did point that out. They actually stopped right before Lara went missing. His unsubstantiated theory was that killing the girl might have been the ultimate escalation after killing and injuring the livestock. But we needed facts, not theories. Be back from your wild goose chase by eleven, you should be able to get back to the shed after that.' He walked off and Sage over to Felix.

Felix was scratching around the memorial stone as she approached. 'Good morning. I've got a couple of hours to help you, if you like,' she said. 'To interview your witches.'

He looked up and smiled, squinting into the early sun. 'What's this stone about?'

'I don't know. I'd like to dig it up but I have to get permission from the landowner first. It looks too old to be related to either girl. Look, the edges are smoothed off, and it's limestone; many decades of acidic rain have eroded the cut edges.'

He stood up. 'You're right. That lichen has been there a long time.'

'It's extensive, and slow growing, so yes, fifty years or more. And the stone fell over a long time ago.' She looked around. 'How are they getting on with the building in the woods? I've got the GPR equipment weighing down the back of my car.'

'They are waiting for the forensic technicians to examine all the footprints that were identified by the drone for trace evidence. In the meantime, they want me to reinterview a couple that knew Lara Black at the time.'

Sage nodded. 'I've been talking to DCI Lenham. He's sending us into the woods to interview the witches. Do they have a really big oven?'

He laughed. 'You can judge for yourself, Gretel.'

The contact details Felix had been given for the 'Wildwood Coven' led to the middle of one of the forest's larger villages, Chilhaven. A mid-terraced Victorian brick cottage, it was covered with ivy that tapped against the guttering and crept onto the slates. It was the home of a couple in their seventies, the Parrises. Felix introduced them, and the man remembered him and shook his hand. He welcomed Sage and told her to call him Oliver. He showed them into a living room lined with books and filled with large sofas, and through to a sunny conservatory at the back of the house.

Sage stood, looking over the walled garden. Every surface was planted, there was no lawn, just a stone path packed with pots wandering into drifts of plants in beds and covered with low trees. 'Wow. That's beautiful,' she said. The brick walls were covered with climbers, some breaking into flower. 'Everything's so early.' Trained apple trees were already in flower, and blossoms were opening from shrubs all around the walls.

'Thank you.' An older woman smiled at her. 'I'm Sky. You're Sage, the police told us to expect you. And I remember Felix, of course. How are you?' To Sage's surprise she kissed Felix's cheek and showed him to a wicker chair. 'You were so kind to us when the press were banging on our windows every day. Maybe they will finally find that lovely girl.'

'I hope so,' he answered. 'As Sage was saying, your garden is even more advanced than when I was here before in 1992.'

'We just love the plants and they love us back,' Sky said simply, as her husband brought in a silver tray with two teapots and a stack of cups and saucers. 'Felix said you were an archaeologist. You must be aware of the earthworks at Hound Butt, then.'

'We are.'

'I've always wanted to see them. Our ancestors created so many sacred sites in the forest. Have you seen Pudding Barrow?' When Sage shook her head, Sky's smile grew broader. 'It has a lovely atmosphere. The builders picked a place full of good earth energy. But

I'm distracting you from your investigation.'

Felix leaned forward. 'I came to talk to you back in ninety-one, about the abuse of some horses. Your insights were very helpful. The police had originally explored the idea that they were ritual stabbings, which we knew was unlikely, at least from any known tradition. My conclusion was the attacks were sexual and sadistic in nature, the work of a disturbed individual.'

'We always knew these were mindless assaults on helpless animals, nothing ceremonial,' said Sky snappily. 'The police are always very wary of the alternative, they wouldn't listen to us. They didn't challenge all the "black magic" and "witches in the forest" headlines.' She softened her voice. 'Your interviews with the press went some way to redirecting the attention back onto the crimes, and away from us.'

'I wish I could have done more,' Felix said. 'When there is a vacuum of information then the speculation can become overblown.' His voice was calm. 'Did either of you know River Sloane?'

Sky and Oliver looked at each other. 'Not at all,' Sky said. 'Of course, we saw it on the news. I thought she looked a little like Lara: same age, height, both blonde.'

'It would help if you could tell us again what you remember of Lara,' Felix said.

Sky nodded. 'We knew her quite well. She was a school friend of my niece and had been to several meetings of our coven.'

Felix glanced at Sage. 'Just as an observer, I remember you saying,' he said.

Sky nodded. 'A spiritual seeker, that's all. She was passionate about nature and the environment. She helped us organise a pony watch in the forest after Oliver found one of them mutilated. Then the police arrested him and our private lives were all over the front pages of the papers—'

'Questioned, I was never arrested,' Oliver interrupted, as he stirred the tea in its pot. 'I was walking our schnauzer one evening when I interrupted an attack,' he said. He looked over the garden. 'Something was screaming – it was a terrible noise. The dog kept barking. I managed to calm him down a bit, and we followed the sound. By the time I got there the pony was lying down, gasping for air, kicking out at me. She had been stabbed, dozens of times, and was terrified. The poor creature must have been in agony.'

'And the stabbing was sexual in nature, which somehow made it worse.' Sky's mouth twisted in distress. 'That poor animal, mutilated and in pain. The vet put it down straight away.'

Sage noted down the details. 'Do you remember the date?'

'It was late in the year, November I think.' Oliver put cups on saucers. 'It was around Guy Fawkes Night, 1991. Because I was the one who called them, they questioned me very closely. They only started to talk to the Chorleighs because Alistair used to walk his dogs in the forest late at night.'

'Alistair Chorleigh would have been very young, sixteen

or seventeen,' Sage said. She wasn't sure why she was defending him, except that she had seen a vulnerability about him when he begged her to look after the dog. Hamish, that was his name.

'Animal mutilations are often done by teenagers,' Felix said. 'They aren't that uncommon.'

'Just horrible.' An image of the beaten-up dead body of River Sloane in his garden flashed into Sage's mind. 'And now he's under suspicion again.'

Sky nodded. 'And it was all too easy for narrow-minded bigots to point the finger at innocent people and talk about animal sacrifices and satanism. Several animal activists were questioned and the local hunt spread rumours about the hunt saboteurs.'

Oliver offered Sage tea: Earl Grey or herbal. She chose the latter; it was rich with chamomile and cinnamon scents and she thought it might settle her stomach. When she said so, Oliver was surprised. 'You know your herbs.'

'My mother is a medical herbalist,' she admitted. 'I grew up on home-grown teas.'

The next few minutes were taken up with the familiar ritual of pouring tea. Then Felix brought out a folder of photocopied newspaper articles.

'I need you to look at these,' he said, spreading them out on the coffee table. 'They are from 1992, after Lara went missing. I was hoping you might be able to tell me about the people in the pictures.'

'It was awful,' said Sky. 'We were pilloried in the local press as devil worshippers and perverts.'

Felix turned one article around. 'But you stayed together as a group?'

Oliver put his glasses on and studied each one. 'Absolutely, although some of the group have died since. We were mostly in middle age.' He held up a newspaper image of his younger self, carrying some shopping out of a post office with the headline 'Forest witches suspected'. 'Every man in the group was considered a possible threat, a suspect.'

Felix nodded. 'Did you have any suspicions of anyone yourself?'

Oliver looked surprised. 'It was hard not to suspect Alistair Chorleigh. After all, he'd been a prime suspect in the animal attacks and he was the last person seen with her alive.'

Sky broke in. 'There had been an odd cloud over the family. First, Alistair's mother ran away with the daughter, then he was expelled from school. No one ever found out why. I didn't even know he knew Lara, but they were at college at the same time.'

Felix nodded. 'What was she like?'

Sky stood and went into the living room, which overflowed with books on every wall, some of the shelves bowing under the weight. 'It's here somewhere.'

'I looked this morning,' Oliver said. 'I'm not sure we still have it.'

'Ah, there. I knew it would come in handy, I've kept it all this time.'

Sky opened a book and brought out a photograph. 'Lara took this. She joined us at a wild camp a few months before she disappeared. That lad is her boyfriend. I didn't know his real name, she always called him Badger.' The picture showed a laughing teenage boy in profile, next to a younger Sky and Oliver. 'I didn't think to show it to the police at the time.'

Sage leaned forward. The photograph had captured the expression of the three sitters, especially the boy. His eyes were screwed up with laughter, and he was leaning on Sky's shoulder as if they were sharing a joke.

Felix took the picture. 'She wasn't living with her parents, if I remember.'

Sky sat back, picked up her herbal tea. 'Her mother shouted at her all the time to get a job.'

'I remember they interviewed the boyfriend but he had an alibi.'

'He would never have hurt Lara.' Sky shrugged. 'They were madly in love, hoped to live together in a community of animal activists. I know he and Lara did fall out over the fox hunt. She was passionate about banning hunting, but he wasn't. He loved horses and worked as a groom. At one time he even worked for the Chorleighs. He thought it was too dangerous for her to go out as a hunt saboteur.'

Felix nodded. 'He was right, a few of them were badly

injured in the eighties and nineties.'

Oliver handed the folder of newspaper clippings to Sage. 'These make me sick,' he said. 'That's how we were all characterised at the time.'

Sage leafed through the clippings. They were savage and ranged much wider than Lara's disappearance, claiming drug use, sexual abuse and animal torture.

Oliver topped up Sage's tea. 'This was the era of the Rochdale and Orkney inquiries, rumours of satanic abuse and hysteria.'

Felix took the folder and flicked through to a large article at the back. 'This is the only story that mentions the Chorleigh family outside of the police interrogation. She was seen, by a motorist, waiting for a bus at the stop down the road from Chorleigh House. She was talking to Alistair Chorleigh.'

Sky managed a dry chuckle. 'No one from the local press would dare write about the family. That was in a big newspaper, they could take the risk.'

Sage scanned the first few lines. 'And this was the reason he was interviewed? He was seen talking to her?'

'No one saw her alive after that, as far as we know.' Oliver sat back. 'Well, he'd been interviewed before, about the horse attacks.' He half laughed. 'They talked to that old scoundrel, Jansen, too. He was the closest thing we had to a satanist at the time. He was the leader of the hunt saboteurs; I know Lara helped him a few times. He once walked a rescued fox right through Chorleigh's garden and grounds late at night. The next day, twenty hounds trampled straight through his land and the horses followed.'

Sky smiled at him. 'She and Badger had a huge fight over it – he probably had to clear up the mess. He was working there as part-time gardener as well as groom. He was questioned too, all her friends were, but he had an alibi.'

'There were always rumours about Alistair Chorleigh, he was awkward with people,' Oliver said. 'Then Lara disappeared opposite their property. That boy was hounded; he became a bit of a recluse.'

'Did you see him after Lara disappeared?' Felix asked.

Sky frowned. 'The strange thing is, we didn't, not for a while. There was a rumour that he was unwell, in a hospital somewhere. I knew the vicar's wife in Fairfield. She and her husband tried to offer support to the family, but Alistair's father was such a bully he pushed everyone away. He got a good lawyer, of course, but he acted as if *he* thought the boy had killed Lara. There was never any evidence that he had, of course. It was a quiet road, anyone in a car could have picked her up. But most of us thought something had happened to her – she wouldn't have lost touch with her boyfriend.'

'Well, thank you for talking to us,' Sage said, looking again at the picture. 'It's a great photograph. She's caught the moment beautifully.'

'She was a lovely girl,' Oliver said. 'A compassionate

spirit, just a little wild. She was drawn to the coven because we shared her love of nature and natural magic.'

'Natural magic?' Sage asked.

Oliver waved at the garden. 'That's natural magic,' he said, smiling. 'Plants flowering months early, because they know they are loved and needed. We know they will protect us, and we nurture them in return.'

Sage struggled not to reveal her scepticism but Sky had picked it up. She smiled at Sage as if she was ten years old. 'I have advanced breast cancer. I was diagnosed as terminal eleven years ago. A lot of herbs and a complete change of lifestyle, but here I am. I call that magic.'

Felix looked at the garden. 'I don't doubt it. I've seen things I can't explain. And your garden is amazing.' He picked up the picture. 'Can we take this? I'll make sure it gets back to you.'

'Of course.' Sky looked from Felix to Sage. 'Be careful, won't you? The forest looks beautiful but it's easy to get lost in it.'

It was almost eleven by the time Felix drove Sage back to Chorleigh House, so she could examine the wooden building in the grounds. Trent had already texted her to say he was on his way.

'There are footprints leading right to the side of the building,' she explained to Felix. 'It's a garage or a stable, it's too big to be a shed. Whoever buried the body may have got the leaves from there.'

'Could they be Chorleigh's footsteps?'

'We don't know yet. They don't appear to come from the house. I'm sure they'll find out what size shoe he wears.'

A police officer lifted the tape to let them enter. The press had dwindled to a couple of people with cameras, who snapped a few shots as the car passed them.

'He may have mutilated a dozen horses and a few cows, remember, and possibly killed Lara.' Felix pulled up in a space on the verge near the house. He grabbed his bag from the back seat as they got out. 'But I have to admit the shallow grave does suggest someone wants to put the blame on Chorleigh, the local scapegoat. I'll come with you to look at this outbuilding, I'm interested.'

As they went through the gate, Trent appeared with a group of police officers. 'Ah, Sage! Where's the GPR equipment?'

'It's in the boot of my car, and it weighs a ton,' she replied, nodding to DCI Lenham. 'This is Felix Guichard, Trent.'

'Professor.' Trent acknowledged Felix before turning to Sage. 'The police are just making sure the decrepit structure isn't going to collapse on us.'

Sage looked at him. 'What about the other case? You went to see a body in a sleeping bag.'

Trent grimaced. 'Probably unlawfully buried but it doesn't look like murder. Benefit fraud, as I suggested.

Grandma dies and the family keep collecting the pension. I'll go back to the grave once the pathologist has had time to have a look at the skeleton. River's murder comes first at the moment, not to mention Lara's disappearance.'

'Shall we concentrate on this building?' snapped Lenham, leading the way down a narrow path made of crushed scrub and brambles. 'I've got to get back to interviewing River's boyfriends – the current one and the ex. We think we've shored up the front wall enough to risk opening the door and I'd like you to have a look inside.'

The door to the large structure had a padlock on it, a pair of young officers working on it with a bolt cutter. Sage could see the front left-hand corner of the roof was sagging onto the top of the door. The whole thing was covered with ivy, and spindly holly trees leaned over the back. She peered around the side, where someone had already cordoned off an area of long grass and small gorse shrubs. Stacked all along the right-hand wall of the building were leaves, piled almost a metre high. She could see how the leaves were funnelled in by the wind, how they could swirl around and settle in the lee of the wall. Along the top were some areas of fresh holly leaves, just yellowed or blackened but still shiny. Between them were three areas where the deposits had been removed almost halfway to the ground.

'That must be where he got the covering layers from.' She pointed, and Lenham, who had followed her, nodded.

'They must have known the building was here, and that

the leaves pile up this way. It's nowhere near the road and on private woodland. Who would know that?'

Sage remembered something. 'There were gardeners here in the nineties, and grooms for horses. Lara's boyfriend Badger was one of them.'

'We're following that up, but we're struggling to identify all of them. Chorleigh paid badly and fired a lot of people.' Lenham folded his arms. 'Let's have a look inside. They had planning permission for a stable in 1989, so it would have been quite new in 1992.' He shivered, shrugging himself into his coat. 'I just hope we don't find Lara's remains tucked somewhere inside. We'll look like idiots.'

'Wasn't it explored when she disappeared?' Sage said, surprised.

'The garden area was searched, briefly, and I like to think thoroughly. But when we went for a detailed warrant for the whole grounds it was refused and our previous limited warrant was rescinded. We didn't get to search again with dogs and more equipment and we never went inside.'

Trent turned to Sage. 'Let's have a quick look, then we'll sweep the floor and look under it with the GPR.'

Lenham walked back to the door and nodded to one of his officers, who leaned on it. It didn't budge.

The PC looked up. 'It's got the weight of the whole roof on this corner, sir.'

Sage pointed at a line of three rusted hinges. 'These don't look so solid.'

Lenham leaned on the top edge and one of the hinges gave way with a puff of wood dust. 'That's better. Trent, Guichard, give me a hand.' The three men forced the edge of the door inwards, creating a narrow wedge of a gap.

Trent leaned forward. 'If we hold it open, you can look inside, Sage. Here, take my torch.' The door creaked and cracked as they pushed, giving way a few more inches. 'Careful, in case it comes down.'

Sage angled the torch into the stable, playing the light over the walls. Old riding tack, white with mould, hung from hooks. Cobwebs trailed almost to the ground. Her eyes adjusted to the gloom. A few holes in the roof allowed a grey light to creep in and brighten the floor. The sight took her breath away. Huge teeth in a yellow mask, eye sockets high on the triangular skull. It was the eerie shape of a horse's head.

'I don't understand.' She leaned on the door some more and with Felix and Trent's help managed to force the hinges forward a few more inches. 'There's a horse's skull on the floor.'

'Don't go inside,' Trent warned. 'The door is holding the frame up.'

She put her head around the doorframe, playing the beam of light around the concrete, over the cobwebs that filled the interior. 'It's a whole horse,' she said, her voice strained. She swallowed the first of her questions. 'I mean, it's the skeleton of a horse. There's some mummification, too.'

'We're going to have to search the stable for Lara Black,' Lenham said. He stepped closer, peering in over her shoulder. 'I doubt if we would have missed the smell of a decomposing horse, so it most likely happened after Lara went missing.' They scraped it open another few inches before the roof sagged onto it.

'It could have happened much later.' She looked around at the stall door inside, kicked almost to pieces. She pulled her camera out of an inside pocket of her coat. 'I think it might have been left in here, locked in. Look at the damage to the walls inside.' She snapped a few pictures. The skull grinned back at her.

The wooden walls were reinforced by metal sheeting, dented with hundreds of hoof-shaped semicircles.

'How long ago did it die?' Lenham put his hand over his mouth. 'It's still a bit rank in there.'

'A decade at least. Look at all the insect damage on the mummified skin over its ribs.' Sage put a foot onto the threshold and peered behind the door. 'Oh, God, there's another one, smaller. They would have lasted a couple of days maybe, without water. Starvation would have taken a lot longer.' She snapped another sequence of shots, the flash lighting up the grinning skulls and leather-covered ribcages.

Felix pulled at her shoulder. 'Come out, it's not safe. Let's get the stable shored up. I think it's mostly held up by brambles.'

She stepped back into the fresh air. 'That's horrible.' She leaned against a tree, took a few breaths. 'I can't see how it relates to River's death, but it might be something to do with Lara's disappearance. We can probably get an estimated date for the horses.' She looked around. 'I can't believe no one noticed the smell of two large animals decomposing for months. The stench must have been awful.'

Felix looked back at the building where Trent and Lenham were looking through the door and talking. 'I don't know, locked inside, maybe it was mostly contained. And it's away from the house and the field. But why would anyone do that? I mean, who would go to the trouble of building a stable for their horses then leave them to die? That's madness.'

Lenham walked over, shaking his head. 'Christ.' He pulled out a packet of cigarettes. 'I'm sorry, do you mind?'

Felix nodded. 'Go ahead.'

Lenham lit up and blew a cloud of smoke away from Sage. 'My daughter has got two ponies.'

'Out in the forest?' Sage said.

He shook his head. 'Stabled outside Lyndhurst. I don't ride but I quite like looking after them. Shit. That's horrible. We're going to arrest Chorleigh on suspicion of cruelty, see if that shakes out anything useful.'

She kicked some of the earth aside from the concrete apron underfoot. 'There's quite a bit of yard out here.'

'I can feel it,' Lenham said. 'I'll call it in, but we can't look under the floor until forensics have done a proper examination. We'll need a vet to do the necropsy on the horses. There could be something of Lara's in there – we don't even know she isn't dead in one of the stalls.' He took another long drag on the cigarette. 'You need to look at those carcasses.'

# 10

'Volume 1 of Baron Abercrombie's book of Bronze Age pottery defines potsherds from cord beakers which predominate in what he calls province 1, Wessex south of the Thames. It is possible to see small areas of geometric decoration typical of these earliest British Bronze Age remains.'

Journal of Edwin Masters, 28th June 1913

Several spoil heaps on oilcloths now dot the ground beside the barrows. Peter has set himself the task of sieving the soil as I trowel it out, and two of his friends from school have helped barrow the earth over to his makeshift tent. As a consequence, he has a sizeable collection of pot pieces and the odd piece of knapped flint that might be the remains of a stonemason's working thousands of years ago.

Hilda Chorleigh, Molly and Peter's cousin, is helping me. She has stopped flirting so much with me now and I like her better. She has taken to wearing jodhpurs and is handy with a trowel. It was she who first hit the edge of the stone that brought us all running.

It was a rough-hewn slab of stone perhaps four feet by two and irregular in shape. Peter and I exposed it slowly, and then a matching fellow, lying alongside it. The shape, roughly grave-sized, excited us all, and even Mr Chorleigh came down from the house to examine it when Peter ran to tell him.

I cleaned away the edges to show its extent, and found the beginnings of vertical supports on which they were lying.

'It's a burial chamber, surely? It must be,' said Peter.

Mr Chorleigh was disturbed by it. 'Don't bother your mother with this. It's bound to be upsetting. Is there any chance of actual remains in that tomb?'

I felt it my duty to reassure him that it was probably an empty chamber.

'I will ask the Reverend Dewey to say a few prayers over the site, just in case.' He looked troubled and I was quick to agree. 'Thank you, Mr Masters,' he said. 'I shall send a note up to the vicarage, then I must leave for court.'

'We won't proceed further until he has been,' I promised.

So we extended the trench to work around what we thought might be a chamber and found piles of rubble loosely fitted at each of the short ends. I checked the alignment with my compass; the feature lay roughly along an east–west axis. I continued clearing an area beyond the western end, which I have already started thinking of as the head end, when I came across a circlet of fired clay.

'Look!' I couldn't contain my enthusiasm and Peter came over with Hilda and Molly. 'We'll have to dig very gently here,' I said, scraping away from the pot.

'What is it?' Molly was crouching on the edge of the trench, staring earnestly into my eyes. 'Is it a whole pot?'

Peter knelt down beside me. 'You'd better wait for Mr Dewey, Ed, if that's what I think it is.'

I concurred, and satisfied myself with cleaning the soil gently from the belly of the pot. Although cracks ran in all directions around it, it seemed complete.

'Why?' whispered Molly. 'What is it?'

'If Peter is right, it's a funerary urn,' I said, brushing gently at the lip. 'Look. It's quite full of earth. Perhaps it had a stopper once, which has rotted away.'

She reached a hand as if to touch its surface then pulled back. 'It seems so strange that a man once shaped this, thousands of years ago.'

'Or a woman,' I said.

She smiled at me. 'Or a woman. Look, Hilda.'

Hilda shook her head. 'I don't want to even touch it,' she said. 'Has it got bones inside?'

'I think this might have been a burial that was added to the barrow after it was finished,' I said, showing the girls where the fingers of the unknown potter had smoothed the raw clay, leaving impressions faintly against the rim. 'The bodies were usually burned and the ashes buried.'

Molly put her own slight fingers into the depressions. 'Definitely a man, I'm afraid,' she said, laughing at the mismatch.

We cleaned up the site a little and sat in the shade of the trees and the awning, drinking the remaining lemonade and eating the last of the biscuits Cook had brought down for lunch. She seems to think Peter is too thin and brings baskets of food every two or three hours. I fed a few crumbs to a curious pied wagtail, and Molly told me that the Hampshire name for them is Polly Dishwasher. She bounced in front of us, flicking her tail, until she took a crumb right from my hand.

'I spent my summer holidays in Norfolk after my father died,' I told her. 'They call tadpoles "Pollywiggles" there.'

'Was that with the general?' she asked, nibbling a little biscuit.

'And his wife,' I said. 'He is the kindest of men. My father's uncle is childless and was generous to me.'

'Don't you have any cousins at all?' Molly glanced at me from under eyelashes that were almost white. I did feel it then, a little breathlessness.

'I have two female cousins on my mother's side,' I said. 'But they have settled in America so I only knew them when I was very young. One pinched me to make me cry.'

'How horrid! I'm glad she went to America, then.'

I smiled at her. 'I'm sure she is much improved now, she is married with children of her own.'

I saw a flash of a black cloak and hastily stood, brushing the dried grass off my clothes. I gave a hand to Molly too, and the others saw me and followed suit.

'Here is the Reverend Dewey to bless the site,' Peter said. We were introduced, then stood in the sun with our eyes closed and hands folded while he droned some prayer or other. I should have listened, but the sound of bumble bees in the honeysuckle at my shoulder almost drowned him out.

'Amen,' he said, and we all echoed it.

'I should be most interested in your findings,' Mr Dewey said to Peter, smiling at him. 'Such a worthwhile endeavour.'

'We would be happy to show you once the barrow is opened,' Peter said, fanning himself with his straw hat. 'We mean no disrespect, of course, and will be careful with any remains we find.'

'These are hardly Christian burials,' Mr Dewey replied, smiling at Peter. 'Just heathens who lived and died without the benefit of our Lord.'

It seemed strange to me. My father lived, and eventually died, for his beliefs. Yet he never bored me, nor applied his faith to every little thing. I also found Mr Dewey strangely overfamiliar, especially with Peter, whose arm he insisted on clutching over 'rough ground' and whom he kept calling his dear boy. Molly seemed no more enamoured of him than I was.

Once the reverend had been shaken off and Peter's cousin and friends returned to the house, we could cover up the stone box and then protect the urn. It was about two-and-a-half feet high and a little less wide, more cracks at the base but still in situ, packed with soil. Around the middle were two lines of small scratches, and two thin lines around the top under the lip. It must have been a handsome piece, probably dark grey with black decoration but Peter detected (he thought) a hint of red in the dots. Time will tell when we get the whole thing out. At the moment the infill keeps its shape.

Molly's pencil flew over a sketch of the pot. She had tried to get the shape right several times and had given up. 'Oh, this blasted pencil.'

'Here, let me.' I took it and opened my penknife.

'I can do it,' she said, staring at the pot. 'You always make it too sharp.'

I relinquished the knife and pencil to her expert shaving. I looked down at the crown of her head, the whorl of ragged curls so like her brother's. 'It's probably mostly full of wood ash. There would have been a funeral pyre.'

'It's strange to think that someone's bones might be buried under the stones, too. It's a bit scary. Peter used to chase me around the garden with an old sheep's skull, I blame him.'

'I wish you were my sister,' I blurted out, which wasn't quite what I meant to say.

Her whittling paused for a moment, then resumed. 'Do you?'

'What I mean is…' I ran out of words.

'I know,' she said, then blew the shavings off her pencil and closed the knife. 'I like you, too.'

Letter from Robert Conway to Edwin Masters, 27th June 1913

My dear Edwin,

How pleasant to have heard from you, I have just finished the round of end-of-term meetings that I most despise. I have examined your potsherds and am quite intrigued. I had to attend a dinner in London so took the opportunity to consult with a colleague in the British Museum.

You are quite correct as to the date, although I think earlier rather than later, say 1800–1200 BC. I was especially interested in the short section of black-rimmed beaker. What was so interesting is that this type of clay is usually Germanic in origin. You may have a precious pot brought by traders or settlers or even invaders in your hands!

The coin is of interest but little value. I showed it to Dr Arnold: he confirms that it is Commodus, an interesting bronze coin from about the second century anno domini – nothing to do with your earthworks, I suspect.

I was unable to exactly relate your Chorleigh House to the old maps of the area. If you let me have your location in more detail I may be able to find it on our own maps in the library here. I am most intrigued by the second of your features, especially the one close to water. Could it be a ceremonial dock? It would be worth looking within the wet area itself for ritual items.

I envy you; the New Forest is truly an excellent location for a holiday, especially with an ancient burial on site.

Yours affectionately,
*R. Conway, Balliol College*

# 11

*Afternoon, Wednesday 20th March, this year*
*Chorleigh House, Fairfield, New Forest*

Two hours later, the police had shored up the front of the stable and Sage had more information. She showed her photographs of the horses to Trent. 'They look as if they just lay down together for warmth or comfort, then died.'

'I hope they were humanely put down,' he said, 'but you'd think they would be separate and laid flat.' He packed bags and a camera into the boot of his car. 'Look, Lenham will tell you what he needs. I have to look in on the post-mortem of the woman in the sleeping bag.'

'I thought that was just benefit fraud?' Sage glanced back at the house. It was dark and quiet.

'That was before they discovered blood in the top of the fabric.' He slammed the boot shut. 'This looks like it might have been transferred before death. I'll keep you in the loop; it might be useful for you to have a look, broaden your experience.'

She waved him off, then stood by her car, resisting the urge to follow him.

Sage was aware how quiet the place was. The press had gone, the road had been opened but no traffic came down it. Although Alistair Chorleigh's car was on the drive there was no sound from the house, even from the dog. She wasn't sure if he was there or not but she knew the police had brought him home. She grabbed her work camera and started walking across the old lawn towards the path to the stable, her clothes and boots brushing the grass and bracken. She could hear her own breathing. Even the birds had fallen silent. *Anything could happen here.* A snap in the undergrowth stalled her, one foot off the ground, and she held her breath, her heart jumping. Sage felt as if the trees and bushes were staring back and for a moment, she was standing right at the edge of the gaping well on the island.

She shook off the fear and stomped along the narrow path, widened by successions of police feet.

She could hear Felix's voice as she approached the stable. 'That's – heartless.'

'You can see where the horses kicked the stall doors down. They couldn't get through the main door but they did some damage to the frame.' Lenham turned as Sage reached the entrance to the stable. 'Look at the flat-backed water buckets; there was no automatic system for filling them.' He kicked at the remains of a feed pail. 'Bastards.'

The front of the stable was now propped up, and light

flooded through the door, highlighting the skull of the larger animal. The smaller one was beside it, its head leaning against the forelegs of the other horse as if they had lain down together to die. It made tears spring to Sage's eyes. The mummified skin appeared bone dry and cracked with age. Thousands of holes peppered the skin, blowfly maggots burrowing out, she imagined, as well as beetles burrowing in.

'Is it safe yet?' Sage didn't wait for the answer but stepped forward to Felix's side, just inside the doorframe.

'It is now.' Felix pointed up at the roof. Sage could see small holes but the ivy had covered any larger gaps. 'They've jacked up the roof at the back as well.' He looked down at her. 'I'm staying on for a few days. This looks like it might relate to the animal attacks in the 1990s.'

Lenham waved an arm around the stable. 'I need you to go over it like another crime scene. I have to concentrate on River and the grave in the garden, but we need to know if Lara is here too, if the two girls ended their lives in the same place.'

She looked around the floor, seeing piles of ancient straw, flattened by the animals. In the corner was a heap of rubbish, newspapers and card. She lifted what turned out to be the remains of a blanket and a flat cardboard box.

'Ah.' She turned the box to the light. 'Equicura wormer.' She dusted off the label with her glove. The information on the prescription label had faded to nothing, but the manufacturer's information was clear. 'Expires August 1993 but I can't see when it was dispensed. We can't be sure when the horses died but it might narrow it down.'

'The Metropolitan police had an equine crime unit here until 1993,' Lenham said, holding out a bag for it. 'Forensics might be able to get more information. The dates are around Lara Black's disappearance.' He picked up a newspaper, blanched on the outside but legible on the inside. He took it into the light to read it. 'July 15th, 1992.'

Sage nodded. 'We heard of an attack nearby, possibly in November 1991, from the couple in Chilhaven who knew Lara. They thought Alistair Chorleigh was questioned at the time.'

Lenham made a note. 'I'll look into it. Of course, he was a juvenile; we didn't keep every interview back then.'

Felix started sorting through the tack. 'If we don't find anything later than 1992 it might connect Lara to the dead horses. I think the disappearance of a girl who cared about animal rights at the scene of the abuse of two horses is unlikely to be a coincidence.'

'Exactly,' Sage said, as much to herself as the men. 'We'll search the stables. If Lara was ever in here, we might find something.'

Lenham shook his head. 'Her body's not here now. God, I hate spiders.' He wiped the webs on his hands onto the back of his notes. 'The stable was put in in 1989, we've checked with building control that signed off the structure.

Trent's going to check under the concrete inside and out once forensics have worked it. To bury a body, someone would have had to create a hole in the slab, dig a grave in the subsoil and concrete back over it but I can't see a patch.' He peered up at the roof. 'We once found a gangster under the floor of his own pub, the patrons never suspected, it was all done overnight. It is possible.'

Sage turned over a pile of straw, welded together with webs, to find a large penknife in the corner, still open. 'I've got something.'

Lenham peered at it. 'Bag it. The blade tip is bent, it's distinctive. Where's Trent?'

'He's been called to the other case.'

Lenham lifted a tangle of straps that might have once been a halter. 'We'll need to get the animals out to look at the floor.'

'I'll concentrate on clearing the stable with the SOCOs.' Sage walked outside, grateful for the smell of grass and leaves. Despite the time that had passed, there was still a stink of decay around the bodies. She stumbled over a line of bramble laid across the thick grass, catching her hand on one of the holly branches beside the stable.

Lenham followed her out. 'I've got a young PC who needs forensic experience, he'll give you a hand. I can't spare the SOCOs for more than a day on an animal case or a tenuous link to a missing person.'

'They will still be too heavy for just two people to lift.'

There was some light sunshine but in the shade the woodland was cold. 'Get Guichard to help you,' he said. 'The animal attacks were his case.'

Laying two tarpaulins twenty metres away and then heaving out the surprisingly heavy remains took over an hour, even with help from PC Stewart and Felix. Sage had decayed horse dust in her hair, up her nose and even inside her forensic suit. There was a wide stain on the floor from the decomposition fluids: the majority of the soft tissues of the two animals had liquefied onto the floor, probably in a boiling sea of maggots which left thousands of pupa cases all over the concrete, and despite the time elapsed, a vile smell.

There was no obvious sign of euthanasia on the skulls, like shooting or captive bolt marks. She supposed they could have been injected with something, but why leave the bodies to rot? She worked her way over the carcasses, until she found an anomaly on the neck of the larger horse. Closer examination revealed another on the pony, although the skin was less well preserved as it had been lying a little under the larger animal. Fluids from decomposition must have bathed the smaller horse. She laid a measure alongside each and photographed them.

They were both small cuts, about 31mm wide, deep stab wounds. She passed a probe into two of them and they seemed to extend into the desiccated muscle; the space had pulled open as it dried. Threads of meat had been pulled out of the incisions at one end. She spoke into her phone's recorder. 'Mention wounds on right side of the neck of both horses to vet doing the necropsy. Query folding blade. Check this odd ragged edge.'

She searched the interior of the stable with the two scene of crime officers. There was no explanation for the damage to the walls other than the animals' frenzied efforts to get away from something, or escape their captivity. In places the walls were almost breached; a little longer and they might have broken free. From her rough measurements she estimated the smaller animal was a pony whereas the larger was a heavily built horse.

'Like a Shire horse?' Felix asked.

'I'm not sure,' Sage said; never having succumbed to a pony fixation as a child she was hazy on the distinction.

'More likely a hunter. Look at the kit,' PC Stewart said, pulling out the edge of decayed saddle. 'These suggest a decent pony, maybe for an older child, and a large horse for an adult. The vet will probably know more.'

'Will the family's vet have records after all this time?' Sage looked at Stewart. 'Perhaps he knew the animals, prescribed the wormer.'

'I was brought up around here. The practice shut down about ten years ago when the owner retired, but I'm pretty sure he still lives in the area.'

Sage looked back at Felix, sorting through a pile of old

newspapers. 'I could take Professor Guichard to ask him about the wormer. We can't do the GPR on the stable floor until it's clear and Trent is here.'

PC Stewart nodded. 'I'll check in with the boss, see if he can arrange it.'

'OK.' She walked over to Felix. 'I'm going to get some coffee. Then I'm headed out to talk to the original vet, if you want to come with me.'

They walked through the woods to the van, the doors open and a canteen of warm coffee in the back. Felix accepted a paper cup and downed it in three gulps.

'Maybe the vet will know something about the other animals that were abused.'

Sage took her time, sipping the black, bitter drink. She remembered the enormous cases of equipment in her car and offered her keys to PC Stewart when he walked up, waving his radio. 'Tell Trent where I've gone, if he turns up,' she said. 'The equipment is in the boot if he needs it.'

He nodded. 'I've tracked down the vet – he's in and this is the address. Trent is holding off doing the floor until the SOCOs have completely cleared the area.'

She took the address. 'It might help with the animal cases and maybe even give us an idea about Lara too. Do you mind driving, Felix?'

'No problem,' he said, dropping the cup into a bag hung off the police van. 'Maybe we can get a decent coffee somewhere.'

\* \* \*

Felix drove Sage through some of the best scenery of the forest. Open country was peppered with mature trees, ponies grazing in small groups.

Sage glanced at her phone the second she got a signal, away from Fairfield. 'Have you ever heard of similar cases of horses left to rot like that?'

'People do leave horses tethered and without water,' he said. 'Or just dump them beside roads. But in both cases they might have hoped members of the public might intervene, which they generally do. There was no hope of that here, in fact every effort was made to isolate the animals.' He glanced at Sage. 'It was oppressive in there, wasn't it?'

'Those poor animals,' Sage said. 'Anyone capable of that would be capable of hurting a teenager, I imagine.'

'Except for the time frame, which is wide,' Felix said, slowing as he approached houses. 'Let's try to narrow down the date a bit by finding out when he prescribed the wormer. Stewart said the vet's retired now, he lives in the village – ah, here we are, Rose Lane.'

He pulled up outside a pretty thatched cottage that looked like something out of a calendar.

'There's good money in veterinary medicine,' he said, squinting up at the house. 'This must be worth a packet.'

Sage got out, stood at the gate while he locked the car and gathered his bag. 'I'm struggling to pay for a one-bedroom flat,' she said.

'It can't be easy for you. I suppose the rest of the time Nick's rattling around that enormous vicarage.'

'It's his work.' When she thought of Nick she recalled snappy conversations in whispers over Max's head, or phone calls to cancel plans at the last moment. His work was immersive. He hadn't yet sorted out a work–life balance – shit, neither had she. Every moment was Max, childcare, work, sleep.

Sage rang the doorbell and waited for someone with white hair to open the half-glazed front door. A deep bark from somewhere in the property was answered by the man shouting back into the hall.

'Shut up, Henry!' He opened the door. 'Come in, come in. Ignore the dog.'

'Mr Westcott? Dr Sage Westfield and Professor Felix Guichard. I believe the police rang ahead?'

'They did, and I'm happy to help if I can. Call me Malcolm, please.' He escorted them into a living room that went right through the property. 'Take a seat.' Malcolm sat in a wing chair opposite them. 'What's this about?'

'We were wondering what you remember of Mr George Chorleigh, or his son, Alistair,' Sage said. 'Of Chorleigh House outside Fairfield.'

'George was a nasty bit of work, chief agister at one point. Rode his horses hard – they were always lame after a few days out with the hunt. Chorleigh senior lived for his hunting. Alistair was a quiet lad, nice enough. My wife knew him better than I did.' He took a deep breath and leaned back in the chair. He stared at Sage. 'Doctor of what?'

'Archaeology,' she answered. 'I'm training to become a forensic archaeologist. Felix is a social anthropologist.'

Malcolm stared at her for a long time. The room was full of paintings, some hanging askew. Half were faded watercolours of flowers, the other half were of dogs.

'I suppose you'll be looking into that missing girl again, Lara Black,' he said. 'We knew her, of course, she used to come to the hunt to wave a few banners and distract the hounds. I was questioned, anyone who'd visited the place was. I couldn't say much about George's character except what I told you. He punished the boy even harder than his horses, I recall that. Alistair was still at college then, but I was surprised when they questioned *him* about the girl. I would have thought he wouldn't say boo to a goose.'

Sage made a note. 'Do you remember anything about Chorleigh's animals around that time?'

'Oh yes, George had a bloody great hunter called Brutus and a pony. He used to have a third horse but he was too heavy for it and he said it was skittish. Sold it to a friend of mine; it turned out to be a sweet mare away from Chorleigh.'

'Any other animals?'

'A couple of dogs, he might have had a cat or two, just to keep rats and mice down,' the vet said. 'Of course, he had the pony for his wife. When she left, Alistair rode her. New Forest chestnut, about fourteen hands. She must have been over twenty at that point. I remember seeing the boy out on her when he was younger. Jenny, I think she was called.' Sage must have winced at the mention of the pony. 'What?' he asked, looking at her.

Felix had his pen poised over his notebook. 'When was the last time you saw the Chorleighs' horses? Either of them?'

The old man leaned back in his chair and chewed his lip. He looked at Sage. 'What has all this got to do with the horses?'

'We were wondering if you saw them around the time Lara Black went missing. September ninth, 1992.'

'Yes, I think so. I went around to the house to do some routine thing, deliver wormer or something. I remember speaking to Chorleigh; he was as puzzled as anyone about the missing girl. We talked about a bridle he wanted to borrow from my wife, I told this to the police. This was in the days after she disappeared – they were knocking on doors all over Fairfield. I can't remember when they took Alistair for questioning; I know he had an accident around that time.'

Sage leaned forward. 'You remember that?'

He nodded. 'What I remember is how furious his father was. We – my wife and I – always suspected Alistair was being hit by his father.'

Felix looked up from his notebook. 'And the horses were all right then?'

The old man shrugged. 'I suppose they must have been.

The records are all gone now, of course. We used a card record system until about 2000.'

'And when did the Chorleighs stop asking you to see their horses?' Felix asked.

'That I do remember. Chorleigh was usually lazy about the bills, and I recall him paying up in full in the autumn. He said he'd sold the horses after all the trouble with Alistair. The boy was in hospital for a while, you know.'

Sage looked across at Felix. 'What happened to him?'

The vet shrugged. 'I was told Brutus had reared up and hit Alistair in the face. But no one really knew. I don't think I actually saw the horses after that, now I think about it. I would have been wary.'

Felix scribbled it down. 'Can you state for the record when you think the last time you did see the horses was?'

'I don't know… before the girl went missing? Ninth, you said? Maybe the month before, I don't think I saw them when I dropped in the wormer that last time. I remember talking out on the drive.' The old man seemed to sink back into his memories. 'I'm not sure any more.' He looked at Sage. 'What is this about? You haven't found the girl, have you?'

Sage wasn't sure how much he knew – or was allowed to know. 'We were called in on a separate case. A recent burial was found.'

'Not that girl, River? I thought she must have gone missing in Southampton.'

Felix leaned forward. 'The body of a girl was discovered in

the garden of Chorleigh House. It was on the morning news.'

'Poor girl, how awful. At Chorleigh?' Malcolm shook his head. 'To be honest, I don't follow the news much, just see the headlines outside the shop when I pick up my milk.' He seemed lost in his own thoughts for a long moment. 'It wasn't Alistair, was it? I mean, I never believed all the rumours with the other girl.' His hands were shaking. 'When Chorleigh senior reminded me that Alistair had been visiting my wife to pick up a hackamore for Brutus, I told it to the police, I didn't question it. Now I'm not so sure.'

Felix shook his head. 'You were just going on what Chorleigh senior had told you.'

'The boy was always here; my wife was very fond of him since his mother left. He probably was here.' He shook his head. 'Bloody hell. I've sworn up and down the forest that the boy didn't do it.' He looked at Sage. 'If I had my doubts it was about his father. He was a nasty bit of work. Not just heavy-handed with the horses, he had a terrible temper, very quick to despatch injured animals in the forest. He beat his stable lad up before he fired him. He said he had been stealing and the boy was too frightened to press charges.'

Sage leaned forward. 'Do you remember his name? The police could talk to him.'

'Jimmy something. Nice lad, a bit wild.'

She took a breath, tried to keep her voice even. 'Do you have any recollection of Chorleigh having his horses put down?'

'He would definitely have called me if they were ill or injured; aside from being heavy-handed he took good care of them. Brutus would have been worth a few thousand. He sold them, I told you. What's this about?'

Sage could see the old man had tears in his eyes. 'Do you know that for sure?' she asked gently. 'Did he sell them locally?'

'I used to be on call to the forest auction. No, he would have sent Brutus up country anyway, to get a good price. The pony wasn't worth more than dog food. Nice little mare, probably all the affection that Alistair ever got since his mother left.' He looked almost as white as his thick hair. 'I need my tablets.' He waved at the coffee table in front of Sage, and she handed him the pill packet there.

'Do you need some water? I could make some tea.'

'Would you? Don't mind the dog, he's all talk.'

Sage walked over to the door he had indicated and opened it a few inches. The deep bark had come from a spaniel who looked as old as his owner and wagged his whole back end at her when she patted him. She soon found the kettle and put it on. The draining board had one plate, one cup, one setting of cutlery. She found two more mugs in a cupboard and set them out. She leaned through the door. 'Do you take milk and sugar?'

He surprised her by coming to the kitchen door. 'Not usually, but I think I will today. I feel a bit wobbly.'

'I'll bring it over.'

The old man's fingers whitened on the door frame. 'You're going to tell me something happened to those horses, aren't you?'

Sage didn't know what to say. Her silence seemed to answer him though.

He nodded slowly. 'Two sugars, please, young lady. There are biscuits in the barrel on the windowsill. I have to keep them up there, away from the dog.'

He walked back to his chair more slowly than he had when he met them, and she put his tea within reach.

'Are you sure you're OK? We could call your doctor.'

'I'm fine. I'm just a bit shaky. I'm shocked that anyone could suspect Alistair Chorleigh of hurting anyone now. The last time I saw him he was too drunk to catch the bus home, so I gave him a lift. It must be a year ago now. He's a sick man, he couldn't manage the walk from the pub.'

Sage nodded. 'Do you remember seeing Alistair after Lara Black went missing?'

The old man took a bite of biscuit and chewed before answering. 'I think he dropped out of college but I don't remember him ever having a job. He used to help my wife in the garden but she said he was moody, depressed. Then he started working for his father and we hardly saw him again. He came to Isabel's funeral four years ago. He made a big fuss of the dogs we had then.' There was a little more colour in his face now. 'I'm down to one, now.'

Felix leaned forward. 'Did you ever think either man

was capable of cruelty to an animal?'

'Alistair, no.' The old man took a deep breath. 'Around that time we had some animals injured in the forest. Horses and cattle were being mutilated, stabbed; I attended a few myself. Had to put a couple of children's ponies down, very sad. George Chorleigh was loud in condemnation of the police, of their inability to catch the person responsible.'

Sage nodded. 'We're looking into it, to see if there's any connection. But neither of his horses were affected?'

'No, no. He built a proper stable for them – he just had a field shelter before and he used to stable them up at Oak Farm in the winter. He installed a proper lock, alarm, everything.' He wrapped his fingers around the cup. 'The horses weren't sold on, then?'

Felix sat back. 'I'm sorry. We can't talk about an ongoing investigation. Let us know if you remember anything else. The police will send someone round to take your statement.' His voice was mild but he stared directly at the old man. 'I must emphasise that it's important to stick to the truth, not protect anyone.'

The vet turned to Sage. 'I still don't see how I can help.'

She leaned forward. 'Do you remember a product called "Equicura"?'

He raised an eyebrow. 'We used it for years. We only went over to a new product because it had such a short shelf life. We were always chucking old stock out. A lot of the wormers were like it back then.' He stroked the dog's ears. 'We went over to Ovasicure around 1992, I think.'

'And how long did Equicura last, would you say?' Sage said.

He shrugged. 'Under a year, certainly. My wife used to complain we got boxes with short dates on, I recall. She worked as a receptionist for us. My daughter was one of the vets, it was a real family business.'

Sage smiled at him. 'That's useful, thank you. And if Alistair Chorleigh didn't do anything wrong, I'm sure we'll prove that, clear his name.'

'I suppose the police will be interviewing him if she was found in his garden.' When neither answered, he sighed. 'You know what a scapegoat is? That's what Alistair has always been. A scapegoat.'

# 12

'Some news from ancient history should astonish our readers, as a tomb from the Bronze Age has been excavated by students from the University of Oxford. Mr Peter Chorleigh and his colleague Mr Edwin Masters have already found what they believe to be a funerary urn, deep inside the mysterious tumuli in the gardens of the house in Fairfield.'

New Forest Gazette, 1st July 1913
Newspaper clipping pasted into the journal of Edwin Masters

The first morning of July was dull and overcast, but we walked with renewed enthusiasm to the dig. An article was in the local *Gazette*, the reporter had visited us the previous day. He was disappointed, I think, that we hadn't found either treasure or bones, but he did write about the urn.

Something had been walking over our spoil heaps overnight, no doubt digging for worms, probably badgers. Molly was uncharacteristically quiet, although she had been filled with laughter over parlour games with her friends and cousins the previous evening. Childish pastimes did not appeal to me, so I sat with Mrs Chorleigh who had joined us after dinner for half an hour. She was very thin and looked frail, but she asked after my mother and after a little while, she talked about Claire, her youngest child. A few tears flowed; she told me that while Mr Chorleigh did not like to talk about their daughter, she believed it did her good. She remembered stories of her three children, and I contrasted their childhood with my own, spent often in the woods around my mother's birthplace of Derby and my great-uncle's in Norfolk. I was able to mimic the local dialects of both, and she surprised me with her own very creditable impression of a rural Hampshire workman. That distracted the others from their games, and after Mrs Chorleigh retired Peter, Molly and I sat and talked until bedtime, a lovely evening.

At the barrows, I helped Peter pull off the excavation covers and the pot was even more remarkable in the morning light. Molly unfolded her stool and sat down to draw. 'I'm going to get better measurements,' she said, not looking at me. 'It's still not quite right.'

We uncovered the base of the pot very slowly, and despite our care, one crack opened up and pulled a wedge off the pot-shaped fill within.

'It was bound to happen,' I said to Peter. 'It's too heavy to support its own weight with the damage. Over millennia, water and frost will have fractured it.'

He lifted the triangle carefully and laid it on a cloth. 'We'll be able to reconstruct it anyway.'

Since it was no longer whole, we could dig away at the centre of the pot, hollowing it out. A few blackened fragments of something, perhaps bone, started to show in the soil. I collected them as I uncovered them, until I found a roundish object that looked like the head of a long bone.

'Is it human?' Peter was almost whispering, and I realised he was looking up at Molly.

I nodded my head. I could see Molly might get upset. 'We should be able to get the whole thing out,' I said in a low voice. 'We'll need some sort of glue if we want to reconstruct it.'

Molly folded her notebook open and showed me the sketch of the urn.

It was remarkable. She could be an artist if she chose, if she wasn't so interested in history and science. We exclaimed over it until she blushed, then she put her pencils away and said she had to sit with her mother that afternoon. When she had gone, we pored over the blackened fragments, looking for recognisable bones.

The back of the pot yielded a handful of teeth: three incisors, one premolar and two molars that could only have come from the mouth of a human being. We were sombre, holding in our hands the essence of a man like ourselves, long dead, cremated then buried.

'This is a secondary burial,' Peter mused. 'Which suggests there might be a primary burial under the slabs.'

'Slabs which may need a gantry of some sort to get off the ground,' I reminded him. 'Perhaps we can rig up some block and tackle arrangement if we can find trees big enough.'

He brushed away at the inside of the pot, added a broken piece of bone to the pile. 'I'll ask at the yacht club,' he said. 'They have all sorts of lifting equipment down there. We used to watch them take the boats out of the water at the end of the season.'

'We?' I was staring at the new fragment with my eyeglass, looking for enamel that would verify it as a tooth. I found a sliver of shiny orange surface that confirmed it.

'Me and Claire and Molly.' Something in his voice made me look up. 'Are you getting fond of Molly, Ed?' He sounded so awkward.

'What?' I caught his meaning. 'No. I mean I like her enormously, she's just the sort of girl one would like as a sister. Or a friend.'

He grinned at me. 'That's good to know. I mean, she's the best sister a chap could have, but I don't want you getting distracted.'

I wondered then if he was warning me off. I turned back to my burned bones, and he took up his brush and trowel. I suppose I would be a very poor match for Miss

Chorleigh of Chorleigh House, when all I have to offer is my scholarship and willingness to work.

'I'll box these up,' I said, my voice somewhat cool. 'I think the professor should see them, what do you think?'

'I think that's a splendid idea.' He shuffled over to where I was sitting on the grass. 'Don't think I meant anything by it, I know you're the best of fellows. But Molly is sensitive. I wouldn't like her to get a crush on a chap.'

I laughed at that. 'I should think not.'

'And Molly is so young, and impressionable. And you're a good-looking fellow. I just don't want—'

'I understand.'

He slipped an arm around my shoulder. 'I knew you would.' He hugged me for a second. 'Let's sort out the last of these burnt bits.'

I hope he doesn't see the hurt his words have caused. I wouldn't have him distressed for the world.


Letter to Professor Robert Conway, Balliol College, Oxford, 1st July 1913

Dear Professor,

We have excavated the west end of the barrow to a depth of three feet eight inches, sieving out several dozen small fragments of pottery and a number of sharp flint shapes. I enclose a sketch of a buried pot, complete and in situ at the western end of the centre of the barrow, adjacent to two fitted slabs of limestone that appear to overlay a void. These stones are raised on an edge of vertical slabs each varying from eighteen to twenty-one inches in height. The pot, when excavated, was found to contain a number of small, burned fragments of bone, a large femur, head much charred, and some teeth (sample enclosed). I would welcome your insights into the finds.

Yours gratefully,
*E. Masters*

# 13

*Thursday 21st March, this year*
*Chorleigh House, Fairfield, New Forest*

Sage spent the next morning working under the direction of the senior scene of crime officer. He was a quiet man who had given Sage the slabs of turf cut from the grave the day before to lay out on a long table under an awning on the lawn. Now Sage could catalogue and preserve finds to be examined in the lab. She looked briefly for obvious fibres, blood, anything anomalous, viewing through different light sources and using a binocular viewer that magnified all the bugs, making them look like they were reaching for her. One particularly large centipede raced over her hand, making her leap up and swear. She pressed her hand over her heart as it thudded, and the creature disappeared under another piece of turf.

She decided it was time for a break and stepped away. In her bag was a flask of coffee she had brought from home. She poured herself a drink and sipped, balanced the mug on the very edge of the table. She dialled her mother's number on the one bar of signal she had.

'*Sheshe*?' Sage could already picture her smiling down the phone.

'Sage. You all right?'

Sage could hear Max banging something in the background. 'How's Maxie? Is he being good?'

'He's being baby, always good. He's playing with wooden spoons, like you did when you were little.' She laughed at something Max was doing and Sage's heart leapt. She had been teaching part-time as well as studying courses at home, and had become used to more time around the baby. 'How's Nick?' her mother asked. 'You did talk to him? You went so early this morning.'

Nick. 'Oh, he's fine.' Even Sage could hear the evasiveness in her voice. 'I haven't had much time to speak to him, he wasn't answering when I got back and then I fell asleep with the baby.'

'But how did big interview go? He's coming back now, yes?' The signal was fading in and out.

*Big interview?* Sage didn't want to ask; he'd talked about a team ministry, whatever that was. 'He said a few days. We'll talk about it when I get back,' Sage said. 'I was just missing Maxie. They've got me sorting through about a hundred clods of earth full of spiders and bugs.'

'Call Nick.'

Standing back from the table she saw something she

must have missed earlier. A flash of white. 'I will, I promise. *Sheshe*, I'm sorry, I have to go.'

She rang off and walked over to where she'd seen the – something. Close up there was nothing so she tried lighting from the side. There, a tiny rectangle of something under a blade of grass. It was a translucent speck that caught the light, a few millimetres wide and a little longer. She retrieved it with forceps and put it in an evidence vial. 'Martin?'

The senior SOCO had been working on the grave, and emerged from the tent with an expression of relief. With the sun out the tent must have been getting hot. 'Found something?'

She mutely offered him the specimen. 'Just this, so far. I almost missed it.'

'Could it have come from your forensic suit?'

Sage looked down at her plasticised paper coverall. 'I suppose it could be. But I think it's more transparent. That's why I almost missed it.'

He held it up to the light. 'It looks like trimmed-off plastic waste from some sort of manufacturing process. Did you document its location?'

'Of course. TRM-133-148. Just at the base of a blade of grass in the section of turf 133 that was piled up.'

'It's contemporary with the burial.' He smiled. 'Good catch. I was talking to Trent yesterday about the barrows.'

She grinned back at him. 'They are fascinating. More my usual job, to be honest.'

'He said they had been dug up a few times?'

'The big barrow was excavated in the early nineteen hundreds. But Trent showed me LiDAR scans showing the features in more detail, with several other indentations and ridges associated with the site. I thought we might ask the landowner if we can explore in the soft ground at the end of the smaller feature, that boggy area, there might be something there. In the future, obviously.' She sipped the coffee. It was cooling rapidly in the slight breeze. 'It's well documented but hasn't been properly surveyed or excavated.' She waved at Trent, walking towards them from the road. 'Trent, we found something.'

Trent walked over, and had a look at the plastic sample. 'Good work. Can I borrow Sage, Martin? I've thought of something about the barrows.'

Sage put her tools down, stripped off her gloves and forensic suit and followed Trent down the path. 'How's the other case?'

'Can't get on it. The sleeping bag remains are at the mortuary so I had a look at the site here,' he said. 'Much of the area around the barrows would be hard to dig for a burial, it's full of roots and stone.'

'So?'

'In 1992 Lara Black disappeared here,' Trent said, looking around. 'Where would you bury her?'

'I suppose in the garden, in the flower beds or under the grass where the soil is easier to dig. The police must have searched back then; even if they didn't have much time, they would have noticed recent digging. And she could be somewhere in the forest.'

Trent shrugged. 'If I was trying to conceal a body, I would have avoided anywhere where dog walkers go. This isall private land. I just wish they had been able to look more carefully at the time, but Mr Chorleigh senior had very good lawyers and was a forest official.'

She thought about it. 'Forensics would be able to tell us much more now.'

'Thermal imaging, DNA, microfibers, so many things we didn't – or couldn't – identify back then. They didn't even run a metal detector over the grounds or get permission to bring in dogs.' He pointed at the barrows. 'How about in the barrows themselves? You could put someone in there and no one would know.'

Sage looked at the long mound stretching along the field boundary. 'The soil would be easier to dig. But they had gardeners working here; they would have noticed the grass and soil had been disturbed.' She thought back over what she knew. 'The Chorleighs fired one of them around that time. The police must have questioned them.'

'The thing is, no one can dig up an ancient monument without a dozen permissions. I doubt if even the gardeners worked up here. If someone dug into the barrow itself and replaced the turf, who would know?'

'So you think we should widen the search for Lara to the barrows?'

'And then the whole New Forest? No. But I could make a case for examining the grounds in more detail, and maybe you and I can have a good look at the barrow along the way. Bonus.'

Sage shaded her eyes to look into the bright spot behind the clouds, starting to break through. 'What about the stable floor? I thought you wanted to get on with that soon.'

Trent shook his head. 'It's going to have to wait. I need to get back to the lab. A cold case where there may not be a murder isn't a priority when we have a body in Southampton and one here. I just came to check up on you and look at the grounds.'

Sage nodded. 'I'll finish bagging the turf and we should have enough to add the evidence to our report about the actual grave.'

'You talked to the pathologist about the body. Any thoughts?'

'She said River was left lying on her side on a hard surface after her death, with her arm underneath her,' Sage said. 'She suggests a time of death on Saturday evening. She wasn't killed where she was found, there's no blood evidence around the site.'

'Odd. They kill her somewhere, then risk being seen driving out here, park somewhere on the verge, carry her into the grounds, dig a shallow grave and cover her with leaves from the woodland – from a stable you can't see from the road.'

'I know,' she said. 'It doesn't make much sense, unless they knew the property very well. Which does suggest Chorleigh. Maybe he thought the grave would be deep enough – out of sight, out of mind.'

'According to the DCI, everyone from around here thinks Alistair Chorleigh killed Lara and got away with it,' Trent said. 'But Lenham's looking into records of people who knew the property – the local farmer, builders and gardeners who knew about the stable, widening the inquiry.'

'So there are more suspects. Have they contacted Lara's old boyfriend? He used to work here.'

Trent half smiled. 'Of course. But right in the middle of the investigation is the man who was present at both events. Alistair Chorleigh.'

Sage finished bagging up the turf by dusk, brushing the larger bugs off as she went, and headed for her mother's home in Winchester just as it started to drizzle again. She managed to find a parking space one street over from the house, in the middle of the town. She walked through the rain, past a hotchpotch of houses from modern to medieval. It had been a bit of a bargain – a Victorian two-up two-down with a sizeable courtyard garden at the back, for less than the house Yana and her husband had sold. Sage was still getting used to her mother being single, while she struggled with her father's new relationship.

'*Sheshe?*' She dropped her rucksack in the hall and looked down to the kitchen at the back of the house. The lights were off. On the kitchen table – the same one Sage had done her homework on as a child – was a note in big letters.

'Salad in fridge. Love you xx'

Sage opened the large fridge, an enormous thing given that her mother was single, and found a plate with film over it. Cheese, salad, chopped fruit. Her mother was keen on healthy eating but something in the fridge caught her eye – a packet of ham, which to her knowledge her mother had never eaten. She had been vegetarian as long as Sage could remember.

Sage lifted the plate onto the table and sat down to eat. There were signs of Maxie's occupancy – two wellington boots covered with grass and mud on the back door mat, a picture of smeared handprints on the fridge, a harness and reins hung on the back door handle. Max was barely toddling but her mother already had him out in the park every day stumbling after ducks, crawling on the grass. He loved it.

Sage had barely finished the food when she heard the key in the lock. With Max half asleep in one arm and the folded buggy in the other Yana hissed at Sage, 'Take baby,' as she parked the buggy under the coats. Max looked up sleepily as he was transferred then leaned his head against Sage's collarbone. She was filled with warmth and love as she looked at his perfect lashes, fanned over his perfect cheek. God, does this feeling ever wear off?

'He's ready for bed,' her mother whispered, pulling off his shoes. 'I put his coat over his sleepsuit.'

'Where were you?' Sage was in no hurry, just the sensation of him sleeping in her arms was intoxicating after a day of the horror of what had happened to someone else's child.

'I went out to my women's group. Mad Cows, you remember?' She bustled about in the kitchen, putting the kettle on, clinking cups together. 'Tea?'

Sage rocked Max in her arms. 'God, yes.' Max was heavy, and, as she wormed his coat off from around him, ready for bed. She took him upstairs, tucked him into his cot under the window beside her own bed and snuggled him under a quilt. 'I love you,' she whispered, kissing him. He squirmed, turned over and sighed into sleep again.

Yana was waiting downstairs with a large cup of chamomile tea. 'Tough day?'

The steam was reminiscent of apples. 'It is tough. I don't know if I can do it, *Sheshe*. It's so sad, it's so horrible, even when she's not there, to try and stay objective by her grave.' She took a sip of the comforting liquid. 'I keep seeing her.'

Her mother sat on the large sofa, put her feet up, leaving Sage the armchair. 'Sit. Tell me.'

'I don't know if I can. It sounds so hard and cold. She was left in a run-down garden, just like a bit of rubbish.'

No, not like a bit of rubbish. Every element of her burial was deliberate – even tender. 'I don't really mean that. But she was killed, and the body – it's just meat, it rots.' She found she couldn't even mention the horses.

Yana nodded. Sage sipped her tea again, the fragrance of citrus and some spice coming off the brew as well. Sage looked around the room. Yana had painted the walls beige, a colour Sage would never have predicted as she knew her mother's passion for colour. Then Yana had covered most of it with an eclectic mix of posters, paintings, a vibrant kimono hung over the fireplace and shawls hung as curtains over the poles.

'What about you?' Sage asked. 'What did you and Maxie do?'

'I had a couple of consultations today so my friend Elaine took Max to a library session for babies.'

'You left him with a stranger?' Sage was shocked.

'Not stranger. Friend. Best friend.' Yana leaned forward, topped her cup up. 'She has two grandchildren of her own. He loves it there, they looked at books and he played with toys. Then they fed the birds in the park.'

Sage opened her mouth, shut it again, and took a breath. 'Oh. Good.' Questions were forming in her mind faster than she could put them away. 'I'm glad you're meeting new people.'

Yana glanced at her. 'Have you spoken to Nick yet?'

'Not yet. I thought I'd have a bath first, wash off the day.'

Yana nodded. 'Is cold, I'll light fire.' She knelt by the wood-burning stove, scrunching paper and piling up sticks. 'Don't leave it too late.'

Sage still couldn't pose the question about Nick's visit to Northumberland for a possible job. 'I'll be upstairs.'

She soaked in a layer of bubbles, bought for Max but they brought back so many memories of childhood she couldn't resist them. She tried to get the sadness of the excavation out of her mind. When she shut her eyes the girl's face was still there under the leaves, the cry of the woman echoing around the forest, the centipede reaching from the turf.

Another flash intruded of Nick lying on the grass, staring at the sky with the knife in his chest. She slid under the water to wet her hair. Nothing had happened to Max and Nick; nothing was going to happen to them.

Yana's shampoo was home-made and smelled of rosemary and lemon; it left her scalp tingling and fresh. She towelled herself down and slid, still damp, into her pyjamas. She couldn't call Nick from the bedroom with Max asleep so she tried from Yana's room sitting cross-legged on the bed.

It was only two days since she had seen Nick and already she was missing him. Her flat was so small, the baby was sharing her bedroom, there was no time, no privacy. But staying at the vicarage was worse. It was in the middle of the village, people knew when she was there, when she stayed, when Nick turned the lights out. The diocese had been starting to pressure Nick to set a date for the wedding, and every parishioner was a potential moral critic. It was like living in a goldfish bowl.

She dialled his mobile, waiting for him to answer. Just as she was about to hang up, the phone clicked.

'Hello? Sage.' He sounded cool.

'Hi. I was just wondering how you were.' It seemed so stilted. A week ago he was in his boxers, bouncing Maxie on her bed, laughing with her.

'I'm fine. Did Yana pass on my message?'

'Actually, she didn't.' Yana really did want Sage to talk to Nick. 'I've been getting on with the case. Where exactly are you?'

'Alnwick. I did tell you I'd be away for a few days. I came to see a rural ministry up here. I just wanted you to know I'm staying a bit longer.'

She couldn't place it. 'Yana said you were being interviewed?'

'There's an opening here. It's a beautiful place. Just south of Scotland, north of County Durham.'

*Wait, south of Scotland? Opening?* She spoke slowly. 'OK.' He didn't answer and she could feel something fluttering in her throat. 'Do you want to move to Northumberland?'

'No. I want to stay on the island and marry you and be Max's dad. But we both know that isn't happening.' Maybe it was the distance, or the tinny speaker in her phone but he sounded very remote.

'I don't know – I don't know what's happening. I mean, I want those things too.' Even as she said it, she could feel her throat close up. 'I want you. But I'm just working out a new career and how to fit it around Max.'

'I'm up here on a workshop looking at the placement,' he said, after a long pause. 'They have places for two rural vicars, empty posts. It's a great team.'

'But Maxie, Yana, my job…' Her voice failed. 'You didn't even consult me, you didn't say anything—'

His voice erupted. 'I have tried and tried to tell you, Sage! You use Max as a reason to justify everything you want. I have a life too, I have needs, a career, a home. I wanted to share those with you.'

She was stunned. Nick was so patient with her, with Maxie. 'I – I know I'm spoiled,' she said slowly. 'I know I've been concentrating on me. The baby, going back to work, the attack.' The moment Nick reeled onto his back, a ten-inch carving knife stuck in his chest. *Don't give up on me now.* Tears gathered in the corners of her eyes and started to spill down her cheeks. She sniffed. 'I'm sorry.'

She could hear his breathing at the end of the phone. 'Don't cry. Let me in, Sage. Let me help.'

'I love you.' It sounded contrived, but at that moment her chest was tight with love, and fear that she was losing him. 'Don't give up on me yet.'

He huffed, a sound she had become familiar with. She

could see the frustration in her mind's eye. 'You drive me mad, do you know that? I'm not giving up on you, I'm exploring possibilities.'

'I know. But I do love you and I'm trying to deal with it all – I know I'm not handling it very well.'

'It's called PTSD, Sage. And unless you get counselling it's going to ruin your life, and mine and Max's.'

She sat on the colourful quilt and let the tears fall in her lap. The urge to howl came more and more frequently now. 'I know. I know you're right.'

'So you thought looking into violent crimes would help?'

She wiped her face with her towel. 'I know you don't understand – but this way, I can help someone, maybe the parents of that murdered girl. We felt so helpless when we were the victims, remember? Families deserve to know the truth.'

There was a long pause at the end of the phone before he spoke. 'I've been on a tour of several villages, I've met all sorts of people and tomorrow I get my interview proper. Here I can help people, really make a difference. The landscape is stunning, and the communities are close-knit, just like the island. I'd love to work in a team ministry like this one.'

Sage put her arm across her stomach over an ache of longing for him. 'What happens if they offer you the job?'

There was a long silence at the end of the phone. 'There

are four candidates. They might not want me.'

'They will. You're a brilliant vicar.'

'We'll talk about it then, if it happens.' His words were calmer than his tone. 'You do use Max and your job to make all our decisions, and we can't go on like this. You try and keep a distance between us. I love him, we've bonded and I'm not threatened by his birth father. But I feel as if I have to make appointments to see him.'

'I never stop you seeing him.' Sage knew the moment she said the words they weren't true. It was easy to say she was tired or Max was asleep – how many times did she push him away to stop Maxie getting dependent on him? 'I know, you're right.' She caught her breath for a few moments, crushed by the thought of losing him. 'You're so good for him. And I love you, you know I do.' She wasn't sure how much of her garbled words he understood. 'I'm just scared.' *Scared of needing you, scared of needing anyone.*

'We'll talk when I get back. Are you still at Yana's?'

'Yes.' She swallowed her tears back. 'Yes. I'm still processing the crime scene.'

'I'll be driving back in a few days. I'll call Max at breakfast time, as usual.'

She took a deep breath. 'We can talk about it when you get back. But – Northumberland? That's like four hundred miles away.'

When he spoke, there was a little warmth in his voice, a lightness. 'Almost. It took me eight hours.'

'God. That's a bit harsh for a weekend together. Max throws up after five miles in the car.'

'We'll talk about it. I have to go.'

'Yes.' Yes, they would. If that's what it took to keep him. Maybe she should tell him that.

'Bye, Sage.' The phone clicked before she could say anything.

'I love you,' she said to no one.

# 14

\* *Buy more film from chemist, also twine and brown paper for finds. Plaster strip for blisters, pencils and drawing paper for Molly.*

Journal of Edwin Masters, 2nd July 1913 (pencil in margin)

The next day Peter and I boxed up the burial urn in three large pieces, all padded with newspaper, and a number of smaller pieces of the rim in a paper bag. The human remains, I'm afraid, found a safe home in a biscuit tin.

Using the calculations of the size of the blocks and the density of limestone, we were able to estimate the weight of the stone at a hundred and fifty pounds per cubic foot. The thick slabs are about four feet by two feet, so an estimate of about six hundred pounds each, an astonishing weight! It's certainly more than we can lift, even if there were convenient handholds. The boatyard manager, an engineer called Parkright, was called and examined the problem.

'The weight's no bother,' he said, 'but getting straps under it will require stone wedges, or wooden chocks. We have some in the yard.'

The idea was to raise the edges with levers and put wooden blocks under it, so we could pass lifting straps or ropes underneath. Having scratched his head and examined the stones minutely, Mr Parkright made a couple of quick sketches and prepared to retire to the boatyard to fetch equipment and half a dozen men.

'What can we do?' Peter asked.

'Clear as much of that soft soil away as you can so we have a firm base for a tripod,' he said. 'We can use a block and tackle to lift each stone separately. And you need to clear a space to put them, we won't be able to carry them far.'

While he was away, Peter and I moved the spoil heap he had indicated to a location at the end of the large barrow. It had been getting hotter and more humid for the last several days; the work made us uncomfortably sweaty. Since Molly was keeping her mother company in the house, we stripped down to short trousers and worked as fast as we could. The head gardener came and watched us for a minute.

'I could use some of that fine soil,' he said, before Peter had a chance to ask him to help. 'It's the far end of the tennis court, the young ladies have been complaining it runs downhill towards the river.'

I looked at the enormous pile still facing us. 'It's all been sieved,' I said. Once it had been excavated, it could never be replaced in the places it had been removed from exactly, but I was still uncertain and said so. The proper procedure was to replace it.

'I understand that, but it's only going a few hundred yards, and the tennis court does run down in the corner. Very well, McNally,' Peter said. 'Only, please take the soil from the pile we're trying to move. We need the ground level ready for Mr Parkright to set up his lifting rig.'

McNally was a whiz with a wheelbarrow; he worked fast and we soon cleared the ground to the hard-packed surface of the excavation, level with the base of the tomb. Then we created a space for the two slabs to lie separately, and finally walked down to the river for a swim and to wash off the mud.

By the time we got back to the house to change into something decent, I was given a letter that had come in the morning post, having crossed the note I had sent to Prof Conway.

Letter from Robert Conway to Edwin Masters,
1st July 1913

Dear Edwin,
    A little research has uncovered an interesting map of the area, circa 1772 (see my scrawled copy). As you see, the

whole area belonged to Blazeden Farm, the home of Mr
Adam Blazeden at the time, who also owned properties
up to and including a street in Fairfield Village. You
will notice the mounds are marked side by side, not end
to end as you found them, so I assume the mapmaker
had not seen them for himself. Beside the mounds runs a
waterway called 'Brock Water' which appears to meander
along a field boundary. I notice on your site plan there
is a ditch, perhaps this has been adapted. But the main
thing I can see is that Brock Water appears to arise at
the barrows, as if it is a natural spring. Perhaps your
second earthwork is arranged around the spring head. I
enclose a most rudimentary tracing of the original plan,
for which I apologise, but I believe the main features
are represented correctly except the earthworks. I look
forward to further information as it is exposed.

Yours affectionately,
R. *Conway*

The afternoon brought fresher weather, and equipment and
men from the boatyard. They quickly assembled a large tripod
from poles, and we helped them lever up the edges of one
of the stones on top, slipping large wedges under each side.
Peter was tasked with the job of sliding straps underneath,
which were fastened about it at each end. Finally, a block and

tackle took the weight and we started to take up the slack.

The first slab was truly heavy. It was also stuck with mud at points, and when it finally yielded we could see the black soil of the interior. Over millennia, worms and other creatures had brought soil into the tomb, along with rain washing into the narrow spaces between the stones. Only a few inches of void remained, dank and earthy in smell. We swung the whole slab, perhaps a quarter of a ton in total, and lowered it onto the prepared ground.

We rested before we tackled the second slab, smoking and drinking beer provided by the kitchen. One of the gardener's boys was helping, and he soon entertained us with stories of the barrows.

'Fairy mounds, they call 'em,' he said. 'Everyone knows it. My grandfer used to tell me stories of fairy horsemen leading ponies into the barrows to live underground.'

Peter swigged his beer straight from the bottle. 'I love these stories. My mother's family used to believe their ancestor was a changeling.' He grinned at me. 'There's a picture of Great-Uncle Harold over the stairs. He's the ugly one. I can see why they called him a changeling, he looks nothing like the rest of the family.'

I recollected the swarthy-looking gentleman beside a photograph of Mr and Mrs Chorleigh's wedding. 'He's certainly not Saxon fair,' I said, looking at Peter's golden hair and blue eyes. 'Perhaps an ancestral link to an older generation.'

Peter laughed at me. 'There is an easier explanation,' he said. 'My great-grandmother was very close to the Rothschild family, especially one of the younger sons. He bought her some jewellery, my mother inherited it. Several fine diamonds and a huge sapphire.'

I was reminded that it was Mrs Chorleigh who was considered to have the breeding and money in the family; Mr Chorleigh's family have only been prosperous for two generations.

The second slab was a little lighter, and came up relatively easily, exposing fine black soil, riddled with worm holes. Tool marks were still visible on the surface of the stone, all done with flint axes, I suspect. We took as many pictures as we could, then I borrowed Peter's bicycle to take the rolls of film into the chemist's in Fairfield. It was good to get away from the oppressive grave, an ugly dark rectangle now the slabs were removed. Both of us were certain it would yield buried remains but it was too late to start. I left Peter to cover up the grave site for tomorrow. He promised he wouldn't even trowel off the top layer without me there.

The chemist's assistant, a friendly gentleman around my own age, took the films and gave me the packets of prints we had previously ordered. I slipped the envelope inside my shirt.

'The whole village is talking about you digging up the dead,' he said chattily, as he handed me a few pennies change. 'People are saying you shouldn't disturb the past.'

'People always do,' I said. 'Thanks for the prints. I'll be back for the new ones.'

'Next Tuesday,' he said. 'Maybe Monday if I get time to do them.' He followed me out the door and watched me climb onto the bicycle. 'If you ever fancy a pint, the Royal Oak is good.'

I looked over my shoulder at him. 'Thank you. For the recommendation.'

'I'm in there most Wednesday and Friday evenings. I'd be happy to buy you a drink.'

His words were familiar, in a way I didn't like. 'Really. Good day,' I said, wobbling the bike into the road then setting off to Chorleigh House. His tone was impertinent; I wondered if I had led him to believe that I wanted a closer acquaintance. I searched my own behaviour but I couldn't see that I had encouraged him.

When I got back, I told Peter, laughing off the encounter.

'That's Matthew Goodrich,' he told me, his face twisting into a wry smile. He pulled an oilcloth and some sacks across the top of the tomb. 'We were friends, when we were younger. That's all.'

'Friends?' I packed up my tools as he opened the packet of pictures.

'Years ago, when we were at school. Come on, let's get washed up for dinner, Cook has a couple of capons in the oven.' He stopped, a look on his face caught between happiness and grief. 'Oh.'

I stood at his shoulder, and he showed me two pictures of a fair-haired girl, just a child really, grinning at the camera with much the same expression as Peter's. She looked both plumper and a merrier sort of person than Molly. 'Is that your sister, Claire?' He nodded, and I put my arm around his shoulders and hugged him. 'I'm sorry, old chap.'

'Mother will be pleased,' he said, his voice thickened by tears that also sat on his lashes. 'I know it will be sad, but also happy. The last picture she thought we had was from a school photograph. But I don't want to upset her…'

I squeezed his shoulder, and he turned to me for a moment, letting me hold him. 'It's all right, old chap,' I said, glad to be of some comfort. 'They are happy pictures, at least.' He hugged me, and I felt the wetness of his unshed tears on my neck.

He let go and looked at the two photographs. 'I'd better give these to mother before dinner. It's bound to make her feel a little wretched.'

'But grateful,' I reminded him.

# 15

*Friday 22nd March, this year*

Sage had had another broken night, the rain hammering against the window, which disturbed Max several times. Eventually, she snuggled him in with her and hoped he wouldn't fall out. She woke early to him kicking off the duvet and babbling like a bird.

As Sage drove to Chorleigh House she couldn't get the conversation with Nick out of her mind. She had turned her phone onto silent but was aware of it buzzing so she pulled over at the entrance to the national park to check her missed calls. It was Trent.

'Sage, I'm going to be delayed with pathology. We can't ID the skeleton in the sleeping bag.'

'Can I do anything to help? Anything to get away from the wild woods.'

'That bad?' He sounded amused.

'It's just so empty out here. I never thought of the

New Forest as being creepy before.'

'You'll be finished soon, and in a nice dry laboratory with about two million decaying leaves. Why don't you make an appearance at the station in Lyndhurst for Lenham's briefing? One of us ought to be there, anyway. It starts at nine.'

'OK, will do. What about the concrete scan?'

'I'll be there for that. Meet you about eleven?'

Sage agreed and rang off, rumbling over a cattle grid on the forest road towards the police station.

Lenham was in his office, gathering up papers ahead of the morning meeting.

'Hi. Trent's been held up on his other case.'

'So I heard. We'll have to manage with you, then.' He nodded to her and she looked around. 'What about the radar scan of the stable floor?'

'We're going to do that later this morning. Trent's got some staff and students from his department coming in to help,' she said. 'They will do all the related scans like magnetometry as well. If there was a body under there, they will pick up something, even if it's just new concrete or disturbed soil.'

'OK.' He looked up at her. 'He seems more interested in those old barrows than Lara Black.'

'I promise you, we're just looking for any sign of a burial. I'll be looking at special aerial scans that were done in this area recently. We're hoping to see any unusual shapes in the surface of the soil around the house and the field opposite.' She stopped – he clearly wasn't that interested. 'Any more news on River?'

'It's early days,' he said over his shoulder as he walked into the incident room. 'Listen up, everyone. Those of you who don't know her yet, this is Dr Westfield, our archaeologist.' She recognised a few of the officers and PC Stewart lifted a hand.

'Right, Martin, tell me about the shoe prints in the grass.'

The forensic specialist stepped forward. 'Common shoe, I'm afraid. They came from a work boot with steel toecaps, the sort of thing used in lots of light engineering firms. They were from a style introduced in 2015 and are still in shops, so nothing distinctive about them. There wasn't enough detail to narrow down wear patterns, but they were size ten. Chorleigh takes a twelve.'

Someone nudged Sage. It was Megan, holding an armful of papers. 'You OK?' she whispered.

'Fine. Quite glad not to be at the house,' Sage murmured back.

Lenham nodded at Martin. 'Thanks. How about you, Megan?'

'Time of death probably no later than midnight, no earlier than about eight o'clock, Saturday night,' Megan said, walking forward. 'I've narrowed it down, that's as close as I can get it, and it's always an estimate. I'm ninety per cent sure of the window, though. The other thing is the shoe pattern on River's face and body, which Sage and

I uncovered at the scene and at the PM.' She put several close-up images on the board marked 'pathology'. 'There are a few partial bits of the sole and toe, as you can see. The best composite is image D, which has also been enhanced on the computer – it looks like a size five from the size of the pattern on the tread. We swabbed the bruises for the forensic team; they came back with oil, metal dust, dried mud – basically, garage floor dirt.'

Stewart put his hand up. 'Any match on the shoe?'

Lenham waved at another officer; Sage recognised her from Chorleigh's garden as PC Patel. 'Priya?'

'It's a rare import, a fashion boot from China, mostly sold on the continent but we had a shipment come into Southampton last year. We're trying to track down who bought them, but a lot of them would be sold for cash at the market.' She held up an ankle boot. 'They came in black and purple; this one comes from customs and excise so we're showing it around colleges and in the press.'

'Good,' said Lenham. 'Check the family homes and ask friends. What about the boyfriend?' He looked at Sage. 'We have an ex-boyfriend, Ryan Wellans, and a current one, Jake Murdoch, in at the moment. If we don't get anything in the next few hours we'll have to let them go.'

Sage folded her arms. 'Do either of them have a car?'

Lenham answered. 'Both. What are you thinking?'

'The body was two hundred plus metres from the road and the leaves were another seven hundred metres into the woods,' Sage said. 'They carried her in, dug a shaped hole, created a border and covered her with leaves. That took time and energy. I imagine the person who did that couldn't do it all without a car and some sort of spade and trowel. They definitely used a curved digging tool, I don't think it was a tool of opportunity.'

PC Patel stepped forward. 'Ryan and his girlfriend Soraya have been dissing River online, saying she was more interested in her animal causes than people. I've talked to Soraya, her alibi was: "I was home, in my room, watching TV." She could have been anywhere; her parents were out with friends. Ryan's tyres don't match the ones found on the verge but he takes a size ten shoe.'

'What about Jake?' Lenham said. 'He is very close to the family.'

Patel consulted her notes. 'He attended a demonstration at the university against animal experimentation on Saturday evening, and expected River to be there. He claims to have been in bed in his student accommodation, with no witnesses that night. We haven't seen either car coming from Lyndhurst or Lymington but there are no cameras across the forest to pick them up. His tyres don't match the impression we took at the scene, although we don't know if that's related to the burial yet, and his shoes are size eleven. We're checking other family and friends.'

Lenham nodded and allocated tasks to people. Sage walked over to him. 'Anything for me?'

'Trent promised me you would look at the scans of the garden, see if you can see anything like a grave from 1992. I was hoping she would come forward alive and well but that's looking increasingly unlikely. You will also have to supervise the examination of the leaves.'

She nodded. 'Did you find out more about what happened to the horses?'

He brightened. 'Actually, we did. The vet said both horses were killed with what's called carotid sticking, just below the jaw. It takes training, some skill, and a blade at least five inches long. The forest agisters might have that training.'

'The knife in the stable was about that long.'

He pointed at a picture on another board, this one filled with – on closer inspection – pictures of injured or dead animals. 'Forensics found horse blood on the knife. I'm trying to decide whether we need to spend the money to match DNA to the animals. I can't prove it's directly related to Lara but—'

'There could be human blood on that blade as well.'

He slowly nodded. 'I'll send it for detailed examination. Go find me a burial site.'


Sage headed out to Chorleigh House. The place was quiet, just a few cars parked on the verge, including Trent's and Felix's. She walked through the grounds, calling out to Trent but not getting a reply. She felt uneasy, like she was trespassing, and wondered where Alistair Chorleigh was. To put off the moment when she had to examine the stable, she clambered up the side of the intact barrow and checked her phone for messages, the only place she knew she might get a signal. There weren't any but she had a great view of the surrounding field and forest. She turned slowly, forty-five degrees at a time, as she'd been taught.

The post and wire stock fence stretched for maybe three hundred metres. On the other side of the field was more forest. She could just see the roof of the church beyond the trees, a small spire projecting over the red-tiled roof. Turning again she could see the sloped end of the second earthwork on the ground. From this angle it looked taller and there was a dark edge to the slab on the top.

Continuing her rotation, she stared into the trees and at the corner of the stable. Hopefully Trent would be setting up to scan the floor. She turned again, and all she could see was the middle section of the trees, the trunks packed together, crowding each other out. There was no planting plan here, the trees had just seeded themselves where they could. They could easily all have grown since the stables were abandoned. Looking along the barrow, she could see how the middle was sunk in a little. Maybe Trent was onto something; there could have been something buried here a generation ago that had collapsed. She crouched down to look for changes in flora, any evidence of an interment.

Her phone beeped: it was a message from her mother.

*I'm taking Max to the adventure park with Elaine. Be back later.*
The signal was already gone when she tried to reply but by
waving the phone around in several directions it finally went.

She walked down the other side of the barrow and
started up the flank of the second, truncated earthwork.
The grass and ferns were crushed in places; she had
to walk around a few bramble patches that looked
impenetrable. Right at the top the scrub gave way to an
area of rough grass with mosses and lichens filling in the
middle. She could see stone underneath, a few high points
pushing through the green. Looking back she could see
that the whole top could be an enormous capstone some
three or more metres long and at least a metre and a half
wide. A light area caught her eye and she crouched down
on the grass, looking along the stone.

Someone – probably Trent – had scraped away some
of the grass and soil. It was a finished slab, fairly flat and
certainly not the natural surface of a riven stone. She could
see a couple of tool marks at the very edge. Even the type
was unusual: the vertical stones were limestone but this
was slate which must have been imported from somewhere
else; Hampshire didn't have any. It must have been far
too heavy just to top a burial chamber. It made it more
likely that it was some sort of early water tank, built over
a natural well.

Sage glanced over at movements against the distant
hedges on the other side of the field. Deer, a dozen of them,

all standing alert, heads up, scenting the air. She crouched down on the grass beside the stone to the edge. The slab was slippery and the drop into the mud seemed longer now, so she was careful.

The top seemed to be surrounded by the edges of a limestone framework, perhaps for the cavity of a well head or burial. Again she could see where Trent had scraped away. Slowly, she exposed the edges of flat stones, three buried in the soil and forming some sort of box. The LiDAR data had suggested the feature was originally about thirty metres long and ten wide. Both mounds might even have been one big barrow.

Burial cists were normally a few feet across, but she knew the one at Gaulstone in Ireland was more than two metres by one and a half, even bigger than this one. There was a carpet of grass; she could lift it up at the edge where Trent had loosened it. She caught a sound, a man's voice. It was coming from the stable so she dragged herself away from the Bronze Age to see if Trent had any results.

Two students and the geophys expert, Marina, were setting up the heavy equipment on the swept floor of the stable. Trent was watching them.

Felix was checking his phone. 'No signal,' he said, putting it away. 'I've been doing some research.'

'I got a bit of signal on top of the barrows,' Sage said.

'Did you find anything interesting?'

'I've found some strange legends about Hound Butt. Or rather "Wolf Butt", as it used to be known.'

She sniggered, immediately feeling really stupid. 'Sorry, childish. I'm a bit nervous about what we're going to find under the concrete.'

'Don't worry,' he said. 'I had PC Patel helping me in the library all day yesterday, she was just as amused at "Wolf Butt". Do you think Lara is under there?'

'We didn't see any irregularity when we cleared it out. They would have had to replace the whole floor to do it.'

Marina waved at her. 'Just starting. We'll try electrical resistivity as well.'

Sage and Felix moved a few paces down the path. 'I was wondering about the history of the area,' he said, 'and its relationship to local mythology. There were stories of a curse on the burial in the barrows.'

She sighed. 'That's what people always think about when they talk about archaeology, you know that. Mummies, treasure and curses.'

'The thatched building beyond the field is Blazeden Farm. That's the farm that owns the land around Chorleigh and once owned the estate. They must have sold it to the Chorleighs to build on in 1888.'

'OK.'

He pointed in the direction of the house. 'The locals claimed that a giant supernatural dog haunts the land,

and the farmer was glad to get rid of it.'

'Oh. One of those giant dogs, Hound of the Baskervilles and all that. What's that got to do with River?' She remembered the grave, the dead girl, and the intrusive memory made her feel sick. 'Or Lara.'

'It might have everything to do with why someone chose this garden to bury her in. Apparently the Chorleigh family has had nothing but bad luck since they have lived here. Peter Chorleigh was sent away and didn't come back until after his father died some years later. His sister died young, too. Then, in this generation, Alistair Chorleigh's mother left with his baby sister. He must have felt abandoned, especially if his father was difficult.'

'And we know his father was brutal, if he beat Alistair up and possibly killed the horses.' She stared into the woodland. 'But I still can't see that this has anything to do with River Sloane being killed, or Lara Black disappearing.'

'If I wanted to distract attention away from a murder, this is the can of worms I'd want to open. I think they are related, somehow.'

She let his words settle, make sense. 'Any more research on Lara?'

'Quite a lot. Unfortunately, not all digitised and online yet.' He scrolled through pictures on his phone. 'The thing is, most of the papers ran this image from 1992.' He showed her a picture of a wild child in hippy chic, holding a banner for an animal rights organisation, Liberation Wild. The banner had pictures of tortured rabbits. 'But the local paper ran this one.' An angry older man was yelling, shaking a fist over his head, and at his side, looking straight into the camera, was a young man. Just a boy, but still recognisable as Alistair Chorleigh. Behind him, in profile, was Lara Black. The headline read 'What happened to Lara?'

'So that was George Chorleigh?' Sage couldn't decide if the boy looked angry or scared. Overwhelmed, perhaps, at his father's anger at the young girl's banner. 'Are the press using these pictures of her now? I saw how much coverage the linked cases are getting on the news.'

'These images aren't available online, I had to get them from the *New Forest Weekly Journal*'s archive. It had a very limited run at the time. If it hadn't been written by a Hampshire author it would have sold even fewer copies. But the article was very pro-Lara and did suggest the hunting lobby were aggressive.' He glanced in the direction of the house. 'Where is Chorleigh?'

'I don't know,' said Sage. 'I haven't seen him.' Marina stopped the machine and waved to her.

'Looks like she has something.' Sage walked over to the stable to stand by Trent.

'Sorry, guys.' Marina shook her head. 'It's a completely normal slab of concrete. I'll try electrical resistivity and the metal detector again, but I can't see any voids, no bones, nothing obvious. I don't think it's worth digging up.'

Sage's feelings were mixed. It was a relief that the girl

wasn't under the stable but the question remained: where was she?

In the afternoon, Sage, Trent and Felix headed back to Trent's office at the university. He started opening maps, laying them out on the table.

'Make yourself at home, Felix,' Trent said. 'As you know there's nothing obvious under the concrete, nor under the ground immediately around the stable. The bits we could get to, anyway,' he said. 'But I brought you back to look at the grounds on the LiDAR.'

Felix looked at Sage. 'LiDAR is…?'

'Light Detection and Ranging. It's a mapping technique that helps us see the ground under foliage and forestry,' Sage said.

'I found some historical photographs of the barrows, too,' Trent said, sitting back. He pulled up an old black and white photograph of the barrows on his laptop, the grass overgrown even then. A newish-looking barbed wire fence surrounded both, she recognised the remnants. 'Does the top look sunk in or not?'

Sage stared at the photograph. 'It does, a bit. Is this from before Lara's disappearance?'

'It is,' Felix said, pulling out his tablet. 'That I do recognise – it's a picture from an article I read about some bones discovered in the excavation.'

'Really?' Sage said.

Felix started to read the article out loud. "'Local magistrate and verderer Mr James Chorleigh has announced that an excavation by a team of archaeologists and historians from Oxford University have found the remains of a Bronze Age chieftain with his faithful hound." That's a bit of a leap, isn't it? When was this? July 1913.'

'As far as we know the only "team of archaeologists" was Edwin Masters.' Trent pulled up another article, with the banner 'Mysterious Disappearances on Haunted Tomb!' 'Then he disappeared. Shortly after this dig, there was an outcry from the local church demanding a Christian burial for the bones in the barrow but the Chorleighs reinterred the remains themselves.' He sat back. 'It's a hell of a coincidence, isn't it? Two people disappear and one is buried, all on Chorleigh land. I just can't see the connection. But then I found *this*.' He pulled up an image on an interactive whiteboard that ran along one wall.

Sage looked at the brightly coloured lines and shapes of the LiDAR scan, looking for landmarks. Trent unfolded the ordnance survey map on the table.

'This is the Chorleigh estate.' He ran his finger over the map. 'There's Blazeden Farm, almost exactly south. Chorleigh House faces south-east; I suppose that's why they orientated it side-on to the road, to get the sun.'

Sage bent over the sheets. 'This is an old map. You can still see a clear area around the house now, then a defined area of forest encroaching here.' She ran her finger along the edge of the lawn. 'It's all overgrown now, there are trees advancing into the garden.'

Felix leaned forward. 'There's a shape there, by the house. Vegetable garden?'

'That's the old tennis court,' Sage replied. 'River was buried there, towards the far corner. That's where we picked up small Bronze Age potsherds. I saw an old picture of the manicured lawn and flower beds, then the tennis court. All shaved grass, it must have taken hours to mow.'

'They probably had staff, gardeners and stable lads.' Felix peered at the map.

Trent pointed at the LiDAR image. Even low features showed up in contrasting colours. 'You can see here, the tennis court is still exceptionally flat, whereas the rest of the garden runs gently down towards the south-east.' He turned the image to line up with the map. 'The land on the other side of the house runs down to this ridge, the river's floodplain is beyond.'

'It would have made a great view from the back of the house,' Felix said. 'Lots of evening sun.'

Trent pointed to the mess of lines and splodges over the earthworks. 'I was hoping to see some anomalies around the barrows, where the ground would have been easier to dig.'

Both Trent and Sage studied the images but nothing jumped out.

Sage then studied the whole area for comparison and

noticed something by the house. She pointed at a splodge of pink at the edge of what might have once been a flower border. 'What's that?'

It almost looked like a computer glitch; the edges were a little smudged and lines ran into each other. Trent zoomed in. 'It's small and very close to the house. Only about a metre by a metre and a half. That's why I didn't notice it immediately.'

'It's rectangular.' Sage's heart started to bump unevenly. 'Could it be a grave? Could that be where they buried Lara Black?'

'I think it would have been an unlikely place for a burial. It would have been a very obvious excavation at the time, just in the border beside the edge of the lawn,' Trent said, leaning forward to squint at the printout. 'Look, you can see the profile of the lawn itself, quite regular, gently sloping to the side boundary with a deep border of shrubs running into the woods. Someone edged that lawn for decades; it's made a little raised feature.' Returning to the screen he enlarged the image until it was almost too fuzzy to read. 'This would have been right in the flower bed adjacent to the grass. Someone would have noticed a recent grave in the nineties, surely? They were looking for a missing girl – even the postman would have seen it.'

Sage compared the rectangle with other features on the fields around and the garden. 'Look, the edge of the drive is much sharper. Someone could have buried her after the police stopped looking. And it is in the flower bed, with exposed earth – maybe it looked like they just created a flower bed. It's raised, unlike most burials.'

Felix shook his head. 'I was there in 1992. We would have noticed it.'

Sage nodded. 'It looks shallow, maybe it's older. Surely the Lara Black investigation must have included sniffer dogs? Trent once spent two days digging up a feature like that we found in a park. It turned out to be a pet Labrador.'

'No dogs; the investigation was curtailed in 1992,' said Trent. 'The search warrant was challenged by Chorleigh's solicitors.'

Felix stood up, sighing as he rubbed his back. 'So what do you do next?'

'We need to talk to the police,' Trent said. 'Lenham thought we would have a confession by now and there wouldn't be any urgency about the leaf evidence but now we need to organise that. Sage, swing by the mortuary and talk to Martin or Megan about how they want you to work. Then we need to excavate this site to rule out a burial.' He looked out of the window. 'But we can't do much tonight. Look out there.' The rain was running down the windows in sheets and the sky was almost dark. He looked at Sage. 'Let Lenham know about the anomaly you found on the LiDAR, and tell him we need to dig. Maybe we'll find Lara Black buried right under our noses.'

# 16

'As Williams-Freeman stated, archaeologists are in the scientia scientiarum, and all other sciences are its handmaidens. As I look over the wilderness I have never been more aware of my need to be a geologist, a historian, a mythologist, an osteologist and anatomist as well as a natural historian.'

Journal of Edwin Masters, 3rd July 1913

Today we found the first bone within the stone tomb, in the centre of the barrow. Peter was standing beside the upright slabs of stone, brushing away a layer of black dirt. He gave a little yelp when he realised what he was looking at. He called me over and showed me what must be a fragment of pelvis, including part of the curved hip socket.

We slowed our scraping to brushing and feeling our way gently with trowels. Peter stopped us at intervals to take pictures with a ruler for scale. Molly, who was pale but resolute in the presence of the ancient bones, found a comfortable perch on the unexcavated barrow and started making sketches. Our laughter and chatter stopped; we worked in silence.

'I think there is more than one individual here,' Peter finally said. His cheekbone was smeared with mud; a little drizzle had at least cooled us down but it made the earth sticky.

'I agree,' I said, looking at the bones. Something was very odd about them. There was a knee and a kneecap, a fibula and tibia. The remaining straight leg bones were twisted and fine. 'Are they animal bones?'

'They might be. Can you follow them down to the foot? That would be different, surely?'

I had spent many hours in comparative anatomy, identifying sheep and cattle bones from human. These did not resemble either.

Molly stopped drawing. 'It's sad,' she said. She shivered. She was wearing a light summer dress with her cardigan around her shoulders, huddled under a large umbrella. It had stopped raining, at least.

'Take my jacket,' I said, pointing at my bag with my trowel. She got up and put it on.

Peter called out. 'Here, Ed. Look at this.'

At the bottom of the grave was a jumble of bones. The

smaller ones were crumbling away at the edges, soft like wet, yellow chalk. The toe bones were all wrong, angled oddly, the leg bones slim. 'I think it's a dog,' I said. 'Look at the metatarsals.'

Peter waved to Molly. 'Come and draw this, Molls.'

'I don't want to.' I turned to see her standing behind us.

Peter scoffed a little. 'Don't be silly. It's just a few old bones.'

'I don't care,' she said. 'I think they're creepy.'

I nodded. 'I don't think you're being silly at all. It is a bit strange to think of the man and the dog, lying there all those years under the ground.'

She looked at me. 'It's just seeing them.' I held out my hand and she put her cold fingers into mine. 'You understand, don't you?'

'I do.'

Peter waved. 'You'd better do it, then, Ed. You're a better draughtsman than me. And I'll get a few photographs.'

I let go of Molly. 'Let me know if you change your mind. You're such a good artist compared to me.'

'I'll be all right,' she said. 'It just gave me a shock, seeing the bones like that.' After a few minutes, she came and joined me, and started drawing for me, correcting my rather shabby effort. 'I'm all right now,' she whispered. I remembered she was in fact only seventeen years old.

\* \* \*

Letter to R. Conway, Balliol College, Oxford, 3rd July 1913

Dear Professor,

Exciting news! At last we have revealed the central structure of the mound, a stone case for bones, human and animal. We are fascinated by the discovery, despite there being no other materials in the burial chamber itself, we have found the bones of a person buried with what we think is a dog. Using Pearson's method of estimating height from the femur we find that the individual, buried lying on his side with his knees a little drawn up, was at least six feet. Among the human leg bones are those of the animal, the foot bones being mixed up. Although the smaller bones are crumbling the larger bones are in good condition.

I have never heard of such a burial, and I wondered how much you know of animal interments with a human? It was entombed with some ceremony, it would seem, the bones lying above the man's (assuming such a large person was likely a male). The pelvis of the dog lies somewhat in front of the man's, its neck arched backwards. We have not yet uncovered the skulls although we can already see the tip of a lower jaw. We believe they were not covered with earth, as we have found two pockets of air within the soil, which I believe has been washed in from the overlying sediments.

Instead, they were enclosed in a rectangular stone tomb (see enclosed sketch, photographs to follow). I will write tomorrow when we have the skulls. My friend Chorleigh's sister is a remarkable artist and I will ask her to make a copy of her sketch for you.

It would be strange to find a dog in a barrow known as Hound Butt, perhaps for thousands of years. It fits with many legends of ghostly dogs in the area, a lot of superstitious nonsense but having a grain of truth at their heart, perhaps.


Best wishes,
*E. Masters*

# 17

*Later, Friday 22nd March, this year*

Before she headed to the pathology department, Sage had called Lenham to organise digging up the rectangle on the edge of the lawn. Then she drove through the rain to the mortuary. She checked her watch: five-thirty already. Maxie would be having his tea, or maybe a bath.

The mortuary was as threatening to Sage the second time, and she was relieved to be directed to the conference room rather than to the body. Megan was there with a folder with 'River Sloane' written on the front.

'Hi Sage,' the pathologist said, with a small smile. 'I just wanted to let you know we've set up the leaf and soil evidence in our forensic lab at the back of the building for tomorrow. They've all been refrigerated to stun the bugs and delay decomp. I just have a couple of suggestions about how you work; Trent asked me to brief you.' She sighed. 'I have to organise a viewing of the body first. River's stepfather is coming in, he wants to say goodbye.'

Sage's heart fluttered with adrenaline. 'OK. I'm happy to wait.'

'Her biological parents have already been in, separately. Everyone is heartbroken.' She looked up and Sage could see tears in her eyes. 'This one is getting to all of us. My daughter's thirteen; she's already taller than River was. You make connections, even though you have to remain professional.'

'But behind closed doors—' Sage tried to smile but it must have looked more like a grimace.

Megan took a deep breath. 'Anyway. The poor kid's been cleaned up as best we can. The funeral director will be able to cover up the staining on her face, but we don't do that. You can wait for me in the forensic suite if you like or you can see how we handle family.'

Sage hesitated momentarily and then decided to ignore the fluttering in her stomach. 'OK, that would be useful,' she said. Sage followed Megan into a small room by the main door. A stocky man was already waiting; Sage recognised him from the TV appeal. His face was pale; a teenage girl sat next to him holding an older boy's hand.

The man stood up. 'I've come to see River,' he said. 'I'm Owen Sloane, her dad.' He looked down for a moment; his hands were shaking. 'Stepdad. I've been her dad since she was seven years old but I suppose I'm her stepfather. I just wanted to see her. You know, to say goodbye. This is my daughter Melissa and River's boyfriend, Jake.'

'Of course, Mr Sloane,' Megan said. 'She's in our viewing room, waiting for you. She's been tidied up as best we can, but you understand she was left in the elements for a time.'

Sage stepped back against the wall, not knowing what to do. Sloane looked at Sage. 'Have you seen her? Her mum said – she warned me she's changed quite a bit.'

Sage looked at Megan. 'I have. Are you sure you want to…?'

'I have to. Do you have kids?'

Megan stepped forward. 'We both do, Mr Sloane. She's just in here.' She opened a door on the other side of the corridor marked 'Viewing Room'. 'Are you ready?' She looked at Sage as well as Sloane.

He looked over his shoulder at the girl. 'Melissa, do you want to…? Just to say goodbye.' His voice was strained.

'No, Dad. We're just here for you.' The girl glanced up at Sage, impassive. The boy was looking down, his shoulders shaking as Sloane left the room.

Taking a deep breath, Sage followed Mr Sloane and Megan. A tiny form lay under a huge sheet that almost touched the ground. River's outline was childlike. A female police officer stood at the foot of the table, her face tense.

Megan stepped around the table and asked Mr Sloane: 'Are you OK?'

He nodded and Sage caught her breath as Megan exposed the girl's face. She looked different now, less swollen. Much more like a teenage girl. Her face was unnaturally pale but not the grey colour it had been in the ground, in the fading dusk. Her eyes were properly shut, she looked clean and her hair was laid around her head, wavy, dry.

'Oh, God,' the man said, and put his hands over his face. 'Oh my God. It didn't seem real before.'

'Your wife said the same,' Megan said, staring down at the girl. 'I think that's a very natural reaction.'

'She was such a lively little girl. Funny, really classy. She used to do ballet, she was really good at it. She only gave it up last year because she started going out with friends.' He started to cry, wrenching sobs. Sage could feel her eyes prickling in sympathy as she listened. Megan just nodded.

He sniffed back tears and looked up. 'My kids are all taller, you know? Melissa is a year younger but half a head taller. She's usually the one you have to watch, always taking risks, staying out late. We haven't let her out of our sight since...' He looked back at River. 'Do you know what happened to her?'

Megan shook her head. 'I'm afraid you will have to wait for the inquest.'

'But you must be able to tell me a bit.'

'I'm sorry,' Megan said. 'I can tell you that she didn't die where she was buried.'

'The police told us that. Do they know where she died?' He held his hand over River's forehead but didn't touch her. 'They questioned me. Nine hours straight. They always suspect the parents, they said. They needed to rule us out of their inquiry.' He pulled his hand back. 'They've done that, now. They even searched both houses, her dad – her other dad's house too. They talked to all of us.' He wrapped his arms around himself and looked at Sage. 'Are you one of the doctors?'

'No, I'm a forensic archaeologist.'

He shook his head. 'What does one of them do?'

'There's a whole team involved. We all add our bits of information to understand what happened.'

'Did you see her – you know, in the ground?' Tears were running in two trails down his face. 'I'm sorry. I just can't bear to think what happened to her. What he did.'

Sage was struck by something in his voice and glanced up at Megan.

'He?' she said gently.

'Alistair Chorleigh. He killed a girl before, you know. Lara Black.'

Megan stepped forward. 'I'm sorry, Mr Sloane. We don't know anything for certain.'

Sage watched as the police officer escorted him away. He broke into tears again in the doorway where his daughter and the older boy were waiting. The young man reached out a hand, squeezed Owen's shoulder. The girl stared at Sage, her pink-dyed hair half across her face, which she brushed back with painted nails. She half nodded to Sage before she turned back to the boy and took his hand.

When the family had been accompanied from the mortuary, Sage followed Megan into her office. 'It's hard on the family. I thought I recognised the boy. River's current boyfriend, I forget his name, I saw his picture at the briefing.'

'Jake, I think. Mr Sloane was very upset; it's hard to comfort them.'

Sage sat in the spare chair. 'I thought he would ask if she suffered rather than blame Chorleigh.'

'He was breaking down. Reality hits, they can't pretend to themselves that it's all a mistake, someone else's child.'

Sage thought about it. 'He was very quick to blame Alistair Chorleigh. And to link the case to Lara Black.'

'No more than the press have been.' Megan pulled out a book and opened it, riffling through the photographs of the body. 'I do this job all the time, so I switch off a bit. The usual reassurance people are hoping for is "she didn't suffer" and we can't say that in this case. She was beaten to death and died hours later. It was a cruel death.'

'Do we know how the investigation is going?' Sage asked.

'Alistair Chorleigh, as far as I know, is still a suspect, and there's the historical disappearance to worry about. But otherwise they're all still hypothetical. She had an older boyfriend, an ex without a good alibi, both a biological father and stepfather, her mother and stepmother. I think we can rule out the younger half-brother Henry. Owen Sloane's biological daughter, Melissa, who we saw just

now, was ice skating all afternoon and had a sleepover with friends that night. Though since we don't know exactly when River was attacked, that's no longer a compelling alibi.' She closed one book of photos and opened another. 'Two of her friends, her stepmother and her stepsister all take size five shoes, but we can't find a match for the boot. The police are still looking. There's another briefing tomorrow morning, you can catch up.'

'OK.' Sage made another note. 'When?'

'An early one, I'm afraid. Seven-thirty, at the police station. Bring your charming anthropologist friend too.'

'Felix? I'll ask him this evening, we're meeting for dinner.' Sage looked up. 'You had suggestions for examining the leaves?'

'We have set up the evidence bags in the big lab, and I've found a forensic tech who is free to help. We only want to look at the evidence once, so use different light sources, record and preserve anything anomalous. Ask forensics for the choice of preservatives.'

'Great.' Sage mentally ran through the list of things she needed to do. 'What do we need for the case briefing?'

'Can you rough me out a preliminary report by tomorrow? Soil types, your archaeological finds, the edges and deposition of the leaves. I will add humidity, temperature, et cetera, and my estimate of time and cause of death. Then we can present when she was buried there, what the sequence of events was, what knowledge they must

have had and how it was done.' Megan raised her eyebrows. 'I also understand you've identified a possible second burial on the grounds – you'll need to look at that. Maybe you'll find Lara Black. That would leave Mr Chorleigh with a lot of explaining to do.'

Sage had arranged to meet Felix at his hotel in the New Forest, pulling into the car park at eight. She left her notes and the albums of pictures in the car, determined to snatch a couple of hours away from the investigation before writing up her report.

Felix met her in the hotel lobby.

He peered at her. 'Are you OK? You look tired.'

She winced. 'I'm not sleeping very well. The horses, the body – they all play havoc with my dreams. And I'm sharing a room with the baby; he's not sleeping as well as he does at home.' They walked into the hotel restaurant and approached the bar.

'I booked a table for two under Guichard?' Felix said.

The woman behind the bar took a couple of menus and escorted them to a table near the dark window. Sage made herself comfortable and watched as Felix manoeuvred into a chair, wincing.

'Are you all right?'

He sat down and looked across at her. 'I was in an accident last year. I broke some ribs, had a nasty bang on the head. I get creaky by the end of the day.'

'Oh. I'm sorry.' She handed him a menu. 'Are you OK now?'

He leaned forward to take it, resting his arm on the windowsill. 'The thing is, I'm physically better than I am mentally. I suspect you are too.'

Her stomach was growling. 'I know I've been a bit – preoccupied. God, I'm starving.'

'I've only had a sandwich all day myself.'

'I've been more worried about my relationship than me,' she said.

'Nick?'

'I think Nick has given up on us. I can't move into the vicarage, and my flat's too small and too far away from his work.' Emotion made her voice rough. 'I think he's giving up on *me*. He's gone to Northumberland, for a job interview.'

'He couldn't go much further and not be in Scotland.' He smiled a little lopsidedly.

'I know. I don't really want to bother you with it. We'll work something out.'

He looked at her for a second, as if he wanted to say more. 'I hope so. What do you want to eat?'

They both ordered steak, and sat back with a bottle of wine to wait for their food. 'I'd better be careful, I'm driving,' she said, sipping hers.

He poured himself a large glass. 'It's been a complicated day. We seem to be pulled in several different directions. I found out George Chorleigh, Alistair's father, was suing Lara for criminal damage.'

Sage sat back. 'Was he ever a suspect?'

He shook his head. 'Honestly, Lenham was young, less thorough back then. He really thought she had run away. I was the one who thought Alistair Chorleigh knew more than he was saying. The police are looking into Chorleigh senior now, as well.'

'Before I forget, did anyone talk to you about the briefing tomorrow, seven-thirty?'

He nodded. 'They did. I'll be there, even though it's ridiculously early.'

She looked at him, seeing grey streaks in his dark hair that hadn't been there a year before. 'So, tell me. What happened? This – accident.'

He half smiled. 'You wouldn't believe me.'

'OK.' She tried to read him but couldn't. Felix was a world expert on reading body language; he also knew how to conceal it. So, she waited.

Finally, he spoke. 'Do you believe in magic? Really, under all your rational thoughts?'

She knew most people did, on one childlike level. 'I suppose there was a time when I wondered if Bramble Cottage was haunted. Remember the poor woman who lived there? She seemed overshadowed by something supernatural. But it turned out to be physics, ultrasonic sounds tricking us.'

'I've spent my whole career disproving magic. Witch doctors in West Africa, *mambabarang* in the Philippines, *suangi* in New Guinea. Traditional magic workers, spell casters. Often the victims of superstition and abuse. But every now and then I meet someone who can do things that defy all explanation.' His voice was as serious as she'd ever heard it.

Sage looked up at him. 'Until they are explained, lots of things seem like magic. To a Victorian, antibiotics would be magic potions.'

'Yes.' He hesitated for a long moment. 'Jack – my partner – she went through something, a kind of psychological treatment. And whatever it was, it affected me too. I was knocked out.'

'Wow.' Sage was trying to find anything to say that didn't sound sceptical or mocking, but he went on.

'When I came round, she was dying. She only survived because the man we were with was a brilliant first aider. He saved her life. And now I can't get that moment out of my head, when she was just lying there, lifeless.'

That Sage could identify with. How many times did she see Nick falling back with a kitchen knife in his chest?

Felix carried on. 'I was diagnosed with post-traumatic stress disorder. I got help – it sounds like witchcraft itself. You look at some moving lights while you talk about what you saw. It sounds absurd, but—'

'EMDR,' she said. 'My doctor suggested it. It does

sound ridiculous. I don't even know what it means.'

'Eye movement desensitisation and reprocessing.' He sat back as the food arrived. 'Thank you.'

'Did it help?'

Felix looked down at his steak. 'It helped me. And that helped *us*, as a couple. I couldn't have coped with the flashbacks otherwise.' He looked up, smiled crookedly. 'It's made a huge difference. I think we're settling down now. Happy.'

'Maybe I will try it.'

The food was delicious, and hunger blotted out more questions. She thought about the flashbacks she was having. So many things set them off. A sharp knife or sunlight glinting off metal or a man's voice, shouting. When the flashbacks burned into her consciousness she couldn't react to Max or listen to Nick, she just wanted to be by herself. The unpalatable fact was that even Max – centre-of-her-world Max – was enjoying time with his grandmother who was really there for him, instead of hearing 'not now' or 'in a minute' a hundred times a day. She often dreamed of the attack just before she woke up; she could feel Elliott's fingers digging into her wrist, hear him scream as the well collapsed. Felix had saved her life that day, he'd saved them all. The thought killed her appetite for a moment. She pushed a few peas around the plate.

'Do you ever think about what happened at the cottage?' Her voice was smaller than she expected.

'On the island? I do, sometimes. I'm just sorry we

couldn't save everyone,' he said. 'I do wonder, could I have seen it coming, could we have done something to stop Elliott acting out? I don't know why he behaved so irrationally – perhaps it was the ultrasonics, or maybe it really was some evil spirit trapped in the house. We'll never know.'

'I'm starting to think forensics isn't for me,' Sage admitted. 'Looking at that girl's body – that's a long way from interpreting a few bones from hundreds of years ago.'

He half smiled without any humour. 'I can't forget Isabeau's skeleton.'

The girl in the ghostly remains of a dress, buried four hundred years before, still haunted Sage too. She smiled back. 'OK, even bones from the past are disturbing. But people's intentions are horrible. Someone hated that poor girl, River, enough to beat her to death.' She looked around in case anyone was close enough to hear them. 'And maybe Lara Black too if she's buried on the site, beside the lawn.'

'Does the anomaly on the LiDAR look like a grave to you?'

'Not really.' She pushed her cutlery away. 'To be honest, it's a bit raised, not what you'd expect from an old grave. No matter how hard someone compacts the soil, it's always looser after being shovelled in on top of a body. Which shrinks over time, lowering the profile. Sanctioned graves are normally mounded up to allow for shrinkage. I think you're right. If there had been a large mound of fresh soil by the lawn in 1992, the police would have seen it. I suppose he could have hidden the body away until after the police left, but where? And why have this right in plain view, next to the path? No, I think it's something else.'

'It does seem an odd shape, too. Squarish, not long and thin like a grave.' He smiled at the waitress as she took their plates away. 'Pudding?'

'That would be great,' Sage said, her appetite surging back. Her phone beeped with a message. 'Sorry, it's my mother. I'd better call her.'

It was fine, Max was OK, she just hadn't got the message that Sage would be late.

'That nice professor, yes?' Yana asked.

'Yes, Mum. That nice professor.' She smiled at Felix. 'No, I won't be too late, I have work to do. And I'll call Nick when I get in.'

Sage rang off, tucking her phone away from sight in her bag.

'A bit of pressure about Nick?' Felix asked, looking up from the dessert menu.

'I'm finding life hard enough without Nick to consider.' There, it was out, the uneasy feeling she'd been squashing down with a barrage of work and study. 'Maybe you're right. I should try this therapy. I can't feel much worse than I do now. I have dreams sometimes about Steph, falling into the well, only I can't save her and she's just floating, smiling up at me...'

'I can recommend the clinic in Bristol that I used, if you

like. A few sessions and you'll be able to think clearly.'

'I nearly lost Nick and the baby.' She dashed away a single tear tickling her cheek. 'I feel like people expect me to carry on as normal. I saw River's stepfather today. He'll never be the same again.' She looked down at her hands. 'Nick would make a brilliant father to Max. He does already when I give him the chance.'

Felix looked up as the waitress approached. 'I'll have the cheesecake, please,' he said. 'Sage?'

'Crème brûlée, please.' She waited until the woman was gone. 'Sorry. I don't want to burden you with my problems.'

'What you're feeling is completely natural. No one else is expecting you to carry on as normal. Just you.'

'I know.' He was right, she could feel a softening in her spine as she slumped back in her chair. It was only anger that was really keeping her upright. 'So, what do I do?'

'Spend more time with Nick and the baby, stop worrying about the future, enjoy the moment.' He shrugged. 'It's the only useful thing my father ever taught me, and he only learned it at the end of his life. Grieve properly, then move on. You can't live in the past and the future may never happen.'

Their food arrived and Sage was lost in the crunchy sugar and smooth custard for a moment. 'Being in the present, huh?' She smiled.

'Exactly. Concentrate on the facts of the case not on the tragedy. That's how I manage the World Health Organization stuff, anyway. Think about that girl. Think about the story of how she got there, not the awfulness of it.'

'And the story is that someone put River there to be discovered, and deliberately implicated Alistair Chorleigh.'

He leaned back and watched her until she had eaten the last scrap. 'Sage, just be careful around Alistair Chorleigh. Stay objective.'

'He's just pathetic,' she said, remembering his concern for his dog. 'You heard what the vet said, he's the local scapegoat.'

'So was the Lanarkshire Strangler. When he was interviewed by a psychiatrist, he was hugely upset at not being allowed to talk to his wife while he was being interviewed. He cried.'

Sage couldn't imagine it. He'd attacked a dozen women and killed three, if she remembered the news correctly. 'Crocodile tears?'

'Compartmentalisation. Just stay wary, stay focused. Chorleigh may be being framed for River's murder, but he may equally have killed her and buried her in a fit of drunken remorse. And he is still the last person we know to have seen Lara Black alive.'

After she left Felix, Sage drove back to Winchester. She couldn't park anywhere near her mother's house so late in the evening, so she had to walk through the quiet town, past the cathedral green, its towering frontage ghostly in the lights focused on its saints and windows. Yana's house was dark when she fumbled the key into the lock.

She crept in in case her mother was asleep, but heard the murmur of voices, and when she pushed the door open realised there were just a few candles burning in glass lanterns around the living room. Someone – a woman maybe in her fifties – was curled up on the sofa, her mother in the armchair opposite.

'Ah, Sage,' her mother exclaimed, then put her own finger to her lips. 'Oh, sorry, Maxie has just gone down again. He woke – bad dream I think, poor *bobek*.'

Sage came in the room. The wood burner was filled with glowing embers; it had made the room uncomfortably warm. She undid her jacket. 'I'm sorry I was a bit longer than I thought.'

'No trouble.' Yana stood and took Sage's jacket off her like she was five years old. 'Sit, sit. This my friend, Elaine.' She walked into the hall with the coat.

Sage took the offered hand. 'Hi. I've heard a lot about you.'

Elaine smiled. She was striking, dark hair streaked with grey.

'Likewise. And your son has won my heart. He's adorable.'

Sage sat in her mother's chair. 'He can be.'

An awkward silence grew longer. Yana returned, carrying a large mug of hot chocolate. 'Is cold out there,' she said, holding it out for Sage. Elaine sat up and made room for Yana. 'So, you meet.' Yana smiled at them both and squeezed Elaine's hand. 'Two of my favourite people.'

Sage concentrated on her hot chocolate while Elaine laughed for a moment. 'Yana, you have to give Sage a bit of time – me too – we've only just met. And there's bound to be a bit of awkwardness when your daughter meets your new partner.'

'Are you? My mother's new partner?' Sage looked over the rim of her mug at the woman. Elaine had dark eyes, they looked black in the low light. She was too tired to be having this conversation, and she needed to see her son. 'I'm sorry. I ought to check on Max and I have a report to write before an early meeting.'

Yana frowned – even in this light Sage could see she was displeased. 'There is no need to be rude.'

'She isn't being rude.' Elaine picked up a scarf from the end of the sofa. 'She's being direct, I like that. She's had a long day and you spring this on her. Yana and I are in a relationship. I don't know where it's going but we're seeing a lot of each other and having fun.'

'Thank you.' Now Sage felt awkward and her mother was glowering at her. 'You're right, it's been a very long day and I really do have a report to compile for tomorrow morning. I hope we get to know each other a bit while I'm over here.'

'That would be great. And your son really is adorable,' Elaine said, smiling at her, and stood up. She was tall, as tall as Sage. 'I have two delightful but horribly spoiled grandchildren. Max makes them look naughty. Of course, he's only young, there's time.'

Sage nodded. 'A couple more weeks with my mother and he'll be just as bad.'

Elaine laughed, and even Yana smiled, looking from Elaine to Sage and back again.

'Actually, I have paperwork to do before tomorrow's clinic,' Elaine said.

'What do you do?' asked Sage.

'I'm a doctor, a dermatologist. You can't imagine how many arguments about alternative therapies we get into.'

'Not alternative,' Yana broke in. 'First therapies. Herbalism predates your medicine by thousands of years.'

Elaine held up her hands to fend her argument off. 'I know, I know. And most therapeutic agents are based on molecules derived from plants. But it's too late to get into that now.' She wound the scarf around her neck. 'Nice to meet you, Sage.' She leaned forward and kissed Yana on the cheek. 'See you tomorrow?'

'Stay over. Stay.' Yana looked at Sage defiantly.

'I will. Tomorrow. Good night, all.'

Yana saw her out, and Sage finished the hot chocolate. Before Yana could say anything, Sage spoke. 'She seems nice. Really nice.'

Yana took the empty cup from her. 'I like her. It seems – it seems magical, not to have to hide, you know?'

'Actually, I do,' Sage said, smiling up at her mother,

remembering the sneaking about she had had to do during her affair with Max's father, who was married. 'It's nice to be out in the open.'

'Elaine has always been out,' Yana said, sitting opposite Sage. 'Even when she had her daughter. It's different for her.'

'Mum, I'm OK with it. I've just had a shitty day.'

Rain hit the window and Yana pulled the damper open on the stove to burn out the embers. 'It's been really wet, on and off. Trees are down on the main road. I hope she gets home OK.'

'It's not too bad out there. Have you heard from Nick?'

'He called for Max,' Yana said. 'Spoke to us for a few minutes. I know Maxie doesn't say words but he understands loads. They were both laughing.'

Sage struggled to get out of the armchair. 'I'm shattered, I'd better get on with these notes. I have a very early meeting.'

'You will speak to Nick, won't you?'

Sage faltered at the bottom of the stairs. 'Tomorrow, *Sheshe*. I promise I'll call him. But it's too late now.'

Too late. After scribbling two pages of notes she lay in bed but sleep wouldn't come. Instead she thought about Nick, looking for a job in Northumberland. Just south of Scotland; she'd looked it up on the internet. Wild, stark, beautiful. Another world from the island.

# 18

'My dearest Edwin,
The sunshine has done wonders for my health. Your
aunt and I are now walking to the church every day,
which as you remember, is quite half a mile each way.
I look forward to your letters and such a tale! I should
probably be quite squeamish about handling human
bones but I'm sure you have become accustomed...'

Letter held in the cover of the journal of Edwin Masters,
5th July 1913, signed 'Mother'

It was hazy sunshine before breakfast so I stole outside
with my camera to get some shots of the earthwork in
the good light. Two days of excavation have revealed much
of the skeletons. I got some good views of the human and
animal remains, intertwined in the grave with what looks like

ceremony. Several bones in the arms show deep scratches, and I puzzled over whether some animal attack had killed the man or he had held his arms up against a weapon.

My mother has written to tell me she is much better, which is such a relief. I have thought so often about these last months, about how our funds have been spent on my education while she manages on shillings in a house my father would not have kept a dog in. The doctor's bills are all paid and with a little economy we shall manage until I find a permanent position. I am promised three evenings a week in my house library while I study for my master's degree. Thank goodness my fees are already paid from the trust fund established by my father, and I have a bursary to live on from his old college. I know he always hoped I would take orders, but I have not been drawn to the church.

Peter came and found me on the terrace and took me into breakfast. He says his father will not be offended that I had come down so early, before the family, and that I must treat the place exactly as my own home.

What kindness his mother has shown me, unlike Mr Chorleigh who, I fear, thinks me a very feeble fellow. I was thrashed at tennis yesterday evening by Hilda Chorleigh. She is a jolly girl but a bit inclined to flirt in a way I find distasteful. The court runs downhill at one corner, and Mr McNally the gardener is building it up with the extra soil from the dig, so no more tennis for the rest of my stay.

We prepared to excavate more bones today. They rested

under an area of silt which needed careful removal. Peter and I had our plans drawn in a systematic manner, and laid out the schedule for the rest of the guests to help. I suspected their enthusiasm would soon pass, except for Molly. We assembled some buckets and trowels, a couple of mattocks and spades and some old sheets to put out any more finds. Peter put up a tent to sieve the spoil in the shade. I rolled up the sides and it made a very pleasant space with an old table in it. Cook provided jugs of lemonade and water for us, all covered in pretty lace hats.

Two hours later, the eye socket of a great hound stared at the sky over a row of the sharpest teeth I have ever seen. The burial itself was almost in the middle of the barrow, as we had predicted. Our volunteers were drawn in by the finds – none left us until late in the afternoon. Even Mr Chorleigh himself came and looked at the massive head, larger I am sure than any living hound today. Molly sat on the unexcavated part of the barrow, sketching under a huge straw hat. She claimed it was to prevent freckles, but I told her I liked them. Both she and Peter were covered; their fair skin was reddened by the sun, their hair growing sandier every day.

'Look, Ed,' Peter called me, crouching awkwardly on the edge of the hole, scraping carefully with his trowel. 'I think this is the man's collarbone. Here, under the edge of the animal jaw.'

We had wondered if the man and his hound had been

buried together since finding the kneecap of a human next to the back leg of the dog. We could see the ghostly edges and curves of the skeletons, the dog laid along the man's bones, almost the same height from back feet to snout. The man had been tall too, as tall as Peter anyway as I am no great height. I imagined him as fair, the distant ancestor of the Chorleighs, a giant like Peter's father.

As Peter and I lifted the dog skull, still packed with earth, a housemaid trotted up to give me a letter. She screamed when she saw it and dropped the missive. She was comically shocked by the remains, talking of the haunting of the barrow, an old story told to frighten children in the forest.

'That's the devil's own hound,' she told me, refusing to come closer. 'And a sinner beside him.'

'There's nothing supernatural, Evie,' said Peter, climbing up the side of the excavation. 'Just a warrior chieftain being buried with honour with his faithful hound.'

She dared to lean over to see the skull laid upon its canvas. 'No dog was ever that big, sir.'

I laughed at her, perhaps unkindly, given her lack of education. But she turned and looked at me as if I was the deluded one.

'They tell of a black dog, Black Shug is his name. He runs so fast he flies over the forest, even over the trees. He swallows people whole.'

'Well, this dog can't harm you,' I said, to reassure, but she trotted away faster than she had arrived. The letter was from the professor and I put it away to read before dinner.

Molly, who had been sitting above us, on the edge of the dig, looked troubled.

'What is it, Molls?' Peter asked, pulling himself up to sit beside her.

'I know there's no such thing as ghosts...'

'None at all.' He looked at me. 'Come on, Edwin, back me up.'

'I don't think there is a ghostly dog that eats people,' I promised.


Letter from Professor R. Conway, Balliol College, Oxford, 4th July 1913

My dear Edwin,

You have come across a remarkable find. I remember reading of a burial of a man and a dog once before in Germany, but none in England. You must write it up for your master's thesis, it will make an excellent demonstration of your scholarship.

I have further examined your excellent drawing (your friend's sister has a fine eye for scale and detail) and the intact burial will tell us a lot about the rituals of these people. I agree that the burial chamber was likely not filled in. The soil in the New Forest is known to be largely acid; I suspect few remains would have survived had they been buried below the water table without the protection of the stone cavity (also beautifully drawn by your young artist). I am returning your finds but retaining a piece of corroded metal. I believe it might be possible to use the chemistry department's fluoroscope to determine its original composition.

As to the coincidence of the name of the barrow relating to its contents, well, we have seen that before in place names. Such research into folk memory and lore can be useful if not slavishly followed. I should certainly look into local legends.

The teeth you sent me are indubitably human.

Yours affectionately,

*R. Conway*

# 19

*Saturday 23rd March, this year*

Sage and Felix were early for the briefing at the police station. They were offered coffee and pastries from a large box courtesy of DCI Lenham. They found chairs towards the back of the room, surrounded by over a dozen police officers and a couple of the forensic specialists Sage recognised from Chorleigh House. Megan Levy, the pathologist, was there too and Trent was standing at the back. Sage had a few minutes to review the necropsy report from the Home Office veterinary surgeon, who had examined the horse carcasses.

She read through quickly, pausing at the photographs of the small cuts she had found in the mummified skin. '...
Evidence of a deep cut to the left external carotid artery. The animals were found in a passive resting position; it is unlikely that they would stay down for the fatal injury unless already impaired. Normal field despatch would need

a blade at least 130 millimetres long to sever both carotids and the windpipe, and death would ensue within one minute. From this I can suggest that they were incapacitated in some way from sedatives or illness, or posed in this way after death.'

She skipped down to the end of the report to find cause of death. 'Both horses bled to death from a deep injury to the carotid, just under the right side of each animal's jaw. The incision was made with a blade with a width of approximately thirty to thirty-five millimetres. Muscle fibres drawn out of the wounds suggests the knife was imperfect, and the one found in the stables had the tip bent over by four millimetres.'

There was a highlighted line. 'A similar defect was seen in wounds in the bodies of horses and cattle in the Hampshire area from January 1990 to September 1992, where sadistic assaults on horses and cattle were associated with sexual abuse. The author of these attacks was never discovered. DNA was not archived. Comparisons are being made with a folding knife found at the scene.' Sage looked up as the briefing started.

The room had a hum which quietened when Lenham started talking.

'Thank you for giving up your weekend, not that we gave you much choice. I'm especially sorry for anyone who had tickets to see Southampton play, particularly me.' After a ripple of laughter, he introduced Sage and Felix to the room and went around announcing the forensic team as well as senior officers.

'Dr Levy has established our timeline. Time of death is estimated at eight p.m. Saturday to midnight Sunday morning with a plus or minus of two hours. She was attacked some time before that, possibly as early as lunchtime. River Sloane was reported missing by her biological mother, who she lived with, at three-forty on Saturday afternoon. She had last been seen at about twelve-forty. This was some hours before she died. Obviously,' he continued, 'we are looking at Alistair Chorleigh because River was found in his garden. But we have a large pool of potential suspects. We have identified one of River's classmates at school who bullied her online over two years and an ex-boyfriend, Ryan Wellans, eighteen. They broke up over her passion for cruelty-free research. His new girlfriend, Soraya Brown, alibied him but she also bullied River online. Ryan has a car, so had the means to move the body. River had a current boyfriend, Jake Murdoch, who is nineteen and also has a car. Both vehicles have been searched for trace evidence but we found nothing. Neither car matches the tyre tracks we recorded, but we can't link that decisively to the burial. We have a biological mother, a stepfather, a biological father and a stepmother who, thank God, we can rule out as she was away in Aberdeen. There's a fourteen-year-old stepsister, Melissa, but I think we can rule out the six-year-old half-brother. We must also keep in mind that unknown party or parties might be involved. Keep working.'

'Anyone standing out?' asked another officer.

'The boyfriend isn't that convincing. He's acting guilty about something, even if he's upset about River's death. But we've seen lots of murderers crying crocodile tears. We're applying to extend his interview. Meanwhile, we're widening the search to other family.'

'Grandparents, sir?' asked a young officer.

'Two deceased, one in Canada, one has dementia and is in care.' He pulled out a note. 'We also looked at River's step-grandfather, Owen Sloane's dad. He's sixty-nine-year-old Dave Macintosh, has a record for breaking and entering from thirty years ago. He's a reformed alcoholic. I'm not seriously looking at him at the moment. He works weekends, twelve-hour days as a security guard at a shopping centre in Reading, and was on shift all day Saturday.'

An officer put up her hand. 'Sloane's father is called Macintosh?'

'Exactly. Perhaps you could have a dig around and find out why they don't have the same surname. There are a number of friends and Patel is looking at social media. Any updates?'

'Yes, sir,' PC Patel stood. 'We've been looking at the memorial sites and various platforms she used. There's a lot of sympathy and support for her family, which is mum, stepdad, his daughter Melissa who lives with them, and her six-year-old half-brother, Henry.'

'It is a bit of an unusual setup.' Lenham looked around the room. 'Can family liaison provide some background?'

A tall man stood up. 'The girls didn't get on well. Melissa moved into River's family home three years ago so she could attend a better school. Also, her biological mother was having discipline issues and had just had twins with her second husband. Melissa, known as Lissa, spends some weekends with her mum but not this one—'

Patel interrupted. 'Melissa's received a lot of sympathy, from both her own friends and River's. I've noticed something that might be significant: River's boyfriend Jake Murdoch has been spending a lot of time with her, and she seems to be clinging to him.'

The liaison officer nodded. 'Mum says Melissa was naturally jealous of River's popularity and used to flirt with Jake when he came over.'

Lenham nodded. 'Probably not significant but keep an eye on the situation. Stewart, what about the tyre evidence?'

'Yes, sir. The track parallel to the verge was checked against the database. It's a common brand, KV69, used mostly on small vans but also some cars. It doesn't have much wear, so might be quite new. There's nothing distinctive about it and the tracks weren't detailed enough to be able to match it to a particular vehicle. We've excluded our vans and the press.'

'We'll see if we can match it to any of our other suspects' vehicles. Work vans too.' Lenham turned to Felix. 'We called Professor Guichard in to investigate attacks on horses and cattle in 1991. He was then consulted when Lara Black disappeared. We are now considering whether the cases of the two girls are linked. Can you summarise your inquiries so far, Professor?'

Felix stood up. 'You will see the report from the vet who examined the remains of two horses found in the stables. The distinctive wounds demonstrated a faulty blade, maybe one with a bent-over or damaged end. This matches findings on live and dead animals found in the early nineties, when seventeen horses and cattle suffered sexual abuse that escalated into piquerism and eventual killing. Although the horses at Chorleigh House were killed with a similar knife, they only suffered a single wound each.'

An officer waved a hand. 'By piquerism you mean…?'

'Stabbing or cutting for sexual arousal and release. Basically, penetration was more exciting with a knife for this man. I say man because these animal abusers, so far, are always male and usually young.' He looked down for a moment. 'My conclusion at the time was this was an adolescent male who was likely to escalate to a human victim.'

The silence in the room built up, and Sage could see people turn to Lenham. He cleared his throat. 'One of a number of possible lines of inquiry that we considered at the time was that Lara became that victim. We questioned her family and friends, employer – no one stood out.' He waved at the pictures on a large board set up with Lara's name at the top. 'The main question marks remained over her animal activist friends, some of whom were violent and had been locked up. A new geographical profile on the animal attacks has suggested a focus on an area with Fairfield at its centre as the most likely home of the offender. This also leads us back to Alistair Chorleigh, who was also the last person to see Lara.'

Sage tentatively put her hand up. When Lenham nodded at her, she cleared her throat. 'What about Lara's boyfriend?'

Lenham turned around and looked at the board. 'Go on?'

'We were told that she was with someone. His nickname was Badger. Sky and Oliver Parris gave us a photograph of him taken by Lara when Felix and I visited them. They said Badger worked for George Chorleigh but was fired.'

Felix chimed in. 'The local vet identified one of the Chorleighs' employees as someone called Jimmy. I wonder if they are one and the same. I can't find a name in my files, but if so he had a grudge against the Chorleighs and could have had a personal issue with Lara.'

Lenham nodded. 'Work on this with the team, see if you can match this photograph to anyone in her animal groups and friends, there must be pictures. It might be helpful to review the interviews from the time. Anything else?'

Felix opened a second folder. 'I've been looking for Lara's name in association with animal rights organisations all over the south. Although young, she was engaged in various activities including demonstrating against hunting in the New Forest. She certainly met Chorleigh's father on at least one documented occasion, when she was protesting against fox hunting. Also, we're revisiting Lara's belongings – her rucksack found at the bus stop and her camera in the woods behind St Aldhelm's Church, a mile away. The case had been immersed in water at some point, the camera and film canisters were filled with water, but there was no body of water nearby.'

'Right,' Lenham said. 'Patel, you're with the professor. Follow up the animal activist angle, see if you can find any more connections, and have a look at whatever's left of Lara's belongings. See if there's any overlap with River's affiliations. Dr Westfield, tell us about the new archaeological evidence.'

Sage presented her evidence, and she felt an increase in tension in the room when she mentioned the anomaly on the LiDAR scan. 'I don't know what it is,' she said. 'But it's distinct and *could* be some sort of burial.' There was a buzz as people looked up and started whispering. Trent gave her a thumbs up from the back of the room.

Lenham shushed his colleagues. 'Could it be Lara Black? From 1992?'

'Probably not but we do need to rule it out.'

Lenham nodded. 'I'll assign you some help. But make it your first priority, the leaves will have to wait.'

* * *

Sage still felt tired as she drove to Chorleigh House to start the dig. Trent had to get back to his other case, so the full responsibility of the new excavation would fall on her shoulders.

She pulled up alongside a couple of police cars. Lenham had got there ahead of her.

He met her as she walked over to the edge of the garden, in front of the house. 'Let's get on with the new grave.' He was bouncing on his toes with impatience. 'From the scans.'

She was surprised he wasn't interviewing suspects, and said so.

'I want to know if this is Lara Black. I want to know I didn't make a mistake twenty-seven years ago.'

Sage shook her head. 'I said it was probably not Lara Black. It might not be a burial at all.'

'Well, whatever it is, I can't see it on the ground. You'll have to direct me.'

Sage glanced up at the house. The door was wide open, and Alistair Chorleigh stared down at her. 'He's here.'

'Has been for a while, but has stayed away so far. We couldn't hold him, but if this is Lara…' Lenham waved at a couple of other officers. 'We're going to find this second grave.'

'It probably isn't even a grave—'

But Lenham wasn't listening. He marched off to talk to someone standing nearby in a forensic suit.

It was hard to see on the ground but Sage could see a

slight difference in the foliage of the browned brackens, the rank grass. The young birch almost exactly east of it was a lot bigger than on aerial photos, but was clearly the same tree. Comparing it to the LiDAR scan she estimated that the feature was about eleven metres from the trunk. She crouched down to see the slight rise and waved to a waiting officer. 'About there,' she said, pointing at the ground. 'You need to allow a couple of metres all around because I am guesstimating here.'

The officer helped Sage mark off an area six or seven metres across and taped it. Sage walked over to the police van to pick up a forensic suit and booties, past the fallen stone marker. Lenham was there, already suited up.

'Do you mind if we dig up that stone as well?' she asked. 'It might be related in some way.' Sage looked at him. 'Are you helping?'

'Dig up what you want. I'll help, I know enough not to get in the way, and I can carry buckets.' He looked down. 'I've been looking for Lara Black for twenty-seven years. I'd like to find her.' He waved at three officers getting ready. 'They will do the grunt work.'

The first, back-breaking task was cutting off the turf, itself a deep layer of bracken, gorse and shrub roots. The officers were handy with shovels and the area was soon cleared between them. It became clear that there was a slight difference in the layer underneath, a lighter rectangle within the rich soil.

Sage turned a small piece of the fill in and crumbled it in her fingers. 'This has been disturbed, but quite a while ago. These roots have grown deep into it.'

'How long? Can you estimate?'

'More than twenty years, certainly, and we know it was after the house was built and the garden established in the eighteen eighties,' Sage said. 'We need to excavate more carefully now.'

Having set up an area for the spoil, Sage started trowelling down neatly. The officers helped as far as they could, but left the actual digging to Sage. 'We could really do with Trent,' she grumbled. 'Have you got any idea how long he will be? I don't have any signal on my phone.'

'He is digging up the whole garden in Southampton,' said Lenham, lifting a bucket Sage passed him and handing it up to another officer. 'But I reckon we'll find something first.'


The work progressed, layer by layer. Lenham was soon called away to speak to his officers, but Sage worked systematically, passing the spoil up to be dumped on a tarpaulin to one side. Finally, she reached a lump of corroded iron, attached to a few threads of what looked like canvas. 'Get DCI Lenham,' she shouted up, and he arrived in a minute.

'What is it? Is it her?'

'It's cloth, old cotton or hemp,' she said, looking at it through her hand magnifier. 'Hemp, I think. Like an old military kitbag – there's some sort of insignia too. I saw something like this on a dig in Flanders as a student.' It was far too rusted to see what it represented but there was a discernible symmetrical pattern. She was able to get a good close-up with the camera. 'The weave of the fabric has left a pattern in the soil over it,' she said, snapping a few pictures.

Lenham crouched down. 'Could this bag contain the body of Lara Black?'

'I don't know yet.' She worked her trowel around the edge to give her a clear area to lean on beside the bag. 'These coarse fabrics lasted a hundred years in France, they are still finding them on First World War battlefields. I can't think it would get to this state in only twenty odd years. There's something inside.' The deepest part of her excavation, barely half a metre below the surface, was slowly filling with water. She swept the wet dirt away. A hole in the fabric revealed a familiar curve. 'Here,' she said, quietly. She looked up at Lenham, a smear of dirt across his forehead where he'd swept his grey hair aside. 'This is bone. We need to get this back to the lab.'

She outlined how to dig around and under the bag in order to keep it intact as they lifted it out. Lenham followed her, taking notes for her as her hands were covered with sticky soil. He was impatient with her reticence to open the bag. She lifted enough of the torn fabric to see what looked like a jumble of bones.

'Are they human?' His voice was quiet. She wondered

if he blamed himself for giving up on the investigation all those years ago.

'I'm not sure.' She eased the small area of disturbed linen up further with the end of a probe. 'Yes.' A pen torch lit a dozen jumbled bones inside. 'Metatarsal, vertebra, looks like a thoracic one, T11, T12 maybe and...' She tried to visualise the rest of the spine sticking out at an odd angle in the jumble of bones. 'These must be disarticulated bones – this isn't a body buried and left to be skeletonised. But I don't recognise this one.' She tried to get an image with her phone camera. 'I think that's an animal bone. We need to have a good look at them.' She showed Lenham the image on her phone. 'I can't tell if it's Lara Black. The human remains look quite big to me and we know Lara was short and slight, like River. The texture is crumbly, eroded over many decades if not centuries. I need to get the remains back to the lab. I don't want to lose any other evidence in the bag.'

Lenham looked down at the ground, blew out a frustrated huff. 'This has to be your main priority. Balance of probabilities? Could this be Lara?'

'I'm sorry,' she said, snapping a last picture. 'I think it's probably too big and the bones look older. Let's concentrate on getting the bag out in one piece, if possible. We need the pathologist and the forensic team to take a look and I need to let Trent know.' She outlined what the forensic team would need to do to preserve the fragile textile.

He walked up and down a few paces, nervous energy making his movements jerky. 'It would be a hell of a coincidence, wouldn't it, one dead girl, one missing and a skeleton under the lawn? Chorleigh has to be involved in it all somehow.' He stopped, looked at her. 'Is this anything to do with that mound of earth at the back of the land?'

'I don't know. If Alistair Chorleigh is one common thread to this, so are the barrows.' She hesitated. 'They could be the remains of the missing archaeologist from 1913. But I think the bones might be even older than the bag – they may be Bronze Age.'

'We have to work from the assumption that they might be Lara until proven otherwise.'

'Of course.' Sage stretched her trowel hand, flexing the stiff fingers. It had been too long since she had actually excavated anything.

'Trent still wants to have a look at the barrows,' Lenham said. 'It's possible someone buried Lara there. Would he dig?'

Sage shook her head. 'We want to do a geophysics examination, non-invasive. It's a scheduled monument. For an archaeologist, finding something of historical interest and being able to write about it in an academic journal – that's a career-building move. But you have to have all your paperwork and permissions in order first.'

Lenham looked back towards the house. 'Back in 1992 the locals told us about treasure hidden in the barrow. Handed down the family, along with a curse.'

Sage snorted a laugh. 'Curses and treasure stories come from the early excavations of Egyptian burials. No, I doubt if there was any treasure, or a curse. If some valuable artefacts were handed down the family, wouldn't Chorleigh still have them? Or there would be a record of a sale.'

'We didn't find anything in the house,' Lenham said. 'But it's in chaos, I doubt if he's thrown anything away for twenty years.'

Sage looked over at the muddy rectangle that contained the bones. 'We'll look at the LiDAR again, see if there are any more burial places, smaller ones.'

'Could you show us non-archaeologists the scans, interpret them for us?'

'I'll try.' She dropped her trowel next to the hole and picked up a handful of paper towels to clean her hands. 'Trent printed off scans of the forest that showed the full extent of the barrows beyond the grounds.' She brushed her forehead on a hanging branch; it immediately splashed her with water from the recent downpour. She swung her rucksack from her shoulder.

She pulled out Trent's scan of the site. 'Here's the main earthwork, this big colourful collection of lines. There's the other one – you can tell the stonework has been exposed for a long time. There are furrows and ridges around the cut edge where it goes into that pond area at that end. The main earthwork was originally much more imposing than it is now. The edges have been ploughed out in the field, and you can see the middle sags a bit, maybe where they excavated.'

Lenham peered at the map. 'Or maybe where they buried someone.'

'We just had a quick look to see if there was anything obvious.' Sage was reluctant to accuse Trent of any impropriety. 'But it's possible, remotely so, that there's a recent burial in the barrow itself.'

Lenham looked around the garden. 'It would be a good place to put her, if it's so difficult to get permission to dig it up.'

'I don't think we can just dig it up based on a hunch.' Somehow Edwin Masters, Lara Black and River Sloane were linked through the Chorleigh family and their connection to this ancient landscape.

She turned to Lenham. 'Can we have a look at the memorial stone?'

He nodded. 'They've already turned it over for you, although it's hard to read.'

Sage walked over to the stone which had left a deep scar in the ground. It was bigger than she'd expected, the size of a proper grave marker but thicker, like a milestone.

'It's limestone, expensive, well carved,' she said as she scraped. '"In Memoriam, Edwin George Masters, vanished from this spot, July 12th 1913. Much-loved friend. *Requiescat in pace.*"'

Sage couldn't ignore the coincidence: people were coming to this place and disappearing. She just couldn't see the connection yet.

# 20

'On this day in 1900, my father died of wounds and infections acquired in the Battle of Magersfontein, after a long illness and an arduous journey back to England. Requiescat in pace.'

Journal of Edwin Masters, 5th July 1913, later that day

We were so excited by our finds and by Professor Conway's excellent reply that Peter introduced the topic before dinner, while we had drinks in the library. As a rule I do not partake of strong drink, but I permitted myself a small celebration sherry and secretly toasted my father. Mr Chorleigh, though dismissive of me as usual, was much taken with the sketches of the bones.

At dinner he chastised Peter for not spending more time with Trixie, warning him not to let such a corker of a girl slip through his fingers. Peter bore it in good spirits but allowed his father to understand he did not think of their engagement as binding.

'Well, make it binding, you fool! Put a ring on her finger and secure her future as well as yours.'

Peter slid a glance at me. 'Sir, perhaps we should keep this conversation between the family. It must be embarrassing to Edwin.'

The older man harrumphed; he looked as if he would snap again, but his generation can be appealed to on their manners. He turned to Molly. 'And you, girl. Your cousin and aunt are going into town tomorrow with the motor. It's about time you got some new clothes.'

'Oh, Father!' Molly tried in vain to argue but was overruled.

'We won't make any momentous discoveries without you, I promise,' Peter said. I was secretly a little pleased. While I like Molly's company, it's good to focus on the dig, just the two of us.

'And you, Mr Masters.'

'Sir?'

'If your professor wishes to visit, we will be very happy to accommodate him for a few days. Get a proper historian to observe, what do you say?'

I was pleasantly surprised and quick to accept the offer. 'That is very generous, sir. I will write to him this evening.'

\* \* \*

Letter to Professor Robert Conway, Balliol College, Oxford
5th July

Dear Professor,

I enclose the latest drawing of the peculiar burial we
have exposed. I should very much like your thoughts on
the remains.

Which brings me to an invitation made by Mr
James Chorleigh of Chorleigh House, to visit the site
for yourself, and perhaps offer your expert opinion as
well as establish the likely history of the barrows. It is a
large house, and Mr and Mrs Chorleigh would be very
pleased to welcome you.

The huge skull of the animal has caused some
controversy in the household. Perhaps this man was
buried with his faithful hunting beast or guardian.
They must have made a striking pair, the warrior and
his hound. The local area abounds with tales of demonic
dogs; I wonder if the name of the barrow, Hound Butt,
owes something to the burial as well as the legends.

We have uncovered a number of other finds,
including pottery fragments, a couple of what I think
are stone axes and a piece of bronze wire twisted into
a knot, uncovered by the daughter of the house. It has
been a most rewarding dig and I should be very happy
to write it up.

I hope you will be able to get away for a few days.

The location is most picturesque and the Chorleighs are excellent hosts.

Yours affectionately,
*Edwin Masters*

The next day at the barrow, or grave site as I should call it, went well, but the intricate mixing of canine and human bones was difficult to sort out. The dog seemed larger than any I had seen before. We measured it as far as we could; the tail bones were lost under the man's feet. But we estimated that it was almost two yards from head to tail, quite as big as a mastiff.

I laboured over my notes and sketches while Peter scraped and Molly, returned from her shopping trip and pensive, drew. Occasionally, I caught her looking at me. Finally, she brought the drawing of the animal's head over to me.

I suppose her imagination had made the creature's skull seem almost alive, as if it were caught in mid snarl, the head thrown back, jaws wide. The empty sockets were shaded deeply, and seemed to stare back at me.

'Gosh, Molly, this is very good.'

'It's the best I can do without my paint box.'

'No, pencil is better, more scientific.' She looked upset as she turned to go away. 'Molly,' I said, catching her hand. 'I hate to see you troubled. They're just a few old bones.'

She looked down at our joined fingers and I let go. 'It's not that,' she said, and walked away.

# 21

By late that afternoon, the burial had been laid out on a metal table in the mortuary. The retrieval team had done an amazing job, bringing the intact canvas bag and capturing some of the soil underneath it.

The door pushed in and a suited-up Megan walked in. 'Hi, Sage, I'm down the hall working today, shout if you need anything. I need you to be absolutely sure and make certain there's no trace of Lara Black in there so treat it as possible evidence. Trent's just getting you both some coffee.'

Sage took a deep breath. The room stank of wet mud. 'I just don't want to miss anything significant.'

'Trent will help, and remember your training. It's not that different from digging up ancient burials. I'm lending you someone from my department to help.'

What had her tutor said? Treat every burial as a crime scene, even if it's historical. *Gender, age, height, race, trauma, disease, date and individual identity.*

'OK. I'm ready.'

When Megan left, a young woman with a number of piercings and bright pink ends to her ragged hair came in and introduced herself as Jasmine.

'Call me Jazz. I've helped Trent loads of times. I want to train as a SOCO.'

'Scene of crime officer might be just what I need,' Sage said. She zipped up her suit and snapped on a glove as Trent came through the door, carrying three paper cups. 'Great.'

'I always need more caffeine on the weekends,' he said. 'I got you a soya latte, Jazz.'

'Thanks.'

Jazz and Trent stood back as Sage inspected the tray of instruments she'd been given.

'Gloves, hood, mask. I don't want to add any trace fibres or DNA to the remains,' she said to herself. 'I'm not going to cut the knots or stitching, they can tell us a lot of information.' Sage felt a sense of calm fill her as she leaned forward to look at the small hole at the top of the bag. 'I'll make an incision in the best-preserved part of the bag. Close the door, will you, Jazz?' She tented the bag with forceps and ran the scalpel into the body of the fabric, allowing the tension in the fabric to help guide the incision. 'Here we go.' There was a shiver of excitement for Sage – this was proper forensic archaeology.

Jazz reached over her to press a switch overhead. 'If you

talk, we'll have a permanent record and I can use it to type up the report for you.' She spoke into the microphone a foot over their heads. 'Doctors Sage Westfield and Trent Reynolds, forensic archaeologists, and Jasmine Thomas, pathology assistant, attending case 34851-AH. Unknown burial at Chorleigh House, retrieved earlier today, 23rd March. So, you're making a single cut in the fabric? There's a camera, by the way. Do you want me to photograph and collect specimens?'

Sage breathed a sigh of relief. 'If you can, that would be brilliant. Just a shot inside the bag, I'll hold back the edges – oh. Wow.'

'What?' Jazz leaned in to get a closer shot, then jumped back. 'God, what is that?'

Sage smiled at the girl's reaction. 'That's an upside-down canine skull. A very large one. Look at that, Trent.' She pointed at a pair of fused vertebrae.

'Not another Labrador,' he said, leaning in.

'It looks like it's going to bite me.' Jazz snapped another few pictures for different angles. 'Is it just someone's dog, buried in the garden?'

Sage used a probe to point to the bones. 'I'm afraid not. *That's* human.'

Over the next few hours, Sage gently exposed the underside of a human pelvis, caught up with a canine femur and a scattering of tail bones, all packed within the canvas. The bones looked old, but were in good condition, and she knew certain soils could age skeletons quickly. They didn't make them bigger, though, and she could confirm these weren't an adolescent female's remains.

She called Lenham with the news and Trent left her to work, with strict instructions to update him if she found anything unexpected.

She and Jazz worked well together. 'Definitely not Lara, then,' Jazz said, laying out more paper sheets to receive individual bones. 'What about Edwin? Could it be him?'

Sage thought about it. 'I think this is an older man and that wear pattern on the teeth would be from a much more fibrous diet and a couple more decades. It doesn't look like someone in his early twenties. I think this is most likely the Bronze Age remains excavated in 1913.'

The pelvis had the remains of a piece of string caught through the bone, from a label perhaps. This reminded her of the old specimens she had studied as a student, bones catalogued in Indian ink on card tags, stored in cardboard boxes labelled with exotic locations like 'Knossos, December 1902' in florid script. She managed to free the pelvis in two halves, laying the pieces out for Jazz to wrap up and put in the largest evidence bag she could find. It was a tight fit. She tried to estimate the height but there wasn't much to go on until they had the long bones. The impression was of a male individual with a heavy skeleton, large by modern standards. The dog was equally large, she guessed about four feet from nose to the pelvis, and probably six feet to the end of the missing tail vertebrae. She arranged those bones on a separate table as she released them, and could see the smaller foot bones were missing as well as the spine. Even allowing for her inexperience with canid remains, the animal had enormous femurs and a correspondingly large head with an underslung lower jaw. She could easily match the remaining top teeth with the scratches on the human radius and ulna.

'Look at these scratches, there's no healing visible. Whoever he was, it's possible he had a violent death. It looks like he was bitten on the arm.' She held her own arm up to demonstrate. 'Classic defensive posture against an animal.'

Jazz straightened the human skull. 'You're sure it's a "he"?'

'Pretty sure by the pelvis alone.' She brought the front of the skull forward and ran a gloved finger over the brow ridges. 'The face looks male, too, although it's not definitive. I once had a skeleton we could only sex definitively by DNA. There are no fillings, and a high level of wear which could be prehistoric.'

'I thought you had a werewolf or a circus freak for a moment. You know, Jojo the dog-faced boy.'

'Two skeletons, two heads. I think we can rule out werewolves, but this could be a wolf skeleton. If this is the Bronze Age remains from the barrow excavation, wolves lived all over this area. It's unusual though; mixed burials were rare in Europe. It's possible they were originally buried separately and just reinterred together, but the bones are in the same condition, and look about the same date. I suppose they didn't know what to do with the remains once they had dug them up, so put them back in the garden.' Thinking back to the history of archaeology, it didn't make sense. 'At this time, they might have given them a Christian burial, put them in a museum or even reinterred them in the barrow. I don't think an archaeologist would put the bones under the lawn.'

'I'll ask DCI Lenham what he wants done with the remains, shall I?'

'That would be helpful. I just need to finish up here and we can start on the leaf evidence from River Sloane's grave site.'

Jazz made the call. 'He's happy to release the remains to the university, once we confirm it's more than a hundred years old.'

Sage pulled off her mask. It made her feel claustrophobic, and her face was sweaty. 'Sure.'

Jazz walked back to the table. 'I'm sorry it's not Lara, for her family. They've been waiting for news for so long. Every time a body turns up, they come in.'

Sage leaned against the wall. 'I'm not sure what's worse, holding onto that last bit of hope or knowing that she's dead.'

Jazz started wrapping more bones in bags. 'If she was a

bit older she might have started a new life somewhere, but at sixteen?'

'It does happen, though.' *How would I feel if it was Max?* 'Suppose someone took her and still has her?'

'That's how parents think. In real life, most people are dead in the first four hours, almost all in the first twenty-four.'

'Well, I *am* a parent.' Sage looked up at Jazz as she wrapped the dog skull in an evidence bag. 'I'm sorry we haven't found Lara. You better tell Megan.'

The pathologist formally concurred that the bones weren't Lara's. 'Dentistry might suggest an era, or isotope dating would tell us if the bones were formed pre nuclear testing in the nineteen fifties,' she said. 'The animal bones are odd. I'd say dog but they are enormous.'

'Canid, definitely,' Sage said. 'Remember, the whole area was covered with dense forest. There were wild animals like bears and wolves. The recently domesticated dogs were probably half wolf at that time, and not very tame. Heavy bones for big hunting animals.' Sage stopped. 'We're confident this isn't Edwin Masters.'

'If it's more than a hundred years ago we wouldn't treat it as a murder, anyway. But until we date it, we can't confirm, so we'll hang onto the remains for the moment.' Megan half smiled. 'Do your isotope dating, confirm it for us. But I agree, I think it's prehistoric. Keep the bones bagged up until we can rule them out of any inquiry.'

'Trent will be thrilled to get his hands on anything from the barrows,' Sage said. 'I'll call him.' When Megan left she turned back to the table, covered in bones arranged roughly into the shape of two bodies. 'Let's pack these away safely. We'll need to preserve the bag, too, it's part of the archaeological story.'

Jazz packed the dog skull into a plastic box with other canine bones. 'Which still leaves Lara. Alistair Chorleigh was seen with her in the bus shelter. She disappeared, leaving her belongings. Sometimes the simplest answer is just the truth. She's probably still on his land somewhere.'

'So murder is the most likely explanation for a girl's disappearance?'

Jazz shrugged. 'Experience suggests it.'

'Well, I have to go back there so I hope you're wrong.'

'Why do you have to go back?'

Sage looked at the skeleton sheet she had filled in as she went. 'We're missing vertebrae, some bones from the left hand and the right clavicle. I want to check they weren't thrown in around the bag.' She lifted the lump of corroded metal and held it to the light. 'I'm pretty sure this is an old military badge or button. It might suggest a date range.'

Jazz looked at the sheet. 'I'll put these into storage.'

'OK, good idea,' said Sage. 'What about the leaves? There are thousands of them.'

'They're in cold storage. It's too late to start now – we

can do them on Monday once I've cleared the lab.' Jazz reached up to turn the recorder off.

When Sage got back to Chorleigh House, Alistair Chorleigh was standing next to the hole she'd dug. He looked as dishevelled as ever and the appearance of his clothes suggested he had been wearing them for several days. The dog raced to Sage, jumping up and barking.

Sage bent to stroke Hamish and catch his collar. 'Mr Chorleigh. I'm glad you got your dog back all right,' she said. 'Here, Hamish. You look very smart.'

The little dog was clean; the kennels must have groomed all the knots out too as his coat was ragged but soft.

'You're that archaeologist. I heard you found another body.' He sounded upset; his eyes were watery and red like he'd spent the night awake. Or drunk.

'We did, but it looks like an old burial. We took it back to the lab and we've decided it was the remains of a man, probably over thirty, and a large dog.' She ducked under the tape around the area, and pulled back the weights they had used to hold the tarpaulin down. 'I can show you, if you like. The area showed up on a radar scan of the forest, just an odd blip on the map.'

He looked down at the hole. 'The police weren't exactly polite – they acted as if I knew all about it, they questioned me all over again.' He looked straight at Sage. 'But I didn't hurt Lara Black, and I've never buried anyone, let alone in front of my house.'

'Were you able to explain that to the police?' Sage crouched down to stroke the dog again, scratching his back.

Chorleigh grunted. 'I never tell them anything. They'll use it against you, I wasn't risking that. My solicitor told me to shut up, make them prove I did something. But I didn't do anything to that new girl, and there won't be any evidence that I did.'

She could see he was curious and something else. Sad, maybe. 'The bones we found buried here on the edge of the lawn were in some kind of bag, they may be very old.'

He peered over her head at where they had been digging. 'So who was that? Could that be the archaeologist who went missing in 1913? My grandfather Peter told me about him.'

'We don't know. It looks like even older remains, perhaps the ones that came out of the barrow. Come and see.' He moved towards the excavation and she pulled up the police tape for him to come closer. 'We think a person and an animal's bones were interred here in a bag of some sort.'

Chorleigh looked into the hole. 'I assumed they put the bones back where they found them. That was the family story.'

'What do you mean?'

'My great-grandfather let his son Peter dig up the barrow. This was before you had to get permission; it was on our land so they thought they could do what they liked. They found a skeleton but then things started to go wrong.'

Sage looked at him. 'What went wrong?'

'Well, Peter's friend, the actual archaeologist, disappeared. He left stuff here, his wallet and clothes, even his glasses.' He picked up the dog, who was trying to get into the hole. 'People have always blamed my family. Peter left, he didn't come home until his father died; he always blamed him for his friend disappearing. And when Lara went they blamed me.'

'I'm sorry.'

He stared at her, then his expression changed and he looked back in the hole. 'Grandpa Peter and Edwin found a man buried with his dog, if I remember right,' he said. 'My mother showed me sketches of the dig when I was a boy.'

'I'd love to see anything you have about the original excavation.' Sage gently put the canvas back over the hole; she couldn't see any loose bones. 'I'm an archaeologist, I'd be really interested to see any records you have from back then.'

Chorleigh seemed to be thinking as he gazed over her head. 'My father kept a few bits and pieces belonging to my grandfather. I think there were some notebooks and letters and so on. No one ever claimed them; we hung on to them and they ended up in the house somewhere. I remember seeing them years ago. There were a few bits of pottery, too, in a tin.'

Sage climbed back onto the path and did her coat up. 'It

would be helpful to see that. Perhaps he made a field sketch
of the burial as he found it? That's what we would do now.'

'I'll have a look.' He paused. 'Thank you for showing me
this. It's nice to be treated like a human being for a change.'

'Don't you get on with your neighbours?'

He looked down at Sage. 'My neighbours believed I killed
Lara Black when I was a teenager. No one speaks to me.'

'I don't understand,' Sage said. 'Why didn't you sell up
and start somewhere else?'

He half smiled at her. 'Leave Chorleigh? It's home, it
was always home, especially after the old man died.' The
smile faded. 'I wouldn't know how to live anywhere else.
And the landlord of The Forest Gate still serves me.'

He turned and walked into the house, the dog at his
heels. Sage couldn't help feeling sorry for him. She had
arranged to meet Felix at the pub to discuss his progress,
so secured the site. She would have to come back and fill it
in when she had time.


The Forest Gate served food and it was only a mile away.
Sage parked alongside Felix's car. He had chosen the
warmth and comfort of a fireside chair and waved her to
the spare one.

She put her hands out to the smoky stove. 'I can't get
warm today.'

'That's the problem with March – if it's sunny, it's cold,'

Felix observed. He shrugged his jacket around his shoulders.

'I'm just tired.' She checked her messages on her phone now she had a signal. There was nothing from Nick or Yana. 'The burial in the lawn turned out to be a canvas bag filled with old bones. Not Lara, probably not Edwin Masters either. So it's most likely the Bronze Age burial.' She grinned. 'Do you know how brilliant that is?'

'For an archaeologist, yes. For a crime investigator, no.'

'At least it's clarified the situation. People can concentrate on River's murder again.' She stretched her hands out to the log burner, which was just starting to flare up. 'My hands are frozen. I hardly ever feel the cold, normally.'

'I do,' he said. 'I spent of lot of my childhood in Africa. Really hot summers. My father was a diplomat.'

'Oh.' She studied him. There was something a little different about Felix; she had always liked his face. His skin was tanned, even in the winter, and his green eyes stood out against it. His dark hair, although ruthlessly brushed back, had a wild curl in it. 'What part of Africa?'

'Côte d'Ivoire,' he said, picking up the menu. 'My mother was born in Yamoussoukro. They were a prominent cocoa-bean farming family.' He looked up at her. 'My father was a French speaker but he couldn't be more English. The only vaguely imaginative thing he did was marry a mixed-race African woman, who was about twice as intelligent as he was.'

'Were they happy?'

'They never stopped loving each other, but no, they weren't happy. My father's life was his work. My mother's life was me, her art, her humanitarian work, her friends and the family back in Côte d'Ivoire. She missed Africa terribly. She moved back there for the last fifteen years of her life.'

Sage picked up the menu but thought about Nick. *They never stopped loving each other, but no, they weren't happy.* With an uncomfortable jolt, she realised that she was more like Felix's father than mother. It was she who was prioritising work over Max and Nick.

'Are you OK? You look pale,' he said.

'I just need to eat something warm,' she said. 'A bowl of their chilli would be good.'

Felix went up to the bar to order. She checked her phone again, but no messages. She started typing a message to Nick. *I love you. Hope you're having a good day, call you later xx.* She knew he would call back, and she wasn't sure she could talk to him yet.

Felix sat back down and his eyes stared into hers for a long moment. 'It's a stressful case. Missing girls, dead bodies.'

'Seeing River's body did make me think back to Nick being attacked,' she said. She could feel the usual jumble of feelings that gathered when she talked about Nick. 'It's like I'm still terrified he will die, and put me through that again. And angry, really angry that he made me feel that way, that he made me love him so much.' She blindly noticed someone had brought warm drinks and cupped her hands around hers. 'I didn't order coffee,' she said.

'I did,' he said, watching her. The coffee was milky, sweet and had a head of froth. 'I thought you could do with the sugar.'

'Thank you.' *I could try this EMDR treatment. Maybe Nick will give me more time.* She sipped her drink and thought back to the shambling, broken Chorleigh. She'd looked into his bloodshot eyes and just seen confusion and fear for his dog. She leaned towards Felix, keeping her voice down. 'Chorleigh just doesn't come across as a murderer.'

Felix leaned back in the chair. 'I've met dozens, probably hundreds of people who have murdered, maimed and kidnapped people – even killed children – who are as genial and friendly as everyone else.' He looked up as a woman with two plates came over and placed them in front of him and Sage. 'Thank you.' He waited until she had moved out of earshot. 'We were very suspicious of Chorleigh in 1992. He wouldn't say anything to exculpate himself, just mumbled "no comment" on the advice of an overbearing solicitor and an even more overbearing father. They made him look guilty.'

'How could anyone speak to hundreds of murderers?' Sage asked.

'It's the type of cases I investigate for the WHO,' Felix explained. 'In 2011, a farmer called Jean-Pierre Ndayizeye went missing in Burundi. Half the village turned out to talk to the World Health Organization task force – me

included – and told us how worried they were. He was nineteen, the sole breadwinner for his widowed mother and his younger siblings.'

'Where was he?'

'What was left of him was in an old fridge on the outskirts of Bujumbura, the capital.' He pushed his plate away. 'We already knew that. I had to listen to the villagers tell me, time after time, that they knew nothing about it. "We loved that boy", but always in the past tense. They already knew he was dead.'

'What happened?'

'Jean-Pierre was born albino. He was worth more than three or four years' harvests to the villagers. He was butchered for body parts, sold, and the rest left to rot.' He looked at his hands. 'The local people, although ostensibly mostly Christians, believe in witchcraft. If they don't believe in magic directly, they do believe in profit. He had been targeted before. When he was eight, he was grabbed by some men in a truck. They only took his right hand that time.'

'It sounds mediaeval. He must have been terrified.' Sh
flashed back to the moment Elliott came at her holding
knife towards her pregnant belly. She squeezed her han
together under the table and tried to control her breathi

'I wanted to help the investigation,' he went on. 'I loo
for deception markers, tells. I listened to the wee
neighbours, the distraught mother, joined the can

vigil they held at the church where they sang all night.'

'And some of them knew?'

He looked up. 'They all knew. Even his mother, who was rewarded with eight thousand US dollars and a new heifer.'

She was shocked. 'You knew they were lying?'

'We did, but when we saw her grief we did wonder if we'd got it all wrong.' He grimaced. 'We hadn't. Jean-Pierre had been dragged from her own kitchen.'

'But why?'

'Witchcraft practitioners in Malawi, Tanzania, Burundi and Mozambique use the body parts to do prosperity spells. But albinos are also raped by people who believe it will cure their HIV, and some cultures believe they have golden bones.'

It sounded far-fetched, but Felix's expression was bleak. 'That's terrible.'

'So when Alistair Chorleigh tells you he didn't do anything, hugging his dog with tears in his eyes, remember he is facing life imprisonment if he's convicted.'

'Don't believe anyone. Got it.' She didn't fancy the last few sips of her cooling coffee.

'On the other hand, he's not the only suspect.'

'There's the family, of course. I met the stepfather.'

Felix put his fork down. 'There's always the family. River lived with her mother and stepdad in Southampton, and his daughter, Melissa. It must have been tense with two unrelated teenagers. You could imagine an overstressed

parent losing it, especially as they also have a six-year-old.'

'They haven't ruled out Melissa's biological mother and her partner, either. Apparently they thought Owen Sloane and his wife unfairly favoured River over Melissa. And there's her boyfriend, Jake, I met him as well. He has a car, he could have moved the body. It does seem like a frenzied, emotional attack, doesn't it?'

Felix nodded. 'It does look very personal. Maybe she fell out with Jake and he lost his temper.'

'There was a previous boyfriend too, Ryan something. Both of them had size ten or eleven boots, they could have left the footprints at the house.'

Felix dragged a folder out from his shabby briefcase and consulted his notes. 'Ryan Wellans. I do know something about him. I've been researching local animal welfare groups.'

'That River was interested in?'

He swiped his phone screen. 'She was actively protesting about animal testing. This is security footage from a medical research laboratory in Cambridge recorded last year.' The short clip showed a young girl banging on the doors with a banner, shouting. Sage was shocked to see River alive, energetic, emotional.

'God.' She looked up at him. 'Can I play it again?'

He handed it to her and she watched it a second time, then a third, this time concentrating on the faces behind the girl. 'Owen Sloane is with her.'

'Is he? I didn't see that.'

Sage paused the clip and blew up the image. 'I need to see this on a bigger screen. But that image reminds me of Badger, Lara's boyfriend. See, without the beard, and a lot slimmer and younger. Have you got the photograph Lara took?'

Felix pulled a battered tablet from his bag, which he booted up as he explained. 'I think the key to this case is why they chose to bury the body in Alistair Chorleigh's garden. Someone who knew about Lara Black chose to set Chorleigh up, so it's more likely to be a local person, and someone who was old enough to remember the case.'

'Exactly.' Her mind skittered back to the terrible grief on Sloane's face at the morgue. Maybe it was guilt she was seeing.

'Right,' Felix said. 'There's the tape, that's him. That's Owen Sloane, protesting about animal experimentation.'

They looked at each other. 'If he's Badger, or Jimmy, he worked for the Chorleighs,' Sage said. 'He knew about the stable and the leaves getting caught down the side wall.'

'But why would he kill River? There's no evidence that he's been anything but a loving stepfather and even shared some of her interests.' He swiped the tablet again. 'This is what I wanted to show you.'

It was a newspaper cover, a picture on the front page. He could zoom into various parts of the picture. 'Here, look at this.'

A headline came up: 'Snow White and the Huntsmen'

with a close-up of Lara shouting at the person taking the picture. Another picture in the article was of half a dozen people on horseback on the drive of Chorleigh House.

Felix tapped and swiped the tablet. 'This was in a local journal, *The Magical Forest*. It was written by someone calling himself Herne and relating the strategies the hunt supporters would use to protect themselves. The author called on local witches and warlocks to defend the forest and its creatures. He declared himself the forest's satanist guardian.'

'There are crazies everywhere,' Sage said.

'Definitely. But there's more to it.' 'Animal lover takes on magistrate'. The article focused on the efforts of George Chorleigh to limit access to the forest for known agitators and criminals. The author was the same writer, Herne. 'He accuses Chorleigh senior of persecuting certain hunt saboteurs. He stops short of naming Lara but it's implied in the picture.'

She sat back. 'So you're going to follow up this Herne person. I wonder if the police can track him down?'

'I've done a bit of research already and DCI Lenham has arranged for me to visit.' He reached into his pocket for his wallet. 'I'll get this. I'm going to meet up with this Herne tomorrow morning. Would you like to come along?'

This was getting interesting. 'I'm going to ask the police to follow up any aliases Owen Sloane has had, then I'd love to come. Not too early, though? I'd like to spend some time with the baby. I'll pick you up from the hotel around eleven.'

# *22*

Letter from R. Conway to Edwin Masters, 6th July 1913

My dear Edwin,

Your letter came as a wonderful surprise. As you know, the long vac has already started. I was quite at a loss as to what to do next – the oppressive atmosphere of the empty colleges is weighing on me. I shall, with your approval, travel down to Dorset to visit a friend there, stopping for three nights at Chorleigh House upon the way. I shall arrive on the 10th July. I enclose a charming legend, courtesy of Annie Wilde's *A History of Haunted Hampshire* for your perusal. I believe it relates to your dig.

Hand-typed page inscribed: *copied for Prof Conway*
'The Black Hell-hound held in much awe in Devonshire

has its cousin in the Black Shug of the village of Twyford, near Winchester. It is believed that this creature only appears from its grave, in Hound Butt near the village of Fairfield in the New Forest. The great creature, reputed to be as large as a shire horse and able to jump a house in a single bound, is responsible for hunting deer and ponies that graze within the forest. They are found utterly spent, having been run and gashed about their necks and shoulders by the jaws of the great beast, which plays with them like a giant cat with mice. The barrow concerned is one of two to be found on the land of a farm adjoining the forest, which has exceptionally fine stonework revealed. The farmer, a Mr Bartholomew Chiverton of Blazeden Farm, when asked if he had ever dug about the tumuli, said 'he dursn't', for it would disturb the creature and bring his family bad luck. Some years ago a Rev. Wm. Walker was holidaying in the New Forest with his two sisters, when they were roused from their slumbers by the howling of the beast, which seemed to be running around the cottage they had rented for the summer. In the morning giant footprints could be seen in soft ground under the ladies' bedchamber window, and deep scratches up the limed walls. A local gamekeeper could not explain the marks, which extended up to the window frame itself, some eleven feet from the ground.'

Edwin Masters' journal entry, 8th July 1913

Trust my old mentor to find me a ghost story, and one much better than I might contrive myself. Molly will be interested, I am sure, even if her sleep is disturbed by tales of monsters. It is a curious coincidence, however, that within the barrow named after a giant hound we do find one, though not as big as a horse. It is the largest I have ever seen; it must have been a magnificent beast, quite a yard high at the shoulder.

I have some misgivings about giving the tale to Molly, however, as that sweet creature seems somewhat distant and I wonder if I have offended her. I am in the habit of treating her as if she were my own sister (had I had one) and I noticed that she has become shy around me. Peter teased me a little, for I had not seen it myself. My mother says I am like my father, a cool creature who lives in my thoughts. Mr Chorleigh seems unimpressed by my lack of family or prospects, barely addressing more than a few words to me, then, quite by accident, I seemed to win him over. Mr Chorleigh asked me who my people were, at dinner. I dread these questions, but I cautiously said my father was a chaplain in the 3rd Division at Stormberg, in the Boer campaign. He warmed to me considerably. He fought at Magersfontein under Lieutenant General Lord Methuen and expounded at length about the general inferiority of the Boers, the blacks, and any troops but his own. I didn't tell him that my father abhorred all violence and war, and went to relieve suffering wherever he felt called. When Mr Chorleigh found out he had died of an infected wound received at the battle he seemed quite avuncular. He was scathing of my mother allowing me to attend a grammar school but approved of my full scholarship to Oxford. When Peter called across the table that I had achieved first-class honours for my degree there was a round of applause from the family.

I was embarrassed, I fear my face was flaming, but Molly kept up her questions about the dig throughout dinner and I tried to answer as many as I could. She is quite as intelligent as her brother and I asked if she had given more thought to going to university. Mr Chorleigh laughed off the idea, saying she would soon be busy with her wedding. I asked her about this but she went quite as red as I had, and said her father was speaking in general, not about anyone in particular.

'Besides,' she said to me, under the cover of the general conversation, 'who would want someone like me when they could have Trixie or Hilda? Father says no one wants a clever wife.'

'I would only want a clever wife,' I answered, truthfully. 'And I know plenty of chaps who would feel the same.'

She picked at her food, a piece of fresh-caught sea bass I had seen delivered by bicycle that afternoon. 'Really?'

'Absolutely.' I qualified my answer. 'If I ever get married, that is. I can't imagine it.'

Again I was aware of Mr Chorleigh listening and attended to my food. Molly, too, seemed conscious and changed the subject to the dig.

'How long ago were the barrows actually made?' Mrs Chorleigh asked, glancing over the table.

'Something like 1800 BC until about 1200 BC,' I said. 'Or so we believe, if they are Bronze Age. We think they are the remains of two oval burial mounds. The pottery suggests the date.'

Peter's mother leaned forward, her eyes shining. They were very much like Peter's, who has beautiful flecks of brown in his blue eyes. 'How wonderful. Are they definitely both barrows, then? One is just a heap of stones half covered in grass. Molly has been telling me about your excavations.'

'Indeed, I think it was originally a barrow,' I affirmed. 'Someone has dug it out leaving just a few stones and the incline of half the oval. Perhaps it was flattened to grow crops or turn a plough around. But the professor will tell us more. You will like to meet him, I'm sure, Molly. He makes history so interesting.'

'I should love to help you tomorrow,' she said. 'But I have promised to read to my mother in the afternoon.'

Mr Chorleigh glanced over at his wife. 'Perhaps your mother could forego your companionship,' he said. 'While the good weather holds.' When she agreed I looked down at my plate.

Of course, Molly would be welcome to help again. But part of me would have preferred the companionship of Peter alone.

# 23

*Sunday 24th March, this year, the New Forest*

Sage had reported back her observation that Badger and Owen Sloane might be one and the same person. Lenham told her that Sloane's car didn't match the tyre track outside the house but one of his work vans had the same brand. She promised to email all the evidence to him and, meanwhile, she would help Felix interview Herne, the author of the articles that mentioned Lara.

As she drove through the dark forest, Felix leafed through his notebook. Sage had seen it before; it was decorated by a sketch of a dog on the front cover. 'Did you draw that?'

'Sadie did, my partner's teenager. She draws all the time, I think she's got quite a talent. Of course, we can't say anything or she'll never draw again.'

'So you're a stepfather too.'

'Sort of. Jack is her guardian. We live together whenever we can – it works.'

Sage looked out the window as trees closed overhead, making a loose tunnel of the road. 'Nick's all the dad Max has ever known. Marcus doesn't have much to do with him – he's trying to save his marriage.'

'But they have met?'

She took a tiny turning on the left after Felix pointed it out. It was barely a track, with a crooked sign saying 'Keep Out'.

'His wife arranged a couple of picnics and walks where we'd all sort of turn up at the same time, partners and kids in tow. Fliss is nicer about it than I thought she would be, now she knows I'm no threat.' She smiled at the memory. 'I think she likes Nick and she was charmed by Max. She seems to have forgiven me but I don't know if she's forgiven Marcus. The thing is, her children are Max's half-siblings.' They were lovely kids; Sage had seen a resemblance when he met them.

Felix smiled. 'That's a nice thought. I hope you can work it out for Max's sake. Here's the house,' he said, as she pulled the car up on the grass beside an old van. 'I got Lenham to find out more about this Herne, and PC Patel told him to expect us. His real name is Philip Jansen, and he has a long record for trespass, criminal damage and affray. The Parrises mentioned him.'

'The satanist?' Sage looked at the front windows, which were obscured with tattered net curtains and piles of books.

'Apparently,' Felix said. The front door had no knocker

so he hammered his fist on it several times. When Sage started to look down the side of the decrepit old bungalow, Felix caught her elbow, pointing out a dark tangle of twigs and leaves hanging on the wall. 'Don't touch it,' he warned. 'They're traditional charms. Those things can be dangerous.'

'What is it?'

He looked like he didn't want to say. 'It's an old trick to disable unwelcome visitors. At the very least, it's full of poisonous berries, thorns and possibly needles.'

'You know your sorcery,' a voice said from the other side of the cottage door. It opened a foot, and revealed a thin, older man, with a shock of grey hair loosely tied at the neck and a beard that was woven into dreadlocks. 'It's a hex bomb, a magical anti-personnel mine.'

'I've seen one before. I'm Felix Guichard, I believe you're expecting us, Mr Jansen?'

The man ignored the outstretched hand and turned to Sage. 'I don't want to talk to the police.'

'You opened the door,' Sage blurted.

'He knew about the hex bomb,' the man said, looking her up and down in a way that made her feel a bit uncomfortable. Not sexual, she decided, just very curious. 'Who are you?'

'I'm Sage Westfield, I'm an archaeologist. We're investigating the burial of a girl at Chorleigh House but we're not police.'

The old man opened the door fully. 'OK then. You can come in, but I'm a busy man. I don't have much time.'

They were shepherded into an old-fashioned but pleasant living room. Sage was waved to a sofa. The house smelled of wood smoke; there was a lazy fire smouldering in the grate. Posters on the wall were against fox hunting, mink farming, abattoirs. They showed pictures of abused and dying animals. Sage wondered how he could stare at them every day.

Jansen pointed at one bloody picture. 'All for your bacon in the morning,' he snapped. 'Don't look away, it's happening all around you.'

Felix remained standing, and brought out his tablet. 'I believe you wrote this article.'

The man took it and squinted at the page. 'I did.'

'And included this picture of Lara Black. You were very critical of the Chorleighs.'

'The father, George Chorleigh, yes. He was an evil bastard. Tried to restrict the right to roam over the forest.' Jansen handed the tablet back to Felix. 'He threatened me, he threatened Lara.'

Sage caught his eye. 'We wondered if you can tell us more about that time.'

The man looked at Sage from under bushy eyebrows. His eyes flicked up and down her person then looked to Felix. 'I have some pictures from that era, yes. I kept them because no one cared enough to find the girl.' He reached up to the top of a bookcase and brought a folder down. He thumbed through the photos and brought out a large black

and white print. 'This is the original. I "confiscated" the
film from a local news photographer.'

The picture showed a much broader scene. Lara and
two men waved banners at the camera; one was a young
version of Philip Jansen. Sage looked back at him. 'Was
that legal?'

He shrugged. 'I threw the camera back.'

The younger of the two men was shorter, turning away
in a blur. He looked familiar and Sage wondered if it was
Lara's boyfriend – Badger.

She pointed to him. 'Do you know this person?'

Jansen glanced at it. 'Jimmy Mack, Lara's boyfriend at
the time – she called him Badger. He was camera shy, not
like Lara.'

'Mac?' Sage glanced at Felix. 'Owen Sloane's father is
called Macintosh.' She could see a slight similarity but
the boy was thin, obviously very young, and clean-shaven,
unlike River's stepfather.

'Follow it up.' Felix was leafing through the stack. 'Was
Lara involved in other activism? Releasing laboratory
animals, for example.'

Jansen shrugged. 'That was her business.'

Felix looked at him, one eyebrow raised. 'If it led to her
being killed it's the police's business. She was also a pagan.'

'That didn't get her killed. She was part of the
Wildwoods, I know that. Making pot pourri and singing
to the moon, mostly,' he said, sniggering. 'You'd have to ask

them, they don't exactly invite me to their moots.'

Felix nodded. 'So you're solitary?'

'Just me. And Satan, obviously.' He looked at Sage. 'Just a bit of old-fashioned cursing and magick with a k.'

'Do you believe in all that?' Sage said. 'Like the thing outside, it's just folklore, isn't it?'

'A sceptic.' Jansen stared at her, then at Felix. 'You believe though, don't you?'

'In Satan? No.' Felix turned to Jansen. 'I've seen things that I can't explain, though. I'm much more interested in your animal welfare activities.'

'Magic is all about intent,' Jansen said. Sage must have looked confused, because he elaborated. 'That's how I protested against fox hunting in the forest. Banners, sabotage, the odd spell. I don't like trespassers, right? So I set up the hex bombs around the sides of the house, where people could get in. All my intention to keep them out is locked into them. If they touch them, boom! They get all the hate and rage and warding I can muster. My place is a haven for wildlife.'

Sage could feel herself frowning. 'But how will trespassers know how you feel from the bomb thing?'

'It's woven into the brambles I make them from, slathered with greases I rub on, imagining how they'll feel when they touch it.'

'Has it ever worked?' She didn't know whether to laugh or pretend to be serious.

'Not yet.' He grinned at her. He'd lost a few teeth and

it made him look like a naughty six-year-old. 'No one has risked it so far.'

'So how do you know it will work?' Sage looked at Felix for support but he was studying the picture again.

'I know. I can feel the energy coming off it.'

Felix held out the print. 'This is George Chorleigh, the magistrate?'

'Master of hounds, that's him. He and his friends hunted all over the forest, killed cats, foxes, a swan one time. I saw them take down a half-grown deer once and the master just let them. They hadn't got a fox that day and the dogs were desperate for a kill.' He looked at Sage. 'They keep the hounds like that, aggressive.'

Felix pointed at the image. 'How well did you know his son, Alistair?'

The three of them looked over the photograph, Sage in the middle. His clothes looked filthy, the man smelled like smoke and the outdoors. He reached a stained finger straight to the young Alistair. 'He was odd, quiet. A bit strange, I thought, very intense.'

Sage pulled back. 'Did he show any interest in Lara?'

'We were all interested in the girl. You have to remember, I wasn't that old then, thirty odd. Alistair Chorleigh was about seventeen. She was passionate about animals, and she was sexy. Flirty.' He turned around. 'Here, I wrote an article about the hunt saboteurs in the forest.' He pulled out a stack of home-made magazines and looked through

the front covers. The leaflets had coloured paper covers
with lurid images of goat gods and green men on them.
'We used to sell fifty or sixty every quarter, mostly by post.
But one sold well, about three hundred copies. Hold these.'

Felix took the pile of discarded magazines. 'What was
special about it?'

But Jansen was already moving to a cupboard behind
Sage. 'That article on your computer thing, that was
written for a local magazine. It's all online now. I still write
a few bits a year for them.' He pulled a battered magazine
out of another heap. 'But this was old school, actual paper.
Here you go. That edition sold more than all the others.'

He held it out to Felix.

Sage looked at it with him. There were hand-drawn
illustrations and strongly worded articles about the forest
ponies, wildlife and conservation. It had an article about
the hunt and the picture. 'That's the one. Who's seen this?'
She looked at the date on the bottom of the page. '2012?'

'There was a twenty-year anniversary investigation of
Lara's disappearance. I wrote this for *The Magical Forest*
that year.' Jansen tapped the front cover. 'We sold a hundred
copies, then went back to the printer a couple of times. It
sold through the tourist office.'

The first article was called 'Justice for Animal Lover
Lara'.

'We definitely got justice,' Jansen said, grinning
unpleasantly.

'Which was?' Sage watched Felix leafing through the magazine to an article in the middle.

'George Chorleigh died of cancer. He got it bad, he rotted from the inside out. I doubt if anyone grieved, especially his son.'

Felix showed Sage the page. Crudely reproduced in black ink was another picture from that day in the New Forest. This time the elusive Jimmy was caught in profile and Alistair was snapped staring at him with absolute hate on his face. Lara was captured just turning her head to look at him; she must have caught his expression out of the corner of her eye because her face had an odd look, her long hair whipping around her head as if alarmed. Maybe Alistair or his father had just said something. Then Sage saw what Felix was trying to show her: Chorleigh senior's raised arm, the riding crop lifted right over Lara's head.

Sage turned to Jansen. 'This picture. Do you know if there are any copies in the library that we could show to the police?'

The old man scowled. 'There used to be. I nicked it back.'

Sage looked at him. 'Why?'

'It's for people like me, not for bored housewives and silly teenagers.' He looked away. 'And the Chorleighs threatened to sue me.'

'For this?'

Jansen shook his head. 'You don't understand what it was like back then. The fucking landowners versus the real foresters. They could get away with anything. Take the horse rapes.'

Felix interrupted him. 'Do you know anything about those?'

'We knew beasts were tied up and abused, and the forest officials did nothing about it. Some of the animals were so terrified they had to be put down even if they weren't badly hurt. Kiddies' ponies, a few heifers. Vulnerable creatures like the fox cubs they use for their own amusement.' He looked away. 'George Chorleigh was an agister; he could go anywhere, do anything, he was the law in the forest.' He handed Sage a copy. 'You can have that one for the police.'

Sage took it. 'Thanks. What do you think happened to Lara?'

'I know old George could have killed her in a fit of rage. She was a thorn in his side,' Jansen said. 'Not just making him look like an idiot with the hunt but asking questions all the time.'

Felix shook his head. 'I don't remember Chorleigh senior ever being identified as a suspect. I'll look into the files again.'

'I tell you, he was untouchable.'

Sage pointed at the young man in the picture. She could see the resemblance to Owen Sloane again. 'Do you know any more about this man?'

'Badger? He was all right. He had worked for the Chorleighs at one point but he hated them. He was always in trouble with the police, they probably have a record for him.'

'We'll look into it.' Sage ran her eye down the list of articles. There was one entitled 'An Experiment in Sex Magick' as well as 'Flying Ointments and Magic Mushrooms'.

'You might like the sex magic story,' Jansen leered, nodding his head towards Felix. 'You and the professor.'

Sage blushed and found her lips tightening. 'Felix and I are just colleagues,' she said, her voice coming out primmer than she had thought possible.

'Ah, well.' He waved them towards the door. 'That's all I've got to say, anyway.'

Felix held out a card. 'If you think of anything more about Jimmy or anyone else who spent time with Lara, could you call me? It's very important.'

'I don't have a phone,' Jansen said, but he took the card. Before he shut the door completely he looked at them through the gap. 'But I'll call from the village. Alistair Chorleigh deserves a fair chance. Drunk or not, he's isn't stupid enough to bury a girl in his own garden and then leave her for a dog to find.'

He shut the door and Felix looked at Sage. She glanced to the 'hex bomb', or whatever he'd called it. 'Load of rubbish,' she said, with feeling. But she avoided it anyway.


By the time she dropped Felix back at his hotel in Lyndhurst she was starving. She checked her watch: one-thirty – she hadn't eaten since an early breakfast with Max. She drove into the pretty village of Fairfield and parked outside a tea shop that was open on Sundays. She selected a piece of chocolate cake and a large hazelnut latte.

The shop was quiet, just a couple of women with toddlers in the window, so she tried to call Nick.

'Hi, Sage.'

His voice brought tears to her eyes. 'I'm glad I've got you,' she said. 'I tried to call you last night. I was hoping you were coming back.'

'We've been at the retreat house; I decided to stay a bit longer. No signal, no telly, nothing. We ended up playing footie in the garden by the security light with a few people. It kept going off, which made it harder.' His tone changed. 'Is everything OK? You sound a bit wobbly.'

'Everything's not fine – and I'm not fine either.' She looked over at the two women, laughing at something one of the children had done. 'It's this case. Both cases.'

There was a long silence. 'There's another body?'

'No. It turns out another girl who was about the same age as River went missing in 1992.' One of the women turned sharply to look at her and she lowered her voice. 'Two girls, just teenagers, one disappeared and one dead. The man who owns the house might be being framed because someone buried that girl in his garden, maliciously, to put the blame on him. But he was also the last person to see Lara Black before she went missing in 1992.'

'That's awful, those poor girls.' That was his first

impulse, the caring streak that ran through him.

'Even if he was involved in the disappearance, would he have drawn attention to himself by burying this River in his garden? And there isn't any obvious motive.' She sighed. 'They say he might have been drunk, and done it on impulse. But the girl went missing in Southampton, and they seem to think he doesn't go out much, just to the pub and back.'

'Is Trent helping you? Talk about being thrown in at the deep end for your first case.'

'He's been busy with another murder. But Felix is here. They called him in to investigate the torture of some horses back in the nineties, then he got involved in the investigation of the missing girl, Lara Black.'

'Her parents must be devastated,' he said. There was a sad note in his voice.

She remembered he'd lost his own wife a few years ago. 'We found some bones but it wasn't her. But now I really want to find her.' She swallowed back tears. 'Look, I'm sorry. I'm not sleeping, and I keep having bad dreams when I do.'

'If it gets too much for you, let them know. Tell Trent, at least.'

'I would, but he's run off his feet with another case.' She rested her head on one hand and curved the other around the cup. 'It would be great if we can find out what happened to Lara, as well as River.'

'You can't do everything by yourself, Sage.' The sigh at

the end of the phone sounded defeated. 'Look after yourself.'

She took a breath, remembered why he was so far away. 'Have you heard about the job?' The elephant in the room pushed everything else aside. 'You need to tell me what you're thinking. Are you considering moving to Northumberland?'

There was a long silence. 'I don't know. I can't stand the idea of never seeing you or Max. That's hard, but the idea of seeing you only two or three days a week feels almost as bad.'

Again, that feeling of the pull to him from somewhere in her chest, in her gut. The idea of losing him was uncomplicated, while the idea of living with him was filled with frustrations and stress. 'Don't leave me.' It wasn't what she meant to say at all. 'I mean, let's talk about it properly when you get home.'

'We will.' His voice was softer. 'Look after yourself. And, Sage—'

'I know. I love you too.' It wasn't until after that she wondered if that was what he was going to say.

# 24

NB: The Butts, cluster of bowl barrows. Maps and articles held by library in Lyndhurst; enquire for Mr Askwith, any afternoon except Thursday.

Note in Edwin Masters' Journal, 9th July 1913

The family allow us much time to concentrate on the dig, which is generous. But they also want to spend time with Peter, naturally, and I am expected to also attend these social events. This morning, we planned to ride out in the forest and I became aware of some secret scheme for the day between Peter and Molly.

The family have horses stabled less than a mile away, at a large livery yard at Blazeden Farm. I was curious to go there, as Chorleigh House had once been part of their holdings.

The farm itself was of great interest to me. It had been

built over and incorporated parts of a mediaeval farmhouse. The hall, the centre of operations for the farm with its stock books and office desk, had crumbling daub walls infilling ancient, somewhat wormy timber panels. The chimney was large enough to stand two men inside, and lined with tiny Tudor bricks.

The rest of the place had a more modern wing with a comfortable parlour and what smelled like a kitchen. The farmer's daughter looked me over, and suggested a lively gelding called Horace, her own steed. 'He'll be kind to you, sir,' she said, 'if you've little experience of riding in the forest.'

'I rode as a child,' I confessed, 'but haven't been on a horse for years.'

'You don't forget it,' she said, 'and Horace is a gentle horse. Watch Mr Peter's mare, though, she nips him and he might shy. She's a bit spiteful, and they haven't had much exercise recently.'

'Oh?' I followed her out to the stable yard and admired the big bay she showed me.

'Not since Miss Claire – you know.' She turned her head so no one else would hear. 'Mrs Chorleigh and the young ladies rode most days, when the weather was good. But not now.'

The young daughter of the house, dead from diphtheria at fifteen. The reason the family were so tense, and why Mr Chorleigh was so uneven of temper. I resolved to be more patient and judge less.

Hilda Chorleigh, Peter's cousin, was riding with us on a heavy mare. We set out down one of the forest trails, Mr Chorleigh staying behind to talk to the farmer. Despite my resolve to be more understanding, I was somewhat relieved.

Horace had a comfortable gait and seemed to know every bump and hollow in the path. Molly brought her horse alongside mine, as the track widened. 'I'm glad you got Horace. He's one of ours, we sold him to the farm.'

'Was he your sister's horse?'

She was quick to reassure me. 'No, Claire's horse was too small for any of us, my father sold her to a neighbour.' Her voice softened. 'I see her out sometimes, it's good to know she's nearby.'

'It must be difficult for you.'

She smiled at me through tears. 'I try not to think about it too much. But it has brought my mother very low, which is why it's been so nice to have you here.'

I had enjoyed my brief conversations with Mrs Chorleigh, but our exchanges were mostly about Peter and Molly. I said as much.

'Ah, but you see, we haven't had anyone stay since the funeral. Mother wasn't well enough. Getting your room ready, keeping Father off your back – it has become a valuable distraction for her. She has even been down to annoy Cook about menus. And she has talked about Claire to you – she doesn't even do that with me.'

I smiled, somewhat wryly. 'I hope I haven't been too much work for your mother.'

'No, no. I think Father likes you a bit better now he knows your father was a military chaplain.'

I couldn't imagine why – the two men could hardly have been more different. Peter was riding ahead with Hilda, their horses putting successive waves of birds to flight. A group of outraged rooks lifted, then landed on branches over our heads, cawing.

'Here, Ed! What about this, then?' Peter called back to me.

Ahead lay a large clearing, maybe two acres, surrounded on all sides by trees. In the rough grass, the ground was uneven. Bowl barrows, a group of them, sat in undulating sward. I put Horace to the heel and he cantered up to the first of the features. 'I don't remember these from the map!'

He laughed. 'They were only found after the map was made. They will be in the next one, don't worry. Local people have known about them for centuries; around here they're called "The Butts". There must be two hundred prehistoric barrows in the forest, maybe more.'

They were three main features, maybe only three feet at their highest, with a shallow ditch outside each. The side of one mound was much pitted by rabbit holes. Peter slipped off his horse and tied it to a sapling. I followed suit, and Hilda took my horse for me.

We walked up the slight slope to see the other barrows from the central one. They were quite small, I estimated eleven or twelve yards across. The rabbit-pocked barrow appeared to have a sagging contour. Perhaps some inside feature had collapsed. Another two slight mounds could just be seen, lying under trees.

'This one used to have a huge badger sett in it,' Peter said, pushing the hair off his face. 'People thought it was just an uneven bit of the forest, full of animals. But when there was a fire here, the year I was born, the barrows were revealed. As you can see, nature is trying to reclaim them.'

I looked around the site as I had been taught, forty-five degrees at a time. It was a level landscape with possibly five barrows in it, each with its ditch. They didn't intersect and remained distinct from each other, but they appeared to have been built around the same time.

Horace's nose nudged me as Hilda allowed him to come forward.

'Are they all burials? I mean, do they have bodies inside?' she asked.

I shook my head. 'We don't know that, but probably not. Most round barrows, when excavated, have no bones at their heart.'

Molly slid down from her horse. 'Will someone dig these up, too?'

Peter reassured her. 'These are in the National Park. They are protected by the new schedule.'

'Well, aren't ours?' asked Molly.

It was a question I had been turning over in my mind.

'Yours is neither scheduled nor in public ownership. It belongs to your family.' But, the question whispered in the back of my mind: should we have destroyed evidence, as we no doubt have, for the purpose of our own curiosity? I know we took every precaution to document and to preserve, but I am conscious that had we attempted this a hundred years ago, as so many historians did, we would not have had even a camera to document our findings. Perhaps better techniques will be available in the future.

I used the stump of a tree to help me mount the patient Horace. The forest path took the four of us beyond the barrows and along a grassy track, and the question of legacy weighed heavily on me. We were impetuous, certainly, and I comforted myself with the thought that ploughing, tree roots and felling, badgers and rabbits have all taken their toll. One of our barrows is half robbed out altogether.

'Edwin! Race!' Peter put his heels to his horse, a beautiful creature I understood belonged to his mother, and she surged forwards. I'm afraid poor Horace was disinclined to even canter, falling into a tooth-rattling trot whenever he could. Peter, Hilda and Molly soon disappeared around a bend in the road before I realised my mount was favouring his right foreleg. Climbing down, I saw that his shoe was loose, so began to lead him.

The forest is a strange place. The trees somehow absorbed the sounds of the riders ahead, and the susurration of leaves in the wind drowned out our own noises. The creak of saddle and harness, the jingling of Horace's bit, they all seemed to become part of the forest. Even my riding boots, borrowed from Peter and a size too big, seemed to be cushioned by the grass and moss underfoot.

Someone was watching me. I stopped. I could feel someone – something – gazing at me, listening to me. I spun around, expecting to see some verderer or farm lad there, but nothing. My instincts became sharpened, and something had also bothered the horse. He flattened his ears back, snorted, looking around him. As I stood, catching my breath, my pulse leaping in my throat, I strained my eyes into the green shadows between saplings and under trees. No one. I have never been so sure someone was there in my life, and had to resist mounting poor Horace and riding him, to hell with his feet.

I somehow managed to control the impulse and walked instead, murmuring something soothing to the horse, and he, great trusting creature, nudged me with his nose as if I would protect him. I looked around from time to time, and listened for footfalls, but nothing. As I walked the horse around a huge oak tree, I saw Peter and the girls had dismounted, and were resting in the shade beyond.

They exclaimed at my ill fortune, and I took Horace down to the spring where the other horses were drinking, and we sat on the bank and shared the picnic Cook had made for us. I hesitated to appear foolish, and made a joke of thinking I was being watched. Hilda scoffed at the notion but neither of the Chorleighs thought me a fool.

'It's as if the forest looks at you,' concluded Molly. 'You can see why so many people believe in ghostly ranks of ruffians, lying in wait for travellers, or the spectres of huntsmen or poachers lost in the forest.'

Peter laughed at my serious face. 'We've all felt a bit lost, but I can assure you, old fellow, you were perfectly safe. Although in the rut, the stags can chase you. My school friend Alfie told me he was chased three times around a tree by a stag while the girls' school looked on.'

We walked back on foot, having knocked Horace's shoe back on with the heel of my boot. When we returned, Peter had a letter which made him stop, read it again. He frowned as he folded the note up and put it in his pocket. He mumbled something to us and ran back into the house, leaving Molly and I to stare at each other and Hilda to look to Molly for an explanation.

I shall ask him after dinner if everything is quite all right, for I have never seen such a look on his face. I would say it was fear, dread. I hope it is not bad news.

# 25

The following morning, Sage was in the corner of a lab with dozens of bags of leaves to sort through. A quick look had determined that the ivy and especially the glossy holly leaves could potentially hold a fingerprint as well as hair or fibres. With Jazz's assistance, she started poring over the leaves with a magnifier, back and front, carefully sorting them according to how close they were to the body. Different light sources could reveal smudges that might take fingerprint powder.

A tiny piece of plastic tape caught her eye – not the first one, she remembered finding one in the grave site. She held it up to the light under the binocular scope: a single blue line ran through the flat tape, which was about eight millimetres long and barely two millimetres wide. She put it in a tiny evidence box and tagged it.

'Look for anything like this,' she said, showing Jazz. 'We

found one before, but Martin, the forensic co-ordinator, thought it might have come off a forensic suit.'

'I'll keep my eye out. Are we really looking for fingerprints and trace evidence on old leaves *all day?*'

'I'm afraid so.' Sage sighed and lifted out another stack of leaves. A fine white mould seemed to have developed since they were collected – God was it only seven days? There were no obvious fingerprints so far. Since the body was clean, she had to assume that the killer had some knowledge of forensic countermeasures, perhaps from watching television shows. It seemed likely they had at least worn gloves.

She turned over more leaves, skeletonised oak mostly, and a little of the brown humus the leaves were collapsing into. The holly leaves were in better condition. They dropped all year, rather than all at once in the autumn, leaving the tree covered year round.

'Another piece of that tape,' Jazz said an hour later, peering at something on the end of forceps.

Sage handed her a vial. 'Label it up, will you? They need to be analysed.'

Jazz bent over the bench again, her sigh muffled in the mask she wore. They were both dressed in forensic suits; Sage thought they must look like ghosts against the subdued greys of the lab. The leaves started to blur after a couple of hours but they were getting through the bags.

She caught the squeak of the door opening and glanced up. 'Sage?'

'Felix!' She introduced him to Jazz, then excused herself for a coffee break.

He opened the door for her. 'How long will it take to examine all the leaves?'

She pulled the mask down. Her face was hot and damp from exhaled breath. 'We've done about fifteen bags so far. It's going to take the rest of the day, maybe longer. How are you getting on?'

'I've been talking to the leaders of animal rights groups around at that time. Some are in prison for offences they have committed over the years. Police are following up leads, but the people they interview aren't telling us much – they see the police as part of a corrupt system they have to fight against.' He paused outside the canteen. 'Anything more on the bag of bones?'

'I'm sure they are the Bronze Age remains dug up from the barrow. As certain as I can be before the radio-dating comes back, anyway. Do you want to sit in the canteen?'

He shook his head. 'Actually, I think we should go outside, get some fresh air.'

'OK, great.'

Outside the lab was a narrow strip of garden with a few benches. They looked over a park, and it was strange to sit in an evidence suit watching children play. They must be used to the strange clothes, as hardly anyone gave Sage a second glance.

'Have you found anything about Lara's friends?'

Felix opened his case and brought out a few copied sheets. 'There are two strands to my investigation. One is the animal rights lobby who were into liberating animals from testing labs. They released mink from fur farms, causing untold damage to the native wildlife, by the way. A naïve approach. Many of the same people were against the fox hunt; there was a large group of hunt saboteurs in Hampshire. Lara and her friends made a lot of enemies, including George Chorleigh. Interestingly, he dropped a lawsuit against Lara three days after she was reported missing.'

'Well, that's odd. Did he know she was dead?'

'He claimed he didn't want to add to the family's distress.'

Sage snorted. 'He didn't mind upsetting them when he sued their sixteen-year-old daughter.' Sage sat back, let the weak sunshine warm her face. 'And the other strand?'

'It's the water in an old camera case they found after Lara went missing.' Felix grimaced. 'I know the police don't think it's significant but it seems strange to me. The case was found on the edge of the village graveyard, and inside was Lara's camera and an empty film canister, everything saturated like it had been soaked in water. This was pre-digital cameras, remember. The film case was filled – to the top – with water. They tried to develop the film in the camera without success but they sent the canister off to identify the location of the water. These are the items.'

'Give me the highlights,' Sage said, looking at the pages.

'The water was very clean, with very few microorganisms.'

'OK.' That didn't make any sense. 'That's odd. If it was a pond or puddle the water would be teeming with life.'

The pages showed photographs of a branded backpack and a drenched case for the camera. 'Tell me more about the water.'

'The report concluded that it was not river, bottled or even distilled water.' He handed her the paper. 'It had very low levels of bacteria, some ions of dissolved calcium and the like. They also found the tiny spores in it, but not pollen, which you might expect from a puddle or even a stream that was open to the air.'

'So we should look for unusual water sources around the Chorleigh property,' she said. 'The barrow has water coming out of it. It might be the well head for a spring.' She remembered the water seeping into the hole where they had retrieved the bones.

'Have you ever been around the back of the house?'

She frowned. 'I've had no need to. We were focused on the burial itself.'

'There's a broad terrace, some overgrown shrubs and more grass. It's just as overgrown as the front. It must have looked down towards the river at one time. It's got trees fifteen, twenty feet high all over it, and a lot of gorse.'

'OK.' She couldn't work out what Felix was trying to tell her. 'So?'

'There's an abandoned swimming pool around the back, covered in plastic, half filled with rainwater.'

'So Lara could have been around the back of the house, lost her camera in the pool? That means someone retrieved it later and left it where the police or public might find it.'

'If I'd killed a girl I would want to refocus the police away from the area,' Felix said. 'It was found about a mile away.'

Sage turned to the water analysis. 'Low nitrates,' she said. 'Much less than you would find in pond water. No chlorine, so not drinking water or pool water. Even if a swimming pool had been neglected, algae would have produced nitrates, and lots of organics would have accumulated. I don't know much about rainwater, but there's very low carbonic acid, too.'

'You've lost me.' Felix stretched his feet back and looked up at the sky. 'Are you talking about acid rain?'

'Basically, as rain falls through the atmosphere it dissolves small amounts of carbon dioxide, nitrogen and sulphur oxides too. They all create a slight acidity. But the pH of this is almost neutral, even slightly alkaline.'

'So, is it purified water?'

She ran through the other results. 'Any filtering and buffering system would clean out some of the contaminants but they would also have picked up – these things.' The tiny green shapes had been photographed under a microscope. 'They don't look like any pollen I recognise. I know a bit about common ones found in peat and soil, but nothing like these.' There were searchable databases she could look at. 'I'd better get back to my mouldy leaves,' she said, without enthusiasm. 'Then I'm going to reward myself by asking Alistair Chorleigh if I can have a look at the finds Peter and Edwin dug out of that barrow.'

He frowned. 'I still think he knows something about Lara.'

'I'll be fine. I'll make sure the police know I'm going.' She smiled up at him. 'I'm quite capable of managing one drunk. But first I have a load of mouldy leaves to examine.'

After several more hours of sorting leaves, Jazz was happy to continue the laborious searching by herself. She was young, and looking for lab hours to bolster her profile with the department. Sage managed to get a gruff agreement from Chorleigh when she phoned to ask to see the pottery he had mentioned. She drove through the forest just as the light began to fail.

She banged on the door. 'Mr Chorleigh?' It swung open and the dog barked and jumped up to her knees.

'Hi, Hamish,' she said, bending to stroke him. 'Where's your dad gone? Mr Chorleigh! It's Sage Westfield, the archaeologist.'

He clattered down the stairs to the hallway. 'Oh. It is you, good. I thought it was those bastards back to question me again. How many people do they think I've killed?'

'I'm so sorry to bother you again.' She patted the dog one last time. 'I was wondering about the finds your grandfather made in 1913 when they excavated the barrow. You said you'd got something I could look at when I phoned.'

He shook his head as if trying to clear it. 'It's in here, I remembered where it was. I put it in the kitchen years ago, after the old man died. It's in an old biscuit tin with horses on the front, somewhere in the dresser cupboard.'

She looked past him. The hall was cluttered, heaps of coats on the newel post of once-elegant stairs that swept up the centre of the lobby, then divided. 'Wow. Lovely stairs.'

'Draughty,' he said, but he pulled back so she could pass. 'Bloody freezing in the winter. One of the windows on the landing is cracked.'

Sage waited for him to lead the way through the passageway towards the back of the house. They passed open doors either side, with boxes and piles of magazines and books sliding onto the floor in places.

'The police searched everything, smashing stuff, throwing it about.' Chorleigh shuffled past the side of the stairs, pushing open a smaller door at the back of the corridor. 'They left the biscuit tin though.'

Searching the house must have taken days, and the police had left the place upside down. Looking around at the dust, the grime on the wall up the stairs, Sage wondered what it had looked like before the search. Chorleigh didn't look capable of sorting it out, not in his present state.

'Great. It will help with the old bones your ancestor buried outside the house,' she prompted. 'We've confirmed the bones are thousands of years old, and most likely have come out of the barrow.'

Chorleigh led the way into a surprisingly large and comfortable kitchen. The draining board was piled high with clean plates and cutlery, a few clothes were draped over an airer near a radiator. The floor was filthy, dark patches where the dog was fed and came in from the garden, Sage supposed.

He waved at the dresser, a whole wall of cupboards and shelves. At the end of the room were double doors in the middle of a pair of windows. The house was on a rise; it looked down over shrubs to the sloping land running to the river.

'Wow.' Sage walked over to check out the view. Even through the smeared and dusty windows it was stunning, the silver ribbon of water weaving in lazy loops along the valley floor. 'That is beautiful.'

Chorleigh stood next to her. He had a sour, unwashed smell. 'It's the main reason I haven't sold the place,' he said. 'We don't own the land right down to the river, just a hundred yards of the slope. But that view – my mother loved it.' She could see the edge of a dirty plastic sheet that must be the pool cover, just at the corner of the house.

He pointed along what she realised was a mossy and grass-covered terrace. 'I put seeds out for the birds. We get all sorts in the garden. We had a goldcrest last summer, and a lesser spotted woodpecker. Look!' His excitement was infectious, despite the wave of unpleasant scent as he raised his arm to point at one of the feeders, hung from a sapling. 'Treecreeper. We get them in the spring sometimes.' The creature slithered around the trunk of the tree like a feathered rat.

She smiled. 'You must get squirrels and deer as well.'

'I put pony nuts out for them.' He looked away, pulled his arm back as if to protect himself. 'The police asked me about the horses, why I didn't go for help when Dad left them to die... I tried to get to them, make sure they were fed and watered. He went nuts, hit me. I don't remember much else. When I got back I found them dead, in the stable. He said he'd put them out of their misery once they were too weak to fight back. It was horrible; it was supposed to teach me a lesson. I've never been near them since. The police questioned me for hours but I would never have hurt them. Not our own animals.'

'That must have been awful,' Sage said. There were tears just balanced on his eyelashes. She turned to the kettle. 'Can I put some tea on, if that's OK?'

Chorleigh nodded, staring at Sage. 'I haven't killed anyone.' Sage opened her mouth to say something but found she couldn't. She didn't trust him that much and wasn't sure how much he was allowed to know.

'It must be really difficult for you,' she said eventually. He nodded, and walked over to get a couple of cups from a cupboard. 'We've already ruled out your involvement with the bones in the garden. We're just trying to find the truth.'

He pointed out teabags and the fridge to Sage, and walked over to the dresser. Someone had obviously gone through it and stacked everything back inside. It didn't take him long to pull out a pile of books and an old biscuit tin.

'Here we go,' he said, hefting the box, which rattled. 'I remember my mum showing this to me and Carol, my sister. We used to play with the bits of pot when we were kids.'

'When did your mother leave?' She was curious about him. He wasn't as old as she had thought; if he was a teenager in 1992 he could only be in his mid-forties, but he looked sixty at least. Only his bushy hair was youthful, just streaked with grey.

'Before Lara disappeared. She lives in Spain now with her second husband. She took my younger sister when she left and the old bastard said she didn't want me. Later he told me she'd passed away. I found out the truth when he died in 1995. Carol went to university in the UK; she got in contact a couple of times but we lost touch again.'

He struggled to get the top off the tin; it looked as if it had been rusted shut. Clearly the police hadn't been too bothered. Inside were a number of old plastic bags and bits of newspaper. When he pulled one open to reveal a piece of pottery about half the size of his palm, he dropped it into her hand.

'Wow. We have to be careful though,' she said. 'That could be four thousand years old or so. Someone rolled the clay into a pot, fired it and probably cooked in it for years so it's going to be brittle.'

It was typical early Bronze Age, in that it was crude but defied simple classification. Each potter group would have had their own preferred clay and style. It was thick, and the edges were sharp, despite the hundred years of being handled.

Chorleigh unwrapped another and handed it to Sage.

'Hold on,' she said. 'Have you got any plain paper?'

'I can take some from the printer.'

Sage noticed that he had a modern-enough computer on a battered desk in the corner, beside a sofa with a sleeping bag on it. The dog's bed was at the head end. *This beautiful house has given him nothing; he's camping in this one room.*

He cleared the end of a table and laid a couple of pieces of paper down. She started arranging the pieces of pot, seventeen in all. There were a few pieces of fragile corroded wire in what looked like a copper alloy, and two fragments of carved animal bone. 'This is the rim of a cooking pot,' she said, lifting it carefully and placing it on his palm. 'That smooth indentation? That's from the potter's thumb when they were making it.'

He put his own thumb into the smudge, and it almost fit. 'Amazing. That's wonderful, like stepping back in time.'

'Isn't it?' She walked back to the kettle. 'That's what got me into archaeology.' She filled the cups and added a splash of milk to each. 'No sugar, is that all right?'

'I don't think I have any.' Chorleigh prodded another

sherd. 'I always thought this was the same pot as the one with the thumbprint.'

'It's quite likely. They may have included whole pots in the grave goods with the bodies. For the dead to take to the next world with them, or to honour them in some way.'

She lifted one of the pieces of bone. It looked like a bit of sheep rib and when she smoothed it gently, she could see it was pierced in a lacy pattern. 'This is great.'

'They did find that in 1913,' Chorleigh said, dropping the other fragment into her hand.

'How do you know that?' Sage looked up at him.

'I don't know. I must have been told.'

Sage tried her most reassuring voice. 'When you were little, you were probably around your grandparents discussing it. You might know a lot more than you think. Do you mind telling me?'

He sat heavily, curving his hand around his mug. 'I'd probably remember a lot more with a drink inside me.'

'I'd hate you to start drinking because of something I said.'

'Don't worry,' he said, his eyes intense. 'I'm going to drink anyway.'

Sage lifted one of the pieces of pot. 'When was the first time you remember seeing this, for example?'

Alistair held his hand out and she dropped it gently into his fingers. 'As I said, it was with Carol and Mum. We looked at it because my dad was away.' He looked around. 'She showed us the book and the drawings as well.'

'Book?' Sage's heart did a little loop in her chest.

'A little leather book like a diary. And some folded sketches. Grandpa Peter found them after his father died.'

'Do you still have them?'

'I don't know. They were just bits of paper, I'm not sure where they are now.' He pushed the finds roughly towards her. 'Here, take them. I'm tired.'

Sage sipped her tea, then carefully wrapped up the finds in the original plastic. 'I shouldn't take them. They belong to you. If you want to donate them to the local museum, I know they would be grateful.' It almost hurt her to say it.

'I may as well chuck them away.' His attitude had changed the second he mentioned the book.

'Please don't. I'll look after them and get them photographed, and bring them back to you. Maybe you will find the notes and this book, they might be pivotal to understanding the excavation.'

He seemed to stare right through her, like there was someone else in the room to look at. One of his painful memories, she guessed.

Eventually, he nodded. 'I'll have a proper look tomorrow. I'm going down the pub to get some food and a few pints.'

'OK. Thank you for lending me the pottery, it's an amazing collection.' There must be more, God knows where it all went; the fragments were from more than one large pot. But she could already see the same reddish brown as the pottery in the grave site, from under River Sloane's body.

# 26

'Readers will recall the strange case of the spectral hound of Fairfield, when visitors to the Forest suffered an attack on their cottage by an unknown, ghostly hound. We have received reports of an excavation on private land of the burial of such a great dog, and eagerly await the scholarly explanations of several visitors from the University of Oxford.'

*Fairfield Recorder* dated 8th July 1913, cutting pasted into the journal of Edwin Masters

Yesterday, on the ninth, our mentor and friend Professor Conway arrived in the early evening in the same trap I had. He is a man of medium height and he has a bad knee, giving him a limp. He will never explain the injury but I suspect he was a soldier at one time. He never talks about the Boer campaign, yet he knows a great deal about it. He wears his hair longer than is customary and has a fine beard, and I thought neither would find favour with Mr Chorleigh, who is clean-shaven and has iron-grey hair so short you can see his scalp. But Professor Conway soon charmed Mr Chorleigh, and his knowledge of the New Forest impressed the whole family. Indeed, he entertained us with the latest theory about the round barrows at Fairfield Common, just recently described in the journal of the Society of Historians and Antiquaries, of which he is a fellow.

The two older men sat up talking the first night over a decanter of port, while we were sent off like children to play cards in the parlour. They seemed to reach an understanding, and the very next morning, Prof Conway was ready to see the barrows.

He approached the dig very slowly, checking alignments with his compass, framing the barrows in his hands, and standing with his back to the excavation to look at the forest background. Finally, he took off his jacket and looked at the hole itself, nodding at our care in sieving the spoil and keeping it well back from the excavation. Finally, he walked to the grass beside the barrows, crouched low, then laid down flat to observe the land around the earthworks.

I offered him a hand up when he had finished, and he struggled onto his good leg. He looked over at the half-barrow. 'I think you have something quite interesting here,' he said, pushing his hat back on his forehead. 'If you look at the large mound, you can see the other feature would have overlapped it, had it been the same shape and size. Also, I fancy it is on a slightly, slightly I must emphasise, different alignment.'

We nodded; we had already remarked on the length of the first barrow compared to the second. Had it matched the second feature, it would have overlaid it by some ten yards or more. We had also discovered it lay at a slightly different angle, which his expert eye had seen at once.

'Were they built at different times?' I asked.

'I suggest that *this*,' he said, walking briskly up the slope of the second barrow with the aid of his stick, 'was always something entirely different, it was never a complete barrow.'

Peter, who had only a slight acquaintance with Prof Conway, having studied mostly modern history in his degree, was diffident in putting our theory forward.

'We did wonder if this was a well head, over a natural spring.' Peter had been a little subdued since his letter had arrived, but he had laughed off my concerns.

Prof Conway clambered down and walked around to the cut end of the feature. 'No, I think it was always like this. It provides an excellent lookout point, don't you think?' He walked to the base of the wall of stone, moving with care between the muddy spots, and laid his hands upon the two upright slabs. They were covered with green and yellow lichens and mosses. 'Is it possible?' he said, as if to himself. 'I wonder. I have seen something a little like it, in Poland. Or was it Lithuania? I forget, but I certainly recall sketching something similar.' He turned to me. 'Show me the bones, Mr Masters. Let us interrogate them.'

'Please,' I stammered, 'call me Edwin, sir.' Indeed he had in his letters.

'Only if you will call me Robert,' he answered, smiling at first me and then Peter. 'At least away from college, we are just three antiquarians digging into Britain's past.'

We showed him the bones. The man's skeleton lay *in situ* as we had been removing the animal skeleton. Peter showed Prof Conway – I will never be able to call him Robert – the sketches Molly and I had done, and called her over from the trees where she was observing. He admired the drawings, suggested ways to make them more scientific and to annotate them, then turned his attention to the head of the great hound.

He smoothed the great skull as if stroking a dog. 'A large beast.'

'I've never seen a dog as huge,' I said. 'Unless it was a mastiff or some other such breed.'

'A mastiff or a Great Dane, perhaps,' he said, 'but these muscle attachments are particularly impressive. I'm no zoologist, but you should seek an opinion from one. If you don't mind, I should be happy to send a sketch up to a fellow I know at Magdalen.'

Molly was immediately asked to do another drawing

from the side, and since she was the best artist among us, we set her up in the shade with the skull. 'Only,' she whispered to me, 'don't leave me alone with it. It scares me.' I laughed at her but without malice; I could hardly judge when I had been nervous in the forest myself only a day before.

Prof Conway was keen to see the other finds, declaring himself no expert on the Bronze Age then astounding us with his scholarship. He was knowledgeable about the two hundred or more sherds of pottery, and was able to discern a spiral of copper wire in a lump of corrosion. But his respect for the burial made us all stop and think about the fellow whose bones were laid to rest under his hound.

'I have no doubt he was a prominent fellow,' the professor said, gently scraping at the edge of the burial with his own trowel. 'Look at his size. He was well fed and exercised, and his bones show no sign of deficiency in his growth during childhood. Observe this shoulder muscle attachment on the right side. This was a man who trained with a heavy weapon, perhaps every day. I see the scratches on the bones; certainly it looks as if an animal attacked him.'

I peered into the hole. 'We wondered if we might find a sword in the grave, or a shield boss.'

'Perhaps, but they are usually laid across the body.' He stared acutely at the skull, as if he could see the face of the dead man. Perhaps he could, perhaps he could look at the shapes of the bones and the hollows where tendons, ligaments and muscles once lay, and could divine the man's physiognomy.

'No, I am wondering about the hound, as you call it.'

'Surely, it has been given a high-status burial?' Peter said. 'You can see where it was despatched. Ed found a cut in the animal's neck bones.'

The professor stood, favouring his better leg, and stepped over to Molly. He smoothed his finger over the vertebra. 'Indeed.'

Peter stepped forward to look. 'We were thinking about the story of Gelert and Llewelyn.'

Conway raised an eyebrow and we subsided. Clearly he didn't agree with our suspicions of a great dog, dying to save his master. Or slain to accompany him into the next world, like some Egyptian king's hound.

'Let me get your sister's sketch off to my friend, and we will see,' he said. 'I should like to know what landscape features and settlements were here in the Bronze Age.'

I rattled off the little I know, supported by Peter. Between us we could contribute information about the many known barrows and the main road through the forest, said to predate the Romans. Peter naturally contributed the most to the discussion, which became lively. But I saw the professor turn his eye again and again to the strange well head.

'I see there is a void at the top of the stones,' he said. 'Perhaps it would be possible to see inside.' Peter told him a stepladder from the house could be used to get a look at the interior with a torch.

With some excitement, Peter and I ran back to the house

to get the equipment. He vanished upstairs and returned with an electric torch he had received on his birthday, exactly for the purpose of excavating tombs. He checked it worked, the batteries were good, and he added it to our supplies along with a length of rope and a short piece of plank in case we needed a solid platform for the ladder. We felt like two schoolboys off on an adventure, and our excited speech alerted Mr Chorleigh in his office. He decided he should come and see too, and it was quite a party that walked through the woodland back to the barrow.

Professor Conway was standing on top of the 'well head', inspecting the grasses that grew half over it. 'Perhaps you should start by excavating this top stone. It seems solidly set in the grass but when I stamp, I detect some hollow sounds. Have you thought about digging around it?'

Since we had brought the ladder and Mr Chorleigh wanted to see inside as well, he was soon persuaded to climb down and look inside the cut side of the barrow instead. Above the two stones that formed the upright was the top slab, projecting out a few inches. Although the whole was overgrown, the gap was just visible, a dark slot perhaps three feet wide and ten or twelve inches high. We carried the ladder over; it was easy to prop the feet firmly into the softish ground and get the gardener to help me steady it. It was agreed that Prof Conway should climb up first, as he would be able to interpret the void from his superior knowledge. He climbed up five steps, leaning towards the letterbox-shaped hole at the very top.

'It is a small cavity, maybe a yard deep,' he said, brushing away hanging mosses and grass and dropping them down to me. 'Hand me my stick, will you, Mr Masters?' I passed it up to him, and he probed the back of the hollow, then used Peter's torch to look into the space. 'There is a lot of moss growing in the lighted area,' he mused. 'It appears to incline down at the back. There is an internal architecture of some sort dividing the two, like two chimney flues, one behind the other.' He climbed down carefully, taking care with his bad leg.

Peter was up next. The space was roughly box-like. Peter managed to rest his arms on the entrance and wiggle his head inside. 'The prof's right,' he called back. 'There's another small channel running down the back, like a gullet.'

When I clambered up, I found it disturbingly so, like a stone giant's throat. The cavities were divided by a rough septum that seemed a natural layer rather than contrived. I guessed that over millennia, water had forced its passage along a softer stratum in the rocks, which had been lifted to vertical by some ancient upheaval. I could see the walls were of hard limestone; perhaps the carved-out area was a mudstone or chalk layer, eroded away by a natural spring. I put my theory forward, and Prof Conway concurred.

'These slabs of stone may have been erected to contain clean drinking water,' he said, tapping the top stone with his stick again. 'I think these walls could have contained it, like a prehistoric water cistern.' He looked around at Mr Chorleigh. 'These natural springs were much prized, and often worshipped. This would be an extraordinary discovery.'

Even Peter's father looked interested. 'And the name of the barrow? It's known locally as Hound Butt, but the earliest map we have calls it Wolf Butt.'

Conway nodded. 'Is it clear which of the two is called Hound Butt?'

Peter shook his head. 'There are two earthworks shown, but just as low mounds. They are drawn as the same size on the old map, but it is not accurate.'

Prof Conway smiled at us all. 'A real mystery. Tell me, Mr Chorleigh, who would you recommend as a local folk historian? Someone who has lived in the area for a good many years.'

Peter's father thought for only a moment. 'Old Bessie Warnock, I suppose,' he said. 'But she's not well regarded around here. She must be eighty years old, if not more.'

Molly managed to get a few words out, although I think she was still shy of Professor Conway. 'She was ninety last year. Mother and I took her a basket on her birthday.'

Her father barked a laugh. 'I'll bet she was ungrateful. Miserable old besom, I've had her up before the bench a dozen times for grazing her stock illegally.'

'Not now, Father,' Molly interrupted. 'She's given up her animals.'

'Except her poultry,' he said. 'Her geese are forever

chasing people around the green.'

'Perhaps Miss Chorleigh would come with me to interview her,' the professor asked. 'I often find good information comes from local elders.' He smiled at her.

'Mr Masters?' she asked. 'Will you come, too?'

Peter clapped his hand on my shoulder. 'I'll come as well. We'll all walk up after tea.' He seemed to have shed his anger or dismay at the letter and was quite his old self.

# 27

*Tuesday 26th March, this year*

A new morning, a fresh pile of leaves at the lab. In the plastic bags the dampness had condensed and fed a network of fine moulds. Even Jazz's enthusiasm was fading as they sorted through more stacks. 'Trent's at the briefing for the sleeping bag murder,' she said, holding up a leaf then dropping it. 'This is a needle in a haystack. With no guarantee of a needle.'

Sage snagged her glove on a leaf, not for the first time, and was tempted to throw the whole lot in the bin. As she disentangled the spine of the holly leaf from her glove, she noticed a tiny drop of blood in her glove. 'Shit.' She peeled off the glove to have a look, but it had barely broken the skin, just enough for one tiny droplet. It gave her an idea.

'Jazz, start looking at the spines. We need something that will highlight blood.'

'What are you thinking?'

Sage held up her hand. 'We've said all along they probably wore gloves, right? So while we're looking for fibres and hairs, we don't expect to find fingerprints, although we have to check. But what about blood? These spines are like steel needles, they go through anything.'

'Could we spray with luminol to speed up the search?'

Sage shook her head. 'I think that would dilute any evidence. Anyway, it's not good for DNA testing, and we need to keep looking for fingerprints, just in case. A high intensity light source should help, though.'

Jazz looked at the pile of bags they had already sorted. 'Do we have to go through them all again?'

'I honestly think that you would have seen a blood spot, looking for a fingerprint. But check all the spines back and front from now on.'

It took another two bags then Jazz shouted out. A minute smear of something dark red on a spine, and on a leaf stacked with it, another drop.

Sage started recording, photographing under different light sources, before she called the forensic team.

'Could it be animal blood?' Jazz was leaning on the back of Sage's chair as she meticulously labelled the specimen pots she needed.

'It could be. Maybe from the dog that found her body, or a wild animal. But those leaves were gathered from the lee of the shed, and then placed in distinct layers. What's the chance that a dog or some other animal deposited blood on a leaf *inside* a stack without disturbing the top layer?' She checked the plan of the grave from where they had taken the leaves in bags. 'These leaves came from the leg area, where the body was still covered.'

'But the blood could be River's.'

Sage nodded slowly, focusing for another shot. 'Very unlikely if she was already dead. DNA will tell us for sure. But I think her body was laid out very carefully, then she was covered with leaves, like a shroud – from the top of the stack by the stables. Then other layers, these older ones which are a bit mushy and stuck together, were added on top. If this leaf came from that layer – which we think it did – then it probably never touched River's body directly.'

'I don't understand what he was doing.' Jazz leaned back, looking over at the bags. 'It seems mad to kill someone then cover them up with so much care.'

'It is odd.' Sage looked back at Jazz. 'But I do kind of understand about the leaves. I wouldn't want to put earth straight on the face of someone I cared about.' She filled in the form for the bloody leaf sample with as much location information as she could.

The door banged open and Sage waved at Martin, the SOCO she'd met at the burial site, who walked along the examination table.

'What have you got? Lenham wants to put a report together from the burial.'

Sage held up her own ruined glove. 'I caught myself on

one of the holly leaves, and wondered if our killer did too. Jazz found traces of blood on the spine of one.'

He glanced down through the camera lens that Sage had fixed to a stand. 'I thought you and Trent were insane, preserving and bringing all those leaves in. The rest of my team are just glad they don't have to look through them.'

She shrugged. 'It could be River's blood but it's unlikely. It could be the person who handled the leaves.'

He smiled at them. 'Great work.'

'We found this, too.' Sage held up one of the pieces of plastic she had found in its glass vial.

'Interesting, another one. How many?'

'Three so far.' Sage handed him all the small tubes. 'We put them in glass so you can analyse them. We found one at the grave, too.'

'I remember, we wondered if it was off one of our suits. Is that a blue strip running through this one? I'll let you know what we find. Well done, both of you. Back to work – let's find a fingerprint as well.'

'No pressure then,' Sage said.

He laughed. 'Well, a signed confession would be good, too. Keep looking.'

Work progressed slower now they knew what they were looking for. Another tiny piece of tape turned up; Sage held it up to the light. 'You're going to think I'm going mad,' she said. 'But this smells funny, sort of medical. It's longer, too.' Another cautious sniff suggested something mentholated.

The odour was fleeting, but she noted it down anyway. Jazz took it and cautiously smelled it.

'What do we call the smell?' Sage asked.

'Like mouthwash?' Jazz suggested.

Sage looked down the microscope at the specimen. It had a faint blue stripe down the middle. 'Could it be dental floss or tape?'

'It could be.' Jazz waved at the computer. 'Why don't you ask the chemists?'

By the afternoon, the plastic tape had been confirmed as a type of dental floss, nylon coated with polytetrafluoroethylene, flavoured with an artificial menthol compound found in mint. Amazingly, the crime lab had stock samples on file from a local company, Burdeck and Young. DCI Lenham came down to get the details of where and how they had found them.

'Do they help your investigation?' Sage showed him the couple of pieces they had found since the lab results. 'That's four – no, five in total, found under the leaves. You heard about the blood we found?'

'Of course. You two have to keep this completely to yourselves,' Lenham warned them. 'But we're interviewing someone who works at Burdeck. We've taken his DNA for comparison along with Chorleigh and all River's family and friends.'

Sage handed over the last of the samples.

Jazz squeaked with excitement. 'Oh my God, can you tell us who?'

'Not officially.' He smiled at her. 'But River's stepfather Owen Sloane works with plastics. Sage already brought him to our attention. He did live with River so she may have been exposed to the tape before. But since her body was stripped and cleaned, the plastic almost certainly came from the person who buried her.'

'Have you confirmed he was Jimmy Mac?' Sage asked.

'He was born James Owen Macintosh but took his stepfather's name after he got a record for getting involved in animal protests.'

'I met him, at the morgue. He seemed so upset. But he's not necessarily the person who killed her?'

'Not unless we'd found plastic in her wounds, no, we can't be sure,' Lenham said. 'Which we didn't.' He shrugged. 'But the vast majority of people who bury a body also kill them. He's being questioned again right now.'

'Which would put Alistair Chorleigh in the clear.'

'Which is my other reason for coming over. He's left a message for you. Apparently he's found a book you were looking for.'

'Brilliant.' She turned to Jazz. 'Can you do these last two bags? I'd like to follow this up.'

Lenham waited until she had packed up her bag and phone, and he walked her out to her car. 'Is the professor going with you? Chorleigh is still a suspect, at least until that blood DNA comes back.'

'Felix is working on Lara's belongings, the ones they

found after she disappeared. We're looking into the water found in the camera case.'

'OK.' He tapped the car bonnet. 'Just watch yourself with Chorleigh. Sober he's just pathetic, but drunk, he's a different man.'

She glanced at the clock in her car. 'It's two-fifteen. I'll be fine, and you know I'm going. I'll just let him know I'm on my way.'

Sage drove through the forest, the afternoon sunshine dotting the road ahead. She had to slow for a couple of ponies on the verge, and again as a buzzard defiantly stopped traffic each way to drag some squashed furry thing off the road. Apart from being excited to see the book, she needed to landscape the site of the Bronze Age man and wolf, if that's what it was. She had sent photographs to an osteologist friend, but there wouldn't be enough money from her university budget nor Trent's for a DNA analysis on something unconnected with the investigation. Hopefully the osteologist would be able to tell her more about the deterioration and possible age as well as species of canid.

She parked her car alongside Alistair Chorleigh's, and he was waiting by the door as she crunched over the drive. He managed a small smile.

'How are you?' she asked.

'Better now they've stopped questioning me. Maybe they

are looking at someone else. It's horrible being suspected of this girl's murder.'

'So you've found the book and the notes?'

'They were on the desk in my father's study. I don't touch anything in there normally. The police must have moved them onto the desk; I was going to put them back in the drawer.'

She stepped into the kitchen, which was at least warmer than the draughty hall. Hamish made a fuss, jumping out of the basket to greet her and sitting on her foot when she settled at the table.

'Here.' Alistair dropped a parcel in front of her. It was packed in oiled card and stank of linseed. She could only hope the sketches weren't impregnated by it, but when she opened the folder everything was protected by layers of paper. She gently opened the package, to find a leather-bound book darkened with age and with a film of white powdery mould on the cover, on top of a stack of folded sheets of paper.

'You haven't looked inside yet?'

'I was waiting for you. Do you want some tea? Or coffee, I have coffee.' He was eager to please, knocking a cup from the draining board into the sink.

'Coffee would be lovely. Black, please.' The milk had been none too fresh the day before. She gently removed the book and laid it on the covering. Beneath it was what looked like fine tissue-like paper packets, she remembered her grandmother using something similar to send letters to her sister in Australia when she was a child. It had the faintest blue pigment and inside each was a heavier sheet, creased into what looked like quarters. She opened the first one and unfolded the paper inside.

It showed something in fine pencil, and it took a few seconds to see it was a site plan from above, with the area of the excavation marked with comments. 'Finer sand', 'pot A–D', 'small rock fragments'. The dig had only just started, by the look of it, just after the turf had been removed and the covering layers scraped away. She had to squint to read the faint inscriptions, in tiny writing. It was fascinating, she couldn't wait to enlarge the image and see it properly. She took it over to the window to get a photograph.

She carefully unfolded the next plan, which had a partially laid-out skeleton in the diagram. The drawing was a lot finer but somehow Sage knew the artist wasn't so knowledgeable about the archaeology. The first drawing had been made with an eye to the stratigraphic context. But the second picture was of the face of the animal she had excavated herself, the powerful features standing out from the earth. The tip of the canine's snout rested at the skeleton's side, just under his arm. Had he really been buried with the animal that killed him? Or was he attacked by a wild animal and maybe his dog had defended him?

She started unwrapping more papers, carefully placing each on its cover sheet. More plans showed different parts of the dig. The pictures were jumbled; some showed later stages of the dig, some earlier. Finally, two smaller papers just folded in half.

The first showed a young man sitting on a heap of spoil, a notebook beside him that he was jotting in, the other hand holding a pipe. He was wearing what looked like a straw hat, and looked unaware of his portrait being taken.

In the corner was a signature: 'P. Chorleigh'. At the top, more legible was the simple title: *Edwin*. The picture was done with care but also affection, she thought. This was an artist who had caught the young man's profile, the eyelashes dark along the eye, a focus on the narrow nose and curved lips. The other paper was another portrait, of a young girl, clearly aware she was being drawn. She was laughing straight at the artist, fair hair tumbling over her shoulders, a hat on the back of her head and her hands pulled around her drawn-up knees. She was sitting on the smaller mound, the grass reaching over and almost obscuring the flat stone along the top. She was pretty, but the artist hadn't lingered on her features like he had on the other one.

'Molly,' she read, turning the paper over to see the pencil inscription. Underneath was a line of inked words. She read them aloud. 'Mary Evelyn Chorleigh 1895–1918. RIP.'

'She was Peter's sister,' Alistair said, putting her coffee down a little unevenly. It splashed a few drops on the table so she moved the papers away from the liquid. 'The story is she went overseas to nurse in the First World War.

Grandpa Peter was a captain, I have a picture somewhere. He fought in France for three years, he was wounded twice.'

'I'd love to see it.' She looked around, saw a tea towel on the back of a chair and carefully dried the table and the bottom of the cup.

'Don't worry about that, it doesn't matter.' He seemed suddenly different but not drunk. 'The picture's on the landing upstairs. There's a few of the family. Come and see them.'

Sage suddenly felt awkward. She shrugged the feeling off; he'd never been anything but polite to her. For a moment she remembered how she had trusted Elliott. But Chorleigh was different now, nothing like the intense young man who had nearly killed her. She took a breath, blew it out. 'OK. Lead on. I'd love to see more. Did she die in the flu epidemic after the war?'

'I don't know. I suppose she could have done. She died in France, I know; she isn't buried in the churchyard in Fairfield. Peter is, and his wife and daughter Claire.'

Standing on the wide stairs which were shallow, perfect for Victorian evening gowns, she could see rows of framed photographs. The carpet was filthy, covered in dog hairs and grass from the garden. Underneath she could just see the remains of a flowered pattern, all it needed was a good clean. 'Do you know when the house was built?'

'Actually, I do. It was started in 1886 and took two years to build. It was on the site of a smaller building that was bought by the family, for the land. There's a bit of the original kitchen left, housing the boiler and the water pump.'

'It's a lovely house.' The high ceiling above was stained brown in places and was bulging around the skylight that brought light down into the stairwell.

'The roof leaks,' he said, pointing at the corner where black staining had travelled down the wall, paper peeling away. 'I can't get anyone to fix it.'

She wondered where he got his money from – clearly he didn't work. He pointed towards a landing where a large painting dominated the photographs.

Sage stared at the man in the picture, who stared back. He was good-looking in a heavy-jowled sort of way. Very dark, just a hint of silver at the temples, and piercing black eyes, quite different to Alistair, who had watery blue eyes and brown hair. But there was something about the way he tilted his head and the modern dress that identified him to Sage. 'This is your father?' He looked younger than in the photographs from the early nineties.

'That was done when he became a verderer. Or when he was chief agister.'

'What's that?' Sage couldn't take her eyes off the brooding portrait.

'An agister looks after the forest animals, makes sure people abide by the bylaws. My father used to be called out to injured ponies and deer on the road; he'd be responsible for putting them down if they were badly hurt. He had a special rifle for the job but he often just cut their throats if he was in a hurry.'

She could see this powerfully built man killing injured animals. He looked like he could do anything. There wasn't a hint of softness in the picture; she wondered if the artist was nervous of him. She looked away and turned her attention to the photographs.

She immediately recognised Molly in a party dress that made her look even younger. She had tucked her hand into the crooked elbow of a fair young man who was smiling at the camera. Here she could see hints of Alistair, the hair curling back from the crown, softness about the mouth which suggested a smile. 'Her brother Peter?' she said, to herself as much as Alistair. 'They were a good-looking pair.'

'That was before they went to the war.' He was standing close, a bit closer than she was comfortable with, and she stepped aside to get a better look at the picture he indicated. A smaller snap, it showed the two in uniform, Peter holding his officer's cap, Molly in flat shoes and cape barely up to his shoulder. They both looked gravely at the camera, as if they had already been swept into the storm of the trenches. 'This was the moment they went back after leave in 1918, in Scotland. The family didn't see Molly again. Peter was there at her funeral; he wanted her buried in France and not back here.'

'Why not?'

'Well, this was their father, my great-grandfather.'

The painting showed a balding man with a massive handlebar moustache, broad-shouldered and leaning towards the artist. He looked powerful, stern. Alistair's presence was oppressive, and now she could smell the spirits on his breath. He was standing closer; she was wedged into a corner of the stairs.

'He was a bullying bastard, like my father. He went to Cheam as well, and joined the army at the same age. He was an agister too, responsible for shooting injured horses. My mother told me Grandpa Peter hated him.'

'Cheam?'

'Prep school, we all went there. I went on to Winchester College. My mother insisted. It got me away from my father, but I got chucked out at sixteen. Then I went to the local college.'

She wanted to ask why but couldn't frame the question. She looked back to the pictures. There was another portrait of Molly and Peter, presumably with their mother. She was seated, looking frail, a wispier, paler version of her daughter. 'Did Peter attend Winchester College too?'

He nodded. 'He was a bright student, I think; he was sent off to university afterwards. The family story is that Molly wanted to go too, but her father wouldn't let her.' He leaned in to look at the portrait, his shoulder brushing hers. 'There was some sort of scandal about the excavation, maybe between Edwin and Molly. She and Peter were sent away to Scotland to stay with their grandmother after the dig. The local gossip was that she was having a baby. I never heard of one being born, though.'

'Oh.'

He turned to her. 'This family, always in the local gossip somewhere.'

'Well, thank you for showing me that.'

'That was my dad, with Brutus,' he said, pointing to a colour photograph of a heavyset Chorleigh senior in huntsman's uniform. The animal was glossy, dark, powerful. A young man holding the horse's bridle made her look again. 'It makes me sad to see that.'

'Is that Jimmy?'

'It is,' Alistair said.

She leaned forward to stare at the grave face looking straight at the camera. 'Can you tell me anything more about him?'

'His dad was in prison,' Alistair said, leaning forward too. 'He worked for us for a couple of years. I have more pictures in my father's bedroom,' he said, pointing down the hall.

The darkness on the landing was brooding and strange, and seemed to have an effect on Chorleigh.

'Perhaps another day,' she said, sliding past him down a couple of stairs. 'Now I'd like to have a proper look at those site plans. It's a wonderful record of a unique excavation.'

'And the journal. It's a mess, but you might be able to read something in it.'

She slowed her steps, trying not to give the impression

she was speeding away from him. The dog was sat at the bottom of the stairs, for once subdued. 'That would be interesting.' She pushed through the kitchen door and turned to him. 'This is very helpful of you, Mr Chorleigh.' She kept her tone formal.

After a moment, he turned away and lifted the battered leather book from the table. 'My mother told me about the notebook. It's got pictures and letters in it too, only they are stuck inside. Maybe you can get it open. The only thing we could read easily is the name inside the cover.'

'Whose name?'

He pulled the cover open a few inches and Sage winced in case he forced it. She could see it was a leather-bound notebook, about A5 size or slightly bigger, with irregularly cut, thick pages.

Chorleigh looked inside and held it up so she could see the confident pen strokes in black ink. 'The archaeologist who disappeared. Edwin Masters.'

# 28

*'If I ever had believed in witches living in cottages in the woods, my beliefs were confirmed by this evening's visit to Mrs Warnock.'*

Edwin Masters' Journal, 10th July 1913, evening

Mrs Bessie Warnock was bent over like a shrimp, peering out from under white hair in what was probably a bun twisted onto the top of her head some days before. She recognised Molly with a series of incomprehensible statements while staring at us. One of her eyes was milky with cataracts, I'm afraid it was hard not to stare.

Molly pointed to the gate beside the cottage. 'Mrs Warnock says I can make us all tea, if you would be so kind as to sit on the bench in the garden.'

She disappeared into the grey interior, and we followed the little woman through a tall gate and into a surprisingly well-kept garden. There was a wicker rocking chair covered with cushions like a throne, and Mrs Warnock sat in it and waited for the three of us to dispose ourselves on the old bench. It sagged under our weight, but thankfully held. Professor Conway immediately introduced us, speaking clearly.

'I'm not deaf,' she announced. 'What d'ye want to know?'

'We are excavating an old earthwork at Chorleigh House. Hound Butt.'

She rummaged in the front pocket of her apron for a long-stemmed pipe. She appeared to look, fruitlessly, for some tobacco. Peter sprang forward, holding a tin of his. She laboriously loaded up the pipe, packing it with an orange thumb. When she went to return the tobacco, he asked her to keep it, blushing to the roots of his fair hair.

The pipe was lit, and we watched as she finally got a good draw and sat back. 'Nay then,' she said, rocking slowly. 'It'll be bad luck to go digging around that butt. They say the spirits of wolves haunts the mounds. Back in them days, before my time, before my granmer's time, there was wolves in the forest. And bears, too. I see'd the bones when I was a girl.' She pointed through the trees in the direction of the church. 'The vicar, he knows. The bones used to be up the church, skulls and suchlike.'

The professor leaned forward again. 'Mrs Warnock, what

makes you think the barrows are associated with bad luck?'

'I knows it. My cousin Arthur went up there courting, when he was learning to be a cattleman up at the old farm. Before the new house was built, this was. He heard such a wailing and crying from the barrows he ran away, broke his ankle in a ditch, had to give up farming. He ended up working as a butcher's assistant in Lyndhurst.' She made it sound like a terrible fate. 'And the girl, Cissy Alton, she miscarried her baby, though folks reckon that was a good thing since she weren't wed.'

Prof Conway nodded. 'Many of these ancient places are associated with magic and curses. Even witchcraft.'

'Well, I dunno about that, I'm a God-fearing Christian.'

Molly appeared, carrying a large tray with cups and saucers and an enormous pot of tea. 'There's no milk,' she whispered to me, 'but I put sugar out.'

The ritual of tea pouring went on as Prof Conway asked more questions. If he wanted to speak to someone who knows about witchcraft, who should he approach?

'I s'pose I know about as much as anyone,' she finally conceded. 'As my granmer was a bit of a white witch. Kindly, like, and a churchgoer.'

'I'm sure she was,' he said.

She flapped her apron at a hen that was pecking around her feet. 'Get off, Flo,' she said, then slurped her tea. 'There were a few girls here, needed to be kept regular, if you takes my meaning.' She nodded to Molly. 'Not wanting to offend the maid. And some people likes their future read. Cards and such like. I don't know nothing like that. I was taught tea leaves, that's good enough for me.'

'And for me,' Conway agreed, and sipped his own tea.

For a sixpence each, she agreed to read each of our cups, swirling the leafy dregs around and turning the cup onto the saucer.

We were a sad bunch. Molly would travel overseas to find her destiny, Peter would have the most pedestrian of lives with four children, two of each, coming back to live out his life in the forest. She foretold a journey for him, a long journey, where he would be away for many years. The professor she struggled with, saying he was a 'fateful' person, most hard to predict a future, but she guessed that he would have a love late in life that would break his heart. My future puzzled her the most.

'Well, sir, it could go any way. There's no clear path for you. But you will know a great love, one day. Soon, I reckon. It's getting in the way of seeing your future.'

My heart gave a little leap, then. I had suspected that love was already creeping into my heart, even though I have always thought myself a cool creature.

'Tell me, Mrs Warnock,' Conway went on. 'Are there any stories about why the barrows were built?'

'That's a longer story, sir,' she said, her good eye staring at him. He held her gaze with an amused patience, like he might to a small child. Finally, she gave in. ''Twas a story of the people who came here, before Christian times. They worshipped their heathen gods in the forest – there are those who say they still do.'

He nodded, and waited for her to continue. I noticed his signet ring, then. A design was deeply carved into the face and it looked heavy, like an old seal.

'They was terrorised by a monster, some say it was a giant wolf. It killed their best warriors, and still they couldn't stop it. Then it took the son of the king, a child protected by guards. Finally, the king himself fought the giant beast.'

'And?' Conway prompted.

'Well, he cut the animal's head off with one stroke, and where it fell water bubbled up in a spring. They laid the wolf's head in the water and it flowed, winter and summer, even in the worst of droughts. The king put up a stone cage to stop it getting out or being stolen. They says, if you takes the wolf head out the spring will dry up, all the springs in the forest will stop running. All the animals will die and the trees will blow away like ash.'

The story was surprisingly close to what we had discovered. I glanced at the professor, wondering if he too suspected our hound was indeed a wilder beast. 'We shall certainly bear that in mind,' said the professor, sounding sincere. 'For no one should ignore the wisdom of our ancestors.'

* * *

When we got back to Chorleigh House I noticed a bicycle leaning against the gate post, and Peter grabbed my arm. 'It's that little tick, Goodrich. From the chemist. He's probably brought the pictures up. I don't want to see him, could you deal with him? Don't let him speak to Father, he never liked him.'

'Are you still friends, then?'

'He's all right. He's not a bad bowler, plays for the village team. Just deal with him.' This he hissed, and he jogged around the side of the house.

I was perplexed. I suppose Matthew Goodrich might have been overfamiliar with Peter too, taking advantage of their acquaintance at school. I walked into the hall to see Tilly, the maid, arguing with Goodrich.

'Can I help?'

Goodrich stepped back, smiled at me while his eyes glanced around behind me. 'I was hoping for a word with Peter.'

'Mr Chorleigh is detained,' I said, a little stiffly.

'Well, I have his photographs. But I would prefer to put them into his hands. Some of them are personal.'

'I can assure you, the pictures are of a project we are working on together.' I was aware of light footfalls behind me and Molly at my elbow.

'As his sister, I'm sure I can be relied upon to deliver these to Peter, surely?' Her light, amused tone was just right.

'Very well, Miss Molly. But the letter is for his eyes only.'

'Of course.' Molly held out her hand and after a moment he dropped the package of pictures and a heavy envelope into it. 'I will be sure to get these to my brother as soon as he is back. Good day, Mr Goodrich.'

She walked with dignity to the library and he walked to the door.

As he turned I saw his face, flushed with something, maybe anger. 'Tell him he owes me an answer. Do you hear? Or I shall take my story to his father.'

I followed Molly into the library to find her trembling. 'Well done, Molly. You were just the right amount of haughty. What a fellow!'

'He used to be a friend of Peter's so I suppose we gave him too much licence around the family. My father could never stand him in the house.' She managed a laugh, put the envelope and packet down and pressed the back of her hand to her red cheek. 'Gosh, I was a bit scared of him, he looked so cross. Where is Peter, by the way?'

'He sneaked around the back. I'll get him.'

'Thank you,' she said, snatching up the envelope and the packet of photographs. 'And give him these.'

# 29

Chorleigh allowed Sage to take the journal as it was so damaged, but he wanted to hold onto the drawings. He agreed she could come back another time to properly photograph them. She was glad to leave the house; his presence was oppressive. A few drinks seemed to make him more confident but more resentful. But standing in the garden at dusk, looking over the raw earth of the excavation of the Bronze Age bones reminded her even more of the girl-shaped depression beyond the house. Those young people, Peter and Molly, had played on that tennis court, maybe had sunned themselves on the lawns or the terrace and swum in the river. The storm of the Great War was just over the horizon for them in 1913. Both Molly and Edwin were dead in their twenties.

She had tried to open the journal in the house but the pages were solidly stuck together, mostly along the cut edges but some more extensively. She could see loose papers tucked within the pages, revealed by an edge here or an outline there. Some looked like photographic card, which was particularly exciting. The pencil in the journal had fared badly, but the ink looked better. The book smelled mouldy, and was as solid as a brick. She put it on the passenger seat of the car and walked over to the deposition site of the man and the wolf. It had been recently filled in and trodden flattish but was bare.

It didn't relate to either crime. She got a can of grass seed from the car, and sprinkled a layer on the soil, bending to mix it in a little. The light was fading. At her back was the edge of the forest which seemed to be leaning in to watch her. The sound of an animal scuffle in the brambles under the trees made her flinch, hurry to fold up the muddy tarp and gather her last tools. It took two trips back to the car and she needed a torch to see if she'd forgotten anything. The house was dark and silent beside her. She could almost believe Chorleigh and the dog weren't there.

She checked her phone, getting one bar of signal on the lawn. Nick had tried to call but she probably hadn't had enough signal to connect. She stood in the dark while she listened to the message.

'Hi. Well, I've been offered the job. Not that surprising, really – they had four candidates for two jobs and one of us hated the place. Too dark, too cold, he said.' There was a long silence. 'It seems a bit stupid to try and negotiate our whole future by text and missed phone calls. I liked the people, the job is great, the landscape is fantastic. I think you'd love it here, too. Think about it. Call me back. Love you. I really do.'

For a moment she had forgotten where she was, but a sudden cracking sound behind her made her jump. It was almost completely dark, the shadows between the trees had run together and as she swung the pathetically narrow torch beam she was aware of something else being there. Whatever it was had frozen too. Sage picked up her bag and shouldered it, wishing the entrenching tool wasn't in the car. She almost called out, but it probably was some animal, not a human.

She could feel her breath coming faster, her heart paddling in her chest. A hand from behind gripped her shoulder and she tried to gasp in a breath to scream, but was frozen. Panic made her sway with dizziness even as she registered who it was.

'Shush.' The sound came from above her head – it was Alistair. He didn't do anything else, just let go of her shoulder. In the almost-darkness she could just make out the silhouette of his arm, pointing into the woods.

'You scared me.' It was a pathetic whisper, as she tried to edge away from him, gauging how likely it was that she would fall over on the rough ground to the car. She was trembling, her breath coming raggedly. All she could think about was the dead girl in the leaves.

'Look.' A far bigger beam lanced the shade of the trees and picked up a pair of eyes near the ground, glowing back. It took a few seconds to recognise the shapes, broken up with shading. Badgers, two, then three of them. 'I put food down for them in the cold weather.'

'You frightened me half to death.' She was angry now, relieved, still cautious of the man. The panic was still making her shake. He reeked of something, whisky maybe.

'I'm not going to hurt you. Neither will they.'

'A week ago there was a murderer in this garden, Alistair, of course I'm nervous. People sometimes come back to the scene of their crime.' She stumbled back a few feet, still uncomfortable being too close.

'I hadn't thought of that.' He scattered something on the grass in front of Sage, then turned to go back to the house.

Sage followed the torch beam and stopped on the edge of the gravel. She looked back, but it was too dark to see. A crunch suggested the badgers had found the food.

'Do you always feed them?'

He turned at the door, the movement activating a security light which picked up the animals. They paused for a second, then carried on crunching. 'Every night, when I get back from the pub. Once I've let the dog out for a pee last thing or he'll eat them. They're only early because I've been distracted; I've missed a couple of days.'

'What about the night River was buried in the garden?'

'Late, I think. I was out later than usual.'

The light went off and Sage moved. It didn't turn on. She walked around but it still wouldn't work. 'How do you set it off?'

He waved over his head and it came on again, showing the grey shapes on the lawn. 'I moved the sensor higher so it only comes on if I walk along the side of the house. Otherwise the animals set the thing off all the time.'

'What about the night River was brought here?'

He seemed to be thinking back. The dark descended again and he raised an arm to bring the light back on. 'I was drunk. I walked back; it's only a mile and the bloody landlord threatened to call the police if I got in the car. I told the police this. I got home about midnight, settled Hamish, threw the biscuits out for the badgers and a few pony nuts for the deer. I fell asleep on the sofa in the kitchen, at the back of the house, must have been half past by then. I didn't wake up until morning when I went out for food.'

'Why didn't the badgers disturb the body? I mean, it was out there in the garden, barely covered.'

'They hang about in the garden until I feed them. Then they go off foraging. I've never seen them come back after they've eaten. The sett is in the forest, at The Butts. They have a great sense of smell.'

'You know they don't come back?'

'I don't usually sleep much. If they are around they scratch at the bin, dig along the wall for snails, they wake me up. The deer come in at the end of the night. I don't think they like the badgers. They graze the lawn and nibble at the shrubbery until dawn at this time of year.'

'Do you remember seeing any deer that morning, the day they found the girl?'

He shook his head. 'I know they had been down, though.'

She looked around. The pool of light sharpened every blade of grass. 'How?'

'I put pony nuts down for them. They were all gone when I went out to Fairfield in the morning. They wouldn't have come if someone was in the garden. When I got back home the police were there, it was chaos.'

She smiled up at him. 'Thank you, Alistair. Did you tell the police all of this?'

He shook his head. 'They didn't ask. I didn't want to say something that they could twist around to get me into trouble.'

'This might actually help.'

He seemed surprised. 'I don't see how.'

'Think about it. I can't believe the badgers wouldn't have disturbed the body in some way if it had been there, a hundred yards from where you feed them. So the body can't have been there until after you fed them when you got home.'

'Well, I didn't see anyone at twelve-thirty, and the dog didn't notice anything, and he barks at them.' The light clicked as it went off.

Sage stretched up and waved her arm, and it came back on. 'So they came later. Then deer came down for their pony nuts. If they are shy of people, anyone in the garden could have scared them off. But you said they ate the food.'

'I wouldn't expect them to come down much later than five, six at the latest. They disappear in the day, down to the woods along the river or over the back of the farm.'

She was excited. 'So the murderer came and dug a shallow grave, laid the body out and covered it with leaves and left between, say, two and six. From your experience with the animals.'

'How does that help me? I was also here the whole time.'

The light went off and they both waved. 'The truth will always help you. They are looking at a range of burial times.' She hesitated before she spoke. 'I can't tell you much about the investigation, but there are other people being questioned, people with alibis for different times, people whose cars might have been picked up by traffic cameras in that time frame. Say one to six. That could make a big difference to the inquiry.'

He started up the two shallow steps to the open front door. 'I didn't think they were looking for anyone else. They acted like they were only interested in me.'

'One last question.' She rummaged in her jacket for her car keys. 'The leaves. They came from the side of the stable, down by the holly trees.'

'I'll have to take your word for it. I never go down there.'

'Who else would know about the stables?'

He seemed to think about it. He switched on the light

inside, and she could see his jaw working. 'I don't know. Anyone who worked here in the eighties or nineties, I suppose, after it was built. We had a gardener and a couple of stable lads while I was away at school.'

'When did you leave your school?' She didn't like to say expelled.

'When I was sixteen. My dad sacked the stable boy, Jimmy, and made me do his work.' He looked away, his whole face set. 'I don't like talking about it.'

'OK. Thank you for the information. It might help find the real murderer.'

He turned to look at her and for a moment she saw a glimpse of the emotion banked inside. 'You believe me. You think I'm innocent.'

'I'd like to think so,' she said.

He half closed the door, his expression bleak. 'No one is innocent.'

The door shut with a snap, leaving Sage standing in the glare from the security light. It lasted just long enough for her to get into her car and lock the doors.

# 30

'The weather is sultry and hot, and everywhere is covered with small insects, called "thunderflies" by the maidservants. They gather in great numbers on drying linens, and are said to presage storms.'

Edwin Masters' Journal, 10th July 1913, very late

T he last few days of sunshine had to yield, eventually, to rain. It came in a great tempest, the sky lit by huge flashes, then the house shook with great claps of thunder. It must have been close: the interval between blinding light and deafening booms was only a few seconds. Peter came into my room and we kneeled on a padded chest under my window, gazing out at the jagged storm tearing the sky.

'The dig will be wrecked,' he said, his voice hushed by the grandeur of the weather.

'We covered it up fairly well,' I said, but in my heart I knew the rain would probably fill up our excavation. 'Anyway, if it does flood it we can bail it out. Remember that dig on Salisbury? The water was a yard deep but it all disappeared in a couple of days.'

'It has been so dry,' he said. 'Do you think it's Bessie Warnock's prophecy coming true?' I could see the flash of his teeth as he grinned.

'Probably,' I answered. 'The forest looks pretty dry already. Maybe we'll miss the rain, and the winds will blow the trees away in a giant dust storm.'

Another flash, so great that it seemed to be nearby, made us exclaim. I leaned my chin on my forearm laid along the windowsill. I could feel Peter's warmth beside me, his shoulder resting against mine, and felt strangely content. Here we were just two brothers, watching the storm together. I remembered the strange letter.

'Peter,' I started to say. 'I don't want to intrude, but you seem a bit upset about that note…'

'Now,' he whispered. 'Look.' Under the fruit trees that were scattered in the grass beyond the terrace, a few shapes moved. 'You'd think the lightning would drive them off.'

Another flash lit them up, dark shapes with white stripes down their noses, snuffling in the grass. They were badgers, some small with their mothers. There must have been more than a dozen. 'What are they doing?'

'At this time, about half of the baby apples drop. It's to

make room for the big fruit later; the gardener explained it to me. But they love them, they eat loads. This happens every year.'

Each flash lit up the creatures then the dark seemed to press against my eyes again. They looked like they were playing musical chairs, frozen in each flash. 'Peter. About Goodrich…'

'It's nothing important. I'll sort it out,' he said. A boom overhead coincided with a flash. 'That's hit one of the trees,' Peter said. 'Look, it's scared the badgers off. They know it's nearby.'

The strangest smell, like hot metal, came to me, then the stink of smoke.

'Come on,' he said, jumping off the ottoman. 'Let's go and see.'

So we rammed on shoes and went, Peter grabbing my hand and pulling me onto a path through the trees.

'Is it safe?' I asked, thinking of the trees above us.

Peter let go of me and turned; a flash bleached him for a second, making his hair look spiky and wild. 'Nothing's safe, you idiot. But what's the chance that the very tree you happen to be standing under will be hit – among millions of trees?'

I followed as fast as I could, slipping sometimes on the track as it inclined towards the river. 'Where are we going?' I was panting with the effort.

'The water meadows!' he called back. I could see

something up ahead, a dull orange glow, and I could smell the wood smoke.

The tree was standing by the river; it must have been the oldest in the area, its limbs hanging onto the main trunk by white-fleshed threads of wood. The heart of the tree was ablaze. Smoke poured from it, occasionally engulfing us, making me duck. The power of the strike had been enormous; the tree was flayed open, dying.

Another flash and the first rain hit me. When they came, the drops were huge, and before we had time to find shelter it was falling almost as hard as hail. Peter whooped and ran back, zigzagging as if under fire. I could see him in the dull orange light, and ran behind him, feeling my adult composure shed as I ran. We raced through the trees, and as he knew the way he pulled further ahead as the light died. I stopped just short of a large tree hearing the gasping of my breath amidst the rain, as I listened for his footfalls. I had never felt so alive, so euphoric. I started walking up the incline; I knew it must come out at the terrace somewhere. My heart was full of joy, of feeling alive.

When I crept in the back door, trying to be quiet despite the storm overhead, I saw movement, a pale shape flitting into the kitchen. For a moment a dozen ghost stories made my heart thud, then the shape turned to look at me. Molly, her face as pale as her nightdress.

'Edwin. You made me jump.' She flinched as another flare whitened her, standing in the doorway. When I walked towards her, blinded still, I felt her shoulder brush my arm. The crack of thunder made her gasp, and she turned towards me. It was easy to open my arms, to offer comfort. She slid against me despite my damp shirt, and I felt her shaking.

'We're quite safe,' I murmured into her hair. Holding her, this creature breathing and shaking against me, made me feel as if the world was trembling around me. This was what my restless thoughts had led me to. I could see her face if I shut my eyes. She nestled against me, no longer jumping at every noise. When the next flash came I saw her looking up at me, and it seemed the most natural thing to bend down until her lips touched mine. We clung together and I kissed her warm lips. She rested her head on my shoulder and it was the easiest thing to hold her close. But for a moment, a flash like lightning, I thought of Peter.

'I'm sorry, I shouldn't have—' I started to say.

'I'm not,' she said, and I could feel a shudder through her at a flash and a boom overhead.

I tried the switch on the wall. 'The lights aren't working.'

'It's going to hit the chimney,' she said, pulling away a little, looking around her in panic.

'No, it's not.' I pulled her back into my side. 'Let's find Peter. It's very unlikely to hit the house, and it won't hurt you if it does.'

We walked up the stairs, and I fancied the lightning flashes were a little further apart. Molly clung to my arm, and when we reached the landing Mrs Chorleigh was there in a long dressing gown, holding a lamp.

'There you are, silly girl! Thank you for looking after her, Mr Masters. Peter said you went down to the water meadows.'

Molly let go of my arm and sheltered next to her mother. 'Peter likes storms,' she said, still wincing at another flash.

'There's a tree down by the river,' I said, still distracted by Molly's kiss. 'It was struck. I don't think the fire will spread.'

Rain spattered the skylight overhead.

'No, I think the rain will put out any fire,' Mrs Chorleigh said. 'Thank you for looking after Molly. She has such a terror of storms.'

I must have blushed, I could feel the heat in my neck and face. 'Not at all,' I stammered. 'I'll go back to my room, now.'

Peter was there, sat in the window, watching the last of the storm. He didn't say anything while the water streaked down the window, lit up occasionally by the last of the lightning.

'Go to sleep,' he said. 'We've got a lot to do in the morning.' There was the oddest note in his voice, a little distance. Had he seen me kiss Molly? Or was it the letters that made him seem withdrawn? He walked over to the door. When he turned to look at me I could see the gleam in his eyes. 'Sleep well, Ed.'

My heart did that loop again, as it had when Molly had put her lips to mine.

# 31

Sage curled up on her mother's sofa, nursing a glass of wine. She'd invited Felix home for dinner, and he was chatting to Yana in the kitchen. She hadn't had an opportunity to speak to Nick again, and now she had the time she didn't want to. She had left a message for Lenham, passing on the information about the timing of the animals visiting Alistair Chorleigh's garden.

She heard a bump from upstairs, probably Max turfing something out of his cot. She found him standing holding onto the bars, his face solemn. He lifted his arms mutely and she picked him up, holding him close for a long moment. He smelled like bubble bath and clean laundry washed in lavender and geranium, the way her mother had treated her own clothes in childhood. She curled up on the bed and he clung to her, half in sleep.

'Bad dream, Maxie?' He settled into her, his body

perfectly fitting into hers no matter how much he grew. She had never thought she wanted children of her own, but now she had Max she could hardly remember life without him. 'I heard from Uncle Nick today.'

'Dada.' He wriggled as if looking around for him. *Is he Daddy for Max already?* She could never remember either of them using the name, yet Max went straight there.

'He'll be back soon. When we get home, he'll be there.'

Max twiddled the hair over his ear and relaxed against her. She settled back on the pillows and remembered Nick packing last weekend. A flash of memory, quickly suppressed. Nick, a kitchen knife buried up to the hilt in his chest. With the memory came all the feelings of terror; they left her trembling and tense. It was hardly surprising she had flashbacks, but she had believed the sooner she got back to normal the quicker she would get over it. Only ignoring it wasn't working. The baby wriggled on her lap and she loosened her grip on him.

'I love you so much, Bean,' she mumbled into his hair. 'I will get help, I promise.'

She became aware of someone in the doorway. Felix smiled, but looked troubled. 'Your mother sent me to get you,' he said softly. 'Dinner's ready.'

'OK.' She hefted the sleepy child, feeling how heavy and relaxed he had become, and laid him in the cot. She pulled the blanket over him, stopping for a second; the breath stilled in her throat at how much she loved him, at how beautiful he was.

Felix half smiled. 'I've got something for you.'

'I hope it's good news,' she said, brushing past him to go down the stairs. 'Because it's been a really long day.'

The food was vegetarian and delicious. Yana had made samosas and a spicy chutney that made Felix grimace with the sour heat. 'Wow.'

'Mum likes her chillies.' Sage grinned at him as he took another cautious bite.

'I grow them.' Yana passed Felix a bowl of yogurt. 'Cool down.'

'Thank you.' The conversation had been mostly sparked by Yana, who was fascinated by Felix's specialism, especially when she discovered he had been to Kazakhstan a couple of times.

Sage was happy to eat and listen, until Yana accepted Felix's help to wash up and Sage had a chance to unwrap the precious leather-bound notebook. It felt, as she held it, as if it contained a pocket of history in its pages. The hand inside the flyleaf announced Edwin Masters, June 1913.

The first page was easiest to read, it was a thicker paper than the others, but it had missing and smudged words. She started copying out the text into her own notebook.

'The invitation to excavate an ancient barrow had come at the right time, at least for me. My mother, laid low by a fever, was convalescing at the house of her sister, and there was no room for me in the cottage…'

'Sage?' Felix sat beside her.

She showed him the first page. 'This is the journal Alistair Chorleigh gave me to look at. From 1913.'

'Peter Chorleigh's journal?' He took the book when she offered it, holding it carefully.

'No, it's Edwin Masters', the archaeologist who went missing. I wonder how it got so badly damaged. This looks like it was immersed, then dried out, but the papers at Chorleigh House were pristine and preserved.'

He brushed his fingers over the wavy pages, but the edges of the sheets were clumped together. 'I've found out quite a lot about him, the mysterious Edwin Masters.' He read the front endpaper inscription. 'He was a brilliant student, by all accounts.'

'Was there any suspicion of where he went?' She corrected a word in her copy.

'He didn't have many places to go. He was a scholarship student, his family couldn't afford his fees. It was a difficult period for poor students. There were bursaries for exceptional students but you had to be sponsored by an alumnus of a college to apply.' He broke off to smile at Yana when she came into the room. 'Thank you for a lovely meal.'

'My pleasure,' she said. Yana seemed to have warmed to Felix too. Suddenly, Sage saw her mother as she was, probably only a few years older than Felix, vibrant and sociable. Elaine seemed to have released something in her.

'Mum, tell me more about your new friend.' Sage received the book from Felix and started to wrap it back in the protective paper.

'Have made many friends. Yoga, ramblers, herbalist guild.' Yana's accent was always stronger when she was evasive.

'I meant Elaine.' Sage turned the book over to see the heavily stained back. It was covered with mould as well as water marks, and there was a darker blot that suggested ink or paint.

'Elaine? She is good friend.' She disappeared and returned with mugs of coffee. 'Drink.' Her voice was pointedly strict. Clearly she didn't want to discuss her new relationship in front of Felix.

'Yes, *Sheshe.*' There was an awkward silence while Sage sipped her hot coffee and Felix looked from one to the other.

Finally, Yana's face softened. 'Elaine has grandchildren too, we are both divorced. We are going on holiday together in the autumn, to Italy. Venice.'

'Great. Wonderful.' It was, too. Yana smiled at Sage.

'This journal, if you can get into it, will be fascinating,' Felix said. 'I need to get back home soon. I ought to get back to Sadie in the next couple of days, she hasn't been well.'

'Sadie is daughter?' Yana asked.

'No – yes, she's my partner's adopted daughter. But she has health problems, she needs a lot of looking after.' He stood, stretching his back. 'But I wanted to tell you what I found in the Imperial War Museum archives.'

'About Edwin?' Sage said.

'His father was a chaplain with the 3rd Division, in the Second Boer War. He died of his wounds months after the battle at Magersfontein, leaving his mother to care for young Edwin on what I imagine was a pretty small pension. Anyway, he attended a grammar school near Colchester, and did well. His headmaster was an Oxford man, so was his father, so he applied there. Edwin was eligible for a scholarship from the university and the church paid him a small grant towards his living expenses as well.'

'How on earth did you get all this information?'

He looked awkward for a moment. 'I was at Oxford myself.'

'Old boys' network?'

He shrugged. 'To be honest, like many students I got in in much the same way as Edwin. My father was a diplomat so I had a scholarship to go to his old college. I still had to get the grades, which wasn't easy. It's different now.'

'So, what else do you know?'

He sat back down. 'When Edwin disappeared, the police were called by Peter and Mary. He'd been missing a few days by then. There was speculation about why the police hadn't taken it more seriously at first.'

'Mary – I suppose that was Molly. Alistair mentioned her name and showed me her picture.'

'Sage, he was still the last person we know who saw Lara alive.'

'He feeds the badgers in his garden,' she said, 'and puts

pony nuts out for the deer. I am keeping an open mind – he does creep me out sometimes. He's an odd man, sad, abused.'

'Healthy, happy people don't usually kill teenage girls,' he said. 'It might be worth you doing a few criminology or psychology classes if you're going into forensics.'

'I'm not.' The answer popped out, surprising Sage almost as much as the others. 'I already know I'm not cut out for it. I think I was drawn to forensics because of what happened to Nick and how Steph died.' She choked back tears. 'And how someone could hurt a sweet girl who did nothing wrong.' She could feel a tear running down her cheek. 'Now look what you've made me do. Thinking about River brings it all back. She was campaigning for animal rights, she had a boyfriend, school. She's a real person, not just a case.'

Her mother passed her a tissue. 'Better out than in, yes?'

Sage dried her eyes and blew her nose. 'I know what you're saying, Felix. I am being careful with Chorleigh; I tell someone I'm going there and I check in afterwards.'

'I saw some of the tapes of Chorleigh being interviewed.' Felix leaned forward. 'I do think Chorleigh is hiding something, even if it's not the murder. After two days of hardly saying a word, he suddenly talked about his father brutalising him, killing the horses, lying to him for years about his mother. The old man told Chorleigh his mother was dead, can you imagine that? Just because she left him to get away from a life of domestic violence.'

'I get that. It was a shitty childhood,' Sage said. 'Do

you think George Chorleigh killed Lara?'

'Maybe. When he talked about his father, I thought he was going to go berserk. The hatred he carries for that man is banked down inside. But I don't think Alistair believes his father killed her, although maybe he did. And almost killed Alistair to prevent him saying anything incriminating.'

His words triggered a memory. 'Alistair was expelled from his private school. Do we know why?'

'Public schools offer very high levels of confidentiality and they claim they don't have records from that far back,' he said. 'I'm concerned that he might have been anti-social even then, although it wasn't referred to the police. They're working on interviewing teachers from the school. It will take time – they all signed non-disclosure waivers and some have died.' Felix half smiled. 'I have met a lot of smiling, friendly murderers. Ones who love their dogs while they lash out at people.'

'Can we talk about something else? I'm fine, I'm being careful. You said you found something about Molly – was that at the War Museum as well?'

'It was.' He rummaged in his briefcase and pulled out a handful of papers. 'They emailed these over to me.'

The copies were of drawings, most were originally in pencil but a few were ink. They were pictures of men, injured, dying, one at least looked dead. 'These are from the war?'

'Molly was deployed as a nurse from 1915 onwards, under her real name Mary Chorleigh. She took it upon herself to record the faces of the injured and dying, the ones that couldn't easily be identified, because the photography of the time was both expensive and needed good light. Many of the Germans didn't keep their ID on them, hoping to get better medical care from the British. Molly recorded them so their relatives would at least know what happened to them.'

He showed her another sheet, a portrait of a thin young man, his eyes closed. The image of the reverse of the page had two lines of handwriting at the bottom. 'Gerhard Schmidt, aged twenty, said his brother was Wolfgang. Died of wounds 15th November 1916.' 'She wrote whatever she could find out about the patients on the reverse of each picture.'

Sage got an image of Molly, sat beside a dying soldier in a ward of dying soldiers, sketching by lamplight. She looked up, tears prickling in the corners of her eyes. 'These are so good. Was that the Battle of the Somme?'

'It was. She made almost two hundred sketches and notes while nursing the German wounded.' He handed her another sheet. 'She has a whole archive in the Imperial War Museum, and the local record office has a few more of her drawings. She had the makings of a great artist.'

Sage could see the individual faces in each of the dozen drawings Felix had printed off. They were young men, so very young, so real. 'It makes me want to find out more about Molly. Hopefully she's mentioned in the journal.'

Felix shrugged. 'I hope you can read it, it seems to have been badly water damaged at some point.'

'Alistair Chorleigh's mother showed him and a stack of drawings of the excavation. Not just the dig, but a couple of sketches. One is of Molly and one is of Edwin.' She looked at Felix. 'It really feels like Edwin, Lara and River are connected somehow.'

'It does, doesn't it? I can't see the connection to Edwin, though.'

Sage shuffled the papers into some order. 'Are you around tomorrow?'

'I've done what I can here, I just have a lot of statements to read. I was going to drive back tonight, carry on researching from home.' He looked at Sage. 'I suppose I could hang on for one more day. But I let my hotel room go.'

Yana stood, collecting the empty cups. 'That's easy. You stay here. Big sofa, yes?'

He looked taken aback. 'That's very kind. I don't want to be a nuisance.'

'Don't be so English,' Yana teased. 'Say "yes, please" and I get duvet and pillow.'

Sage laughed at Felix's confused expression. 'Welcome to Kazakh hospitality.'

It was close to midnight when Sage phoned Nick. She had already texted to make sure he was awake, and his voice was neutral down the phone.

'Hi, Sage. I assume you got my message?'

'I did.' She kept her voice low, although Max was sound asleep in his cot on the other side of the room. 'I've been thinking about you – us – all week.'

'I'm driving back tomorrow. I'll meet you at Yana's, we can go back to the island and talk about everything.'

Sage nodded to herself. 'One other thing.' She started to smile. 'Maxie called you Dada today.'

'He did?' His voice had gone up at least an octave, and he laughed out loud. 'Smart boy. Now we *have* to work out how to live together.'

Sage smiled. 'We definitely do.'

She said goodnight and rang off. She glanced at the clock, it was late and she had an early start. She pulled her notebook over and scribbled 'look for spores – water in film case' and 'Alistair expelled?' before she put her head on the pillow. When she closed her eyes, she could see flashes of the yawning mouth of the well she had excavated last year, the well that had snuffed out lives. The black water, the damp stones like teeth around a maw – she put the bedside light back on and sat up. Her notebook had the name of the therapist Felix had been seeing, somewhere in the front pages. She started searching for him on the internet.

# 32

*'NB Check preservatives suitable for crumbly bones.
Possibly alcohol?'*

Footnote in Edwin Masters' Journal, 11th July 1913

The day dawned dryer than I had expected, as the storm had flown past the forest in a couple of hours. I had fallen asleep to its rat-a-tat on the window, and despite our midnight excursion, I had slept well. Mr Chorleigh was already at the breakfast table with the professor, who waved at me when I entered.

'Have you checked the excavation yet, gentlemen?' he asked.

Peter was sat next to him, reaching for the butter. He usually ate a large breakfast but now was picking at a piece of toast. I took some warm bacon from a chafing dish on the sideboard.

'Not yet,' Peter said. 'We couldn't do anything about it so we didn't see any urgency. All being well it won't be under a foot of water, the bones are crumbly as it is. I just hope we don't have to scoop them out with a spoon.' His voice was flat. I raised my eyebrows at him when he glanced at me, but then he looked at his father.

'Peter!' Molly sat opposite her father. She smiled at me. 'That's horrid. You've quite put me off my eggs.'

'Sorry.' He grinned at her though, and she pushed her tongue out at him.

The professor took another piece of toast. 'Water won't do any more damage to – begging your pardon, Miss Molly – the remains. It might even make getting underneath easier.' He turned to Chorleigh senior. 'The ground is quite compact after thousands of years. Almost like stone itself.'

Molly picked up a teapot. 'Are you coming down to the dig today, Father?'

'I'm at the magistrates' court all day,' he answered, nodding to her for some tea. 'I have a particular case, one I feel needs a firm hand.'

The professor smiled at Molly while she filled his cup. 'Oh?'

'A sad case for a lady in Burleigh who gained a divorce from her husband in—' He harrumphed when he saw Molly. 'Sad circumstances, shall we say. Unusual circumstances.'

'Why are you seeing the case if there's already been a divorce?' Peter glanced over at me, but I shrugged.

'Offences were discovered when the divorce evidence

was aired,' Mr Chorleigh replied. 'And I am not going to discuss it further. We should break for luncheon; I may come down to inspect your progress later.'

'Which leads to another question from me, I'm afraid,' said Peter. 'Can we lay the bones out in the house, to check that we have both skeletons? Last night's storm has showed me how vulnerable they are. I was thinking we could put canvas on the library table. We can wrap them in newspaper and box them up.'

'I have no objection as long as you clean the table thoroughly afterwards. We must decide what will be done with them after that.' He finished his tea and nodded to Molly to pour him some more.

One of the housemaids came in, carrying a letter which she handed to the professor. He opened it and ran his quick gaze over it.

'Good news. It's Miss Molly I have to thank, I believe, for this remarkable information.'

Molly looked fleetingly at me before she turned her attention back to the professor. 'Was it the drawing? Did your friend identify it?'

He smiled and handed her the letter. 'I think you should read it out. It is certainly your discovery and a remarkable one.'

She read through the first few lines silently, presumably the greeting between friends. 'Ah, here it is. "I thank you for the remarkable drawing —" oh, gosh "— of the skull recovered from the barrow known as Hound Butt. I agree it is definitely canid and not ursine—" Is that bear?' When Conway nodded she carried on. '"But I agree it is not a dog. This is a wolf, I suspect similar in anatomy to Canadian timber wolves I have examined in the museum. It must have been an enormous specimen if the artist's measurements are correct."' She turned the sheet over. '"Domestic dogs are known from ten or fifteen thousand years earlier; this does not appear to share many characteristics with those remains, of which we have a whole drawer here in the museum." Then he sends his best wishes.'

'Well, gentlemen, lady, what interpretation do you make now?'

I looked at Peter. 'I suppose it is possible that the wolf attacked the man, and killed him. But why would they bury the two together?'

'Mr Masters, have I taught you nothing?' The prof pretended to be wounded. 'We cannot apply the tastes and mores of the modern world to the lives of these people. There are scratches upon the man's bones, we have all seen them. Imagine that they were caused by those canine teeth, and not spears or arrows. And the animal, mortally wounded, was despatched by some blade. What more fitting memorial for a warrior: forever battling with the creature that killed him?'

The maid, Tilly, gave a little squeak. Mr Chorleigh folded his newspaper with a snap. He spoke to the air somewhere between me and Peter. 'The whole thing is morbid. The servants are making up all sorts of stories, curses and whatnot. By all means record your discoveries and then put the bones back where you found them.'

'But we've only just started cataloguing.' Peter stood, and I felt compelled to follow. 'We have so much to learn.'

'Not only is the excavation disturbing, but your mother is feeling the strain. I will not have her senses overcome again. Perhaps having visitors so soon has been bad for her.'

Peter grew red in the face. 'That's unfair. She's loved having Ed here, she told me so the other day. She said it was a distraction from her sadness.'

'Well, it is a dangerous distraction. I'm sure you understand, Mr Masters.'

I was quick to agree. 'Of course. I'll make arrangements.'

'There's no urgency,' Mr Chorleigh said gruffly. 'But it is time to repair the damage to the barrow and bury the bones. I shall be taking Mrs Chorleigh up to see her sister in London for a few days. I hope the excursion will be good for her.'

Peter turned to Molly. 'Are you going?'

Molly looked at her father. 'I would rather stay here. I know Hilda would keep me company.'

Professor Conway took another piece of toast. 'And I can be out of your hair before you get back. I am so grateful for the visit, Chorleigh, you have a wonderful house and your family have been very kind.'

Mr Chorleigh nodded in acknowledgement, then left

the room, leaving Peter and I standing awkwardly.

The professor accepted Molly's offer of another cup of tea. 'Goodness, your poor mother. I had a conversation with her yesterday; she says she is looking forward to doing a little shopping. The heat in London would be too oppressive for me, I must say. I only venture into hotter climes when I am sailing.'

'We have a boat on the river, but I am the only one that sails now.' Peter sat back down and nodded to Molly as she topped up our cups. 'Thank you, Molls. I'm so sorry he is being so awkward, Professor.'

'Not awkward at all. I think my remaining time might be best taken up with helping you record the remains,' the professor said. 'I noticed you have a camera. Why don't we set up a tripod and document the bones for posterity?'

I took my cup from Molly. 'Thank you. Should we just try and return the bones to the same positions we found them in?'

'Certainly not. My own thought is that they should be better placed in a museum.' The professor sipped his tea. 'I suggest you gather all the bones in a bag or box and bury them where they can be easily retrieved, when your father has a change of heart, perhaps. The stones and soil can be returned to the barrow.'

Molly turned to Peter. 'What was he talking about, the divorce case?'

'I don't know. Some underhand dealings I suppose.'

The professor put his knife down on his plate. 'I'm afraid it's quite common for relationships outside of marriage to force a divorce, if discovered. It happened to a friend of mine.'

'But if there's adultery, that's not a crime any more, is it?' Molly looked up from the table. 'I mean, it's immoral, and I know people speak of criminal conversation but it isn't actually a crime?'

The professor looked at her. 'Miss Molly, it is clear your father does not wish this discussed with you.'

'But I'm not a child. I hate it when I get sent out of the room.' She stared at him. 'I nursed my sister through her final illness, Professor. I want to understand the world, I don't want to be unprepared.'

'Very well, but this must go no further, yes?' He waited for Molly to nod. 'Some men fall in love with people outside of their marriage. They can fall in love with someone they are forbidden to show affection to.'

Molly looked at me. 'Forbidden? Who can forbid love?'

'The law, my dear, prohibits physical love between two men.'

Molly froze. The silence was broken by the maid, Tilly, bustling in again with a fresh teapot.

'Thank you, Tilly,' Peter said, then waited until she left the room. 'Why would a man of that disposition marry a woman in the first place?'

The professor smiled at us all. '"A man of that disposition" is like all men, he may find his earliest affections, or perhaps later ones, will fall upon a woman. He is not so abnormal that he does not enjoy the company of females. And our society demands that a young man is soon married to a young woman. There his natural affections will find a home. But if such a married man meets another man, and falls in love…'

'Like the Greeks,' I suggested. 'Many fell in love with men, it was allowed.'

'But now it is not,' the professor said. 'And people like your father are committed to judging and punishing such men.'

'That is his responsibility,' Peter said. 'I think Father is right, Molls. This is not a suitable conversation for young ladies.' His voice was graver than usual.

'I never really understood,' she said. She looked down at her plate, moved her cutlery around. 'What about women? Do they sometimes fall in love with other women?'

The professor patted his napkin to his lips. 'I'm quite sure they do, and have to conceal their love for propriety's sake, but they are not committing a crime.'

Peter lifted his eyebrows. 'My father would say: except against nature.'

The professor smiled, sadly I thought. 'I'm sure he would.'

# 33

*Wednesday 27th March, this year, forensic lab*

T he local morning news showed an unshaven Owen
Sloane arrested and driven off to the police station
the day before. When Sage phoned Lenham to offer her
congratulations she got a terse answer back. 'We're not there
yet. There's a team briefing at two, make sure you're there.'

'Did you get a match to the DNA we found?'

'We're waiting for confirmation that it's his blood on
the leaves, and there's a strong link to the plastic strip. But
he's not talking. We're interviewing his family again.'

'You got my message about the animals visiting
Chorleigh House at night? Also, George Chorleigh may
have had a motive to kill Lara.'

She could hear his sigh on the phone. 'I don't see how
we can prove it after all these years. I still think Alistair
Chorleigh knows something. I know when I'm being
lied to.'

'He hated his father, he might talk if he knows he's not the suspect.'

He huffed a breath. 'Bloody hell, that opens about a dozen new lines of inquiry for us. I'll put it to Chorleigh when I have time, see what we can get.' Since Felix was still in Hampshire, Lenham asked Sage to request the professor attend the police station later.

Sage had a couple of hours to concentrate on the journal while she waited to receive answers to her inquiries about water sources on the Chorleigh property.

She placed the book on the examination table at the lab, under a large light. She knew from half-remembered lectures that it was possible to unstick pages, but the method partly depended on what materials had stuck. The ink would require one technique, the paper or glue another. She didn't think cold would do any harm, so had left it overnight wrapped in plastic in her mother's freezer.

There, the first stuck page started to yield to a carefully inserted thin spatula. It was less fixed than the back of the book and she could pry it loose. His journal immediately talked about the actual excavation, his enthusiasm coming off the page. Mixed in were observations of Peter – his affectionate focus. Another page sprung free, then a few more, just stuck at the edge. A folded piece of paper dropped out onto the bench as they did.

'My dear Edwin...' The writing was difficult to read; the ink hadn't fared as well as Edwin's own, which was probably one of the indelible inks. She wished she had paid more attention in the few classes she had taken about documents. They were mostly about the conservation of vellum and other ancient materials, rather than modern paper. This blue ink had faded in places, but minute traces showed up under alternative light sources. She photographed both sides. Whoever this R. Conway was, he was obviously fond of Edwin and an expert of the finds. '…quite correct as to date, although I think earlier rather than later, say 1800–1200 BC. What was so interesting is that this type of pot is Germanic in origin…'

She turned back to the pages, lifting each free as she went. Some were persistently stuck towards the spine, but she could still read them so didn't worry. She took pictures as she went, noting pale pencil notes in the margins. She wondered how the family had got the journal, if it was so badly water damaged.

'Sage?' She jumped, but it was Jazz, the assistant. 'I got your message.'

'Thank you, Jazz. I was wondering if you got round to looking into water sources in the grounds of Chorleigh House.'

Jazz nodded. 'You're thinking about the water in the film case, aren't you? There were two wells marked on the original map for the house. I'm waiting to hear back from the librarian at the New Forest Library archive, but they aren't held digitally. She can get them for you if you want

to view the originals, but I asked her to have a look for us.'
She turned her head to look at the pages. 'Wow. Is that
from the original excavation?'

'It is.' Sage showed her the clearest page, filled with
Edwin's enthusiastic description of the dig.

'That's fantastic. Can you get to all the pages?'

'Not yet. You can give me a hand if you like.' Sage showed
her how to peel the pages apart, tugging in different places
to loosen it, not forcing it. Some pages were harder to
reveal, each one a gem of information on both sides. More
letters fell out, some almost illegible with dark mould.
Sage photographed each page as they were revealed. A few
snippets from newspapers were pasted with glue, adding to
the problem, sticking more pages together.

'I can hardly make out the notes in the margin.' Jazz
tried to read the next page, a few notes then a scribbled
sketch. 'This is a voice from the past. I mean, no one's read
this since it was written. How did it get so wet?'

'I don't know,' Sage said. 'This isn't like the damp you
get from leaving it in a wet environment, this is the result
of a soaking and then being left to dry. We can't be sure
when it got wet, but this level of mould damage suggests it
was a long time ago.'

Jazz made a face. 'I like to think it was from 1913.'

Sage grinned back. 'Actually, Alistair Chorleigh said
it has been like this as long as he can remember so it
could date back that far. Did the police get back about the

bloodstains on the leaves yet? Lenham mentioned they were waiting for results.'

'Oh, shit, yes, you distracted me. It's a definite match for River's stepfather. He works at the plastics factory doing quality control on – guess what?'

'Dental floss?'

Jazz took another photograph, squinting down the lens. 'Exactly. And I've finished looking through the leaves, thank God. They're charging him with the illegal burial but they've held back on the murder.' She slid another fragment of a letter out and squinted at it. 'So who's this Conway guy, and why are there so many notes from him?'

Sage read on. 'I think he was Edwin's tutor at Oxford. He seemed excited to be studying under him next year, from what I've been able to read so far. He was planning to do a master's degree in archaeology and antiquities. Shame he never got to do it.'

'Why not?'

'Didn't I tell you? He disappeared.' Sage teased another page but it started to tear and she went back to nudging other areas until it came free. 'He vanished, leaving everything behind, including some drawings. He even left his wallet and glasses.'

'Didn't the drawings get wet, too?'

'No, which is odd. I don't even know where they found the journal. The sketches were OK, I think they never left the house. They were wrapped up in this very fine paper. I haven't seen anything like it, it's like tissue paper but much stronger.'

'It could be onionskin paper, the sort of thing they separated photographs with.' Jazz grinned. 'My major was forensics, but I did a bit of historical criminology as well.'

The term was unfamiliar. Sage looked it up on the open computer, and it looked very similar. 'That looks like it. The sketches were on good white paper, heavy, like cartridge paper.' She had transferred the pictures she had taken at Chorleigh House to the computer. 'These are my quick photos of the sketches but the light wasn't good. I'll try and scan them properly when Mr Chorleigh is feeling less defensive. Hopefully he'll be more friendly when he realises he's out of the frame for River's murder.'

Jazz started looking through them. 'You can see his point of view. They interviewed him twice, and they were pretty hard on him. Of course, at that point they thought he probably did it.'

'It still wouldn't have made any sense to bury her in his own garden under six inches of leaves,' Sage said, leaning forward to see the images. They hadn't come out well, but the sketches of Molly and Edwin were still very good.

'Is that him, Edwin Masters?' Jazz blew the image up until they could get a better view. She sharpened the contrast and brightness and the picture became easier to see. 'He looks so young. Who drew this, the girl?'

'Peter Chorleigh. There's a tiny signature, there.'

Jazz sat back and looked at Sage. 'What happened to him?'

'I don't know much but he survived the First World War. Alistair Chorleigh said he was sent away to Scotland with Molly after Edwin disappeared. I wondered… His picture of Edwin is so flattering and Edwin talks about Peter a lot in the journal, I wondered if they had a relationship. He does talk about Molly, something about his feelings being brotherly towards her. I can't wait to read it all, but the second half is in a very bad state.'

'It sounds intriguing.'

Sage nodded. 'I want to get the whole picture. We know Molly was a nurse in the First World War, and died in 1918. Her drawings are in an archive at the Imperial War Museum.'

'But it's still a bit odd. Edwin going missing, I mean, just like Lara Black did.' Her phone beeped. 'Oh, great. The librarian.' She listened, made a few scribbled notes. 'OK, thanks, that's very helpful. I'll let her know. Bye.'

'Water sources?'

Jazz waved her phone. 'Two. There's an old well to the side of the property. And the house has its own borehole, but I think it's capped.'

The word 'well' still gave Sage the shivers. 'Where?'

Jazz sat on one of the stools. 'At the end of the house itself. There's a boiler room or an outbuilding, it's in there.'

'I would like to find out more,' Sage said. 'Maybe there's a natural explanation, a connection to Lara and Edwin's disappearance. A sinkhole or old mine working that they both fell into, or a cave or something they got trapped in.' Sage smiled at Jazz. 'The briefing is at two o'clock, so I've got time to collect water samples around the Chorleigh grounds. Maybe I can find something similar to the film case sample. Felix sent me photographs of microscope examinations for comparison.'

'Do you want me to go with you?'

'No, I'll be in and out,' Sage said, rewrapping the journal and packing it into a case. 'I'll just grab a couple of bottles and maybe a field microscope. I should be able to rule them out in minutes. I'll see you at the briefing at two, OK? Thanks for your help.'

The sketchy notes from Jazz included the site of a well, marked as disused. That didn't necessarily mean it was filled in, however, but she had scribbled down its general position. The borehole should be easier to find as it was covered by a small building, probably the old kitchen from the original cottage. She hadn't noticed it on the ground next to the main structure, although it was probably only thirty or forty metres from where River's body had been left. She checked the downloaded pictures from the drone survey. She could see something vaguely rectangular; maybe that was the building over the borehole. But it looked as if the roof was falling in. It didn't appear on any of the crime-scene photographs that she'd taken, but then she hadn't been looking for an outbuilding. The huge pile of ivy and brambles in some of the pictures, that could be it.

She checked if Felix was available but he was at the police station observing the interview with Owen Sloane, who still wasn't talking. During the drive through the forest, she took time to relax, focusing on drawing the threads together. Alistair Chorleigh was a strange man, both pathetic and somehow broodingly threatening, but he hadn't killed River Sloane. Everyone knew where Sage was; he wouldn't harm her.

'No one is innocent,' he'd said. She wondered again why he'd been expelled from school. She took a deep breath as the familiar panic started to prickle her skin, make her breath short. She shouldn't have been so scared by Chorleigh the previous night. He hadn't hurt her, he'd just startled her, even though the memory made her shiver. Nick was driving back today, that was the most important thing.

Jazz had told her they had charged River's stepfather with concealing the body and were working towards a confession. She remembered his face at the mortuary, his grief, what looked like agony. Maybe he regretted causing River so much pain, maybe he wished he hadn't done it.

She pulled around the half-open gate and onto the scrubby gravel to park her car next to Alistair's. There were no other cars, no police presence. She opened the original water report on her phone.

'We've tested every water course within a mile, none of them produced spores (labelled a–f in micrographs),' the scientist had written. 'Our ecologist suggests mosses or liverworts, possibly, exact species unknown. The investigation doesn't have a warrant to search for water on the suspect's land.' The enlarged picture of one of the green spores made it look like a Fabergé rugby ball, less than a tenth of a millimetre long.

She had packed her field microscope, and thought she could at least test the water in the wells for similar green blobs, although she would need a much more powerful microscope to get a precise match. She also had a few bits of surveying equipment, although she knew from previous experience how unstable wells could be and wasn't going to get too close. She took a few slow, deep breaths at the thought of an old well, somewhere, maybe with Lara's remains in it. She waited until the flashbacks of seeing the dead face of her student in the well had faded. Time was ticking by. She wanted to have something to take to the briefing in – she checked her watch – less than two hours. Maybe it would help keep Lara's investigation alive if she could find something.

The place seemed quiet. Alistair's car was parked at an angle and an attempt had been made to drag the gate a few feet before it dug into the gravel. Perhaps he was trying to keep everyone out now the police were finally gone.

She still hesitated before she rapped the knocker against the door; it seemed so quiet. The day was overcast. Rain was expected later but so far it was dry and mild. The dog erupted inside the house, barking and getting louder. She could hear Chorleigh shouting at him. When he got close to the door, he shouted through it.

'I don't want to talk to anyone!'

'I'm sorry, Mr Chorleigh. It's Sage Westfield. I just need to test some water. I don't need to come into the house.'

There was a wait before he opened the door and she bent to stroke the ecstatic dog. 'Oh. It's you.' He looked awful; his eyes were red and she could smell the alcohol coming off him.

'I'm sorry to bother you,' she said. 'I just wanted to have a look at two water sources marked on old plans from when your house was built.'

'I'm tired of your people traipsing in without even asking.'

'They aren't my people, Mr Chorleigh, and I am asking. If we can rule out the water sample we have matching any source on your land that helps you.'

He pushed the door open a little wider. 'I don't mean you,' he grumbled. 'I'm tired of it all, the police, the press. I wish they'd leave me alone.'

'They have a suspect in custody,' Sage said.

'Good. Maybe they'll leave me alone.'

Sage pointed down the side of the house. 'Do you mind if I look at the old well marked on the plans?'

'I keep the cover on. I was worried about the dog falling down it.'

'Could you show me?'

The well was in the grounds beyond the house and behind the tennis court. Sage avoided looking at the grave site, now covered with a white tarp. The well had a circular wooden lid, old and covered with mosses and lichens which looked a hundred years old. It might have kept the dog safe but it would never have taken the weight of an adult human.

She gingerly walked closer, worried in case it wasn't stable, but it looked robust enough with four courses of bricks under the lid. Sage managed to get close enough to feed a glass sample bottle through a hole on one edge and lower it on a piece of fishing line. Chorleigh had pulled filthy wellies on and was wearing a dressing gown over his clothes. He still made her nervous.

She pulled up the sample bottle full of brownish water. The water table was high here too; the bottle filled up at six feet or so down the well. 'Thank you,' she said, scribbling a label in waterproof pen. 'Can I see the borehole next?' She was glad to leave the well behind.

'It's in the old boiler room.' He waved at the side of the house. The outhouse was further back than she had thought from the photos, and covered in ivy. No wonder she hadn't noticed it, it blended in with the side of the house, also covered with creepers. She tried the door: it was unlocked and opened a few inches but the roof seemed to have fallen in, dropping debris behind the opening. In the end, Chorleigh put his shoulder to the door, and with a crack it gave way. He was able to open it enough for Sage to lean in.

The borehole was narrow, and had a metal grill over the top that was bolted in place. It was easy to get a sample. There was no chance anyone had fallen down there. 'Four and a half metres down,' she said, filling in the label. She struggled past the remains of an old, rusted machine she guessed was a boiler and out into the garden. She held up the sample: it was clear. 'Is this the water you still use?'

'There's an electric pump in the house. It pulls the water up through a pipe running inside.'

'I saw. What happens if your power gets cut off?'

'We have a header tank in the house. It keeps us going until the electric goes back on.'

'Oh. Good. Thank you for your help.'

He rubbed his hair, making it stick up even more. 'So, what are you going to do now?'

'I'll look at them under the microscope, so I can compare them with water found in Lara's film case in 1992.' She held up the sample. 'I just wanted to rule out the possibility that Lara wandered into either of them.'

'She couldn't get down the borehole.' Chorleigh snorted. 'The police did look down the old well when she first went missing, but they didn't find anything.'

'But it was always covered?'

He shook his head. 'Not always. The stable hands and gardeners used to take water for the garden and for mucking out the stable from there.' He waved a hand at the samples. 'What are you looking for?'

'They found a film case full of water in Lara's camera case. There were unusual spores from a few types of plant in there but the water was surprisingly clean, no chlorine, very low levels of contaminants.'

'Like our bore water? I know that's very clean, we get it checked every now and then.'

'Perhaps.' She lifted her bag onto her shoulder.

He seemed to wrestle with himself. 'You can come indoors, if you like. I'll get cleaned up, make some tea.'

She hesitated as he stomped towards the house, his boots shedding mud from the recent storms. Hamish barked around him, loving the game. Chorleigh might have frightened her last night, but he hadn't meant to. She followed him. The idea of using the scope in a well-lit room was appealing and she didn't have time to go back to the lab before the meeting. He'd never threatened her and it would only take a few minutes.

While Chorleigh went upstairs with a handful of clothes plucked from the airer in the kitchen, she sat at the table and got the microscope out. Dropping a sample onto a clean slide, she looked through the lens.

The specimen from the outside well was teeming with organisms; the rotting cover itself must have fed the well with nutrients as well as insects that had fallen in. It had a slight cloudiness, a hint of brown colouration. There were a few ovals, like green rugby balls that were large enough to be algae but too big to be moss spores. In the sample from Lara's camera, there were just two species. This water definitely wasn't a match.

The other sample was clear and, when she examined it under different magnifications from ten to forty she couldn't find much of anything in it. Higher magnification suggested a few bacteria, but they were too small to identify, nothing like the spores that Trent had picked up.

'Well?' Chorleigh had showered and dressed, and was towelling his hair dry when he walked back into the kitchen. 'Is it the well or the borehole?'

'Neither. I think you should cover the well with something better, though, for Hamish's safety. Wells can be dangerous.' She shivered down the memory of the well collapsing the year before.

'I will.' He hesitated, staring at the microscope.

'Would you like to have a look?' He didn't say anything, but moved a step closer. She pushed the scope over. 'This is your borehole water. It's clean. Better than tap water, really.'

He angled his head to look through the lens. 'I can't see anything.'

'That's good.' She swapped slides. 'Now try *this*, the water from the old well.'

A smile creased his face and he looked back at Sage. 'Good God.'

'I know. It's organic soup. The water saturates the soil

and collects bacteria and bugs from the ground, from the farmed land, animal dung, decaying plants, anything in the soil.'

'No wonder they dug the borehole. They bought the land when the family who owned the farm here died out. No sons to carry on the family business, they broke the farm up into several parcels and sold it. My great-grandfather bought this plot and built the house.'

She smiled back at him. 'If they were using that well we know why they died out.'

His smile faded. 'But there's nothing to explain the girl's disappearance?'

'No.' She started packing up the microscope. 'Lara's camera was found some way away. If we identify the spring it came from, we might be able to place her after she was at the bus stop. Actually, can I have a quick look at the barrows? There's running water there too.'

'They want to excavate the barrows properly,' he said, looking haunted.

'Who?'

'I don't know, some government department. They want to see all the finds I gave you, and look at the drawings. And now you've dug up the bones, too, they will want to see them.'

'Is that OK with you?'

He shrugged. 'It's not just my history, it belongs to the New Forest. I thought, if you have time, you could have a look over the letter for me. I don't want to agree to having the thing destroyed. They can't do it without my permission, can they?'

She was touched. 'Of course not. But they won't destroy the barrows at all. It would be a lot less invasive than the first dig.'

'Well, I think there's been enough damage done. I'm donating all the finds and skeletons as well.' He took a deep breath. 'In fact, I'm thinking of selling up.'

Sage sat back. 'Wow. I think that's a great idea.'

He looked out of the window. 'The thing is, I'd hate to leave the animals behind. No one's going to look after them.'

'I suppose you could sell the house with a nice bit of garden and keep the land. If you wanted to, you could even set up a nature reserve.'

He thought about it. 'You're right. I could. There's thirty-five acres of woodland, and about three acres of garden. It wouldn't cost that much to separate them and fence them off. That way I'd have a say on the barrows' future.' He sighed. 'This house hasn't been an easy place for me.'

She looked around. 'I imagine a house this big in the New Forest would be worth a packet.'

'I could give my mother some money.' He looked at the floor, his voice rougher. 'And my sister. My father didn't leave either of them a penny. It's made them bitter towards me.'

'Have you had any recent contact with your mother?'

He shrugged. 'Only when he died. Then her solicitor

contacted me. But I thought they were probably after the money. That's what he always said, she always wanted something from him.'

'Maybe she was as much a victim as you were.'

He shrugged. 'Maybe. But she could have taken me with her. Why did she take my sister and not me?'

Sage shook her head. She couldn't imagine leaving Max, especially with an abusive partner. 'How about your sister?'

'She did ask me questions about the Lara Black thing when we met. She didn't believe me when I told her what happened.' He sat down at the table, opposite Sage. 'I don't remember much about it. There are things, but I can't place the sequence they happened in.'

Sage tensed inside. She knew he had never talked to the police about Lara, his father's solicitor had made certain of that. 'What do you mean?'

'By the time I was questioned I was too ill to remember. I'd had a bang on the head the day after she disappeared, I was in hospital for a little while. I can't remember how long even, but I was in a rehab place afterwards for brain-injured people.'

'How did you hit your head?'

He shook his head. 'I really don't know. I thought afterwards that maybe it was my father, although he'd never hurt me that badly before. But then I was told I might have had a kick from the horses. Apparently I was found outside the stable the day after Lara disappeared, unconscious.'

'Don't you remember Lara at all?'

'Oh, I knew her, sort of. We used to say hello on the bus. I saw her at college occasionally; her older brother was in the year above me. He was a bully, I got teased a lot.' He shook his head. 'They knew I'd been expelled from my old school.'

Sage waited for him to collect his thoughts. She packed the scope into its case, her pulse starting to skip in her throat.

'I know I got off the college bus at the roundabout and walked up the road,' he said. 'There's a forest bus, but it just goes between the villages, it's not very frequent. She was standing at the bus stop; she must have missed one and the next one was an hour later.'

'So that's where you saw her.'

His face was different, his expression cold. 'She called me over.' He frowned, staring out of the window. 'Someone driving by saw us, but I was just talking. They said that.' He shook his head. 'She was flirting with me. She was pretty.'

Sage swallowed. 'That's natural, isn't it, to flirt?'

'I can tell you what I think happened.'

Sage nodded. The atmosphere had darkened as he wrestled with the difficult memory.

'I think she asked to see the horses,' he said. 'Because I do remember showing them to a girl and I never talked to anyone else. I know the horses were still there then, because I told her their names. Jenny and Brutus.' He seemed to be lost in the past. 'Every day I would get feed, fill up the water then I'd give them a good brush and turn them back out if the weather was good. After college, I'd get them back in, dry them off and water them. I remember her talking to the horses while I went to get water.'

Sage lifted her bag onto her shoulder and waited.

He seemed to look inward, turning away from Sage, his voice small. 'I must have been coming back with the buckets, when I heard something. A scream, a shout, but cut off. I wasn't sure if it was her. I thought it could be a bird or an animal. I searched around but she was gone and her bag was just there, on the barrow. Her rucksack. I don't remember a camera, but I think she had something on a strap around her neck.'

An idea started to germinate in Sage's brain. 'But where was the bag?'

'On the smaller barrow, on the top. You get a good view of the church and the farm from there.'

She headed for the door. 'I need to see the barrows.'

'I'll come with you.'

'No! I mean,' she said, with a weak smile, 'I'm just checking something. I'm going to get a quick sample of the water dripping out of the barrow into that muddy patch. Then I'll come straight back.'

He shrugged, hunching his shoulders up as if he was hurt. 'My memory is all mixed up.' He frowned, shuffled his feet. 'Head injuries do that, they said. I do remember lying on the ground, stunned. Everything was red, I was covered in blood, the paramedic was there.'

Sage stared up at him as he took a deep breath, looking at the ground.

'I think my father hurt me,' he whispered. 'Why would he do that? I did everything he said.'

'Of course you did.'

'I didn't touch the girl.' He looked straight at Sage. 'But my father blamed me, he accused me…' He seemed lost in some dark pain of his own.

Sage backed out onto the front doorstep. 'Don't worry about that now, we'll sort it all out. You were living with a cruel bully, you were very young.'

'I didn't do anything to Lara. I'm telling the truth. I just moved her bag to the bus shelter so I wouldn't get accused of stealing it.'

'I believe you.' She stumbled a little on the rough ground beyond the steps. 'She might have come back for it.'

He walked towards her with an odd expression on his face. 'But now you know about Lara. I didn't tell anyone else. Do you think I should have told the police? They might have found her.'

'I don't know. You did what you could at the time – you did what you were told.'

His face was different now, focused, anger twisting his mouth. 'I shouldn't have told you about the horses.' There was something familiar about his expression, she'd seen it before on Elliott's face as he told her he was going to cut her baby out of her. She started backing away.

'No one blames you for the horses,' she said, and even as she heard the words she started to wonder. The animals were tortured in the forest after he was excluded from school… 'Alistair, it was such a long time ago.'

'They blamed me at school for "inappropriate behaviour" with a pony,' he said, following her. 'I didn't even hurt it, really. But they expelled me, and my dad beat me. He made me work on the land; he said he would kill me if I touched our horses so I never did. Not our own animals.'

Had the animal abuse started at school, with this lonely, rage-filled boy? Sage's reaction must have shown in her face because he reached for her, his face twisted into something like madness. He was between her and the car; instinctively Sage flinched away from him and bolted. His arm lashed out to grab her, his hand looking enormous as the fingers brushed her coat. She dropped her bag and ran back, away from Chorleigh in the front garden, stumbling instead between the trees, along what might have been a rabbit path. *God, where is the path to the barrows?*

She could get out onto the field, across to the farm. She was younger, faster. She could hear him shouting behind her, bellowing her name. She felt in her coat pocket for her phone but almost stumbled. There, through a veil of brambles, the path that had been widened to the stable. She scrambled through almost as Chorleigh started crashing through the trees behind her. The clear grass helped her lengthen her pace down the track. Surely she could outrun an alcoholic fifteen years her senior. She took the left-hand path that bypassed the stable, those poor, dead horses, and headed for the taller of the two features, the possible well head, close to the fence.

It had started raining while they were indoors, now water dripped from the branches. A pheasant burst from the long grass, screeching his warning, making her slip on the wet ground. A hand to a sapling was the only thing that stopped her falling over. She took a moment to listen for Chorleigh. She couldn't hear him, but he knew the grounds better than she did. There was a strange light in the woodland, the sun shining through thin cloud. Looking over her shoulder she could just see the house through the trees. For a moment it looked derelict, every window black. She pushed past a bush that had thorns everywhere, a few spiking her sleeve, then letting go as she jogged towards the barrows.

A snapped branch behind her was close, too close. The stab wounds on the necks of the horses leapt into her mind, as well as the memory of a kitchen knife held by Elliott as he threatened to cut her baby. The thought gave her a last burst of desperate energy as she gasped for breath, staggering into the clearing in front of the barrows. Had Alistair chased Lara up here, had she had the same idea of getting away?

She couldn't hear Chorleigh now, and dragged her phone out. No signal, but she knew it had worked before on top of the half-barrow. If Alistair did appear she was right next to the boundary and could get through the rusty wire and away. She lurched up the slope, tripping on the long grass and brambles that seemed to have sprung back since they left the site.

The sounds were different now, the dripping intense; the birdsong seemed to have stopped. She could feel something building inside her, a feeling that she was being watched. She whirled around but the only sound was her own shortened breathing and the water spilling into the pond. A few drops of rain spattered her face. She could just see the top of the stable roof. There was a creepy atmosphere around the remains of the building; even though taking the doors off had collapsed the whole front, the rest of it was held up by the bushes growing through it.

She looked at her phone, seeing one bar coming and going. *I just need one minute*, Sage thought, spinning around, trying to get a good signal. She dialled 999 anyway. 'Hello? Hello…' The signal cut out and she dialled again. She spun around on the grass, and Chorleigh was there, next to the other barrow, looking up at her.

She waved the phone. 'I've called the police, OK? You can't chase me like that. You're scaring me for nothing.'

'You'll tell them about the horses and Lara.'

'I don't *know* anything, Alistair,' she shouted. 'I believe you don't know what happened to Lara.' She took a step back, onto the flat stone that slightly overhung the dripping cut edge of the well head. The hard surface was slippery and she stumbled to one knee, dropping her phone. It just missed falling off the edge into the deep puddle. The water was filthy. *This didn't fill Lara's camera case*, she realised, the irrelevant thought cutting through her terror. She could see dark foliage spilling from the stone box, bursting out of the slot between them like gushing green water. The roof across the top projected out about a foot. She snatched her phone up and scrambled back to her feet as he walked to the bottom of the slope.

'Alistair, you have to stop this, you're scaring me!' She dialled again, 999. The operator answered promptly, just as Sage got both feet squarely on the capstone and shouted into the phone. 'This is Sage Westfield, I need the police at Chor—' before the phone beeped again and she was cut off.

His face was distorted, hostile. 'I didn't want to hurt you, I liked you. But you can't tell anybody about the horses.' He began stomping up the barrow, struggling with the incline and the weeds. He was fatter, older and out of condition. Sage backed up along the stone until one of her heels just slid an inch over the edge.

She glanced down at the drop behind her. She could see where algae ran down the line between the two upright stones, and had assumed it leaked out. But the join between the stones was tight, and packed with foliage, so water ran out of the top.

The plants were long strands of moss and lichens drooping into the muddy pool. From this angle she could see where the water poured out like a crystal sheet through the plants. Clean water with moss spores...

The wind blew her hood over the back of her head and a few heavy drops hit her waterproof jacket. 'Stop!' she shouted at Chorleigh, holding out her hand. Miraculously, he did. He was five metres away, maybe six, his arms out to stop her getting past, as if he was corralling her to the top.

Sage looked around. The fence seemed close; maybe if she took a run and jumped off the barrow she could clear the barbed wire. She took a step onto the middle of the stone to get a run up, trying to estimate the distance. *Too far, and you'll hit the fence and then he'll be there...*

She felt something move, jerk a few millimetres, before the slab she was standing on leaned abruptly. She staggered back, the stone tipping up a few inches, and dropped her phone at her feet. While she flailed about, trying to get her balance, the whole lid of the barrow flipped up. She dropped onto her back and slid feet first into a void, cutting off her view of Alistair Chorleigh. As she fell, arms fighting to catch the edge, she caught the back of her head and saw stars. The centre of the stone must have been pivoted somehow, the edges had had a few millimetres clearance all round. She'd never stepped on the centre before. She cracked one elbow on the edge but the other hand couldn't reach the opposite side – as she dropped into darkness.

# 34

'Many kistvaens are to be found on Dartmoor, in Devon, England. No doubt many lie undisturbed beneath the undulating scrub and pasture, remains of ancient man inhumed within.' [Is this a kist? EM]

*The Reliquary and Illustrated Archaeologist, Volume 1,* by J C Cox
and J Romilly Allen, quoted in margin of Edwin Masters' Journal,
12th July 1913

Yesterday I was looking through the many pottery fragments we have, trying to collect together pieces that might come from the same large pot, perhaps another funerary urn. I was allowed to use the breakfast table, it was late afternoon. The French doors were open to the garden and now and then a bumblebee would fly in, intoxicated by the roses outside whose scent drifted around the room. I suddenly noticed Molly, leaning against the door. I thought, as I stood back, how pretty she looked, her summer dress so covered in flowers I was surprised the bees didn't follow her. I said something like it, just joking.

'I'm glad you like it.' She didn't smile.

'What is it, Molls?' I asked, quite like a brother. 'You seem a little worried. Is it all the silly teasing?' For her cousin Hilda and that spiteful Trixie were always joking her.

'No. No, it's not that.' She stared at me. Her eyes are blue, like Peter's, although I fancy hers are a little more grey. They both have a brown ring around the edge of the iris. Her hair is fairer than his, just a little, and although short, the curls frame her face.

'Well, can I help? I know I'm not a proper brother like Peter, but I would like to help.' Should I have guessed? I think so, yet when she spoke I was taken aback.

'I don't want you to be my brother.' She took a step into the room. 'You haven't spoken to me about last night, in the storm.' She stood in front of me, her hands folded before her as if she expected a scolding.

'You were upset.' I saw it even as I spoke. 'I can't hold you to anything you did when so distressed.'

'I was. But you kissed me.' She managed a small smile. 'I waited for you to say something. All day. I thought you liked me.'

'I do like you!' I was blurting things out. 'I just – I didn't know what to say.'

'Didn't you like kissing me?'

I looked at her, but anything of that thrill was gone. 'Of course. But I can't offer you anything, I have no prospects. I shouldn't have taken advantage of your distress.'

She stepped very close. I could see her eyelashes, shading her cheekbones. 'I'm not distressed now.'

Her lips were so pink, her cheeks too. Something stopped me leaning down to them. 'I like you, of course I like you, Molly. But I think of you as my friend.'

She put a hand on my chest, the fingers splayed against my shirt. 'What about now?'

I felt miserable; I didn't know what to say. Why didn't I love this beautiful creature, so much my friend? The excitement in the dark, in the storm, had gone.

'I'm sorry, Molly. I'm afraid I'm not really a ladies' man.'

She dropped her hand to her side, her face bright red, tears in her eyes. 'I suppose you think I'm too young.'

'Yes. Yes! You are too young. Molly, you shouldn't be thinking about chaps, you should be looking at a future. Go to university, take a degree, meet lots of new people. You'll soon see how old and stuffy I am.'

She wiped away a tear. 'You're five years older than me. I don't think that's very old.'

'But our lives have been so different. Molly, I haven't lived like you, I don't live in the same world. My mother and I have four rooms in Colchester, every penny we had spare went on my education. Now I will have to earn enough money to support both of us. I couldn't even think about getting married.'

'I wasn't thinking about getting married!' She gulped down her tears, her face red with anger now. 'I just thought you liked me. But I understand.'

I was mortified. I had hurt her, all without trying. I could see the pain on her face, and I had caused it. 'Molly, I'm sorry.' I took a breath. 'It's just that I think it would be dishonest to lead a girl on.'

'You really are a fossil, aren't you?' She had backed up to the doorway. 'My father warned me away from you.'

'Did he? I'm sure he was trying to be helpful.'

There was a long silence when we just looked at each other. I couldn't look away, and she was fighting tears.

She stared at me as if she could suddenly see something new. 'It's true, isn't it? Men falling in love with men.'

I stood, shaking my head. 'I don't know what you mean.'

'Peter's friend in the village, the chemist. He left a picture of Peter.'

I was puzzled. 'What do you mean?'

She had something in her hand and held it out. Tears were spilling onto her cheekbones. 'Peter didn't write back to him, so he sent it to me. He says he'll send more to father or the police if Peter doesn't meet him.'

I glanced at the shadowy, grainy image. Two young men, certainly, lying together in an embrace. I felt a shiver run through my chest. I understood then that

Goodrich was a blackmailer.

'You have to understand, Peter was very young and this Goodrich took advantage of him. He must have set up a camera and staged the shot.'

The curve of a chin, laughing eyes under a shock of fair hair looking back over his shoulder into the camera. The other boy's face was hidden, his hand resting casually at Peter's waist. I was filled with dark emotion, some anger, something else. Shameful jealousy.

I struggled with my fears. 'There must be an explanation for this photograph. Swimming in the river, perhaps, you can see they were outside.' Peter must have been very young and ignorant to allow these photographs.

Molly dashed away a tear. 'And that's why you don't like me. You and Peter—'

'Are friends and no more, I swear to you.' I stepped forward, took the picture from her. 'Molly, there are men who are a little cold-blooded, who don't fall in love easily.' I felt like I was scolding her so I moderated my tone. 'I do care for you, and am terribly upset to know I have hurt you.' I stood before her, and held out my hands. 'Come, can't we be friends?'

She put her cold little fingers in mine for a moment. 'I'm sorry,' she whispered.

'And so am I,' I said. But when she left, turned and fled from me to run upstairs, I was left in turmoil. I looked at the picture, grainy and underexposed as it was. Beautiful in his youthful nakedness, it was unmistakably Peter. I slipped it into my journal and packed up the last of the pottery in the boxes. I had thought my feelings might have turned to Molly naturally, but he was my ideal companion, cheerful enough to pull me out of my darker moments. He shared my greatest interests. My father described how, under fire in the war, he had formed his closest friendships. In fact, one of his friends was now the patron who had secured my place at university. But that photograph burned something dark and arousing into my brain. I knew, in that instant, that I wanted Peter.

I half walked, half ran onto the terrace and around the tennis court. I don't know what it was that I meant to do, just speak to him, say something that wouldn't repulse him completely. The light was fading, the sky a deep blue. The first stars were out as I ran through the long grass on the lawn; it had been too wet to mow after the storm. When I came out of the woodland onto the flank of the barrow, I could see the fields beyond, and shadows under the trees along the hedge. Peter was standing beside the fence in his shirtsleeves, and he turned as I approached. He didn't say anything, just reached out a hand, the pale fingers in my brown palm, and he smiled.

'Here,' he whispered, so close to my ear that he brushed my hair. 'Lie down so they don't see you.' He pointed to the side of the barrow.

So I laid down, my heart almost bursting with love for him, and we waited for our eyes to adjust to the dusk as he released my hand. He pointed and my gaze followed the line of his finger. There, a branched head was lifted, as if to scent the air, on the other side of the field. Then another, his ears flicking back against the sky at the edge of the field, where it sloped up to a small rise. I rolled onto my side, listening to his breathing. It was then that I heard him rustle as he moved closer, felt his warmth as he brushed my face with his hair.

'Ed?' He didn't say anything else, just leaned over me. I felt his breath on my face as he came close. I froze, shut my eyes. Then he kissed me.


What else can I say? We talked, laid in each other's arms, occasionally pointing out a new constellation, freezing at any sounds. The grass was still wet from the storm, so he laid a jacket on the ground for us and for a while, we were happy. Then he lay on his back and lit a cigarette, I could see it blowing above his head.

After a time, he grew quiet and tense.

'Come on, old chap,' I said. 'You can tell me anything. Anything, you know that. What's troubling you?'

He looked at me, hesitated for a long moment. 'It's nothing, really.'

'It's Goodrich, isn't it? I know.'

I knew I had hit the mark by the way he sighed. 'He has some pictures of me. He took them years ago when we were just boys.' He looked away. 'I don't want my father to find out.'

I knew how Mr Chorleigh felt about men who loved men. 'What does Goodrich want?'

'He's asking for money, but if I give him some he'll keep coming back for more. I was stupid.'

'You were too young to know what he might do, maybe, but if this Goodrich is holding them over you, can't you go to the police? That's blackmail, surely—'

'God, no!' Peter leaned in and hissed at me. 'Ed, do I have to spell it out? Those pictures are evidence of a crime.'

Some intense emotion I didn't recognise swept through me. 'I have one of the prints.'

'What?'

I turned onto my stomach on the sloping grass. 'Goodrich sent one to Molly, who showed me. She was worried for you. I have it in my journal.'

Peter looked down and pressed his lips together for a moment. 'Poor girl.' He looked up at me, his face tense. 'I suppose that conversation at breakfast made her think about Goodrich and me. Oh, God, what if she tells someone else?'

'But Goodrich—'

'Damn Goodrich!' Peter turned towards me with such anger I started back, reminded of his father for a second. 'I'll deal with him. It's Molly I'm worried about.'

I waited in the dark, hearing his breathing slow down again. 'How did it start?'

'I always knew I liked other men; I fell in love with boys at school. I have always liked girls of course, Trixie is tremendous fun, but I have never wanted to kiss her. She thinks I am frightfully old-fashioned, poor girl. I have never even tried to put my hand on her knee, let alone seduce her away for a secret weekend.'

'But your family thinks you will marry her.'

'I suppose I will one day.' He sounded sad. 'I thought I would start to see things as other men do, over time.' He ran his hand over my bare chest, tangling his fingers in the curls there, making me shiver. 'But I haven't changed at all, in fact, the opposite.' He found his way to my lips for another kiss, making me groan, whether with passion or despair I'm not sure. Both, perhaps.

'Peter—' I started to say, but he interrupted me.

'Lots of fellows – chaps like us – marry girls. It seems like a sham, but we can't risk being discovered.' He sighed.

I hardly knew what to call it. I knew what we had done was illegal although I couldn't name it. Yet what harm could kissing and touching each other really cause anyone else? 'What do we do now? I don't want to leave you.'

'We'll find a way to meet.' He picked a blade of grass and ran it over my lips. I held my breath, lost in the sensation. 'Matt Goodrich was a good sort, at least to start with. But now he wants money. It seemed like harmless fun at the time. We were so young.'

'What will you do?'

Peter rolled onto his back. 'I will have to pay him, I suppose. At least enough to keep him quiet.'

'Will Molly say anything?'

'No, I don't think so, if I talk to her.' Peter sounded sad. 'I know she won't want to get me into trouble. Do you have it safe?'

'In my journal, which I normally carry with me back and forth to the barrows.'

'She's got it bad for you, poor kid.' He stood up, and I watched him brushing himself down in the moonlight. 'I'll go in the back door, you go in the front in a few minutes. Say you were clearing up here.'

I was cold inside as I sat up. 'But what are we to do now? I must see you again, but my mother can never know. It would kill her.'

'Mine, too. She has such hopes for me now my sister has gone.'

We fumbled our dew-damp clothes on and wandered back through the trees, Peter leading me by my hand in case I walked into a branch. When we reached the edge of the lawn we spontaneously let go.

'What shall we do?' Soon I will have to go back to stay with my mother. I might never see him again, unless we arrange a sordid little rendezvous and pretend to be brothers, or make up some other subterfuge, so we can share a room.

'We'll find a way to be together,' Peter said, his voice

drifting back to me in the darkness. 'When Claire died, I resolved never to let life slip away again.' His teeth gleamed in the light from the hall. 'We shall be Alexander and Hephaestion.'

'Achilles and Patroclus,' I said. 'And we know what happened to them.'

He laughed then, not his carefree voice but a tired chuckle. 'A heroic death awaits.'

The next morning, I tried not to look at Peter or act in any way differently. He was in a teasing mood, so I frowned at him and concentrated on my breakfast. Before we finished our meal, a letter was brought over from Fairfield.

'Oh, what a nuisance,' he said. 'I forgot that I had promised to take the girls riding over to the big house.' The 'big house', I knew, was the local manor and an invitation there was virtually an order to troops. 'Hilda can't have told them you were still here, or you would have been invited too. I'm sure they wouldn't mind if you turn up.'

'I have a lot of work to do here,' I said. 'Not least to stop the gardeners taking more spoil to level up the tennis court. I was hoping to examine at the top of the cistern, to see if we can have another look inside.'

'Well, I shall only stay for lunch. I'll be back by three, and we can have a look together.'

The maid, who had brought the letter, curtsied. 'Mr Peter, we was wondering when those bones were going to be properly buried? In a churchyard, like proper Christians.'

'I'm afraid the man was born many years before Christ, Tilly, and the wolf was never a Christian.'

'It's just unseemly. Cook says,' she qualified her answer.

'Well, you'll be glad to know the bones will be reburied somewhere very safe,' Peter compromised. 'Could you get me my kit bag? The one I took to the cadet training.'

The girl disappeared upstairs. I brushed my toast crumbs off my hands. 'What are you thinking?'

'It's a good, thick bag. It should take both skeletons, and we can bury them under the roses or something, and dig them up when we have more time to examine them. Or when my father agrees to let them go to a museum.'

I thought it a good plan: the bag would certainly protect the remains for a decade or more. I went off to the excavation with Peter's cheerful goodbyes ringing in my ears. I shall tuck this journal in my bag and carry it with me. I couldn't bear for it to be read by another, now, nor the picture found. In the meantime, I will take the professor's advice and just dig around the flat stone at the top of the well head. I think we might find a way to see into the stone chamber and complete the puzzle.

\* \* \*

## *Later*

I hardly know how to write this. I was excavating around the flat stone right at the top of the well head, for it seemed to me that we might be able to peer down the crevice beside it into the two shafts that seemed to make up the well. Something happened, and I woke here, scrabbling blindly in the almost dark. Fortunately, I still had my bag and the remains of a pencil that I stuck behind my ear. I fear my legs are hurt, I cannot move either, although I am wedged almost upright between the sides of the shaft. Above me is the faintest grey light, filtered through the grasses and moss that grow there, barely enough to see what I have written. I have shouted, but no one comes, I do not know how long I have been down here. Perhaps Peter has stayed on for dinner at Fairfield, perhaps it is earlier than I think. I cannot know how long I have been here and my watch is smashed. There is some water by my knees; I have been able to soak my sleeve in it and drink a little. I shall not die here. Peter will see what has happened and come.

# 35

It felt like Sage was being kicked and punched as she fell, darkness enveloping her, slipping down a narrowing shaft. She was abruptly stopped by the shock and splash of ice-cold and her feet finding a solid surface under the water. It immersed her as she crumpled in the narrow space, held up by one arm caught above her. She exhaled a cloud of bubbles as the breath was shocked out of her, and a bolt of pain shot through her snagged arm. One foot pushed against the floor and she stood up, forcing her head and shoulders above the water's surface. She gulped a few breaths of air, reaching up with her left hand to feel along her right arm, caught somehow above her. She couldn't move it at first, wedged as she was in the narrow space. She couldn't pull on it, it was like red-hot nails digging into her shoulder, but with the other hand she could wiggle it in the darkness and finally free it, every movement sending white-hot flashes into her fingers. Her arm slid to her chest where she cradled it with the other. Her shoulder felt dislocated. The pain was agony, burning in torn muscles and tendons. A dull grinding on the front of her chest suggested she'd broken something, collarbone maybe, on the same side.

'Help. Help!' she managed to shout, but nothing came back. *God, she was under tons of soil and who knows how deep underground. This must be what happened to Lara. She died here, probably drowned or hit her head, died of shock.*

It was already starting to spit rain when Sage had run from Chorleigh, it could fill up. Was there even a way out? She thought about the slot at the top, where the water trickled out.

She tried to remember how wide and deep it was – it was shrinking in her mind. No, she had seen it from the ground and thought she could get her head and shoulders in, so it must be reasonably big, but she couldn't even see it. She started to feel down her legs with her good hand, checking for injuries. She was standing on a tiny patch of flat stone, on her left foot. She staggered around to find another footrest ninety degrees to the right. She could push up but only gained a few inches. She stepped back onto her left foot, feeling the cold water sloshing around her chest. Cold. She could die of hypothermia or pass out and drown. At least the water had broken her fall; she could have smashed both ankles.

She leaned her head back to look up into the darkness, the pain in her shoulder making her catch her breath, stopping her reaching any higher. She could feel something warm trickling down her head, tickling around her ear; she must have cut her scalp. She dared not try and use her injured arm in case the dizziness returned; she was terrified she would pass out and drown. Instead, she tried to calm down, concentrate on looking around.

The darkness was so intense it felt like it was pressing against her eyes. But tipping her head back further, ouch, ouch, her shoulder screaming at her not to move her neck – up there was a tiny hint of light. Just a triangle of grey, slowly brightening as she stared. It wasn't quite overhead, there was something in the way, like the shaft wasn't quite upright. She rested her bad arm at her waist and reached out with her other hand. The rock wasn't carved out; she could feel how rough it was, it felt like a natural surface. This was the nightmare that woke her shaking and sweating: falling into a well in the dark. She swallowed the panic down.

Was it a well? She could feel rubble around her ankles, she only had room to stand on one foot and the muscles in her other leg were cramping. She used her other foot to feel about. There were what she thought were rounded rocks, but they were lighter; they moved away when her toe nudged them. Bones, maybe, of animals that had fallen in the top as she had done. God, maybe Lara's remains, maybe even Edwin's. She was able to push her foot up the wall enough to get her other foot to the ground, a relief immediately. Her muscles were stiff from the cold.

'Help! Alistair?'

Nothing. Her voice echoed around her, suffocating her with sound. She could hear something feeble in her tone, something weakened by the cold. Shock, maybe. She didn't know how much of her message the 999 operator had received. Maybe none, maybe they would think it was a prank call.

She took a deep breath and screamed. It was more of a croak at first, but a sip of water helped. It was cold and tasted very clean, like spring water. Like the water in Lara's camera case, maybe, which made her feel even more sick. She found her voice and managed three banshee screeches. *I'll scream every minute. Someone will come.*

Did Lara fall in the same way? Sage was aware of the clunking rounded shapes beneath her feet. Maybe they were skulls – it was impossible to tell through her boots. Did Chorleigh know, did he watch Lara fall and not get help?

He was terrified of his father. So frightened that he didn't tell people what had happened. Perhaps she had been stuck here too, waiting to be rescued, waiting for Alistair to tell people where she had last been seen. Chorleigh had chased Sage up the barrow, and it swallowed her up.

Thoughts spun around her head as she tried to get a better balance on the uneven stone. *Stay positive, keep motivated, don't give up.* She could feel the shock and cold starting to drain away her energy. She thought of Nick and Max teasing her, laughing over bubbles in the bath, asleep together on her ridiculous sofa. She looked up again, even though it pulled horribly on her chest muscles and stabbed through her injured shoulder. The pain, at least, kept her awake. There was a ray of faint light coming in, in strips. The moss, the overhang. The letterbox slot that might be the only way out. Maybe Lara's camera case had been washed out, the film case full of water, after she died.

A band of stinging pain around her shoulder blades made her pull up again. The water was rising. Shit, the cold was already numbing her legs and now it was going to drown her. Her heart clunked in her chest like a machine winding down, and she took a few breaths to control it. At least the trickling from her head had stopped. *Calm, relax, prevent shock. Then scream.* She tried again, except the sound came out more like a wheeze.

She couldn't climb up to the top of the shaft, her arm was agony already and she couldn't feel footholds. Except one, the first one she had felt. She moved her foot around, scraping it up the rock face. There, a tiny ledge under the toe of her boot. She was lighter now, the water was holding a lot of her weight, she realised, more than before. She pushed herself up a foot, the weight dragging on her injured shoulder and collarbone, flashing stars in her vision.

'Help!' It was a croak. She cleared her throat and went for a scream. Her voice was rusty, small, but after a few breaths she got a bit of a screech going.

The water didn't make any sound as it rose up. It must be over an artesian spring or something charged by the water table. She remembered Trent suggesting it, that maybe it was some sort of water tank. It was lifting her, slowly, even as it sapped her strength away. She remembered reading somewhere that when a person stopped shivering they were in trouble.

*I'm going to die before I get to the top.*

For a moment she rested her head against the cool rock. She just needed one free arm. She lowered the damaged arm into the water, feeling first the agony then a welcome coolness as the water rolled over her collarbone. The fingers on the injured side didn't work properly, perhaps she had damaged a nerve somewhere. She fumbled in her pocket with the other hand. Her phone would be drowned and wouldn't get a signal here anyway. A handful of evidence bags, let go into the black water. Car keys, a pen, a couple of soaked tissues. There, the scarf she usually carried stuffed into her pocket. She dragged it out, grateful it wasn't on the other side, and with a little help from her slow fingers on the bad arm managed to tie a rough knot in it. Pulling it over her head was difficult; she didn't see an outcrop of rock by her head and whacked her elbow on it, but having put the sling around her neck she could lift her arm into it. The pain made her scream, and she added a few extra swear words to help. Maybe someone would hear her cursing if they didn't hear the shrieks.

One hand free, one foot on the foothold, she shuffled about for another. There was a tiny ledge a little behind her. She could see the glimpses of the greyness above, obscured by another rock formation. She flailed around with her dangling foot, trying to find the ledge. One end of the ridge was bigger and higher, and with some effort and pulling up with her good hand she managed to get half out of the water. It was difficult standing on a few frozen toes, braced against the side with her other foot. She started to shiver again and realised she would last longer out of the water.

She pushed up again, scraping the other foot around until she found a projection, just a few inches deep. Pulling with her good arm made her scream with pain and effort as the muscles contracted around her chest. Her wet coat was dragging on her injured side. Balancing on toes that were going numb, she managed to slide her bad arm out of the sling, using the pain to scream for help. Then she could slide that side of her jacket down, now saturated, and let it hang free from her other shoulder. It gave her a little padding as she leaned against the rough stone, trying to conserve some heat in it. The shivering was coming in painful spasms, her muscles locking up. She dropped the heavy coat and hauled herself up by her uninjured arm, pushing her legs to stretch her up a little more. The water was now just above her waist, but she could feel it creeping up again. She must be a couple of feet off the bottom, and another hard-won step up helped her find a handhold over her head.

The slot, a wedge of dull light above, seemed too small to get through. She wasn't sure how long she'd been in the water but it was getting dark outside. Overhead she could see an area of missing vegetation where the stone had pivoted, dropping her through the chimney at the back. She was clinging to the rock slab between the two shafts.

It took several more minutes of panting and struggling to find another handhold and one sharply inclined foothold. It dug into the ball of her foot and the other foot had nowhere to go so she shuffled the toe beside the other foot, fighting not to slip. Despite having crept up another couple of feet, the water was catching her up, she could feel it around her thighs. She thought of dropping into the water and letting it carry her up but it was so cold she knew she'd die of hypothermia long before she got to the top. The stone slot had been about twelve feet above her head, but she'd narrowed the distance to half that.

She bellowed as loud as she could but now her voice seemed to be swallowed up by the sides of the chamber, echoing inside her head rather than up to the top. She could feel the apex of the dividing wall and started to inch up towards it, the water dragging her back. She fumbled along the top of the sliver of rock, finding somewhere to grasp and pull up, feet scrambling for new footholds on the rough surface. Finally, she managed to get her good elbow onto the top and heaved until she was half lying on a piece of rock with a flattish edge maybe a foot wide. When she managed to get a good foothold she could kick herself further onto it, the bones in her broken arm grating together in a way that made her gasp and see sparkles in front of her eyes. *Don't faint, you'll fall back.*

She rolled onto the good side of her chest, pushing away from the rocky blackness of the chimney she had climbed, and rested. As her eyes adjusted and the lightshow subsided, she could see the faint greying of the wall above. She screeched again, wordless, but still no one came. How long had she been here? She tried to slow her breathing a little, let her heart catch up and stop knocking in her throat. They would look for her, maybe they had received the garbled call.

It took another few minutes to drag, wiggle and push herself further onto the narrow, slanting ledge. It was only about twelve inches deep, just enough to sit on precariously, while she examined her dangling arm. It felt like it had burning skewers shot through it, and her fingers were numb and limp. She tightened the sling and lifted her wrist up. Her fingers came back to life abruptly, with burning pins and needles.

'Help!' She was only four or five feet below the slit of grey light now. She screamed again, then caught her breath. Both legs were in the water, and a line of cold was working its way up her hip. The water was chasing her up; it would soon fill the whole cavity. She would have to try and stand on the sliver of rock and attempt to slide out.

The angle of the ledge was difficult to climb onto: one false move and she would drop back into the water. Her eyes could pick out the ragged feature behind her, a lump of rock sticking out, pushing her back towards the water. She tried to shuffle around to get one knee onto the rock but the pain made her head swim and the rocks shiver in front of her eyes. *Don't faint, you'll drown. Nick, Nick, Maxie, oh God...*

She coughed, the sound echoing around her. She reached out and caught a good handhold in front of her, a sharp spur on the other side. Thank God she hadn't fallen down that channel, she could have been impaled. She rested for a moment, trying to think. The slab on top had pivoted sharply. But they had been on the earthwork all week, hadn't they? She closed her eyes, trying to remember. Trent had been digging around it, on the barrow; she recalled seeing a line of soil scraped free on either side of the slab. She hadn't wanted to stand on it before, it was green with slippery algae. But when she did, it tipped her into the larger of two shafts. The ancient people who created the mound laid the rocks – could they have designed it to trap something?

She tried to ignore the pain in her shoulder and swung her second knee onto the outcrop, the rough edges biting into her skin through saturated jeans. The water was already several inches over the ledge as she shuffled on. Could she stand? It seemed like there was a handhold above her head, and she scraped one foot up, then pulled on the outcrop with her good arm. It was a lot harder than she expected. Her wet clothes made her feel heavier and the pain – and shock, probably – added to the cold to weaken her. Her foot slipped an inch and she gripped the handhold even harder, until she could balance on both feet. Standing, she could catch her breath.

The opening was only a little over her head but the letterbox-shaped gap was three feet away, on the other side of the other shaft, falling away into darkness. It looked smooth at the top and tapered in. There were no obvious handholds. She screamed again. 'Help! Help me, somebody, help me!'

She rested her chin on her hand, still clutching the handhold for balance. Did she hear something? Her heart hammered in her ears. She tried a rusty scream.

'Sage? Sage!' The voice, Felix's, was sharp with alarm and sounded far away. 'Where are you?'

'Inside the barrow, under the rock.' She could feel tears running down her face in relief, tickling her upper lip. 'The stone is loose at the top. Be careful.'

She could hear more shouting, like Felix was calling to other people.

'Sage, we're going to get you out.'

'I'm hurt.'

'We're coming. Here, Nick—' Felix must have turned away, the voice became muffled.

*Nick?* She rubbed her face on the sleeve of her jacket. 'Nick!' It was meant to be a scream but it was a hoarse whisper.

'Sage! I'm here.' The light above darkened for a moment

and she screamed. When she looked back up she could see a hand in the light. 'We've been looking for you for hours.'

'How long have I been down here?'

'It's late. You've been gone half the day.'

The water was already over her knees again. 'It's filling up with water. I'm afraid I'm going to drown.'

'We're going to get you out. We're getting the fire brigade. Just stay put and talk to me.'

Her fingers were going numb. Standing on a ledge put a lot of strain on the hand clinging to the sharp spur. 'I don't know how long I can stand here. I've hurt my arm and it's really narrow. I'm hanging on but it's so cold.'

'I understand. Just keep talking. We're just waiting for some equipment.'

She rested for a moment, her chest tight. 'I can't breathe,' she said, realising how hard it had become. 'I mean, I can but it's hard.'

'We'll have you out soon. I came in with Felix – we've been looking for you. Alistair Chorleigh is blind drunk but he mumbled something about the barrows.'

'He saw me fall in here. I think Lara Black fell in here too. It's some sort of trap.'

'Sage?' Felix's voice was deeper than Nick's. 'The fire brigade are on their way. Don't move.'

'I'm afraid I'll fall.' Her voice had become small and dreamy. 'I'm frozen. It's full of water.'

There was some scuffling and talking then the light

went altogether, which made Sage scream again. When it came back it was blinding. 'I can see an arm!' Nick shouted, and something warm grabbed her wrist. 'It's OK, it's me.'

She let go of the rock spur and turned her hand to grasp his fingers. Nick could reach in far enough to offer her comfort but she doubted he could hold her weight if she slipped.

'I do want to get married.' It was the first thing that rose to the top of her frozen brain.

There was a long silence as she fought for her balance, gripping his fingers.

'You have crazy timing.' Nick's voice was filled with something. Laughter, joy – he could do joy in a way that Max did, in a way that she held back from. 'Let's get you out in one piece first.'

Her fingers burned with cramp, pins and needles. Waves of nausea washed over her, she could hear a buzzing in her ears blocking Nick out. 'Nick…' She couldn't speak, the dizziness was washing over her.

'Sage! Stay with me. Felix…' She could hear him talking, but the cold was seeping into her. It was climbing now, up to her chest, leaching away her remaining energy. Her breaths sounded louder in her head. She wasn't shivering now, she felt oddly calm as she swayed on the ledge. Max, the baby, only he wasn't a baby any more. She could see him on Nick's lap, laughing, patting Nick's hands in some crazy rhyme he had made up. Dada, Dada, shouted louder and louder. Her hand slipped in Nick's, but it didn't matter, she was so cold it was almost warmer in the water, where she was numb. She balanced for a long moment, vaguely hearing shouting, seeing a crack of light above her head as the stone slid open slowly, a cascade of soil and mosses drifting onto her upturned face.

'Sage!'

The shouts were very far away now, lost in the humming in her ears. Her fingers relaxed, she could feel the grasp around her wrist tighten until it felt crushed in Nick's warm hand. She swayed again, this time feeling the rocks slip under her feet, under the cold, as she slid down. She thrashed her good hand away from Nick, scrabbling for the handhold but missed. The water closed over her head.

# 36

'The missing gentleman is named EDWIN MASTERS, late of Balliol College, Oxford, and recently a visitor at Chorleigh House on the Fairfield Road. We were called to the house on 12th July after Mr Masters was found to be absent after working on a prehistoric excavation he and Mr Peter Chorleigh were carrying out, with the landowner's permission. Mr Chorleigh raised the alarm when his friend could not be found. His jacket and spectacles were retrieved from the top of an earthwork the young gentlemen had been excavating. PC Evans noted that some digging was apparent on the top of another raised bank, which Mr Chorleigh had identified as an old well, but there was no obvious ingress and no one responded to our calls. The stones of said well were found to be wedged with stones and foliage and except for the digging, undisturbed. Upon questioning,

Mr James Chorleigh said his son and daughter (Mary) were on the train to Edinburgh, being called to a family emergency. Mr Masters' belongings have been packed up and are to be held for his return. Mr Chorleigh raised a question as to the young man's character.'

Police report, Sergeant Chance, Chilhaven Police

# 37

*Later, Wednesday 27th March, this year, in the barrow*

A pain through Sage's scalp brought her abruptly round, a burning in her throat forcing her to cough. A hand roughly fumbled under her injured arm and pulled. She screamed until he let go, her left hand grabbing the wrist of the person holding her hair. Hair that had enabled him to pull her head out of the water, anyway.

'Broken,' she spluttered. 'Shoulder, dislocated or broken.'

Another hand anchored her good wrist and started pulling. 'We have to get you out.' It was a strange voice, and for a moment a light attached to a helmet blinded her. 'This is going to hurt for a short time, but as soon as we get you out, we'll give you morphine and get you off to hospital.' He shouted something over his shoulder then turned back to her. 'Stay with me, Sage. A few more minutes and you'll be safe.'

He pulled and it felt like her good shoulder was coming

out of its socket before she got a foot onto the ledge, slipped off, found it again. 'Nick,' she mumbled.

'He's here, they're all here.' She could see the gleam of light on his teeth now.

'Don't fall on top of me.'

'I've got three burly lads holding me. All you have to do is let us pull you up. I can't put a chest harness on you, I think you've broken your collarbone, maybe more. So we'll try and drag you up by whatever we can reach.' He looked up. 'Wedge that stone open, lads, I want to bring her up the way she went in.'

At least she wouldn't have to slide out the letterbox slot. She screamed when they pulled again, her feet lifted off the ledge. Her teeth were chattering. 'I'm sorry, I'm sorry, just do it.'

The rescuer's face was just above hers, the tendons in his neck straining. 'A couple more and you'll be out. Two… three—'

This time she was prepared and managed to contain the scream to a groan, but another pair of hands reached for her clothes, half dragging her by her shirt and her wrist. Then she was face down on the grass of the barrow, sobbing with pain, rolling off her broken bones.

'Nick!'

'I'm here, it's going to be OK…'

She moved enough to throw up away from him.

The man with the torch leaned over her, handed her

something. 'Gas and air. It will help while we get you in the warm.' The shivering was back, great spasms that jolted her shoulder despite the pain relief. Lifting her onto the stretcher made the world white out with pain and she screamed again, but at least the ambulance was bright and warm. They were quick to start cutting her wet clothes off. Every inch of exposed skin was wrapped in blankets.

'Come in, mate.' She could see the rescuer now, in a fireman's uniform grinning down at her. 'Good luck, love. That was a tight squeeze, well done.'

'Thank you.' Tears seemed to flood down her face, scalding her cheeks.

'No trouble.' He disappeared and Nick leaned over her.

'Bloody hell, Sage, I thought that was it.' She could see tears dotting his long eyelashes.

'So did I.' She looked across at where a woman was poking at her arm with a needle. 'Ouch.'

'Sit still. You need some fluids.' The woman smiled at her. 'There you go. Now you can have some pain relief.'

Sage managed a tired chuckle. The warmth slowly invading her extremities was making them burn with pins and needles. 'Good.'

Nick stayed with her as her arm was strapped close to her body – another moment of unconsciousness – and she came around to the rattling of the ambulance in motion. Nick was still by her side. 'You're going to be all right,' he was saying. 'Everything will be OK now.'

The shivering had lessened but she was still cold. 'Hurts.'

'I know. But we'll get you to hospital, warm you up, fix your shoulder.' The pain receded, and the word that came to the top of the stack of things she could say was, 'Felix?'

'He worked out what might have happened. He thinks he knows what the barrow actually is.'

'Wolf trap,' she mumbled, lifting her head to look out of the open doors. 'Dark.'

'You've been gone hours. It's gone eleven.'

'Chorleigh. He hurt the horses in the forest.' She wasn't sure if the words all made it out but Nick was nodding.

'It's OK. We can talk about it later. Everything's going to be OK.'

'No, Alistair told me, then he chased me. He saw me fall into the barrow.'

'He did? He did mumble something about the barrow but he was very drunk.'

The paramedic squeezed something into her arm and a warm numbness spread through her body.

'You're OK,' Nick said. 'You can talk about this later.'

'Hm.' She felt the ambulance slow as she fell into sleep.

# 38

'Yesterday, a search was undertaken by the Chilhaven police and volunteers after the disappearance of an Oxford man, Edwin Masters. Mr Masters has not been seen since 12th July this year and has had no communication with friends or his family. Dog walkers joined the search of farmland and the common lands around Chorleigh House. No clues were found, and railway porters and omnibus drivers were questioned to no avail.

Mr Masters, a visitor at Chorleigh House for the summer, is of tanned complexion, with dark curly hair and brown eyes. Of average height, he is of stocky build and usually wears spectacles. He is twenty-two years old.

Mr James Chorleigh, the householder, had nothing to add to the investigation, and saw no advantage to further searching his lands after a thorough police examination.

Mr Masters' mother, Mrs Alice Masters, is staying in Lyndhurst and has offered a reward of fifty pounds to anyone offering information leading to the whereabouts of her son. Her maternal uncle, General John Bishop, provided the reward and is joining the search with his own men. Professor Robert Conway, of Balliol College, Oxford, is assisting the search and is supporting Mrs Masters. Her late husband, the Reverend William Masters was a chaplain in the Second Boer War, and died of wounds received in that campaign.

Please share any information about Mr Masters, no matter how small, with the Chilhaven police or with Mrs Masters at the White Hart Hotel, Lyndhurst.'

*The Fairfield Recorder*, 27th July 1913

# 39

*Thursday 28th March, this year, hospital*

Lenham pulled a chair up to Sage's hospital bed. She covered her eyes from the sun slanting through the window and he pulled the blind before he sat down.

'Do you feel better?' The chair creaked when he sat back.

'I'll mend. Thank you.' She managed a smile. 'They are going to operate on my broken bones tomorrow. Trent's already been in and I don't think Felix has left.'

'No, he's outside with your partner. Nick, is it? They say you're basically going to be OK.'

'So they tell me.' She couldn't bear to close her eyes, in case she dreamed she was back there. *Great. More nightmares.*

He looked down at her hand, as if he wanted to take it. 'I was really worried we weren't going to find you, like Lara.'

'I was lucky; the water was half filling the shaft. It broke my fall but didn't drown me. But Chorleigh knew, because he had seen it happen to Lara. He herded me back onto the trap.'

'I know. The pressure of being questioned about Lara and the terror that they would find out he'd been attacking horses all over Hampshire made him lie about what happened. His father accused him of killing her, and punished him by refusing to let him care for his animals. It must have been awful for the lad, knowing the horses didn't even have water. Eventually, his father despatched the dying horses; the necropsy showed they'd had their throats cut, very precisely. As chief agister, Chorleigh senior would have known how to put an animal down in an emergency. He didn't want anyone knowing what he'd done to them.'

'And then he beat Alistair up?'

'I think so. Perhaps he still wouldn't tell his father what had happened to Lara. He was hurt badly enough to put him in hospital, anyway. His father covered it all up and got the search warrant rescinded. He probably thought Lara was there, buried somewhere.'

'But she wasn't.' Sage swallowed the lump that was forming in her throat, it made her voice husky. 'She was injured and stuck in the dark waiting to die.'

He seemed to hesitate. 'Lara's injuries were much more extensive than yours. She fell into a dry shaft; the water cushioned your fall. We've retrieved her remains now. She had a fractured skull, it was probably very quick.' He looked at his hands. 'At least her family know what happened now and they can bury her remains.'

She blinked away a few tears. 'I got Alistair completely wrong.'

'He didn't kill Lara, he just kept silent for twenty-seven years. She probably walked up there to look at the view and, well, you know what happened. He should have warned you, or called for help.'

'I could have died.'

Lenham shrugged. 'He's confessed, at least. After he was expelled from school, for sexual experimentation with a pony there, he went on to release his anger at his father on local animals. He was admitted to a private clinic after he got out of hospital, that's why no one could interview him again. They sent him home after all the treatment they could throw at him. Drugs, electroshock therapy, the works.' He looked at her. 'At least it stopped the animal attacks. But what I really wanted to tell you is that we've made an arrest for the murder of River Sloane.'

'The stepfather?' Tiredness was overwhelming her again but the ache in her shoulder, suspended over her head in a sling, kept her sharp.

'No, but the dental tape and blood made us look at him very closely, including his family. Owen Sloane a.k.a. Jimmy Macintosh used to own a lockup garage with his ex-wife, which she got in the divorce. When they split, she let him store things in it, including a set of golf clubs, one of which matched the bruise on River's head.'

Sage rested her head back on the pillow. The cold expression on Sloane's daughter's face had haunted her since the first day at the crime scene. 'Was it Melissa?'

He looked at her in surprise. 'We think so. She's only fourteen. But she cold-bloodedly lured her stepsister down to the lockup on Saturday around lunchtime, and bashed her head in with a golf club. She used trying on ice skating boots as an excuse. Apparently she had a crush on River's boyfriend.'

It was all so horrible. Sage shut her eyes but the memory of River's serene face emerging from the leaves intruded. 'Poor kid.'

'It gets worse.'

Sage shook her head. 'I'm not sure I want to hear it.' She rested for a moment. OK, she was ready. 'Go on.'

'Owen Sloane, who adored both of the girls by all accounts, went down to the lockup on Saturday because Melissa said she was looking for her ice skates, and found the girls. He thought River was dead, so he shut the garage and took Melissa skating as arranged. To establish an alibi, I imagine. I've seen the CCTV tapes at the rink. Owen was sat with his head in his hands but Melissa twirled around on the ice as if nothing had happened.'

'It must have been horrible for him.'

Lenham carried on. 'He went back that night to clean up and get rid of River's body. But he found she had crawled to the doorway and died there, of exposure and shock and her head injury. He was devastated – he could have saved her. He hid the body in the garage, locked it up with a new padlock and devised a plan to bury her in Chorleigh's garden. He had always blamed Chorleigh for killing Lara. Early Monday morning was the first time he could get away as the police were searching. They didn't know about the lockup and at that point it was just a missing person inquiry. You were right about the animals providing a time slot: he went down at two and returned home after four.'

'So she could have been saved on the Saturday afternoon?' Sage was appalled, she could still remember the feeling of almost freezing to death.

'Definitely. If he had called an ambulance, River Sloane would probably still be alive. And his daughter, the little psychopath, would be looking at therapy rather than a conviction for murder.'

It was all too horrible. 'What did she say?'

Lenham peered out the corner of the window, squinting down into the car park. 'Believe it or not, she's blaming her father. Says he lost his temper with River and beat her to death. She then mentioned injuries that she couldn't have known about. Those kicks that came from boots she no longer owns but her mother identified as being similar to our exemplar.'

She looked at his face. 'She kicked River while she was helpless on the ground.'

'Exactly.' He stood up to look out of the window, arms

crossed. 'Melissa was crushed when Owen left her mother to marry again. And River was a beautiful girl, more than a year older, popular at school. She seemed to have everything Melissa wanted, including the attention of Jake.'

'So she was angry, and lashed out in a rage,' Sage said.

'You're right. It could have happened like that.'

'But you think differently?' Sage rested her head against the pillow, avoiding the sizeable lump on the back of it. 'What about her phone. Does it show her luring River there?'

'No, but it's still helpful.' He grinned at her. 'You're starting to think like a detective.' The smile faded. 'We have looked at the family's viewing online. They watched a couple of crime dramas that show that someone's smartphone location can be tracked. She left hers at home. Do you know how unlikely it is that a teenager would go out without their phone? She took the SIM card out of River's and disposed of it.'

'She went there to hurt her sister. It was premeditated.'

Lenham nodded. 'She didn't just knock her over, she hammered into her, kicked her – you saw the body. She panicked afterwards because there was blood on her clothes. We found blood spray as high as the ceiling, thrown up there as she swung the club each time.'

Sage closed her eyes. That child, wiping out a girl whose only crime had been being more popular with everyone, including boys. 'Will she go to prison?'

'Oh, she'll definitely do some time, somewhere. How

long depends on whether they can make the case for premeditated murder. Owen will do time too.'

'For loving her. For protecting the one child he could save.'

'For leaving River to die in a cold garage, afraid and helpless. The temperature that night went down to freezing. He scraped the frost off his car to go and deal with her body.' He took a deep breath, looked down at her. 'You're off to the island soon, back to your partner?'

'Yes.' Yes, she was. She was going to follow Nick, wherever that took her. 'How about you? Back to work on Monday?'

'I won't even get a day off. We need to keep on with the interviews until one of them admits Melissa did this intentionally and deliberately. I think she's a danger to others, she needs to be locked up.' He smiled. 'Either way, I need all your reports as soon as you can write them. Felix's too. I'll be in touch.'

She felt heavier when he had left, her bruises seemed to hurt more. She dozed off, waking abruptly to the sound of Max calling to her from Nick's arms.

# 40

'Peter, Peter, I call but you do not come. I can hardly breathe, I am so cold. I doubt if anyone will read these words, or even if my pencil still makes a mark. But I will say it, because now there is no time for lies. The hours I spent in your arms were the golden point of my existence. If that is sin, then yes, I will die for it. My legs are smashed, there will be no relief. Once I thought I heard your father shouting and I called out for help, but my voice was weak. He stopped, there was a long silence, and for a moment hope surged that he had heard me. But nothing, no rescue. Perhaps Bessie Warnock was right, and the barrows are cursed. Maybe we raised the vengeful spirit of the wolf, who now crushes me in its jaws. I know I am bleeding, my face is cut and there is little skin on my elbow and shoulder. It seeps slowly, but I am stuck here. It is night again, I think, and when I reached down I found water flowing against my shins. My legs no longer have any feeling, it's as if I no longer exist below the chest. Perhaps I have shattered my spine. The pain was agonising in the first day, but now it is gone. I cry out again, not for help but just the animal moans I have left. I am as weak as a baby, and have less voice. If these are my last words, let them be of love for you, my Peter.'

Edwin Masters' Journal, around 14th July 1913

# 41

*Wednesday 1st May, this year*

Sage had her arm out of plaster but still favoured her good hand, and winced out of habit when she leaned on her healing shoulder. Her office at the university was full of her colleague's stuff; he had already moved in but had let her use the equipment to work on Edwin's journal. She had decided to take an extended sabbatical to recover, and sort out their living arrangements. They had already carved out a room in the vicarage for Maxie, who was enjoying the extra space, and she was spending more time with Nick. Living in the vicarage was stressful and public, but for the moment she was enjoying seeing him every day.

She positioned the camera so it focused at an acute angle to the page in Edwin's notebook. The book had been soaked at some point in the past so she couldn't use electrostatic analysis. X-rays hadn't revealed much but she was determined to find all his last clues and entries. She had read Edwin's journal and had discovered the heart-breaking story of his relationship with Peter. What she wanted was to know what happened at the end, because all she had were a few notes at the back of the journal, scribbled in the dark. She wanted to get the entire story before Felix came in with his own research. One thing had been confirmed: the book had been immersed in the same water that had nearly drowned her and had been inside the barrow with Edwin. Mud on the outside suggested it had been washed out of the barrow and into the pond, perhaps retrieved by one of the family or a gardener.

Lara's camera case had been drowned in the same water. Like the notebook, it must have washed out from the stone cistern inside the earthwork and landed in the mud below. The assumption was that George Chorleigh had moved it to distract the police, believing his son was to blame for Lara's disappearance. He couldn't have known that a film canister of water would lead right back to the barrows.

The pages were faded, the writing had not lasted well and mould had eaten away at much of the paper and crumbled the edges. She snapped another picture, this time from above. There, the indentations were obvious, the blunt pencil tearing into the fibres of the old paper. The words had been scribbled across the page over a previous journal entry. She knew how little light there was in the wolf trap;

Edwin must have been writing blind with the remains of an unsharpened pencil. The wood had just disrupted the fibres of the paper enough to show up.

She tried another colour filter until she was able to reduce the ink writing to see the looping letters of another entry. She started to transcribe.

*Later: A night has come, and most of another day. I pray that someone will look at these mounds of rock and soil and see what is under there. A burial mound for a man, and the wolf that killed him. And a trap, forever set to kill wolves that wander in, attracted to the scent of the creatures trapped before. I have no strength left. I can just reach to push my journal up high, since the water is rising, and I shall leave it there. Perhaps it will wash out. If this comes to your hand, know that I would never have left you, nor let any miles come between us. Live long and find new love, my Peter. Find someone to whom you can give every waking moment, as I would have for you. Goodbye, my love.*

Sage sat back, filled with her own memory of being in the wolf trap, of working out how its deadly design had caught her. Edwin, an archaeologist to the last, had done the same. What she couldn't understand was why the person who found it didn't call the police. Even if they had just retrieved his body it would have given his mother some peace. Instead, they kept the diary for all these years.

She read the last faint words again. Perhaps the answer was that the family couldn't cope with the relationship between Peter and Edwin.

She finished the transcription, filling in a few missing letters and words but the gist was there. He had tried to reach the slot to push the book out at least, for Peter. Her eyes were wet, she brushed them away. God, that had so nearly been her. Would Felix and Lenham and Nick eventually have found her body?

Her phone beeped and a text told her Felix was on his way up to her office in the university. He had presented his evidence to the police and was coming by on his way back to Devon.

She had time to organise her notes before he tapped on the door.

'Hi, Felix.'

He came in, hugged her slightly tighter than her shoulder appreciated, then sat down on one of the high stools by the table. 'I come bearing some more clues to the story,' he said, putting a fat folder on the desk.

'Like what?'

'Peter's regiment's war diaries, his service record.' He opened the folder revealing dozens of sheets of photocopied information.

'You did all this?'

He looked sheepish. 'Well, no, I got one of my students to do it. I was too busy tracing *these*.'

He pulled out a sheet with the copy of a newspaper page in it. She checked the date at the top – *The Hampshire Telegraph*, June 6, 1914. He pointed to the article amongst adverts and obituaries.

### 'Missing: Mr Edwin Masters.

*A reward of fifty guineas will be awarded upon the receipt of information leading to the whereabouts of Mr Edwin Masters, alive or dead. Mr Masters is of medium build, dark hair and complexion and has dark eyes. His late mother resided in Colchester. He is a graduate of Balliol College, Oxford, where he studied antiquities and ancient history. Information please to Peter Chorleigh, 44 St Ann's Street, Inverness, or direct to the police at Lyndhurst. Mr Masters was last seen at Chorleigh House, Fairfield, New Forest, in July 1913. His friends anxiously await news.'*

'Peter placed adverts like this for more than a decade,' Felix said.

'So sad that they never found him. The police recovered the broken skull and some long bones that must have been Edwin's. They found Lara too, she had a fractured skull. She probably never regained consciousness. He fell into water, like I did, so survived for a few days.'

'I thought you'd discover the whole skeletons.'

'The water is too acidic, it dissolved the smaller bones over a century.' She read through the advert again. 'Poor Peter. Do we know why they didn't search the barrows?'

'Not for sure. We do have a number of letters the police found in Alistair Chorleigh's house. Peter and Molly corresponded, and he kept their letters after her death. They never gave up looking for Edwin. Molly and Peter were packed off to Scotland after their father claimed Edwin had run away after "dastardly" behaviour. It seems he found out about Peter and Edwin somehow, perhaps related to the photographs. Peter and Molly mention them a few times.'

'He found the journal,' Sage said slowly. 'He must have done, he could see the picture and read the entries. I wonder if he really did leave Edwin to die?'

'But he kept the journal? Why would he?'

Sage thought about it. 'Perhaps to confront Peter when he came home. Only he didn't return to the New Forest until his father died, in 1919, just after Molly.'

'You mentioned a picture?' Felix said.

'This one?' Sage brought out the scanned, enlarged copy of a picture she had found wedged inside the notebook. It was almost black in places but the young man's face was still visible. 'Peter was being blackmailed by Matthew Goodrich, who developed the pictures.'

'I suspect his father was just trying to protect Peter's

reputation,' Felix said. 'He probably didn't know what happened to Edwin.'

'But I think he might have,' Sage said, leafing through her transcription of the notebook. 'Listen to this: "Once I thought I heard your father and I called out for help, but my voice was weak." Maybe he did hear Edwin, but he didn't do anything. Then the book appeared in the pond, so he just tucked it away so no one would work it out.'

'Like Alistair Chorleigh. He knew Lara had gone up there and disappeared, but was too frightened to tell his father about it, so put her rucksack back in the bus shelter. Then the camera case was washed out, and Alistair's father must have dumped it away from the house.'

He put photocopies of handwritten sheets onto the table. She read the direction on the letter. 'Miss Mary Chorleigh. Molly. What did she die of?'

He rummaged through the pages for a copy of a death certificate. 'The cause of death is "Influenzal purulent bronchitis". She was nursing in France looking after the many injured servicemen brought back from the front. The correspondence between the siblings is lovely, they were close. He was already at the Western Front; she was preparing to join him after her training as a nurse. Her letters were returned with her things after she died. There's a little watch as well.'

At the bottom of the certificate, Sage could make out the name of the person registering the death. 'Captain

Peter Chorleigh. Hopefully he was there to offer her some comfort, at the end.' She looked up. 'Do we know what happened to him after that?'

'I noticed his father's death in 1919, possibly also from the flu, and then Peter returned to the New Forest to live. He married Beatrice Elizabeth Marchmont in 1920. They had at least one son, Alistair Chorleigh's father, George, born in 1932.'

'That's amazing.'

'Well, Sadie really got involved in the story and created a whole list of things he did.' He passed her a page covered in scribbled notes and dates in purple ink. 'Peter was chief agister in 1930, and was an alderman by the time he died. He seemed like a very popular man.'

'What about Beatrice? Edwin mentioned her in the journal.'

Felix pointed to the final line. '"Mrs Beatrice Chorleigh is again hosting the mayor's Christmas fundraising dinner in the absence of his wife, who is convalescing in Switzerland." Sadie thinks this is as close as the reporter will get to saying they are having an affair. She was the mayor's unofficial social secretary, and lived in Southampton.'

'So that's where Peter ended up. In a loveless marriage without Edwin or Molly.' It sounded so sad.

'Maybe not. There is a picture from his old age in the *Telegraph*. His secretary had a book published in 1959 about the use of cavalry at Waterloo. We wondered if perhaps this Michael Bishop was actually his partner in later life.' The grainy newspaper picture showed Peter, unmistakeably Peter, with a plume of white hair and eyebrows, smiling proudly down at a younger man, dark-haired and dark-eyed, probably twenty years his junior.

She smiled. 'He had a type, didn't he? Dark, intense-looking. I have something to show you, too. Edwin's final entry, written in the dark with the remains of a broken pencil.'

She read the words out loud, and Felix sat, looking down at the table.

He glanced up with his crooked smile. 'Sad story. It must have been awful for him, waiting to die.'

'It was bad enough for me and I was only down there, what, seven hours? He lasted several days.'

'About that. Chorleigh knew, but he didn't call for help, just like he did with Lara, and just like his ancestor left Edwin Masters.'

'I know. He did try and help once people turned up and questioned him. I'm still angry with him.' She started to put the papers back in the folder. 'Can I keep these?'

'I made the copies for you. Sage, you have to testify against him. He needs to have some consequence for his behaviour. It's going to be hard to prove he left you to die without your testimony. If we hadn't turned up when we did, you could have died.'

'I know. But he was brought up in a violent household, he never stood a chance. Psychopathic bullies ran through his bloodline.'

Felix tapped the closed folder. 'He tortured animals, he lied about Lara's disappearance then he left you to die. You need to help the police build a case against him. The historical animal abuse isn't going to come to court, they can't prove it and it was too long ago.'

She stared down at her hands. There were pink scars on the knuckles of her right hand, a healing cut on her left.

'What about Lara?' she said. 'He told me what he did. He knew where she was, he left her, too.'

'There's no independent evidence that he knew where she was, except what he said to you. If Owen Sloane hadn't buried River in Chorleigh's garden, we probably would never have found Lara.'

'So it comes down to what happened to me.' Felix waited while she sorted through her jumbled feelings. 'I know you're right,' she said. 'Part of me blames him, I hate what he did. He chased me from the house, you know that? But there was something about him – he switched into a different mindset, like Elliott did last year. Like a cornered animal just trying to save his skin. He knew there was something dangerous about the barrow when Lara disappeared. Then he chased me onto the top.' She thought about Lara's family, the agony of not knowing where she was over the years. That could have been Nick, Max, Yana… 'You're right. I'll talk to the police.'

Felix nodded. 'How's Nick?'

She could feel the smile stretching her cheeks. 'Really good.

I think we know what we want now. We're making a fresh start – together. We're looking around for an area where we can both work and we won't be too far from my parents and my sister. They are really important to Max as well as me.'

'I'm glad to hear it.' He stood up. 'I'm sorry to break up the party but I have to get back to Devon.'

She stood, hugged him again, wincing a little. 'I'm still sore.'

'Did you give any more thought to EMDR treatment for your flashbacks?'

She laughed. 'You are kidding, aren't you? I'm seeing a therapist once a week, have EMDR twice a week and I'm on three months' official sick leave. I dream about the wolf trap every night at the moment.' Which was true, but they weren't always nightmares, which frightened her more. There was a moment in some of her dreams when she let go, let the cold and the water take her. 'Oh, and antidepressants.'

'Good for you. Is it helping?'

Even though she was tired all the time, still ached all over and was having bad dreams, every day brought Max and Nick and Yana and a thousand tiny happy moments. 'I'll be OK.'

'How about the career plans?'

She smiled as she followed him into the corridor. 'I don't think I'm ready for a career in forensics, to be honest. But it did – does – fascinate me. I'm just not sure when I'll be ready to sit with a dead body again.' Sage rubbed her sore collarbone gently, relieving the ache of knitting bones.

Felix nodded. 'Good luck with Nick. I'm sure you'll sort it out.'

'I think I will.' She watched him walk down the stairs and stood on the landing, looking through the large windows at the inner courtyard of her building. She let the sun warm her while she did a mental check of her emotional state as she'd been taught by her therapist. 'Nine out of ten,' she said to herself, then smiled. Nick was walking through the courtyard with Max on his shoulders, stopping to look at things as her baby pointed with starfish hands. 'Ten.'

*Acknowledgements*

Firstly, I would like to thank Miranda Jewess and Jo Harwood at Titan, who helped me develop this book from a few simple ideas. Then Cath Trechman worked hard to bring it to life, getting it ready and doing the characters justice. She has taught me so much about constructing a crime story, all with kindness and humour.

I would also like to thank Jane Willis, my agent, who made the strange world of publishing seem easier. She has been a wonderful support throughout.

Lastly, my large and noisy family have helped me, especially my son Carey. He is always willing to read and challenge my stories, which just makes them grow. I am also grateful to my husband Russell for his patience going around yet another archive or museum, often for a single line of dialogue in a book. The life of a writer is a strange one, and plot ideas have often been thrashed out over long journeys and walks.

On that note, I have tried to be as accurate as I can with the attitudes and events of the past, but sometimes imagination has needed to fill in the gaps.

*About the Author*

**Rebecca Alexander** is a psychologist and writer. Rebecca fell in love with all things sorcerous, magical and witchy as a teenager and has enjoyed reading and writing fantasy ever since. She wrote her first book aged nineteen, and since then has been runner-up in the Mslexia novel writing competition and the Yeovil Literary Prize 2012. She is the author of the Jackdaw Hammond series of supernatural crime novels published by Del Rey, *The Secrets of Life and Death* (2013), *The Secrets of Blood and Bone* (2014) and *The Secrets of Time and Fate* (2016). She lives in Devon.

# A BREATH AFTER DROWNING

### *ALICE BLANCHARD*

Sixteen years ago, Kate Wolfe's young sister Savannah was brutally murdered. Forced to live with the guilt of how her own selfishness put Savannah in harm's way, Kate was at least comforted by the knowledge that the man responsible was in jail. But when she meets a retired detective who is certain that Kate's sister was only one of many victims of a serial killer, Kate must decide whether she can face the possibility that Savannah's murderer walks free. As she unearths disturbing family secrets in her search for the truth, she becomes sure that she has uncovered the depraved mind responsible for so much death. But as she hunts for a killer, a killer is hunting her…

### PRAISE FOR THE AUTHOR

"[A] gale-force thriller"
**New York Times**

"Splendid… riveting and addictive"
**Chicago Tribune**

"Brilliant… a dark and stormy novel"
**New York Daily News**

**TITAN**BOOKS.COM

# AFTER THE ECLIPSE
## *FRAN DORRICOTT*

**Two solar eclipses. Two missing girls.**

Sixteen years ago a little girl was abducted during the darkness of a solar eclipse while her older sister Cassie was supposed to be watching her. She was never seen again. When a local girl goes missing just before the next big eclipse, Cassie – who has returned to her home town to care for her ailing grandmother – suspects the disappearance is connected to her sister: that whoever took Olive is still out there. But she needs to find a way to prove it, and time is running out.

### PRAISE FOR THE AUTHOR

"A gritty, riveting thriller"
**Sherri Smith**

"A stunning, compelling debut from a talented new voice in crime fiction"
**Steph Broadribb**

# TWO LOST BOYS
## *L.F. ROBERTSON*

Janet Moodie is a death row appeals attorney. Overworked and recently widowed, she's had her fill of hopeless cases, and this will be her last. Her client is Marion 'Andy' Hardy, convicted along with his brother Emory of the rape and murder of two women. But Emory received a life sentence while Andy got the death penalty, labeled the ringleader despite his low IQ and Emory's dominant personality.

Convinced that Andy's previous lawyers missed mitigating evidence that would have kept him off death row, Janet investigates Andy's past. She discovers a sordid and damaged upbringing, a series of errors on the part of his previous counsel, and most worrying of all, the possibility that there is far more to the murders than was first thought. Andy may be guilty, but does he deserve to die?

### PRAISE FOR THE AUTHOR

"This is a must-read"
**Kate Moretti,** *New York Times* **bestseller**

"Suspense at its finest"
**Gayle Lynds,** *New York Times* **bestseller**

For more fantastic fiction, author events, exclusive
excerpts, competitions, limited editions and more

VISIT OUR WEBSITE
**titanbooks.com**

LIKE US ON FACEBOOK
**facebook.com/titanbooks**

FOLLOW US ON TWITTER
**@TitanBooks**

EMAIL US
**readerfeedback@titanemail.com**